The 12th Victim

ALSO BY KATIA LIEF
FROM CLIPPER LARGE PRINT

You Are Next
Hide and Seek

The 12th Victim

Katia Lief

W F HOWES LTD

This large print edition published in 2012 by
W F Howes Ltd
Unit 4, Rearsby Business Park, Gaddesby Lane,
Rearsby, Leicester LE7 4YH

1 3 5 7 9 10 8 6 4 2

First published in the United Kingdom in 2012
by Ebury Press

A CIP catalogue record for this book is available
from the British Library

ISBN 978 1 47121 312 0

Typeset by Palimpsest Book Production Limited,
Falkirk, Stirlingshire
Printed and bound in Great Britain
by MPG Books Ltd, Bodmin, Cornwall

MIX
Paper from
responsible sources
FSC
www.fsc.org   FSC® C018575

For my grandmothers, mother, aunts, sister, daughter,
and granddaughters yet to be born

CHAPTER 1

When I walked into Mac's home office he turned and looked at me like I'd caught him surfing pornography, and quickly closed his laptop. 'Sorry you saw that.'

The image seemed to linger on the screen even after it went dark: the woman's chipped red manicure digging into the loose muscles of a man's hairy back, her face contorted in either ecstasy or disgust; it was hard to tell which.

'New case?'

'Last week. Wife thought he was cheating on her. He's cheating on her. Slam dunk. Next.'

I crossed the small room to touch his forehead. 'You're burning up.'

'I can't lay in bed anymore.'

'Some people get a flu shot so they won't—'

'Don't say it again.'

Get the flu.

How many times had I told him not to put it off? Our son, Ben; his babysitter, Chali; and I all had our shots two months ago. But Mac, workaholic that he was, couldn't spare the time. Now he was on day one of what would probably be a

1

week of fever, aches, and pains, and already he was crawling out of his skin.

'Go back to bed, dearest.'

He coughed. Shook his head. 'I've got some stuff to do.'

'It's Sunday night. Your client can wait to see those pictures; in fact, you'll be doing her a favor.'

'You're right.' He shut down his computer and looked at me. It was only eight o'clock, I had just put Ben to bed, but the exhaustion in Mac's eyes made it feel like midnight. 'Why do I even do this? I thought I was ready to retire from the police when I did, but now I listen to Billy—'

'Who is overwhelmed, Mac, do I really have to remind you?'

'—and I realize that I will never get another challenging case again.'

'You want to be like Billy, chasing a serial killer no one's been able to find for two years? Haven't you been there, done that? Don't you feel—'

'*Bored.*'

'You're sick, you're tired, and now I think you're delirious, saying you wish you had the kind of cases Billy's been catching.'

'Maybe I should try corporate security again.'

'Come on. Back to bed.' I held out my hand. He took it and stood, pausing to steady himself. He moaned and let me navigate him through the hallway back to our bedroom. I left the room dark and steered him into bed. The musty air felt claustrophobic but it was much too cold out to open a window.

'Sleep.' I kissed his forehead. 'I'm going upstairs.'

He was snoring before I closed the door.

With my two men (well, one of them was just shy of four years old) fast asleep, the house felt peaceful in a way it never did. I crept quietly up the stairs to the second floor of our duplex; it was a typical layout of these brownstone Brooklyn apartments, when you had the lower half of the house, to put the bedrooms beneath and use the high-ceilinged parlor floor for all the social rooms. The floorboards creaked under my bare feet as I passed through the living room. And then, just as I made it onto an area rug, a clatter of noise broke the silence when I accidentally kicked one of Ben's toy trucks toward the opposite wall. I froze, waiting for a reaction from below, but no one seemed to have heard. I switched on the kitchen light and sat at the table a moment, wondering where to begin. An exquisite solitude gathered like fog as I listened to sounds I rarely heard in our home: the ticking of the wall clock, the hum of the refrigerator, dissonant whispers emanating from the radiator.

The dishes: I should do them first. I had made chicken soup, and vegetable skins and crumbs from the sliced baguette were all over the counter. I started by finding a large plastic container to store the soup for tomorrow.

Midway through loading the dishwasher, a text message alert chimed across the room. I turned to look; it was Mac's BlackBerry (mine was in my jeans pocket), abandoned on a shelf across the kitchen this morning around the time he realized he was coming down with something. His phone had been quiet all day, it being Sunday, and the chime took me by surprise. My hands were slick with soapy water. I turned back to the dishes. A few minutes later I closed the tap and looked up – and was startled by my own ghostly reflection in the window that overlooked the back garden. *A tall, crazy-looking woman with messy color-blanched hair stood outside staring in at me.* My heart jumped.

'Get lost!' I waved my arm, and so did she. Then we laughed at each other. Still, she made me nervous.

Mac usually stood here cleaning up at night; I wasn't used to the intensity of darkness directly in front of me and the indistinct mirrorlike reversal of myself. If this was a typical flu, it would be days before he was better. Meantime, I would take on all his tasks, along with my own.

It was still too early for bed, and I had promised myself that before the weekend was over I would quit stalling and enroll in my spring courses. I was eking my way through a college degree while my adult life barreled forward, pretty sure that my twenty-year-old classmates saw me as ancient at thirty-eight. Plus I was a mother. And twice married. My life had been blessed and battered to a ridiculous extent. All I wanted now was to finish school so I could remake my career. Unlike

Mac, in-the-thick-of-it police work did not tempt me anymore, even though I'd been good at it, and despite the fact that I now held a private investigator's license so I could work with Mac on the occasional case. The busier he got, the busier I got; but evolving into his work partner (again) wasn't my goal. I wanted to stand outside looking in, which was why I had chosen a forensic psychology undergraduate program.

Well, that wasn't all I wanted.

I wanted, and would always want, *her* back.

Two hers.

Cece, my sweet little daughter murdered six years ago along with my first husband, Jackson.

And Amelia or Sarah or Dakota – the daughter who was supposed to be, but wasn't. She had miscarried, at six months' gestation, eight weeks and three days ago. Giving birth to a lifeless child was . . . I shook away the memory.

I opened the cabinet drawer where we tossed stuff we might need later and rummaged through the mess for the catalog. It was the size of a magazine, easy to locate, but so much junk had accumulated I couldn't resist grabbing a few things – a small plastic fan that was broken, a playbill from last year, an appliance manual for a toaster oven we no longer owned – and tossing them in the garbage. I noticed a freebie pocket calendar that had arrived in the mail almost a year ago, and was about to throw it away when I realized I should check to make sure no one was using it. I was pretty sure Mac used his BlackBerry calendar exclusively, as did I, but you never knew. Good thing I'd decided to check: When I flipped through the pages I saw half a dozen penciled entries in Chali's handwriting. I remembered her asking if anyone would be using the little paper calendar and telling her she was welcome to it. I tossed it back into the drawer and sat down at the kitchen table with the course catalog.

She was supposed to have been born on January first. New Year's Day. Maybe it had been too neat an expectation to foresee a daughter in my future. It was a dangerous hope, as if Cece could be replaced. Of course that was ridiculous and I never said it aloud, but it was a secret wish. I had felt itchy, pregnant with Leah or Elsa or Caroline, as if having her would scratch away a lingering emptiness. But instead of her birth eliminating a void, her stillbirth doubled it. Pregnancy with Ben four years ago had not brought on that kind of inner discord, but he was a boy, and Mac and I were a brand-new couple, and I was amazed just to be alive.

For the past eight weeks and three days, the hours had felt long and heavy.

And now the holiday season was upon us: Christmas was in two weeks, Ben's birthday was just a month away, and I still hadn't bought any presents or planned any parties.

I started reading the course offerings, wondering how I would find the energy to keep up with the work, and Ben, if I took two classes. I had dropped out at the beginning of the semester when I'd lost the baby, but one of the abandoned courses had intrigued me enough that I was tempted to give it another try: The Role of Malingering in the Insanity Defense: An Introduction. I was still interested in examining the vast gray area where criminal intent overlapped with lying at one end and mental illness at the other. So I dragged my laptop across the kitchen table, booted it up, logged into the school Web site and enrolled for the course again. Classes started at the beginning of February. I still had time to decide whether or not to take a second class.

Another text message chimed on Mac's phone. I wondered who had texted him twice on a Sunday night. It occurred to me that it could be important, so I decided to break an unspoken privacy rule and read his messages.

The first was a Silver Alert from the city, advising of a missing senior. The second was from Billy Staples, a detective at our local precinct, the Eight-four, and Mac's closest friend since he'd married me and moved to Brooklyn to begin the second half of his life. His message was simple, and inexplicable (at least to me):

WARREN NEVINS

I carried the phone downstairs, flicking off lights as I went, leaving what felt like a cold, dark void in my wake. We had set our thermostat to lower at eleven every night, and that the parlor floor was growing chilly told me it was late. I was tired. Ben would be up by six o'clock and I was ready to crawl into my warm bed beside Mac.

I could feel the heat off Mac's body as I came around his side of the bed, intending to put his phone on his dresser.

'I'm awake,' he whispered.

'You got a text.' I handed him the phone.

His face glowed in the anemic light cast by the small square screen. He stared at it longer than necessary to read the two little words. And then he put the phone down on the bedside table beside a heap of crumpled tissues, closed his eyes, and sighed.

Ten minutes later I stepped out of the bathroom in my nightgown, my mouth minty from toothpaste, face moist with cream, and hair static from brushing. And there was Mac: standing in the hallway, fully dressed. His cheeks were pink with fever.

'Huh?' I stared at him; it was the best I could do.

'I have to go out.'

'You have to go back to bed.'

'I'm meeting Billy.'

'No you're not.' I took his arm and tried to steer him along the hall, back toward our bedroom, but he resisted.

'You don't understand, Karin.'

'Mac, you have the flu. This is absurd. You're not going out in thirty-degree weather to see Billy right now. Whatever he needs can wait until morning.'

'This can't.' He started toward the stairs.

'Why not?'

He stopped, turned and looked at me. 'I'm a big boy, Karin. I can make my own decisions.'

'You're really pissing me off right now.'

Half his mouth lifted into a wry semismile. And then a sudden coughing fit buckled him over; propping his hands on his knees, he hacked uncontrollably.

I stepped back into the bathroom and returned to offer him a box of tissues. When he could stand, he took one and blew his nose. I touched his forehead, which was even hotter than before.

'We should take your temperature again.'

He relented and lay back down on the bed, fully dressed. I turned on a lamp and watched him in the golden light, laboring to breathe with a digital thermometer protruding from his lips. After a minute, multiple bleeps announced that a conclusion had been reached: 104.2. I showed him the reading.

'Still want to go out?'

'I have to.' But he didn't make a move to get up.

'Sweetie, what's going on?' I sat on the bed beside him, holding the thermometer in one hand and touching his burning cheek with the other.

'I promised Billy I wouldn't tell anyone, not even you.'

'Tell me what?'

I waited, feeling a growing sensation of nervousness. I didn't like it. Finally he took a deep breath, coughed, and looked at me.

'He'll have to understand.'

'I'm sure he will.'

'I would go if I could.'

'I can call him and let him know you're sick.'

'Don't call him. Just go.'

It was nearly midnight. Freezing out. And dark. 'Where?'

'Warren and Nevins streets. You can walk there; it's close. But I'd feel better if you took my gun.'

Warren Street, Nevins Street – of course. They weren't far from here, though I never went in that direction. 'I won't need a gun.'

'White lady alone in the projects at night—'

'No gun.' The more I'd had to shoot people, the more I'd grown to hate it. 'What's Billy doing over there?'

'Crime scene, probably. He's been having flash-backs at crime scenes, not always, but sometimes. He loses control and it terrifies him.'

'Loses control how?'

'Hallucinates.'

'Jesus.'

'I know.'

A year and a half ago, Billy had lost an eye in a rooftop shootout with a woman he loved. The shock and betrayal had been traumatic on every level – physically, emotionally, professionally – but after a standard leave he had returned to work. Some cops seem able to slough off trauma; others crumble instantly; some come apart bit by bit. You often don't know who is who until some time has passed. We had thought Billy was out of the woods, but maybe we were wrong.

'Is he getting help?'

Mac shook his head. 'The stigma – afraid he'll lose his job.'

Job, full pension, reputation; there was a lot a cop could risk if he showed the slightest sign of vulnerability. Back when I was a cop and I fell apart, people were kind but they kept their distance, as if they'd catch failure if they came too close.

'How long has it been happening?'

'Not sure. He told me about it a couple of weeks ago. Said he'd send me a code, a location, if he felt one coming on again. The deal was I'd show up, wherever, whenever, and help him handle it.'

'You're a good friend.'

'Not tonight I'm not.'

I kissed his forehead. 'I'm on it.' Then I fed him some ibuprofen, turned off the light, and went to get my coat.

CHAPTER 2

The world felt frozen in place as I walked through the midnight streets in a direction that led me away from my usual route. In the three years I'd lived in the area I had rarely ventured this way; normally I headed toward Smith Street with its shops and restaurants and subway, never away from it, toward Nevins. No one else was out. Not even a car. A film of ice covered everything: the front stoops of the sleeping brownstones, the tops of parked cars seaming either side of the street, the unevenly paved sidewalk. I had to tread carefully or I'd slip and fall.

After walking two and a half blocks into what felt like quieter and quieter territory, I turned right onto Nevins. The familiar neighborhood of gracious brownstones quickly gave way to desolation. A shuttered bodega sat beside an empty lot across the street from another empty lot. In the near distance you could see the hard, angular edge of a low-income housing project. It seemed darker here than in the opposite direction and then I realized why: Since turning onto Nevins, there had not been a single streetlamp. Any light here was ambient, bleeding from occasional late night windows. A couple blocks ahead, though, was a bright haze of activity. Half a dozen cop cars and a pair of ambulances sat there, doors agape, blue and red lights flashing. People milled around, shifting through headlight beams before merging back into darkness.

I picked up my pace, heading toward the action, which was where I expected to find Billy. But then, before I'd reached the nearest corner, I heard a voice.

'What the *fuck*?'

I reached into my coat pocket instinctively, now wishing I'd taken Mac's advice and brought his gun. The voice sounded agitated, confused – and familiar. I turned, and in the shadows of a recessed doorway saw a black guy sitting on a step, gripping his knees, talking to himself.

'We'll figure it out.'

I stepped closer, peered through the shadows.

'You're never going to get away with this.'

In a sliver of light, I saw his face.

'Why don't you just put the gun down, Jazz?'

His eye was unfocused. Even this close, he didn't seem to see me.

'We'll figure it out. There's got to be some kind of misunderstanding.'

I knew where he was, because I recognized everything he was saying, though it was all out of order. He was back in that day, that horrible afternoon a year and a half ago when so much that mattered to him pivoted out of control with a single gunshot that exploded his right eye and broke his heart.

He had been unable to shoot Jasmine, because he was in love with her.

But she had had no trouble whatsoever pulling her trigger on him.

He looked at me suddenly, the black eye patch he always wore now angled over the right side of his face. His left eye glistened white in the darkness, centering its attention on me.

'Look,' he said. 'Look. Do you believe this?'

Did he think I was there with him again – because I had been? If I hadn't shown up on that rooftop, chances were he'd be dead.

'I believe it.'

'It isn't happening.'

'It happened. In the past. Come back, Billy.'

He shivered. I wanted to reach down and zip up his blue parka but was afraid that it would startle him. Jasmine had shot him on a warm summer day. Apparently the flashback had returned him to June, and he had unzipped his jacket, despite tonight's frigid December air.

A drop of sweat fell in a rivulet from his forehead down along his temple and landed on the collar of his jacket. He reached for my hand. His skin felt hotter than Mac's.

'Take a deep breath, Billy, like this.' I breathed, held it, let it go.

After a moment he tried it, his left eye locked into mine. We breathed together, slowly in and slowly

14

out. I watched his pupil dilate like a time lapse of a blooming rose.

'Not feeling so good,' he said.

'I know.'

'Where's Mac?'

'Down with the flu.'

'Sorry.'

'Isn't your fault.'

'No, about this.'

'Like I said, isn't your fault.'

He leaned forward to glance down the street toward the flashing lights of the crime scene that had triggered his flashback. 'Not looking forward to getting read my rights.'

He meant his partner, *Ladasha.*

'I'll handle her.'

'I bet you will.' Now he smiled, and my pulse started to slow.

I stood back and helped tug him to his feet. Billy was a bit over six feet tall and I was a bit under. We stood side by side and I wound a supportive arm around his back.

'Want to just ditch this joint?' I asked.

'Can't. I'm on the job.'

'I'll go with you.'

'It's a free country.' But I sensed he was glad I'd offered.

As we got closer, I realized that in the distance what had looked like one crime scene was actually two. The first cluster of police and paramedics surrounded a stretcher on the ground where someone was being readied for a trip to the hospital. A minivan had stopped in the street and a middle-aged woman I took to be its driver was talking to a couple of cops who were noting everything she said.

'I was driving by and I saw someone just lying there.'

'You always out alone this late at night?'

'I was going to the pharmacy to fill a prescription for my son. His fever spiked and the doctor said—'

But the two cops glanced at each other dubiously. The victim looked badly injured, as if he or she had been struck by a car. The woman's van was the only civilian vehicle here, though it was always possible that someone else had hit and run. With no witnesses hanging around, and one of the parties unconscious, it was her word against nothing.

'Neergaard is open twenty-four/seven, in Park Slope, in case you ever need to know.' She reached into her purse and produced a white prescription slip. 'This is the quickest way there; no traffic lights.'

From what I could see there wasn't any blood on the front of her car, though it was dark out. I cringed at the thought of someone ramming whoever it was with a two-ton hunk of metal and speeding off. Either way, I doubted that a garden-variety car accident could have triggered Billy's reaction.

16

'What's going on up there?' I looked into the near distance, at the other crime scene, which appeared busier than this one.

His face tensed. 'Seems my friend is back at it.'

His 'friend,' though, was *not* a friend, and the frustrated bitterness in Billy's calling him that went through me like a swallow of poison. Billy had been hunting for the Working Girl Killer for over a year, to no avail; and now, apparently, the brutal creep feared throughout the city had found his third victim in Brooklyn. For a year before the challenge of catching him, stopping him, had landed on Billy's desk, he had left seven prostitutes dead across Manhattan. Some members of the Manhattan task force had transitioned to a Brooklyn task force, and the hunt continued across boroughs. Looking down the long, dark stretch of Nevins, the forlorn street suddenly made sense: It was a red-light district, without the red lights.

'And then this kid here got hit by a car.'

'Kid?'

'A girl – ten, twelve years old, we're guessing.'

I felt a twist of alarm, then outrage. What was a kid doing out past midnight? Especially *here*.

'Are you thinking she was hit by the unsub on his way out?' That ghostly unknown subject of the ongoing investigation, who struck like a tornado, then evaporated like fog.

'It's a possibility.'

I moved closer to the stretcher and in a dull spray of headlight from one of the cop cars, saw her face:

17

small, with creamy darkish skin as if she'd just returned from an island vacation, and silky hair the color of burned wheat, a long strand of which spilled over the side of the stretcher. She wore small gold star earrings and her fingernails were painted blue, with the perfect sheen of a fresh manicure. Her feet were bare; each toenail was painted a different color.

'Where are her shoes?' I asked Billy.

'Wasn't wearing any, from what we can tell. Got some fresh cuts on her feet.'

'Did she run away from home?'

'Who knows?'

'She looks young for that.' If she had been an older teenager, it would have been anyone's first guess. And if she had been black, there might even have been an insinuation floating in the air that she was out working the streets, despite her tender age. But that fresh blue manicure, and that whimsical pedicure, seemed to tell another story. She was wearing pink flannel pajama bottoms prancing with white sheep. I turned away and closed my eyes.

'Karin, we have no idea why she was out here.' He sounded so sad, and so frustrated, and so hopeless that I automatically reached out to grab his hand. His palm was sweaty but I didn't let go.

The paramedics carefully lifted the girl into the back of the ambulance. One hopped in with her, while the other closed the doors and hurried to the front to drive.

'Where's her family?' I asked.

'We don't know who she is yet – we're canvassing the area, see if she's from somewhere around here.'

But when kids went missing in the middle of the night, sometimes their parents didn't even realize it until morning. What were the odds her parents wouldn't even answer the bell?

A television van drove past us toward the other crime scene. We both watched it swerve around a pothole and finally stop at the nearest edge, adding its headlights to the already bright miasma that had gathered around another dead woman.

'The hooker was still warm when we got here,' Billy said.

I knew enough about the case to understand how unusual that was; normally, by the time they were discovered, the bodies were already decomposing.

'Same m.o.?'

'Yup.'

A prostitute in her twenties, first strangled, then finished off with a knife embedded between her breasts. It was always the same: a single piece of clothing missing, either a top or a bottom; and a Bowie knife, produced in Mississippi in 1963, by a now-defunct company called Stark. The knife hadn't been manufactured for decades, had never been particularly popular, and was hard to find. It seemed someone had stocked up on them pre-Internet, probably paying cash someplace that wasn't good at record keeping. In the years the investigation had been going on, not a single trace of who had accumulated the knives had been found. Ten knives, now, at least . . . or possibly more, if he planned to keep killing. There was no reason to think he wouldn't.

The biggest break in the case came toward the beginning, when the second victim was identified as a twenty-five-year-old woman from upstate New York who had gone missing at the age of eleven and hadn't been seen or heard from since. Of the eight victims the two task forces had been able to identify over time, all had disappeared between the ages of nine and twelve, during the late eighties and early to mid nineties. All had come from states along the East Coast, where they had vanished in transit between their homes, schools, and friends' houses. In each case, they had been trusted to get places alone, and most of them had relished their new independence. In two cases, it was the girl's first solo run without adult supervision. None of the girls were seen or heard from again until the day her body turned up in Manhattan, or Brooklyn, with a cord around her neck and a Bowie knife sunk deep in her chest.

'Another Dead Girl' had become a familiar headline.

It was a new twist on an old story: Kids vanished, turned up ruined or not at all. In this case, it appeared that some angry pimp or maybe an angry john had it in for them – another old story. The first problem was catching the creep who was doing this, and stopping him. The second problem was figuring out where all those girls were hiding, or being hidden, between then and now. It didn't take a leap of imagination to guess that these girls were trafficked into the sex trade, considering the profession they all ultimately shared. But catching their killer was beginning to feel like a leap of faith. Connecting the dots between two known events – the girls vanishing, and the women turning up dead – had proven elusive for Billy and everyone else working the case for the past two years. The task force had swelled to include detectives from multiple local jurisdictions as well as specialists from the FBI; I remembered Billy complaining once that sometimes the investigation felt like it had grown too many legs to move in any one direction, that they were going nowhere fast.

Billy started moving up the street. Still holding hands, I moved with him. The closer we got, the more worried I grew that, like a moth to a flame, he would combust again once he stepped into the eerie brightness up ahead.

'Where you been, a-hole?' Ladasha turned on Billy the moment she spotted him, her long, tight braids cascading over one shoulder as she faced us. She was a short woman, dense-waisted, mother of five . . . baked awesome cookies at the holidays but didn't mince words. 'I been at this myself for an hour!'

A dozen investigators were at work at the scene, along with paramedics and cops. The least busy were the paramedics, as there was no one to save. A small crowd had gathered on the sidewalk, where a photographer was taking pictures of something I couldn't see, presumably the victim.

'Sorry, Dash, I—'

'He's coming down with the flu.'

She looked at me, a glint of humor in her eye. 'You his mama now, Karin?'

'That's right, I gave birth to him nine years before I was born.'

'Oh, you're funny, girl.' A little smile cracked enough to show her gold tooth, one of the upper canines, a detail she clearly relished. 'You know what I'm talking about. Don't say you don't.'

Ladasha had once confided in me that, as the divorced wife of two men and the mother of four sons, she was convinced that 'male-kind' were all children, regardless of chronological age. While both her husbands left and all her sons struggled, her only daughter – a super-competent honor student, athlete, and sought-after babysitter – was proof positive of Ladasha's gender theory.

'Sorry,' Billy muttered.

'Yeah, ain't that what they all say.'

I came up close, into the cloud of sweet perfume she usually wore in abundance. ('Because it beats the sweat lodge of the precinct, the pigsty of my house, and the stink of a dead body,' she once told me.)

'Could be a stomach flu,' I said. 'He was throwing up when I found him down the block.'

She grimaced. 'Thanks for sharing. What're you doing here, anyway?'

22

'I was passing.'

'You in the van with the other white lady? Just passing together?'

I smiled, unsure if she was messing with me in good humor or if it was the generic racial anger she was so good at. At some point Billy would need to explain to her what was going on with him, but it would have to be at the right moment. And this wasn't it. My guess was he'd take her out for a drink one night. Ladasha was better, more relaxed, when she'd had a few; a hard coating melted off and a luscious warmth came on display. I'd seen it once.

'Thanks, Karin,' Billy said. 'I appreciate the help; I'm good now.' But he didn't look good. He looked defeated. I had never had a flashback but had heard they drew you into the past in a way that felt so real it was overpowering; that it was like a movie appearing inside your mind, engulfing you.

'Are you sure?'

He nodded, but wouldn't look at me. I didn't want to leave him like this. But I also didn't want to embarrass him on the job. Then Ladasha saved the day.

'You get the hell out of here, Billy. I can't afford to catch your germs; I've got kids and the last thing I need is a barf fest at home. And I don't need you contaminating the crime scene.'

'I'm fine.' He sounded numb.

'I *said* . . .' She glared at him, and I almost expected her to count to three like he was one of her children.

'Dash is right. You should get to bed.' I looked at her. 'Mac's also down with the flu.'

'Like I've been saying' – Ladasha shook her head – '*men.*'

The cluster of investigators working on the sidewalk had thinned enough that now, when I glanced over, I saw her. The dead woman was flat on her back on the icy pavement, her skin already turning blue-gray, a tiny nose ring in her right nostril flickering in the glare of a headlight. She wore a lacy blue bra. One arm was flung above her head as if he had pulled hard to wrest off her shirt. Her head was twisted at an odd angle; he must have broken her neck when he strangled her, as he had with two other victims. She lay in a pool of blood that had spread around her from the wound between her breasts, where the signature Bowie knife protruded. I had read descriptions of the murders in the newspaper, and Billy had told us some of the details, but seeing it . . . her . . . in the flesh, dead but still bleeding, destroyed by some monster who couldn't understand that she had been a real person with a real life . . . that probably someone out there had loved her, despite her profession . . . that she had been someone's child, possibly a sister, a granddaughter, maybe even a mother. The cold irreverence of the murder shocked me more than the body itself lying there. I had been a soldier and a cop; I had seen a lot of dead bodies. But I would never get used to the horrors, or the

24

randomness, of the twisted motivations that led to this kind of viciousness.

Suddenly woozy, I crossed the street to the opposite curb, braced myself against a parking sign, closed my eyes, and waited for it to pass.

'So now she's got the stomach thing, too?' I heard Ladasha whine.

'Guess so,' Billy said, but my guess was he knew better. I noticed that he kept his back to the dead woman, offsetting the possibility of another flash-back coming on at the sight of her.

I watched from across the street as the body was zipped into a black bag and lifted onto a stretcher. Concealed, the young woman inside the bag looked as small as the girl up the street. The stretcher was loaded into the back of the ambulance, which drove slowly away.

Both ambulances were gone now, one to a hospital, the other to the coroner. I could see from a distance that the other scene was dissipating. The white van drove off up a side street. The last investigator was packing up his equipment.

Billy said something to Ladasha that I couldn't hear. She shook her head, rolled her eyes, and walked away. As he crossed the street to join me, I watched Ladasha approach a forensic tech at the place on the sidewalk where the body had been found. A blood-mottled chalk outline of the young woman's final moments glowed in the dark, a semipermanent reminder that would be gone with the next rain.

'Let's go,' I said. 'I'll walk you home.'

'No, I'll walk *you* home.'

'I came out in the middle of the night to help you, so let me help you.'

'You already did. And now I'm better.'

'Just like that?'

He nodded. 'It hits you like a freight train, and then it passes.'

'Do I look like I want to talk to you now?' I heard the bark of Ladasha's unmistakable voice. Billy and I both turned around: one of the guys from the television van was approaching her with a microphone. He must have been a newbie crime reporter who had never encountered Ladasha before; the veterans knew to wait for the right moment.

'I just wanted to ask a question—'

'What did I just say?'

The reporter stared at her.

'I said, what did I just say?'

'You said—'

'That's right.' She turned her back on him, and got to work bossing the tech, who grinned and said something I couldn't hear that elicited a shout of bright laughter from Ladasha.

'Piece of work,' Billy muttered.

'Call me crazy, but I sort of like her.'

'She's good at what she does. What we do.'

'You'll have to tell her, Billy.'

'I know.'

We walked together along Nevins Street, back in the direction of my house. The spot where the girl

26

had been found was empty now, with just some adhesive backings left behind by the paramedics.

We turned onto Bergen Street and were back in the comforting enclave of brownstones I had come to think of as my neighborhood, a local concept with boundaries measured by the block. Sometimes only half a block could thrust you into another world.

'What time is it?' Having removed my watch when I'd washed the dishes, I'd lost track of time. It could have been one in the morning, or five. All I knew was that it was still dark out, and bitterly cold.

'Time for a drink. Join me?'

We had come to the Brooklyn Inn, a nineteenth-century bar on the corner of Bergen and Hoyt. I had never been inside.

I yawned. The night was already as good as gone. 'Why not?'

Walking into the bar felt like tripping backward into the nineteenth century: dark wood paneling, long wooden bar, wood stools with leather seats, panels of ornate stained glass above a door separating the bar from a back room, gas lamps fitted for electricity but only dribbling light. A surprising number of people sat at the bar, drinking and talking; you'd have thought people would be in bed so they could get up for work on Monday morning. But then I corrected myself; since the economy tanked and the Great Recession started, so many people didn't have jobs anymore that the bars must have been one of the rare businesses thriving as a result.

We bellied up to the bar and ordered a couple of 'seasonal specials' – which, according to the chalkboard above the bar, would come 'hot and mysterious' – from a bartender with a black goatee and diamond earrings. He slid a bowl of peanuts toward us and I immediately dug in, suddenly realizing that I was hungry.

'Do they have food here?' I asked Billy.

He shook his head. 'Just the nuts.'

I took another handful. In the mirror behind the bar I saw the reflection of a round white clock. It was only ten, and I felt relieved for a moment before realizing that it had been midnight when I'd left the house and the clock was reflected backward. It was two in the morning.

Our drinks arrived: mulled cider with rum. The sweet, piping hot liquid went straight to my head, warming and relaxing me so quickly I peeled off my sweater and pushed up the long sleeves of my cotton T-shirt. Billy likewise shed his jacket and unbuttoned the top of his shirt.

We ordered another round.

'So,' I began. 'Talk to me.'

'What can I say?' He leaned back on his stool enough to weave his fingers together over his belly. A powdery whiteness coated his brown knuckles; something about his creased dry skin made me feel what I interpreted as his loneliness. Or maybe it just made me sad that, after his ordeal tonight, the best he could do for comfort was go to a bar with me. He had never married, though I knew he had loved and I knew he had lost. It pained me to think that the most enduring element of his life, his work on the police for over twenty years, seemed to be turning toxic for him.

'How long have you been having flashbacks?'

His dark eye rolled up toward the brown-painted ceiling of decorative tin squares, as if counting backward in time, figuring it out. But I suspected he knew the answer by heart – and didn't want to talk about it. Something like that would have been up there with receiving a dreaded diagnosis: One minute you're fine, the next minute you're dying. You remembered when it happened.

Finally he answered, 'About four months. Just told Mac recently.'

'That's a long time to suffer alone.'

He stared at me. Swallowed once. Looked at us in the mirror behind the bar and nodded his head slowly. I couldn't tell if he was reacting to the part about it having been a long time, or suffering, or being alone, or all of it.

'I didn't want it to be happening. I hoped it would go away.'

'How many times?'

'Tonight was number three.'

'Always at a crime scene?'

He looked back at me and nodded.

'Have you talked to anyone about post-traumatic stress disorder?'

'Only in the psych sessions after I got shot. But I was fine then. And if I was going to get PTSD I would have already had it.'

'Pete Soronack.'

He nodded.

'Des Lee.'

He looked away.

Pete and Des hadn't known each other, but the entire NYPD knew about them, as did much of the city. Both officers had experienced on-the-job violence, both had had three mandatory sessions with psychologists, both had taken a standard leave of absence, both had been cleared to return to work. Then, a year or so later, they came together by chance at a crime scene – both had been patrolling near the Queens neighborhood at the same time when a domestic violence call came in – and when they got to the house and faced the enraged husband waving a loaded gun, both officers froze up. It was Pete's first flashback. Later it would come out that Des had hidden the fact that he'd been having them for seven weeks. Both were suffering from what was called chronic PTSD, delayed onset. So there they were, visiting the past like time travelers who had left their bodies behind, and in the minutes before they came to, and before other cops arrived to back them up, the wife was shot dead and the husband killed himself. All in front of their six-year-old son.

'You should talk to someone now,' I said.

'Karin, I don't want my career to end under that cloud.'

But I had just seen him in the grip of a flashback and I knew he wasn't in control of them. There was no question in my mind that, if he didn't deal with this as soon as possible, his career would inevitably come crashing down. 'I don't think you have much choice.'

He swiveled away from me, glanced at the back room. 'There's a pool table. Feel like hitting some balls?'

I looked into the mirror. It wasn't ten past nine (as if the evening could get earlier as it progressed); it was now ten to three. The night ticked onward, it was almost morning, and there was no point trying to sleep before Ben's regular six A.M. wakeup. With Mac sick, I'd be the one taking him to nursery school at nine.

'Sure.'

The pool table was angled in the middle of an empty room with maroon walls and tall barred windows. Wooden stools lined two walls. There was a musty, airless smell – leftover smoke from past centuries, decades of spilled drinks. On a normal night at prime time this room was probably packed. People's names, presumably from earlier in the evening, were scrawled on a chalkboard waiting list propped against a narrow counter.

We played for an hour, not talking anymore about Billy's looming problem. Or the fact that his *friend* the serial killer had struck again tonight,

31

or that an unidentified girl had been found unconscious and alone on a desolate strip near a murder.
We were both exhausted, it was late, so we just
played pool. At three-thirty, the bartender called
for last drinks. At four, the lights unceremoniously
switched off. We discovered that we were the last
to leave, besides the bartender, who locked up
behind us. He nodded at us before turning to go,
his diamond earrings catching light from a streetlamp, sending two quick flashes into the darkness.
Billy and I were alone on the quiet street.

'Thanks again, Karin.' He leaned in to kiss my
cheek.

'Promise me you'll get some help.'

The way he grinned, I knew he wouldn't.

CHAPTER 3

Having found that a small amount of sleep is sometimes worse than none at all, I made some coffee, ate an early breakfast, and stayed up reading until Ben woke up at six o'clock. I heard his light footsteps in the downstairs hall and hurried to intercept him before he disturbed Mac.

'Mommy!' He paused outside my bedroom door, turned and ran to me at the foot of the stairs. I caught him in my arms, in all his flannel softness, and buried my nose in the mess of his hair.

'Shh,' I whispered. 'Daddy still doesn't feel well. Let's let him sleep.'

We tiptoed upstairs and settled into the usual morning routine. Ben ate his bowl of oatmeal. I drank more coffee and sat with him as he chattered about a red sports car he'd seen on the street the day before. He adored all kinds of vehicles, especially snazzy cars; but I couldn't keep my mind on what he was saying. My thoughts kept falling backward, to last night, to that little girl lying on the sidewalk. For some reason I couldn't pinpoint, whenever I thought of her blue manicure I felt troubled.

'Vroom!' Ben must have had the yellow race car in his pajamas pocket because suddenly he was whizzing it across the table. It flew into the air and landed in his glass of juice. 'Mommy, look! Maretti can swim!' Maretti being an amalgamation of the legendary race car driver Mario Andretti. Ben had begun to show signs that he was drawn to risk, like his mother, unfortunately.

'Now Maretti needs a bath.'

'No, he *likes* it.'

He finished his juice with the car floating in it. When he was through I rinsed it and put it in the dish drainer to dry, then got Ben ready for preschool. Our part-time babysitter, Chali, always picked him up at noon and spent the afternoon with him, to free me up to work with Mac or take classes or both. Today, after I dropped Ben off, I was looking forward to coming home and getting some sleep. He put on his helmet and I helped him into his jacket and mittens. I carried his three-wheeled scooter down the steps and off we went into the bright winter morning. The sheen of ice that had made the sidewalk so slippery last night had melted with the morning sun, for which I was grateful, given that trying to talk Ben out of riding his scooter to school always ignited a battle.

I jogged behind Ben as he zipped two blocks along Smith Street, me dodging passersby as they dodged him. Luckily he was a quick drop-off; we had been spared the emotional drama of separation anxieties that so often flared with early school experiences. He was parked in his classroom and I was out the door in three minutes.

Our routine was so regular that, on my way home, I passed all the usual suspects undertaking *their* morning rush: the guy in a business suit with his coat flapping open, running to the subway; the teenage girl wearing earmuff headphones, probably late for school but walking very slowly; the old Dominican man in his blue balaclava, seated on a bench in front of the Italian restaurant; and my favorites, the Three Musketeers, as I thought of them – three fortyish men in clothes that were always crisply clean but were styled for adolescents, with pants down low, bulky colorful sneakers, sideways baseball caps.

By the time I reached my corner and turned on Bergen, my only thought was: *sleep.*

Hours later I woke up in a bed that felt sweltering and claustrophobic. Mac lay beside me, so still I was certain he was asleep. Between the closed winter windows, his fever, and his flu, the room felt unbearably stuffy. I kicked off the covers, stretched, and yawned.

'You're awake.' His voice sounded rough and thin, as if worn out from coughing.

I leaned on my elbows and peered at the green glow of the digital clock across the room. 'It's after one. Are Ben and Chali home?'

'I heard them come in a little while ago.'

I lay back down. 'Good.'

'So?'

'How are you feeling?'

'Like crap. What happened last night?'

'Oh boy . . . you don't want to know.'

'I wouldn't have asked if . . .' His voice trailed off in a coughing fit that crescendoed before dying down. In the meantime I went to the bathroom and refilled his glass of water. He sat partially up and drank deeply before turning to look at me. 'Please don't make me talk more than I have to.'

I reached over and touched his forehead. 'We should take your temperature.'

He stared at me, annoyed. Obviously he had a fever. He had the flu. What he wanted was the story of last night.

I told him about finding Billy hallucinating on the sidewalk like a lonely derelict, about the girl, and about the murder. About how I tried to talk to Billy about PTSD, and how stubborn he was.

'It's not going to end well if he doesn't get help,' I finished.

Mac lay on his side, looking at me with fluey eyes. 'When I'm better, I'll talk to him.'

'It was really disturbing seeing that flashback in action. It had him under a spell; he was just gone.'

'That's what they say.' He twisted back over to pull a tissue from the box beside his bed, blew his nose, and tossed the crumpled tissue into the trash can he'd pulled up next to him.

36

'How is it Billy developed PTSD,' I said, 'but neither of us did? You could argue that what we went through was at least as bad.'

'Luck of the draw, I guess.'

'Poor Billy. I hated seeing him like that.'

'Maybe I can talk to him later. I don't care how sick I am; I'm not missing it.' Billy was being honored for his heroism and dedication to public safety at the monthly community/precinct meeting being held tonight at the local YMCA.

'No one wants to catch your flu, Mac.'

'I'll stand off to the side.'

'How can you stand when you can hardly sit up for more than five minutes? Give it a rest. I'll go.'

'We'll see.'

'What's the name of that support group for cops?' he asked.

'Can't remember. But he's in such denial, I don't think he'd participate.'

He started to push himself out of bed.

'Where are you going?'

'Get my laptop.'

'I'll get it.'

I went to his office down the hall and returned with his computer. Booted it up, turned on the bedside lamp, and sat on the bed Googling until I'd found the organization Mac was thinking of.

'POPPA – Police Organization Providing Peer Assistance.'

'That's the one.'

I clicked on the link and started reading. 'It says

that about half of all traumatized cops get hit with PTSD sooner or later, but only a few go for help. This group is about cops helping cops. It's a good idea.'

Mac nodded. Blew his nose.

'And it's right here in New York City.'

He leaned in to see the laptop screen. 'That's great.'

'Except it might as well be in Minnesota,' I said. 'If he won't go for help, he won't go.'

'We'll work on him.'

I clicked through to the link titled 'Officer Support Groups.' 'There's a meeting every two weeks in Lower Manhattan. Maybe if you went with him.'

'Good idea.' He was seized by yet another coughing fit and pitched forward to surrender to it. I put the box of tissues in front of him, turned back to the laptop, and opened a new search window. I wondered what the reporter – the one Ladasha had shouted at – had done with last night's murder, and if the news had gone viral yet.

'Tenth Victim,' screamed the headline on the online edition of the *Daily News*. 'Murder Mayhem Continues,' announced the front page of the *New York Post*. 'Serial Killer Strikes Again – Preying on Prostitutes – Tenth Victim in Two Years,' was the meandering headline in the *New York Times*, buried in its city pages. All the pieces briefly mentioned the nearby traffic accident and the girl taken to the hospital, but nothing more.

I dug deeper, and learned that the local blogs had jumped on the plight of the barefoot girl who had been hit by a car. Brownstoner and Gothamist had both done pieces on her, which meant that by tomorrow the traditional news outlets would follow suit.

'She was taken to New York-Presbyterian Hospital in Manhattan,' I told Mac, scrolling down. 'Her name is Abby Dekker, she's eleven years old, a fifth grader at Packer, and she lives right here in Boerum Hill with her parents.'

'Dekker,' Mac said. 'It rings a bell.'

I read down the page. 'It says she's unconscious. She's been put in a medically induced coma to reduce swelling from a head injury.'

'Poor kid.'

'She was so *young*.'

'Is, not was,' he corrected me. 'She's alive.'

'Her family must be freaking out.'

'Google Dekker and see what pops up – I have a feeling I know that name.'

Mac edged closer to watch the screen while I did the search. The fourth item down – below a best-selling thriller author's official Web site, a vacuum cleaner manufacturer, and a management firm – was a company profile for a man named Reed Dekker. A typical corporate photograph showed a middle-aged white man with brown hair neatly parted to the side. He was fairly handsome, with a serious demeanor and smiling eyes that hinted at satisfaction.

'I knew it!'

I looked at my husband, whose weary face had lit up. 'You know him?'

'That's Reed. I talk to him at the gym all the time. He told me he works for a bank.'

We both read the profile. 'He doesn't just work for a bank, Mac. Look at this. He's a senior vice president at Goldman Sachs.'

'You're kidding.'

'Do you know what those guys make? Millions, after their mega bonuses. I didn't know you were hobnobbing with the super-rich at the gym.'

'We sweat together on neighboring elliptical machines, that's about it.'

I read down Reed Dekker's bio. 'It says here . . . he lives with his wife and daughter in Brooklyn Heights. That's funny. The blogs reported that Abby Dekker lives in Boerum Hill. I wonder what's accurate.'

'She was hit in Boerum Hill . . .' He paused to sip his water.

'In the middle of the night. So it's probably Boerum Hill. Maybe Reed put Brooklyn Heights in his bio because it sounds swankier. And it's not like he can't afford the Heights.'

'I liked the guy—'

'He's not dead, either,' I reminded Mac. Though I knew why he'd made the slip: Tragedy changes a family. The Dekkers' only child was hit by a car and was critically injured, in a coma. It wasn't death, but to a parent it would feel too close. And

40

Mac was a parent; he was feeling his gym buddy's pain.

'You're right. Reed Dekker isn't—' He was interrupted by a knock on our bedroom door.

'Ben?' I said. 'Chali?'

'I heard you talking,' Chali's muffled voice answered from the hall.

'Come in.' I swung my legs around to sit on the edge of the bed, switched on the lamp on my bedside table, and waited.

'Put your hand on the knob,' I heard her say in the easy tone she used with Ben. 'Good boy. Now turn.'

But nothing happened. So I got up to open the door. She was standing there holding a tray with two bowls of steaming soup, her long, black hair brushed neatly back into her usual ponytail. Slight, with sparkling brown eyes, Chali wasn't classically pretty but she shone with special vibrancy and goodwill despite the fact that, in India, she was a Harijan, the 'Children of God' caste better known as untouchables. It was a cruel distinction she had escaped by migrating to the great melting pot of New York City.

Chali was the other widow in my life, though hers had been vastly different widowhood from my mother's or mine. Only twenty-six years old, she had a twelve-year-old daughter living back in India with her own mother; Chali had given birth at the age of fourteen after being forced into marriage to a sixty-four-year-old man. I had noticed that she didn't seem particularly aggrieved when she told the story of waking up one morning four years ago to find her husband dead of a heart attack beside her. After a year of struggling in poverty to support herself and her young daughter, Dathi, she gave up and did what so many third-world mothers do, leaving their beloved children in the hands of a family member and traveling thousands of miles to put food in their family's mouths from afar. In this way Chali was no different from scores of other nannies and house-keepers who flee to America, the women who reluctantly leave their own children behind to support them by taking care of other people's families; but to me she was unique. Chali had a bright, unschooled wit, she was a refreshing com-bination of cheerful and honest, and she was reliable to a fault. She had never once let us down and I knew she never would. The longer she worked for us – over a year now – the more like family she became.

Ben pushed the door all the way open, jumped on the bed, and snuggled under the covers with Mac.

'Daddy's on fire!'

'Daddy is sick,' Chali said. 'Let him be.'

'It's okay,' Mac said. 'I could use the hugs.'

'Here, I brought you both some lunch.'

'Chali, that is so nice of you, but *I'm* not sick.'

She smiled. 'So much the better. Now sit and take this bowl before it spills.'

I put one of the bowls on my bedside table, and helped Chali balance the tray on Mac's lap. Together we propped some pillows behind him so he could manage the soup. As we set him up, Chali noticed the laptop screen showing Reed Dekker's corporate portrait. She did a double take.

'I recognize him, but I don't know why.'

'Mac knows him from the gym,' I said. 'He lives in the neighborhood; you must have seen him around.'

'Probably that's it.' She waggled her head in the subtle way she did for emphasis. 'But the name, Dekker, that sounds familiar, too.'

'His daughter was hit by a car last night. That's partly why I slept late – Billy was at the scene and I went to meet him.'

Ben squirmed out of Mac's arms, slid off the edge of the bed to the floor, and darted out of the room.

'Stay in bed and rest,' Chali said, as she went after Ben. 'I'll come back later for the tray.'

I heard their footsteps go up the stairs and then move around on the parlor floor above.

We finished our soup. Then, before getting into the shower, I decided to check e-mail. There was nothing important. I was about to get up when I turned to Mac, who was lying down again with the covers pulled up to his chin.

'Want me to check yours, too?' We had placed an ad on Craigslist yesterday morning, before the flu hit him, for a part-time office assistant to take over some of the paperwork that MacLeary Investigations, his flourishing business, was generating and that had swamped both of us lately. His e-mail address was the contact, and I was pretty sure he hadn't checked it at all.

He nodded.

I ran his e-mail – and opened a floodgate.

'Look at all these résumés!' I turned the laptop so he could see it. 'They just keep streaming in.'

His ad had gotten one hundred and seventeen responses . . . make that one hundred and nineteen, as two more arrived before our eyes. And then another, and another. One hundred and twenty-one people interested in a paltry part-time job. We had advertised office help, twelve hours a week, can pay up to fifteen dollars an hour.

I opened one at random. 'Okay, this one is a woman who has over twenty years experience managing a Broadway theater.'

'Overqualified.'

I opened another. 'Here's someone who has a degree in landscape architecture from Harvard, and helped design city playgrounds for three years.'

'Overqualified.'

'Here's an actor who had a leading role on *Law & Order*. And here's a woman with a PhD in microbiology from the University of Pennsylvania.' I looked at Mac, who was staring at me in shock. 'This is nuts. Why would these people be interested in our little job?'

'"It's the economy, stupid."'

Right. The economy was in disaster mode; all these résumés from vastly overqualified people only reinforced what the news reported every day.

'Maybe your friend Reed Dekker can sprinkle a few extra millions on some of us commoners. Did you know they reported last week that Goldman Sachs is making a huge profit, and salaries and bonuses are back to prerecession amounts?'

'I read that, yup.'

I closed Mac's e-mail account as another résumé came in. 'This is going to be a project. I'll start going through the résumés a little later, make a short list. It could be more time consuming than we thought.'

'We need an assistant to find an assistant.' Mac tried to laugh at his own joke but ended up coughing. I kissed his burning forehead, gave him another ibuprofen, and got into the shower.

Twenty minutes later I was upstairs in the sun-drenched living room, lying on the floor. Ben's tummy was balanced on my feet and I held his hands wide in a flying angel. He loved it when I swerved my legs and dipped sideways, nearly toppling him, and then saved him at the last minute.

At the sound of the doorbell ringing, Ben tumbled down onto my stomach, giggling.

'I've got it!' Chali called from the kitchen, where she was checking her e-mail. She didn't have a computer at home and sometimes borrowed mine so she could keep in touch with her daughter.

'No problem. I'm right here.' I jumped up and went to the door.

On my way, I heard Chali intercept Ben as he headed to the top of the stairs: 'Hold it now, little Hadji, let's put your blocks away together first. Unless you want to build another fortress with me?'

I looked through the peephole and there, to my surprise, was Billy.

'Morning.' He leaned through the open door to kiss my cheek; he smelled spicy clean.

'On your way someplace special?'

'Feeling like a fool about last night. Wanted to stop by and apologize.'

'No apologies necessary, Billy. You should know that. Want to come in?'

Behind him, on the sidewalk, our mail carrier stopped and reached into her cart. She came up the stoop and handed me our bundle of mail, glancing fleetingly at Billy, whose eye patch often drew attention. He ignored her.

'Thanks, Terry,' I said.

'Have a nice day.'

'You too.'

I watched her jog down the stoop and roll the cart forward. When I turned back to Billy, he was staring at the house across the street. It was a typical four-story brownstone, more or less the same as all the others on the block, except for one thing. It was on the rooftop of that very house, in a shootout with his lover, that he lost

46

his eye. I had noticed before that when he came over he seemed to avoid even glancing across the street. This was the first time I'd seen him take such a long look, and it saddened me. I wished I could stop his hurt, all of it, give him back the sight in his right eye and undo Jasmine from having entered his life in the first place. Mac and I had even discussed moving to spare him the distress of revisiting that fateful day every time he came over to see us; but with real estate badly devalued, there was no way we could sell our co-op duplex and afford to move somewhere comparable in the neighborhood, so we'd stayed put.

'Come inside, Billy. It's cold out there.'

I hung his jacket on a peg in the hall while Ben ran to him. Chali seemed to hesitate when she saw Billy; her face blanched just a little – reacting, I assumed, to another distraction stopping Ben from cleaning up the blocks, unless it was something else bothering her. Whatever it was, the flash of agitation was quickly replaced with her usual smile.

'Pirate Bill!'

'Ahoy, matey!' Billy fell to one knee and caught Ben in a hug. 'Where's your hat? You're out of uniform. Do you want to walk the plank?'

Ben hurried downstairs and returned moments later wearing his black pirate's hat with a white skull and crossbones on the front. It had been a gift from Billy last Christmas, and it put an end to our efforts to get Ben to stop pointing out Billy's eye patch every single time he came over. Now it was a game they played without fail.

'What are my orders, Pirate Bill?'

Billy stood tall and stroked his chin in a melodramatic thinking pose. 'Tie up the princess!'

'Aye aye, Bill!'

'Not *again*.' Chali laughed and went to the kitchen to get the ball of twine we used for recycling newspapers. She sat on a chair in the middle of the living room, and Ben got to work.

I led Billy into the kitchen and poured us both a cup of coffee, adding a splash of milk to his. I drank mine black.

'How's Mac doing?'

I shook my head. 'I hope it's a quick flu.'

'It's going around. Couple of people at work came down with it and stayed out a week.'

'Can we talk about last night, Billy?'

'It won't happen again.'

'How do you know that?'

'I feel it.' But in fact there was no feeling in his voice. He sounded numb, even irritated. It was as if a force field of denial had thickened around him in the hours since we'd seen each other.

'There's this support group called POPPA—'

'Don't want to talk about it.'

'You can't avoid it forever.'

'There are more important things than me and my problems, Karin. That girl who was hit by the car last night?'

The thought of her angelic face, her blue manicure, sank my heart. 'Abby Dekker. I looked it up this morning, but no one's reported much besides the basics.'

'She lives a few blocks from here but we haven't been able to reach her parents. I told Dash I'd get over there; she was stressing because one of her kids is in a holiday show at school and she "can't be in two places at once," blah blah blah.' But in recounting Ladasha's words, he smiled and gently shook his head. Sometimes I thought the tension between them made work a little more interesting for him, other times I just thought she ought to stop complaining.

'Mac knows the dad – Reed Dekker. He's a banker at Goldman Sachs.'

'Mac have any private contacts for him? His secretary says he didn't come in today and doesn't know where he is, and no one answers the phone at home.'

'I don't think so. I read that Abby goes to Packer. Did you try the school secretary?'

'Won't give us private information over the phone. All we want to do is locate the parents so they can get to the hospital.'

'Right.'

'The school secretary said she'd call the house, and mentioned that the mom's an at-home parent. I'm going over there now.'

'I'll join you.'

'Come on, Karin—'

'Thanks.' I stood up. 'I'll get my coat.'

'That's not what I meant and you know it. I meant come on, you can't go with me. It's going to start looking unprofessional if you keep showing up when I'm on the job. Or Dash might think I don't think she's a good partner, which is a complication I don't need.'

'I have some errands to run in that direction.'

'What direction?'

It was true: He hadn't told me the Dekkers' address. I got my coat and purse, anyway, and waited for Billy in the front hall.

'Almost done tying the princess, Pirate Bill!' Ben told Billy as he reluctantly crossed the living room in my direction.

'Good work, matey! Now . . . untie her and feed her to the sharks.'

Ben immediately complied, unraveling the twine.

'Thank you, Billy.' Chali smiled.

'I don't think I've ever known anyone so cheerful in the face of adversity,' he said.

'You would be cheerful, too, if your daughter was about to arrive from India.'

'When's the big day?'

'The first of January – New Year's. I just received a flight update: she is now going to arrive one hour earlier. So much the better for me. I'm very excited, indeed.'

'That's great news, Chali,' I said. She must have gotten the e-mail just now, otherwise I was sure she would have mentioned it earlier. She'd been

50

planning this reunion with her daughter for a long time, and I suspected that she secretly planned not to send her back to her mother's in India. The arrangement had worked well for them for the years Chali had been in the U.S. earning a living to send home to her impoverished family – enough to feed both grandmother and granddaughter, and pay tuition for Dathi at the local school – but her mother was older and not in the best health.

'You have no idea how much I miss that blessed child.'

'It's been almost a year since they've seen each other,' I told Billy, as he slipped on his jacket. I opened the front door. 'Back in a little while, Chali. I'm going with Billy . . . that is, I'm going to run some errands around the neighborhood.'

'You're a sucky liar,' Billy said when we were down on the sidewalk.

'How do you know? Maybe I'm such a good liar that most of the time you can't tell.'

We walked together along Bergen Street, back in the direction we'd been last night. When I noticed he'd stopped trying to dissuade me from coming along, I stopped pretending I wasn't.

It turned out that the Dekkers were practically neighbors: They lived two blocks down Bergen between Hoyt and Nevins. It was just past two-thirty in the afternoon, and yet when we walked up the stoop and rang the bell, the house seemed oddly quiet. The freezing day was so bright that

51

the windows shone like mirrors. No one answered. I rang again, and Billy leaned over to try and peek through a window but couldn't see anything. The curtains were drawn, as if no one had gotten up that morning to let in the day.

CHAPTER 4

'You're looking for the Dekkers.'

I turned to my right. A small woman with curly black hair stood on the neighboring stoop, watching us. Her front door hung open, allowing a glimpse of a polished oak floor, the curved end of a banister, a chandelier dripping glittery glass. In the living room beyond the hall was a child-sized easel with a primitive drawing of a tree. An orange cat rubbed its face against the doorway but didn't venture out into the cold.

'We are,' Billy answered.

'Well, who are you?'

I could feel Billy's irritation emanate like heat, and jumped in to intercept a potentially tense conversation.

'It's about Abby.'

She nodded. 'So you're friends of theirs. I'm Gay.' She didn't flinch saying that; she must have been used to it. I noticed she was wearing a wedding ring.

'I'm Karin Schaeffer. I live two blocks up. Do I recognize you from the playground?' A lie; I had never seen her before, but I wanted her trust.

53

'My son, Ben, is almost four. We go there all the time.'

Gay smiled. 'That's probably it. My daughter, Sara, is five. So, what about Abby?'

'I hate to be the one to tell you, but she was hit by a car last night, and we haven't been able to reach her parents.'

Horror and suspicion passed in waves over Gay's expression. She appeared to wonder how it was that we knew about this while she, the Dekkers' next-door neighbor, hadn't heard. Billy must have also sensed we were losing her because he reached into his pocket for his wallet and brought out his police identification.

'Karin's a friend of mine, she does live up the street, but I'm a detective with the Eight-four.'

'What's the Eight-four?' Gay stepped closer on her stoop to get a better look at Billy's ID.

'That's your local precinct.'

'Oh.'

I was shocked. How could anyone not know their local precinct, where it was, how to reach it if necessary? But I kept my reaction to myself.

'Marta fed our cat Orangina over the weekend. I texted her a thank-you as soon as we got home last night but haven't heard back from her, which is strange. She always answers right away from her iPhone. I have their house keys, should I—?' She didn't wait for a response before darting into her house and returning with the keys. I couldn't believe it. What if Billy's ID was a fake? The legion of criminals and cons who could forge documents was mind-boggling. Maybe I was cynical because of my years working in law enforcement, but Gay's naïveté floored me. Still, she had the keys, and she was coming up the Dekkers' stoop jangling them in her hand, preparing to let us in; neither Billy nor I was lame enough to stop her from opening the door and going inside to take a look. As a cop, Billy couldn't legally enter without a warrant; but as a civilian neighbor, I could. It was, after all, how Billy had introduced me: as a local mom, not a private investigator. I wasn't working this case; I was just keeping Billy company.

'We take care of each other's houses when we go away,' Gay said, turning a key in the bottom lock half a rotation, until we heard a click. She tried turning a second key in the top lock, but it didn't budge. 'Huh. I've done this a dozen times.'

'Maybe it's already unlocked,' Billy suggested.

Gay turned the knob and the door opened. 'That's weird. They always use both locks. Now that I think of it . . .' Closing the door, she relocked the bottom and tried it again. 'I didn't think of this before, but the bottom one self-locks, so turning it partway means it was never double-locked. It seems like someone just pulled shut the door and left.'

Billy and I looked at each other.

Gay's dark eyebrows pinched together as she opened the door again and went inside.

'Marta? It's Gay! Are you there? Marta?'

I left Billy outside and followed Gay into a foyer made spacious by having been united with the living room in a feat of modern architecture that had opened up so many of the local brownstones. Antique details had been restored, giving the room a nineteenth-century warmth, and yet at the same time it was almost loftlike in its sense of free-flowing space. There was a lot of carved wood and modern rugs, contemporary light fixtures, antique furniture, high-end stereo equipment. At the foot of the stairs, beside a huge mirror, a pedestal held a tall vase, a twist of orange and red glass I doubted could hold a flower. It sat there like a dare: *Break me.* In one corner of the living room, a shiny baby grand piano was covered in framed photographs: a snapshot of a smiling Reed and Marta, whose dangling earrings were partially obscured by shoulder-length auburn hair that grazed her freckled shoulders; a professional portrait of the family of three; Reed and another man on a fishing boat; and half a dozen pictures of Abby as a baby, a toddler, a little girl, a sassy tween.

'Marta!' Gay proceeded through the parlor floor of the house she evidently knew fairly well. She disappeared through an arched door through which I could see the end of a kitchen island topped in speckled granite, where a ceramic bowl was heaped with Granny apples. I was following Gay, glancing around the dining area, when suddenly she screamed.

In the kitchen, a man lay faceup in a pool of

blood that had been there long enough to spread before drying around the edges. He had the same brown hair I'd seen on Reed Dekker in the online photo, but this man was without a face; it had been blown away, leaving behind a gory sludge of flesh and bone. A constellation of blood spatter was sprayed across the white ceiling and half the nearest wall. I forced myself to look a moment longer before turning away. Reed Dekker couldn't have been there more than a day because there was no sign of maggots. The smell was putrid. I covered my mouth and tried not to gag.

Gay ran past me, shaking, and I heard her crying to Billy out front.

'What?' he asked her. 'Calm down, okay? I can't understand what you're trying to tell me.'

When I got outside, I found Billy standing there, baffled, as Gay dry-heaved over the frozen soil of a clay planter decorated with carved ribbons. Her cat, Orangina, had stepped onto the neighboring stoop and was watching her.

'What's going on?' Billy asked me.

'Reed Dekker – he's dead.'

His jaw dropped, as if a hinge had come loose, and I instinctively watched his eye for a shift in consciousness. Would I be able to see it when PTSD invaded his mind?

But nothing happened. He didn't transform into Mr Hyde. He sighed, reached for his phone, and said, 'I'll call it in.'

Within ten minutes, it began. Cop cars drove up

and parked in the middle of the street, delivering investigators who joined Billy inside the house. The CSI guys arrived in a van that was probably white but was so dirty it looked gray, and hauled their gear up the stoop. Patrol cars closed off both ends of the block. Names of anyone coming onto or leaving the block were listed in a log. When the media arrived in droves, I stepped back into the house because I didn't want to get dragged into the story. Gay was long gone, locked inside her brownstone.

Apparently the Dekkers lived on all four floors of the house, and investigators had swarmed throughout. Quick footsteps thudded above, and out of curiosity I followed the sound. I was amazed that no one stopped me. I knew from experience that it was pretty easy to spot rubberneckers at a crime scene – they tended to exude some combination of fear, confusion, or excitement – and I was good at blending in, having done this so many times back when I was on the force. A detective coming down the stairs nodded at me in passing; I nodded back and kept going.

The second floor of the house had three rooms: a guest room with a double bed and bright Marimekko curtains on the single window; and office with a plain desk holding a pair of flat-screen monitors facing an expensive chair; and a more casual living room than the one downstairs that was probably used as a family room, with a large flat-screen television on a wall opposite a comfy sectional couch. Books and games and dolls were scattered around. I saw only one investigator working on the second floor, which told me that the racket that had drawn my attention was coming from above.

As I climbed the stairs to the fourth floor, the noise increased. I walked past what was presumably Abby's bedroom at the top of the staircase: lavender walls, white built-in bookcases crammed with young adult novels, a messy desk with a white laptop and a jewelry tree dripping necklaces, a twin bed. The sense of chaos increased the farther I got down the hall, past a couple of closed doors to another bedroom at the opposite end.

Investigators had formed a second cluster in the master bedroom, around a king-sized bed. It was a large, apricot-painted room with two matching dressers and another wall-mounted flat-screen television facing the bed. Pale winter afternoon sunlight gave the room a sensation of having been stripped bare. Sprayed blood speckled the wall above the headboard in a weirdly graceful pattern that reminded me of the receding path of the only shooting star I had ever seen. I shifted my attention to the bed and tried to see past a clump of investigators.

From my view in the doorway all I could see was a pair of slender, waxy-looking bare feet. The woman's toenails were freshly painted blue, like Abby's fingernails; they must have recently gone for a mother-daughter manicure and pedicure. An agonizing reminder of my daughter's murder six years ago curdled in my stomach; she, too, had been killed in her bed. Someone shifted and I saw Marta's face – it was gone. I felt my own face screw up. Just then, one of the forensic techs stepped out of the cluster, looked over, and saw me. He was near the top of the bed and his rubber gloves were streaked with blood.

'Can I help you?'

I had dropped my cool, slipped out of character, and he'd recognized an outsider.

I cleared my throat, gathered myself. 'How long has she been dead?'

'Are you a reporter?'

Faces turned to look at me, none bearing an expression of warm greeting.

'No,' I assured them. 'I'm a neighbor.'

'Get her out of here,' he snapped.

A uniformed cop escorted me back downstairs.

Billy came out of the kitchen when he saw me. As I was led to the front door, I glanced at him, concerned he'd tripped into a flashback again.

'You can let her go,' Billy told the cop, calmly; but once we were alone his tone heated up. 'Why are you still here, Karin?'

'You okay?'

'I'm fine.'

'Have you been upstairs?'

'Not yet.'

'Don't.' I worried that the sight of Marta Dekker would bring on another hallucination. Both

Dekkers had been shot in the face as Billy had been, only with more devastating consequences. For Billy, the resonance would be inevitable.

Ladasha came out of the kitchen and saw me. 'You some kind of crime scene groupie now, Karin?'

'I just happened to walk this way with Billy.'

'Do I need to tell your husband you and Billy here are gettin' it on, or what?' She had her hands on her hips and her head cocked to the side. I wasn't sure, but I thought I saw her wink.

'How was your kid's holiday show?'

'Short and sweet.'

Billy put a hand on my arm and steered me forward. 'Karin was just leaving, Dash.'

'So soon? The party just started!'

'See you around, Dash.' I looked at Billy, standing reluctantly at the foot of the stairs, shook my head, and repeated, *'Don't.'*

Outside, a throng of neighbors had gathered behind a front line of media being held back by a pair of cops. Cameras flashed as soon as I appeared on the stoop. Compared with last night's murder of a prostitute on a dark, squalid street, the afternoon slaying of a wealthy couple in a gentrified neighborhood was receiving significantly greater attention. It didn't surprise me, but I couldn't help thinking of the young woman sprawled on the frozen pavement last night. I still didn't know her name and wondered if anyone did . . . or if anyone cared.

The front door shut behind me and the lock clicked. Reporters shouted questions as I came down the steps:

'What's happening in there?'

'We heard two people are dead. Can you confirm that?'

'Can you please spell your name?'

'Is it accurate that there were two murders inside the house?'

'Is the owner Reed Dekker? Is he a banker? Is his wife Martha Dekker?'

Marta, I wanted to correct the young man with a snake tattoo curling up his neck out of his collar and both earlobes tattooed with eyes. *Her name was Marta, not Martha. You don't know anything about these people. I don't know, either. No one knows what happened in there, or why they were murdered.* But I held my silence as I stepped onto the sidewalk and walked down Bergen. The illustrated reporter trailed me, peppering me with questions, until I passed the barricade.

I was only halfway up my front stoop when Billy came walking swiftly up the block, jacket zipped all the way up to the top of his neck, hands thrust into his pockets. I turned around and watched him until he reached my bottom step.

'How'd you get past the reporters?' He was too distinctive to miss – a tall, black detective with an eye patch who had already been written up and interviewed in connection with the city's notorious serial killer who was still on the loose. Billy was practically famous, and he didn't like it.

'Walked fast. Kept my head down.'

'So – you saw her?'

He nodded, but now he wouldn't look at me.

'You okay?'

'I felt a little shaky so I got out of there. Told Dash I was going to the hospital to see Abby.'

'Are you?'

'You coming with me?'

'You want me to?'

'No.' He smiled.

'Let me just see how Mac's doing. Give me a minute.'

Billy followed me inside. The house was quiet; Chali must have taken Ben out to the playground. Billy waited in the living room while I went downstairs to check on Mac. He was sleeping soundly. Back upstairs I left a note on the kitchen table letting Chali know I would be back later. I had already arranged for her to babysit tonight so Mac and I could go to the community meeting at seven o'clock to support Billy; now, unless Mac made a miraculous recovery, it would just be me.

We walked up to Court Street – the main commercial strip that ran from what I thought of as Deep Carroll Gardens, one of the last parts of the linked neighborhoods to be gentrified – to Brooklyn Heights, where we could catch the express train. Along the way, Billy filled me in.

'They were both shot once in the face from close range.'

'Find the weapon?'

'Not yet.' He shook his head. 'Lot of rage there – someone didn't like them very much.'

'Reed's face . . .' I wished I could stop seeing it: obliterated. 'You don't think it was some random whacko who somehow got in?'

'No sign of breaking and entering.'

'So they opened the door to their killer.'

'Or he was already inside. Hopefully Abby can tell us.'

'You don't think *she*—' But I couldn't think that; there was *no way* that little girl in sheep pajamas was a killer.

'It doesn't matter what I think, Karin. I'm just doing my job.'

'Are you running a GSR on her?' Though by now any gunshot residue would have been washed off her skin at the hospital.

'Her clothes are at the lab.'

We turned onto Joralemon Street and headed into the yawning stairwell that led into the subway. Partway down, I turned to Billy.

'Do you think this could be connected to the woman last night? Abby was found so close to the latest victim of—'

He didn't let me finish. 'That's a serious stretch, Karin. The Dekkers' house is right around the corner from Nevins Street . . . something happened in that house, and that's where Abby ran because

64

it was close. The Working Girl Killer kills hookers, and hookers work Nevins, that's a well-known fact. It's the city; you walk one block and you're in a different universe. I wouldn't look for connections that probably don't exist.'

'But what are the odds of all that happening in such close proximity in one day and night?'

'It was a bad day in Brooklyn.'

'Maybe whoever was driving the car that hit Abby saw something.'

'Maybe, maybe not. Along with GSR, the lab's looking for paint and metal trace from a car. It's a long shot, but if it goes that way – if we luck out and find the car, and we find the driver – what are the odds that he killed the Dekkers, abducted Abby, she got away and he mowed her down with his car before pulling over to butcher another prostitute?'

'That's ridiculous, Billy.'

'Exactly.'

'But if he or she saw something—'

'That would be great.' A sarcastic snort. He'd been a detective a long time; you learned not to hang hopes on what you might find, but to look at what was right in front of you.

'I hear you. But I have a feeling—'

'No feelings, Karin. Facts. Keep the feelings somewhere else. What I really need is to talk to Abby, or if she doesn't wake up, find another witness who saw . . .'

His sentence drifted off, so I finished for him. 'Anything at all.'

Billy flashed his badge to the ticket booth attendant, who buzzed open the gate for him. I swiped my Metro-Card and went through the turnstile. We headed down another flight of steps and waited on the platform for a train. The subway had that familiar rotten egg smell, but it was warmer down here. The track started to rumble and soon the front of a train appeared with a green-encircled number five. We stopped talking and crowded in. For the next half hour we rode in silence. When we went back up to the street, we were on Lexington Avenue in Manhattan, the sun was fading, and the sky was turning gray.

It was a ten-minute walk to the river and the Sixty-eighth Street entrance of New York-Presbyterian Hospital, where Abby had been admitted to the Komansky Children's Center. As soon as we crossed York Avenue and entered the lead-in to the hospital's circular driveway, we started seeing media vans with their tall antennas. There were five in all. Reporters hung around the bank of revolving doors, waiting for some action.

They surrounded Billy as soon as they saw him.

'No comment,' he said firmly, twice.

We pushed into the main entrance, a hive of activity beneath a vaulted ceiling, and were directed to the pediatric critical care unit. We knew we had reached the correct elevator when we encountered a few more reporters.

'Any thoughts about all those murders happening so close together,' a woman in a big fur hat asked, 'and the kid getting hit by a car, pretty much all at the same time?'

Billy briefly turned a cold glare on her, before stepping into the elevator and riding with me to the fifth floor.

We stood in the hall outside Abby's private room; we had been told to wait for someone who would fill us in and give us the ground rules of dealing with a coma patient, specifically *this* coma patient. I hated hospitals with their high-gloss floors and eerie quiet punctured by bursts of noise; their awful antiseptic chaos. The only nontraumatic thing that happened in a hospital was the birth of a baby, and sometimes even that was traumatic. I briefly thought of last October (of Julie or Marisa or Zoe) and almost succumbed to the sticky emotional turmoil that reached for me at times like this, but pushed it away before it latched on. I felt a cascade of triumph, then despair. Sometimes I wished for my Prozac back, but it hadn't worked for me, at least not the way it was supposed to. I looked at Billy, wondering if antidepressants would help him. He was leaning against the wall with his eye closed. His breathing was so shallow I couldn't see it.

Finally a woman approached with her hand outstretched. Billy opened his eyes and stepped forward.

'I'm Sasha Mendelssohn. Sorry it took so long.' She was small, with short red hair and freckled skin, and wore a white coat with a name tag that didn't say MD, so she wasn't a doctor. 'I don't know if anyone at the desk explained, but I'm Abby's care coordinator. That means if you have any questions or concerns, or want to speak with the doctor, you ask me, and I, well, coordinate.'

'Detective Staples, Brooklyn Eight-four.' Billy shook her hand. 'This is Karin Schaeffer; she's consulting on the case; we were both there last night and we're following up. Can we see her?'

'We understand that you'll want to question her,' Sasha said, 'and eventually we'll be able to bring her out of the coma, but right now that's just impossible. She's in very delicate condition.'

'Any idea how long it'll be?'

'I wish we knew.' Her gaze settled on Billy's eye patch. 'How did you lose the eye?'

'How do you know I lost it?' His tone was hard, but she'd asked a pitiless question.

'The patch.'

'Maybe I was born blind in that eye. Maybe I have an infection.'

'No one wears an eye patch for an infection or blindness, at least not in my experience.'

'I don't like to talk about it.'

'I'm sorry I brought it up – truly. Not my business.'

'How long before we can talk to Abby?'

'Honestly, it could be days, it could be weeks.'

'She may be the only witness. We understand she's a child, and that she's injured, but it's important.'

'Let me explain,' Sasha said, looking alternately

between us. 'The idea behind putting her in a medically induced coma is to protect her from potential brain damage. The coma helps to prevent swelling that would reduce blood flow to the brain, which could result in a secondary injury worse than the initial injury. It's preventative. But that's not all. She has a broken leg, which is in a cast, and she also has four broken ribs and a broken collarbone, which we tape; for those to heal, the main thing is keeping still. The coma keeps her body at rest and her brain quiet. For her sake, it's the best recourse at the moment.'

'All right.' Billy's attempt at acquiescence didn't match his agitated tone. 'But can't you be more specific than a few days or a few weeks?'

'Billy,' I said to him. 'They have to do what's best for Abby now.'

Sasha hesitated, and then offered, 'I can let you see her for a minute.'

'That would be great,' I said.

'Just a moment.' She quietly opened Abby's door and peeked in, then beckoned us to follow.

Last night, framed in the menacing context of the dual crime scenes, it had taken a moment to realize Abby was a child; here, it was the first thing you saw. She was small and narrow in the big white hospital bed, not taking up much space, a little girl encased in a web of casts, bandages, and tubes. Her broken leg, the left one, lay above the covers. It was set in a cast from hip to foot, with just her multicolored toenails sticking out. Her hands lay still at her sides, with her blue fingernails again evoking a strange feeling in me. I couldn't see her ribs under the hospital gown, but her bruised and battered left collarbone was visible beneath strips of translucent medical tape. She had either been hit by the car on her left side, or had fallen, hard, to the left. Her head appeared to have been shaved; the soft, wheat-colored hair was gone. A white gauze turban hid her head injuries, but you could see that the bruising on her face below the turban was worse on the left side. Tubes protruding from a nostril and her mouth were attached to a pair of larger tubes connected over her chest and extending right and left to the machinery that surrounded and sustained her.

Sasha glanced at me. I held my poker face, summoning the old cop-me who could handle anything (or thought she could). I understood why she had invited us in: seeing Abby like this would have convinced anyone of the fragility of her medical condition. Poor girl; motherless child. I wanted to hug her, but didn't dare. I felt bereft on her behalf, knowing what she would have to learn about her parents' loss when she awoke.

Unless she already knew.

What *did* she know?

That was the big question.

CHAPTER 5

A screeching noise filled the YMCA gym, and the short, gray-haired man standing under the basketball hoop pulled the microphone away from his mouth and winced. Howie Marcus was the president of the Eighty-fourth Precinct Community Council; I didn't know what he did for his day job, but clearly he was not used to talking into microphones. All three cops standing behind him held still, not responding to the awful sound, but in the middle row of folding chairs a man with muttonchop sideburns pressed his hands against his ears until the sound system was adjusted and the feedback died down. Ladasha was farther down from us in the front row, sitting with two young boys I guessed were her sons. I wasn't surprised that she had come out on her own time to show support for Billy when he received his award from the council; for all her toughness, she was a good lady deep down.

'That's better,' Howie said. 'Back to business. As I was saying, or trying to say' – he paused for a spate of laughter – 'before I turn the microphone over to Detective Gates, I want to remind our local children not to smoke, and I want to remind the parents of our children that you are their role models. So don't smoke, either. Detective Gates?'

A man in a dark suit and pink shirt, with a gun holstered on his belt, replaced Howie beneath the hoop. It was a funny place to stand, I thought, given the enormity of the gym. But someone had set up two banks of folding chairs facing the basketball hoop, forcing the speaker into that spot.

'First, let me say thanks to everyone who came out tonight. Like Howie mentioned, we do these meetings every month and they're an important part of our precinct's outreach to the local community. It's our chance to meet each other and your chance to ask us questions. First though I wanted to talk a little about identity theft.'

I turned to glance around the room. It had grown more crowded since we'd first sat down, mostly, I noticed, with older people, though there were a few clusters of the neighborhood's signature hipsters, a sign of the changing demographic. Someday those hipsters would be the oldsters, and a new generation would move in to replace them, just about the time their not-so-cool-anymore tattoos faded and sagged beyond recognition.

Detective Gates reached into his pocket and pulled out a small black plastic device about half the size of a man's wallet. He held it up.

'This is what they call a skimmer – it's a magnetic strip reader. See this slit down the middle? You go into a restaurant, the waiter takes your check and your credit card and goes away for a minute. By the time he gets back, he's run your card through this reader and he's got enough information to reproduce your credit card. You sign the chit, now he's got a carbon of your signature, and he's all set. By tomorrow he's got a dummy card on your account, he knows how you sign your name, and he goes on a shopping spree – on your dime.'

A murmur passed through the room.

'Another thing the guy might do is put a skimmer right over the card slot on your local ATM, so when you dip in your card to take out some cash, you just gave all your information away. The guy standing on line behind you is his partner: He watches you enter your PIN. He memorizes your PIN. As soon as you walk away, he writes it down. Now these sweethearts can duplicate your ATM card and get into your bank account.'

A hand shot up in the front row. Detective Gates pointed at the woman.

'But how can someone put one of those things on a bank machine without everyone noticing?'

'Good question. They wait until no one's around, then the accomplice stands outside the bank window holding a big umbrella, blocking the view, while the guy affixes the skimmer to the card reader.'

'How could someone tell it's not a real card reader?' a man called out from behind me.

'Wiggle it. If it doesn't feel right, don't use it. Go tell someone in the bank if it's during banking hours. If you can, pull the thing off and report it.'

'I never heard of that before,' someone else mumbled.

'That's why I'm here to talk about it. I've been on the precinct's Computer Crimes Unit a year now and the stuff I've seen would curl your hair.'

'I have a question.' The woman's voice was strong and clear. I turned around and saw a young mother holding a baby over her shoulder, patting him with a hand wearing a large diamond ring. 'But it's not about identity theft.'

'Go ahead. Probably one of us can answer it.'

'My husband and I are thinking of buying a house in the area.'

'Good place to raise a family.' Gates smiled.

'That's what I hear. But all the news today about those murders and that little girl getting hit by a car – it freaked me out. And now I don't know if this is such a great place to live after all.'

The room erupted, and more hands shot up. A knot formed in my stomach. Billy's jaw muscles moved visibly beneath his skin; he pointedly did *not* turn around to show his face, though he'd have to eventually. Because he was wearing a baseball cap, the strap of his eye patch wasn't visible from behind; I braced myself for the moment he turned around and people made the connection between the cop being honored tonight and the latest face of the serial killer hunt.

74

Detective Gates raised a hand to calm the crowd. 'We'll address that to the best of our ability. But first, I want to remind everyone here that out of seventy-six precincts citywide, we're number sixty-nine in terms of crime, so this is a pretty safe neighborhood.'

The clamor heightened. One man loudly said, 'Three people murdered in twenty-four hours doesn't feel safe.' Passionate agreement rippled through the room.

Ladasha stood up, faced the room with an irritated expression, but glanced at her children and sat back down.

The cops and detectives present had obviously decided not to throw Billy and Ladasha to the wolves. The only reason they were here tonight was because Billy was about to be honored. It wouldn't be much of a celebration if a throng of outraged citizens vented at him moments before he was handed the plaque we could all see lying on the table behind Howie Marcus, Detective Gates, and the three uniformed officers.

'This is an investigation in progress,' Gates said, 'but I can tell you that from what I understand, one of those cases, the couple on Bergen, was not a situation of breaking and entering. I don't think it's even been classified a homicide yet. And the other one is a separate case totally.'

'It was the Working Girl Killer,' a woman said in such a soft, quavering voice the room quieted suddenly to hear her. 'That's what I've heard. That the killer they've been looking for is right here in our neighborhood now.'

The young mother got up and walked out; she had just changed her mind and wouldn't be buying in Brownstone Brooklyn, after all.

'That case has a task force working practically around the clock,' Gates began, but was cut off by the man with the muttonchop sideburns. He was now holding a pad of paper and a pen: a reporter.

'I thought both cases were being worked by the same detectives. Why is that?'

'Could be. I don't know.' Gates glanced at Ladasha, and then back to the reporter. Ladasha gathered her kids and left the gym. Billy's gaze trailed her, as if he wished he, too, could escape this; but he was on the meeting's agenda and had to stick it out. 'If you're a journalist, why don't you see us after the meeting when we can talk?'

'Why can't you talk now?' a woman called out.

'That's right! We all want to know.'

'I hear you.' The detective's smile was stiff now. 'Believe me, cases like these are an anomaly for our area. We just don't see murders like that very often, and definitely not so close together geographically, or the same day. Not around here. But sometimes crazy stuff happens. We'll get to the bottom of it, that's a promise.'

'It isn't as safe here as you say,' an elderly man directly behind us mumbled, but it was loud enough for Gates to hear as well.

'This is still one of the safest neighborhoods in the city, people. Trust me. These were not random killings. We will catch both assailants. In the meantime, do what you always do and use your judgment about where you go and what time you go there. Don't open your doors if you're not expecting someone. Don't walk alone on dark streets if you have a choice.'

'Don't smoke,' a young man at the back of the room called out, inciting a ripple of sarcastic laughter.

A few people in the back got up, grumbling, and left the room. Howie Marcus came forward and took back the microphone. Gates stood behind him with the three cops.

'Thank you very much, Detective Gates, for informing us about identity theft.' He waited for the obligatory applause, which seemed skimpier than before. 'Now that we're done with all the official community business, I'd like to turn your attention to a special member of our local police force.'

Billy had known for weeks about the award he was going to receive from the precinct's community council. I turned to wink at him, thinking I might earn a smile, but he looked horrified by the attention that was about to befall him. He still seemed raw from last night's hallucinatory migration into the past. I regretted that Mac couldn't be here to cheer him on; he might have relaxed Billy better than I seemed able to. Or maybe it was delusional to think that Mac's close friendship had some special power over Billy; maybe he was slipping beyond anyone's reach.

'Detective William Staples, will you please stand up?'

Billy dutifully stood, his hands clasped together in front of him, and turned to face the crowd. A round of tepid applause was broken by gasps of recognition.

'Isn't *that* the detective?'

'He's been sitting here all along!'

'Why didn't he say something?'

'What's going on with all those murders?'

'Are we safe or not?'

Billy lifted a hand in a gesture of calm and peace. His voice sounded more assured than I knew he felt: 'I promise you, as soon as we know something, we'll tell you. But I can say you're as safe today as you were yesterday. As Detective Gates said, none of the events here over the weekend were random. We're working hard on closing both cases, I promise you.'

'*And now,*' Howie practically shouted, gesturing for Billy to join him at the podium, 'let's get back to the real reason we brought Detective Staples here tonight.' Reading from a prepared statement, Howie continued: 'Detective Staples has been with the precinct for sixteen years, and he has been an upstanding member of our local law enforcement team. But that isn't why he's receiving the Distinguished Officer Award tonight. The reason we're honoring Detective Staples is because any man who puts his life on the line in the course of duty, as Detective Staples does every single day, deserves our recognition and our gratitude. But what Detective Staples did one day a year and a half ago went far beyond the call of duty. He put his life on the line, he took a bullet for our community, and lucky for us, he is not only still here to tell the story but he's still on the job. Now that's courage!'

When the room burst into applause, Billy finally cracked a smile.

'On behalf of the precinct and the entire community, please accept this Distinguished Officer Award for Bravery in the Line of Duty.'

Howie handed Billy the plaque. Billy held it by his side without looking at it. He leaned toward the microphone in Howie's hand, said, 'Thank you,' and returned to his seat.

'Well, I guess that's it,' Howie said. 'Thanks for coming, folks. See you in a month, second Tuesday of January.'

Billy and I waited in our seats until the room had mostly emptied before getting up to leave.

'Thank God that's over,' Billy muttered as we made our way down a flight of stairs and outside to Atlantic Avenue. We stood together in the cold and the dark, cars whizzing past on the busy two-way thoroughfare. Billy leaned forward to kiss my cheek. 'Thanks for coming, Karin. Appreciate it.'

'Billy – wait.' I opened my purse, pulled out the slip of paper with the contact information for POPPA, and gave it to him.

'What is this?'

'Police Organization Providing Peer Assistance. It's the support group I started telling you about before.'

'Jesus, Karin.' He tried to hand back the paper, but I refused to take it.

'You need to talk to people who understand what you're going through. PTSD, Billy; you've got to stop denying it. It's only going to get worse if you don't—'

'Forget it.'

'Let me finish.'

'No.'

I stood there and watched him walk off toward Boerum Place. He lived in Park Slope, twenty minutes away on foot. He obviously wanted to be alone, so I didn't try to catch up with him. I still had one more stop to make before my day was over: I had picked up a prescription for my mother yesterday and promised to have it to her by today. As I turned to walk in the opposite direction, I noticed Billy stuffing the slip of paper into his pants pocket instead of throwing it away. It was reassuring, even if it didn't guarantee that he would follow through.

Court Street was bedecked with holiday lights as far down as I could see; the illuminated stars and snowflakes, slung above the traffic, appeared every November and stayed until January. The decorations always cheered me up, and by the time I'd walked a couple of blocks I was feeling susceptible to the sweet pine smell wafting from the trees being sold in front of the corner drugstore. Another local tradition seemed to be that a small group of French Canadians camped out for a month with their truckload of trees, doing a brisk business right up until Christmas Eve. We were going to spend the holidays at my brother's in Los Angeles this year, and had decided not to get our own tree. But Mac loved Christmas trees, and on impulse, thinking it would cheer him up, I changed the plan.

I pointed to a six-foot Fraser fir, full with silver-green needles and emanating a strong, comforting scent. 'How much?'

'Seventy dollars,' the young man in a red-and-black checked flannel shirt and brown scarf answered in a strong French accent.

'I'll give you fifty.'

'I'm sorry, ma'am. I can go to sixty-five, but no lower.'

'Fifty-five. Because you called me ma'am.'

'Sixty.'

'Deal.'

I paid and arranged to have it delivered in the morning. After stopping at Blue Marble to buy my mother a pint of her favorite black raspberry ice cream, I headed to Kane Street, where she rented an apartment. We hadn't seen enough of Mom since arthritis started creeping up her spine, and I missed her, especially today. She found it difficult to walk the seven blocks to our house, and sitting in a car was no easier. It was hard to imagine how she'd tolerate traveling all the way to L.A. with us in two weeks, but she swore that she'd be fine since her doctor promised to load her up with pain-killers. The trip had been planned before the arthritis hit in full force, and my sister-in-law, Andrea, who was pregnant again, couldn't travel. Mom refused to even contemplate missing a chance to spend the holidays with all of us.

My mother lived on the ground floor of a brown-stone on Kane Street near Tompkins Place. It was a quiet pocket of the neighborhood, leafy except in winter, when the stout limbs of thick old trees shot their spindly branches together in gray lace-work against the sky. Tonight's bright moon cast the scene with a strange clarity. I thought of Abby Dekker, sat down on the nearest stoop, and started to cry. But only briefly. I was overtired and over-reacting. I rubbed my face dry with the palms of my hands, stood up, and continued to my mother's building down the block. I let myself in with my own key, first opening the iron gate and then the inner door.

'Hello!' I called out immediately, so she wouldn't be afraid.

The volume of a television quickly diminished in the living room down the hall.

'Karin honey, is that you?'

'Hi, Mom.' I left my coat and purse on the chair by the front door, picked up the Blue Marble bag, and flicked lights on as I made my way through the hallway off of which sprouted her three rooms: bedroom, living room, kitchen. Off the kitchen she also had a big yard all to herself; it had been one of her stipulations when she'd hunted for a place to live.

She was sitting in the only chair that was at all comfortable for her, a plush white leather recliner that leaned as far back as she wanted it to, resting her feet on a matching footstool. I stooped down to kiss her.

She saw the bag and smiled. 'How did you know I was craving that?'

'Were you?'

'I am now.'

She switched off *Antiques Roadshow* and watched me pass into her smallish kitchen, a starkly modern room that had been renovated, along with the bathroom, just before she'd moved in. I liked the simplicity and cleanliness of this kitchen; it meant business and didn't tolerate clutter, unlike the large country kitchen of my later youth in Montclair, New Jersey, that became a magnet of disorder every afternoon when Jon and I got home from school. Mom had once commented that this kitchen felt 'unexpected' and 'like a meditation.' She had grown used to widowhood and seemed to have adjusted well to the quietude of living alone. I liked to believe that we – Mac and Ben and I – staved off loneliness for her, together with a handful of good friends she'd accumulated since arriving in Brooklyn a few years ago. We had offered to give her Mac's study as a bedroom, so she could live with us, but she'd insisted she enjoyed her privacy too much to relinquish it just yet.

I returned with two of her white bowls holding a couple scoops each of the lavender-colored ice cream. She spooned some into her mouth, and sighed, before speaking.

'How's Mac feeling?'

'He's in for the long haul. You got *your* flu shot this year, didn't you?'

'Yes.' She patted my knee. 'I like it when you mother me. You're a good mother, Karin.' She craned her neck to look closer at my face. 'Were you crying?'

'Just a little. Crazy day.'

'That's why I hate the holidays – they intensify whatever's happening in our lives.'

She meant the miscarriage; we'd talked about it enough for her to know how sad it had left me.

'No, Mom, it isn't that. I've been spending a lot of time with Billy since last night. At two different crime scenes.'

Now she reared back. 'Why?'

I explained what had happened, about Billy's obvious PTSD, but kept the details of the murders minimal. But it turned out she knew all about them anyway.

'Essie e-mailed me this morning after she heard the news about what happened in this neighborhood.' Essie was Mom's good friend from an art history class she had taken last year at the New School in Manhattan. 'She sent me a link and I checked a few online newspapers. Karin, are you telling me *you* were there?'

'I was.'

She stared at me a moment before speaking again. I knew she wished I was completely out of law enforcement; after everything we'd been through already, she couldn't understand why I still worked cases with Mac and was studying to be a forensic psychologist. I had tried to explain to her: It was what I did, what I knew, what I was good at.

'You're a moth to flame, Karin.' She sounded displeased, but dropped it. We had already had this conversation a few times in the past and my mother was not one to attempt the impossible, like changing my mind about something I had already decided to do.

We visited for an hour or so, until a new wave of exhaustion overcame me; it was just past nine o'clock but felt like midnight. I headed home, feeling as if I'd collapse if I didn't get into bed right away.

Chali was sitting in the kitchen, reading a magazine, when I walked into the quiet house.

'They're both asleep?' I asked her.

She closed the magazine and looked at me, her

eyes a little droopy; it had been a long day for her, too. 'Mac's fever is still high – 103.4. I gave him some more ibuprofen and put some ice water by his bed.'

'Thank you so much, Chali. I really appreciate you staying late tonight.'

'How was the ceremony?'

'Not much of a ceremony, really. At the end of the meeting they handed him a plaque and said some nice words. He hated every minute of it.'

'Detective Staples needs to learn to appreciate himself more. And I still say he's a handsome man, even with one eye.'

'I'll tell him you said so.'

'Do *not* tell him I said so, please.' But she giggled.

'You'll be happy to know that I bought a Christmas tree. It's coming in the morning.'

'Excellent. Ben and I will decorate it in the afternoon.' Chali was a devout Christian and, though she hadn't mentioned it explicitly, I knew she'd been disappointed that I hadn't yet made any acknowledgment of Christmas.

'I'm seriously wiped out,' I said. 'Mind if I just head right down to bed?' She had her own keys and was used to letting herself out.

'Yes, but,' Chali began, half rising from the table, and then sitting back down, 'I hoped to have a word with you. I remembered something that I wanted to—'

She had that look on her face, when she started to really talk. If I had one complaint about Chali, and it was an insignificant one, it was that she occasionally talked too much. She was a born communicator who should have been educated and let loose on the mass media or at least the blogosphere. Instead, she had grown up semi-illiterate in a minuscule village in central India, teaching herself to read and write on the sly.

'Do you mind too much if we hold off until tomorrow? I only slept a few hours in the last two days and I can barely see straight right now.'

She hesitated, then stood up. 'It can wait. I'll just go home and take a nice hot bath.'

'You need to rest up, too,' I said. 'Dathi will be here before you know it.'

'January first.' She lit up with one of her smiles. 'It will be a new year in the most perfect way.'

'Thanks again, Chali.'

'Good night.'

Glancing into her dark eyes, I felt a trill of something uncomfortable, a sensation of foreboding. I brushed it aside; it had been a long, difficult day.

'Good night. See you tomorrow.'

CHAPTER 6

I stood back and looked at the tree that now occupied a large space of our living room. Closing my eyes, I breathed in the exquisite pine smell. I wished I'd be able to join Chali and Ben in decorating it that afternoon, but I'd promised to take my mother to a doctor's appointment. It was almost noon. Ben and Chali would be home in about twenty minutes and I still had a lot to do.

I took my laptop downstairs, pausing outside my closed bedroom door for sounds of Mac. It was quiet; he was probably still sleeping. Then I heard the roiling wheezing coughs that had begun to worry me. I waited for it to die down by the cracked open door, wondering if he'd woken himself up. He hadn't. Day three of any flu was like the heart of a storm; you hunkered down while the worst passed. But the sound of that cough – I didn't like it.

I set up in Mac's office where I could get some work done before Chali and Ben got home and had their lunch; I could use that time to review more résumés for the part-time assistant I now felt we needed more than ever. I had gone through nearly fifty résumés that morning, and they continued to pour in. If the flow didn't abate by evening, I would cancel the ad early; it had been set to run for a week. I managed to click open another dozen and sort them into e-mail folders – yes, no, or maybe – when my cell phone rang with a call from Ben's nursery school.

'Karin? It's Alyssa from Open House.'

'Not another timeout.' Ben's nursery school teacher had called once before to report that my headstrong son had refused to give up another boy's color-coded rug spot at circle time; the teachers liked to nip social jockeying in the bud, and keep parents informed every step of the way. But how would kids learn anything if adults constantly intervened in their struggles?

'He's been an angel. I'm calling because his sitter hasn't come for him yet. Was there a change in plans today?'

It was twelve-sixteen according to the blinking icon on the laptop screen, about the time Chali and Ben usually arrived home. 'She must be stuck on the subway. I'll run over and pick him up right now.'

'He's welcome to stay longer, but the full-day kids are settling in with their lunches and he doesn't have anything.'

'No, it's fine. I'm on my way.'

Chali had never been late for pickup before, but you couldn't live in New York City without getting snagged by the subway system sooner or later. I grabbed my coat and purse.

Outside, it was cold and bright. No one else was around as I hurried up our block and turned the corner onto Smith Street, where I nearly collided with the Three Musketeers. They were banded together as usual, talking, heading in the opposite direction from their regular morning walk. I wondered if this was their usual time of return from wherever it was they headed every morning when I was taking Ben to school. The shortest among them, wearing yellow and red sneakers and a sideways Mets cap, jumped when I accidentally came too close. His sideburns were shaped like daggers and his skin had a worn, grainy quality. He smelled like a combination of cigarettes and mint toothpaste. I almost apologized for surprising him but changed my mind when he shot me an irritated look. I shot one back, and walked quickly in the direction of Open House, four blocks down.

Halfway there I stopped dead in my tracks at the sight of two local newspapers displayed on a rack outside a deli. Both showed the front of the Dekker house cordoned off with police tape, bouquets of flowers staggering up the front stoop. A mother I recognized from the playground wheeled her daughter's stroller past and saw me.

'Isn't it awful?' she said, and kept moving.

I nodded, assuming she'd read the alarm in my expression as a reaction to the crime, not the fast-moving ubiquity of the news of the Dekkers' deaths. I flipped open the pages of one of the papers to see if there was anything about the prostitute, but found nothing.

Ten minutes later, jogging back down Smith Street behind my scootering son, I impulsively decided to detour to the Dekkers' house. I wanted to see what was happening over there, and Ben would never notice the deviation from the usual route home. I got ahead of him and kept going instead of making our turn, to avoid passing our building. He dutifully followed, happy just to be whizzing along on wheels. I slowed down and let him get ahead of me so I could keep my eyes on him. When we reached the Dekkers' block, I could see from a distance that the activity had not died down so much as shifted. The CSI vans were gone, but cop cars remained and uniforms still guarded the house. There were more reporters, from the look of it. And the front stoop was now piled high with flowers, candles, balloons, and stuffed animals.

'A party!' Ben shouted, and sped up.

I ran to catch up to him. 'We're not invited. Come on, let's cross the street and go home.' I caught his shoulder to slow him down and maneuver through two parked cars. Maybe it wasn't the greatest move to teach a small child to cross in the middle of the street, but suddenly I didn't want him near a crime scene. Any crime scene. Ever.

⋆   ⋆   ⋆

After lunch I hauled out the box of Christmas decorations and let Ben hang a few ornaments. He was a handful, and I felt acutely aware of how accustomed I'd become to Chali keeping him busy on weekday afternoons. I kept checking the time; it was getting later and later. In just a few minutes I would have to leave to get my mother. The thought of taking Ben an hour on the subway and then having him boomerang around a doctor's waiting room for possibly another hour was exhausting. I tried Chali's cell phone again; and again it was intercepted by voice mail and her cheerful voice promising to call back soon. I left another message and sat there, wondering what to do.

Slow footsteps creaking up the stairs told me that Mac was out of bed.

'Are you okay?' I called down. 'Do you need something?'

'The bedroom's getting claustrophobic.' His voice sounded faint, even as it grew nearer. 'Maybe this wasn't such a great idea.'

I found him halfway up the stairs, steadying himself on the banister.

'Dizzy?'

'Just for a minute.' He continued up. 'But I can't lie there anymore.'

'You're pale.' I touched his forehead with the back of my hand. 'And hot.'

'You're hot, too, baby.' He tried to wink at me, but it wasn't funny and it definitely wasn't sexy.

I steered him to the couch, where he lay, wheezing, with his head on a cushion I arranged for him.

'Nice tree.' He managed a tepid smile.

'I have to head over to my mom's, to take her to see Dr Alderson.'

'Where's Chali?'

'That's the problem.' I explained.

'Go ahead. I'll keep an eye on Ben.'

'That's not a good idea, Mac. You can hardly move.'

'If you close the doors to the hall and the kitchen, I'll be okay. And put out some snacks for him. And hand me the remote control.'

He was right; he could supervise from the couch, and the remote control worked wonders in a pinch. Plus Chali would probably turn up soon. I set out a couple of juice boxes and bottles of water along with a bowl of dry Cheerios, kissed my guys, and took off.

Later that evening, my mother stood between the long dark windows at the front of our living room, beside the Christmas tree, placing the ornaments Ben handed her in the high spots he couldn't reach. She had let her short hair go white, and in the darkness the passing of every car outside and each flash of colored lights from the tree made her glow on and off, unevenly, with a shimmer that would burst and then fade. In her free hand she held a nearly finished glass of white wine.

'"Old age is a massacre,"' she said.

'What?' I glanced up from the floor, where I was slipping hooks into ornaments that didn't have any.

'Philip Roth said that. And Bette Davis said—'

'"Old age is no place for sissies."' She had quoted that one before.

'That's damned straight.' She drained her wine and steadied herself on the windowsill. Her pain management doctor had decided to change her medication and was weaning her off one to begin another. The wine was going to see her through the night. We'd been back at my house three hours and she'd been on her feet the entire time because sitting, she said, felt like a hot poker up her spine.

The doorbell rang and my heart jumped, thinking it might be Chali – but why would it be? She had her own set of keys, and we hadn't arranged for her to babysit tonight. I stood abruptly and loped across the living room to the foyer just as the bell rang a second time.

I paid the deliveryman and took the bag with our dinner to the kitchen. Made Ben a plate of chicken and broccoli with rice and set it by his tall chair. Served my mother and myself some pad Thai with shrimp, and called them to the table. When Mac woke up, I'd bring him some reheated soup.

Mom stood beside the table, washing down bites of noodles with a steady flow of wine. I knew she was going to argue with me about spending the night, but how would I get her home in her state? I wasn't going to mention anything until after I'd gotten Ben bathed and into bed. Maybe then I'd put on a movie. Was there any chance she would fall asleep on her feet and I could just shift her down onto the sofa bed? I wished I could give her my bed, but with Mac sick there was just no way.

'Where does Chali live, exactly?'

I looked up at my mother, standing there with a fork dripping noodles suspended near her mouth.

'Sunset Park.'

'That's Brooklyn?'

I nodded. 'It's not too far from here, probably fifteen minutes.' Fifteen minutes by car, bus, or subway. It was hard not to think about how relatively close Chali's apartment was, how easy it would be to drop in and assure myself that she was all right.

'I guarantee you she's in bed with the flu.'

'She had her shot. And she would have called.'

'You never know.'

Mom was probably right: Chali's flu shot could have backfired this year. Or maybe there was some kind of an emergency with her daughter, Dathi. My imagination did a U-turn and now, instead of seeing Chali feverish in her bed, I saw her at the Indian Consulate in Manhattan, desperate for some reason I couldn't know, begging for help. Had something gone wrong with the visa she had arranged for her daughter's much anticipated visit?

But the visa had already been approved, plane ticket purchased, plans set in place. I shut my eyes. Tried to melt the plank of hypervigilance that had installed itself across my forehead, as if every day now would bring a new crisis.

Chali was *fine*.

Tomorrow she would call me.

The real problem was that I had edged too close to my deep well of anxiety, and was peering in. I couldn't stop thinking about the onslaught of death these past two days. The Dekkers. The prostitute. And Abby Dekker . . . the moment I thought about her and wondered if she was still in a coma, still alive, a wicked headache spread across my skull. The loss of a daughter – mine (twice) or anyone's – opened a cavernous pit in my soul. I told my mother I'd be right back and not to pause the movie; I couldn't concentrate on it, anyway. I went to the bathroom for a couple of ibuprofen. Then, in the kitchen, I closed the door and dialed Billy.

'Is it a bad time?' I heard voices behind him, a woman's voice, the sound of people laughing in the distance.

'Not really. I'm at my sister Janine's on Long Island. She's having her annual holiday party.'

'Are you alone?'

'In the bedroom.'

'I hear a TV.'

'I'm catching the game.'

'Why bother going to a party if you're going to hide out and watch TV?'

'If I didn't come to her party, she'd hold it against me, and it isn't worth it. But I'm tired. Couldn't sleep much last night.'

'Did you call that number I gave you? For POPPA?'

He sighed. 'Not yet, but . . .'

'Billy.'

'I'll call them.' But the way he said it, I didn't believe him.

'Where did you go last night after the community meeting?'

'Headed home, the long way. Stopped for a couple of drinks. I was home before midnight but couldn't get to sleep until around five, and then the alarm clock screamed in my ear at seven.' He paused to sip something, swallow. 'I keep thinking about it, you know?'

I did. But he meant more than the three violent cases that had dropped on him in less than twenty-four hours. In the midst of all that, he'd time-traveled to a bad, distant place where the last woman he'd loved had tried to kill him.

'How is Abby doing? Have you seen her again?'

'No, but I talked to that coordinator a couple of times. No changes. No nothing. No new leads on suspects. Haven't heard back from the lab on traces off Abby's clothes, but whoever's car hit that kid had to leave something behind on her. We just need something to start with.'

'It'll come,' I tried to reassure him.

'It always does. Well, usually . . .'

97

'What about the gun?'

'Nope.' He took another long swallow. I understood his frustration: if they found the weapon, it would yield something to go on. *If.* In the pause, the conversation shifted.

'So . . . Chali didn't show up at Ben's school this afternoon.'

'Hmm.'

'And she still hasn't called.'

That got his attention. He was quiet, but I could tell he was listening.

'I'm worried about her.'

'I'm sure she's fine.'

'Don't try to placate me, Billy.'

'Something came up, Karin. Stuff happens. She'll call tomorrow.'

But that was what Billy did when he knew there could be reason for worry: He intervened with stalwart rationality. I was going to protest. Chali was one of those people who never left you waiting. Who didn't forget or neglect obligations. Who always called. Janine's voice interrupted, though, before I had a chance to argue.

'Get your sorry ass off the bed, William Luther Staples, and come back to the party!'

'Luther?' I chuckled.

'It's an old family name. Gotta go.'

In the morning I dropped Ben off at school, picked up Mom's new prescription, and arranged to take her home later after the new medication had had a chance to make itself known. When I left them, Mac was sitting in the living room, draped over a chair, and Mom was stretched out on her stomach on the sofa bed. I felt like a negligent nurse on a hospital ward; but I needed to do this, and quickly: In two and a half hours I'd have to be back to pick Ben up from school, unless Chali showed up. But something told me she wouldn't. I had the worst feeling.

I found the set of spare keys Chali had left in our bowl by the front door, in case she ever lost hers; the ring held keys for both her apartment and our house, with a small white feather attached with a string that made it easy to pick out of the mass of other keys. The day she'd asked to leave the keys with us was the day I'd understood how few friends she had in New York. She had come to this country to work, to support her family back home, not to socialize. It was a unique paradigm you saw a lot of in the city: immigrants scrimping and saving, plodding along, always looking to the future. I remembered feeling honored that Chali had trusted us as guardians of her keys; it was the moment I'd realized that she was not just working out as a babysitter, but that our relationship had deepened. I dropped the keys into my purse and headed out.

CHAPTER 7

I stepped out of the R train station at Thirty-sixth Street and Fourth Avenue in Sunset Park, into a blistering wind. Lifted my scarf, tugged down my hat, and pointed myself down the wide avenue in the direction of Thirty-third Street. It was a grim procession past a bodega, Laundromat, barbershop, funeral home, two bars, and on Chali's corner a gas station. The utilitarianism of the neighborhood reflected what I imagined to be the flavor of the lives of the people who lived here: hardship, struggle, loneliness, unrelenting work. But the flicker of holiday lights strung around a few of the windows above the stores reminded me that there was always more to what met the eye. Where there were people there were stories, there was life. I thought of Chali and the complexity of the existence she had fled in India, how she had been a child bride to a much older man, how his death had impoverished her but in some ways also freed her. How she had left her beloved daughter behind to start a new life here. How despite the difficulty of that choice, she forged ahead, working steadily and with determination toward a brighter future for them both. You had to admire someone who could do what she did, and as I walked toward her building between Fourth and Fifth avenues, on a block lined with run-down clapboard and a few brick houses, I thought of how much I had come to like and trust and care about her. I wouldn't have come all the way out here otherwise.

I stopped in front of her building: four stories without a front stoop, faced with a red and green checkerboard meant to evoke brick. Dug into my purse for her keys and looked for her name on the strip of four doorbells. Three other names were listed, and a fourth was blank, for the third floor. I pressed that bell. Waited. After a minute I pressed it again, and when again there was no response I let myself in with Chali's key.

The building's front hall was shabby from age but not dirty; someone was keeping it clean and trying, at least, to brighten it up with a vase of plastic flowers and an unframed poster of a Greek village scene. The ammonia smell of cleanser faded as I climbed to the third floor, where outside a single door sat a pair of black boots I recognized as Chali's. One of the boots had fallen over. I knocked on the door, but at this point I didn't expect an answer. I slid in the key but before I turned it, the door pushed open – it had been left unlocked.

'Chali?' I stepped partway inside a narrow living room whose bright pink walls were lined with white shelves packed with books. 'It's Karin! Are you here?'

It was so quiet. The feeling that drew me here, the feeling I'd tried to discount as kneejerk anxiety, grew heavier. Standing in Chali's living room, amid the substance of her private life – the books of literature in English and Hindi, what looked like a manuscript of some kind, a small black notebook with *Addresses* embossed on the front, and countless photographs of Dathi, whom I recognized from a couple of photographs Chali had once shown me – a sensation of dread crackled through me.

I walked through the living room.

Colorful wooden beads hanging in a doorway clattered as I passed through them.

Her bedroom was small, with a white chenille bedspread covering a double mattress on the floor, and half a dozen bright pillows leaning against the wall. A large round painting of a vivid yellow water lily hung above the bed. Across the room, above an old wooden chest of drawers, hung a simple drawing of Jesus Christ. Beneath it, atop the dresser, sat a large framed photo of Dathi and an older woman, presumably Chali's mother – steel-gray hair in a tight bun, wearing a sky-blue sari – facing the bed, where Chali would be able to see it while she rested. Nothing in this room surprised me; this was Chali as I knew her: vibrant, family-oriented, devout. The jeans and sweater she'd worn on Monday were draped over the edge of the mattress; her socks were puddled on the floor. In the corner, near the room's only window, a door stood ajar.

I crept forward and peered through the doorway. Saw the edge of a toilet. White bathroom tiles, scrubbed clean. A green bathmat.

'Chali?' I whispered. I knew she liked to take baths to relax; in fact, she'd mentioned that was what she was going to do Monday night when she got home. She could very well have been in the tub without hearing the bell, or my voice when I'd entered.

'Chali?'

I pushed open the door and stepped into the small bathroom. Beside the toilet was a narrow sink cabinet. A red plastic hairbrush trailing long strands of black hair lay on the edge of the sink. I moved aside to shift the door so I could see the bathtub, but what hit me first, as I took it all in, was the awful smell.

She had slipped down in the bath. Her face was submerged. Her knees, splayed open, jutted above the surface of the water, which was blackish as pungent wine.

And then I saw it: the handle of a knife protruding from the water in the range of where her chest would be. A familiar handle, much like the one I'd seen in the body of the still unidentified woman Sunday night – the hard-to-find Bowie knife that was the signature of the Working Girl Killer.

I backed out of the bathroom. Shaking. Numb.

Light-headed. Sat on the edge of the bed and tried to breathe. But couldn't because it was true: the fears I had nursed like a genuine neurotic; it was true that something awful had happened to Chali. That she was dead. Like the others. I had come here to disprove that feeling, but instead . . .

Staring into my purse, looking for my cell phone, the prosaic objects of daily life seemed indistinguishable. I leaned into a shaft of sunlight angling in from the window until my brain finally recognized the shiny black edge of my phone. I pressed the M, Mac's speed dial, and was so rattled to get his voice mail that all I knew was, whatever I said, it was incoherent. Next I pressed B for Billy. I should have called 911 but I wasn't thinking clearly. I wasn't *thinking*.

Chali was dead in the next room.

Submerged in her bath, into which her blood had drained for . . . how long? Since Monday night. Thirty-six hours lying cold and alone in her apartment, and no one had known. If I hadn't come today, looking for her, how long would it have taken before the smell had crept through her bedroom, her living room, underneath the front door where it would have finally summoned her neighbors?

'Hey Karin,' Billy answered.

'He killed her.' My voice was a hollow rasp.

'Whoa – what're you talking about?'

'*Him*. He was here.'

'Where are you?'

'At Chali's. I came to find her.'

For a moment, neither of us spoke.

'I should call 911—'

'I'll call. You get out of there, Karin. *Now.*'

Moving through Chali's bedroom was like passing through water: weightless and difficult. The strands of beads crashed behind me like a breaking wave and I stood in her living room, drowning in the certainty of what I had feared. *Chali.* The Working Girl Killer had veered off his own path, bypassed his own logic, murdered someone who was not supposed to have been one of his victims . . . and this time, he had taken the life of someone I knew and cared about . . . drawn me into this now . . . and none of it made sense.

Why?

Why Chali?

And why now?

I found myself standing near a photo of Dathi. I knew better than to touch it – this was a crime scene now – so I leaned in and examined the girl's face. She had her mother's big, dark eyes. And her mother's fine, sloping nose. And her mother's clever grin, as if on the verge of telling a joke. But the shape of her face was someone else's; it was wider; the face of the man whom Chali told me had beaten her throughout her teenage pregnancy. Dathi had the shape of her father's face. But I would have bet, looking at the smiling eyes that were just like Chali's, that she had her mother's heart. I leaned closer. Yes: Chali had been lucky:

she had had a daughter. But her daughter was not so lucky, as she was now motherless.

How would she take the news? That she was an orphan now, living with an elderly grandmother who couldn't afford to keep her without the money Chali sent home. The money was the easy part; I could do that myself, and I would. But what about the rest of it? Who would tell these people they had lost someone they loved? Who would have the courage to tell them how it had happened?

The buzzer startled me. My gaze jerked off the photograph and toward the open apartment door. The buzzer rang again and I heard someone rattle the front door downstairs. There was an old intercom unit on the wall by the door. I pressed the button.

'Hello?'

'Police.'

I buzzed them in and then it began: a storm of footsteps up two flights of stairs.

The scene would be documented; Chali's body would be removed and examined; reports would flow from this devastating morning, connecting the past to a projected future.

What did he want?

Why was he doing this?

Who was next to die?

How could he be stopped from taking another life?

I headed downstairs, eager, even desperate, to get out of there. Ben needed to be picked up in an hour, so I had a ready excuse. But by the time I reached the first floor, I'd realized that I was the closest thing Chali had in New York to next of kin. In fact, if she had any relatives at all in the U.S., I was unaware of it. I had to wait.

I would never make it back to Ben's nursery school by noon. And neither Mac nor my mother was well enough to step in and help.

I stood outside the building in the freezing cold while the police did their work upstairs and neighbors gathered to find out what was happening. I pretended to know nothing; they probably thought I was a reporter, the way I was working my BlackBerry. It took a few calls but I was able to arrange for Ben to spend the afternoon at Open House; the school allowed morning kids to extend into the afternoon session, which started with lunch and a nap, for an additional hourly fee. Ben had been begging to stay for lunch for weeks now; I could ask him, later, if he liked his 'surprise' and see how it went over. The deli down the street would deliver a grilled cheese sandwich and an apple juice. So now I had until five o'clock, if I needed that much time.

When Mac called me back, a few minutes later, his baffled tone told me he knew something was wrong. 'Your message sounded, well, *drunk.*'

'I'm at Chali's.' I didn't know where to begin.

'What's going on?'

'She's dead.' I burst into tears. '*He* killed her.'

The chasm of silence that followed was fraught

107

with shock; and Mac's whisper, when he finally spoke, was raw, emotional. 'What happened?'

I told him what I had seen. Explained that Billy was on his way. And that the local cops had already arrived.

'Where's Ben?'

'Staying late at school; I called and arranged it.'

'Okay, good.' Mac coughed. 'What's Chali's address? I'll be there as soon as I can; just hold tight.'

'You're sick, Mac, and the last thing I need is you catching your *death* out here in the freezing cold.' Hammering hard on that haunted word; knowing he would hear me loud and clear: *Do not even suggest doing something that will make you sicker, because if I lose you, too . . .*

'It's just the flu—'

'People die of the flu every year.' I could see him shivering in the frigid afternoon, growing paler, hotter, weaker.

'You're freaking out, Karin. Take a deep breath and—' He must have shifted, possibly stood up too quickly, because something fell over and crashed. '*Shit.*'

'I swear, Mac, if you show up here, I will kill you.' It came out fast and sharp. I ended the call before he had a chance to argue. Slipped the phone into my purse. Jammed my hands into my pockets to keep them warm and waited for the detective who had caught the case.

Twenty minutes later, a blue sedan that looked

like a police-issued unmarked vehicle if I'd ever seen one pulled up next to a delivery truck with *Trevello Bros.* scripted across the side, and double-parked at a careless angle. It was the way he parked that told me the detective had arrived. But then he got out of the car and I thought maybe I was mistaken. I had to remind myself that plainclothes cops in the city didn't dress like the ones I used to work with in the suburbs. Here they covered a distinctly different set of territories, and blending in didn't always mean pressed chinos or pants down low. This guy just didn't look like a cop to me, with his skinny jeans, suede desert boots, short leather jacket, black goatee, purple-tinted glasses, and trendy driver's cap on what you could see was a clean-shaven head. He leaned back into the car and brought out an orange take-out cup labeled *Gorilla Coffee* that erupted in steam when he took off the top. I watched him take three sips before even lifting his eyes to Chali's building, an indifference that irked me for a moment before I realized it probably wasn't apathy so much as preparation. He had probably already heard the stats on this case: immigrant murdered in a downtrodden neighborhood. For a lot of cops I knew, that was a cue for *don't bother caring*. But I reminded myself that I didn't know this guy and shouldn't judge him before he even opened his mouth.

I watched him cross the street before approaching him. As soon as I moved forward, he stopped abruptly and stood there looking at me.

'Didn't mean to surprise you like that,' I said. 'I just wanted to introduce myself before you went inside.'

'You the lady that found her?' He had a chalky voice, as if he smoked, or used to.

'Karin Schaeffer. She worked for me.'

'What makes you think you need to talk to me?'

'Aren't you a detective?'

'Didn't think it was that obvious.'

'I used to work on the force . . . but not here. In New Jersey.'

A little smile crooked up one side of his goatee. He reached out to shake my hand, a gesture I appreciated, despite the thick pinky ring that bit into my palm. 'Retired?'

'From the cops. You bet.'

'You must be loving this, then.' He winked, but managed to make it both warm and sardonic. I liked him. He pulled a rubber-banded stack of NYPD business cards out of his jacket pocket and handed me the bent one off the top: *Detective Jorge Vargas, 72nd Precinct.*

'"Courtesy, Professionalism, Respect,"' I read from the upper corner of his card. 'Sounds good to me.'

'Standard issue.'

'Even so.'

He put the stack of cards back in his pocket. When he removed his hand something flew out and clanked onto the sidewalk. He bent to pick it up.

'My girlfriend gave this to me; keeps flying off my finger.' He slipped the thick silver ring back onto his pinky. 'She got it at the Brooklyn Flea and told me I had to wear it even though it doesn't fit.'

'You can have it resized.'

'I'll have to.'

'Unusual ring.' I took a closer look: a thin rod of roughened silver was melded along the top; it looked like someone had drawn a line across the base of his pinky.

'It's a bar ring, she said. Handmade by a local artist.' He shrugged.

'I see why she likes it.' Though I didn't, really. It was kind of cool, and kind of ugly. I didn't really see the point.

'Can you stick around for a little while?' he asked me.

'Just for a bit, then I'll have to get moving.'

'By the way, everyone calls me George. It's easier, you know?'

I nodded, and he headed inside. A guy on his way out, in a navy jacket with big white letters reading *N.Y.C. CRIME SCENE UNIT*, high-fived him with one of his blue plastic gloves.

'Yo, Georgie boy!'

'Hey Bud.'

'Messy in there?'

'Not really.'

I remembered the drill: a heads-up here, a watch your step there. It was a workday for them. By now everyone knew that whoever that woman was in there had left her body behind like an abandoned meal. What was left was the cleanup. I steeled myself, and vowed to keep it personal on Chali's behalf.

Cops were now starting to canvass door-to-door up and down the block. For a few minutes I chatted with a young reporter, who oddly didn't ask who I was, which told me I was still passing for the press. And then Billy showed up with Ladasha. She pulled up behind George's car; Billy hopped out of the passenger's side before she had fully parked.

He bolted across the street and kissed my cheek. 'What's happening?'

'Detective George Vargas just went upstairs.'

'Seven-two?'

Precinct, he meant. 'Yup.'

'Karin.' Ladasha joined us, both corners of her mouth puckering in frustration. She shook her head. 'I am so sorry about this shit. Did I ever meet her?'

'Don't know. Probably not.'

She shook her head and walked to the building's front door, which was now propped open with a brick. 'This lock?'

'I had to use a key to get in the front,' I told them. 'But Chali's apartment door was open.'

'Broken in?'

'No, just unlocked.'

'So how'd the asshole get in this time?' Ladasha

112

stepped into the hall and looked at the inside of the door.

'Someone probably buzzed him in,' Billy stepped into the hallway, 'or maybe he trailed someone inside.'

I followed them back into the building's vestibule. A cop was canvassing inside, as well, standing outside the first-floor apartment, speaking with a beefy man in a sleeveless white T-shirt who looked as if he'd just been roused from sleep.

'You always home at this time of day?' I heard the cop ask.

'No, just lately.' The man had a strong accent I couldn't place. 'Lost my job last month.'

'You home Monday night?'

'Yes, most nights I'm at home.'

'Monday night, I said.'

'Yes, sir.'

'Hear anything?'

'No, nothing. I heard nothing.'

The cop handed him a business card, told him to call if he thought of something. The man shut his door as fast as he could, but moments later a woman appeared in a five-and-dime housedress, her hair piled in curlers. She was wearing lipstick, and crying.

'Not Miss Chali!' She nearly threw herself at the cop who had just left her front door and was now standing at the foot of the stairs. 'Tell me, please, *no, it isn't true!*'

'Sorry, lady.' He left her standing there, weepy.

Ladasha followed him up the stairs, rolling her eyes. Billy gave her a nod. I touched her shoulder as I passed.

'Where you going?' Ladasha turned and said when she realized I was still with them.

'She's already been up there,' Billy defended me. 'What's the difference?'

The truth was, I didn't want to go back into Chali's apartment, but I was concerned about Billy entering another crime scene. I didn't want him to see it without some moral support.

'Whatever.' Ladasha smirked.

The small apartment felt crowded with nearly a dozen investigators and technicians doing their work or just standing around talking. I could see George Vargas through the beaded curtain separating the bedroom. He had put his orange coffee cup on the desk, right on top of the manuscript I'd noticed before. I went over to pick up the cup and as I was about to touch it – just as I saw that the top page of the manuscript was a poem in Chali's distinctive handwriting – Ladasha barked at me:

'What you doing now, girl?'

'The detective brought this cup in. I was just—'

'Nuh uh!' She wagged a finger at me. 'And you know it.'

I backed away from the poem and the cup and any sense of proprietorship over the things Chali had left behind.

Billy passed through the beads with a rattle of

114

sound, and then stopped suddenly. He stood beside George Vargas – very still, both looking at Chali for the first time.

I came up behind Billy and there she was, laid out on an unzipped black body bag atop a gurney on the floor. But it wasn't Chali anymore. It was a slab of bloated flesh carved open between her breasts. The knife was gone now; it would have been segregated as evidence. Her face in death had distorted into a grotesque parody of her living self. The smell was even worse than before. I turned sharply away, pressing my nose into Billy's shoulder. Through the fabric of his jacket I could feel him shaking. I looked at his face. His left pupil was small as a pinprick, stuck to her body. The skin on his face had erupted with perspiration.

'Billy,' I whispered.

He didn't move.

'Look at me.'

He couldn't.

'Come here.' I tried to pull him away, but he had turned to stone.

'I didn't want to do it.' The remorse in his voice frightened me. 'You didn't give me any choice.'

'What the hell?' Ladasha spoke as she burst through the beads. 'You a piece of work, my man.' I glanced at her and she flashed me a concerned look that betrayed the irreverence of her words. 'You wanna take my pal outside for a breath of fresh air? If you can find any in Brooklyn, that is.'

So she knew. But then why wouldn't she? She

115

spent far more time with him than I did, and his PTSD symptoms weren't exactly subtle.

'What's with him?' I heard George Vargas ask Ladasha as I led Billy out by the elbow.

'He's a whole other story,' I heard her say. 'Always crying out of his one good eye.'

'Where'd he get the patch?'

She didn't answer that. 'You caught the case?'

'That's right.'

'I'm Ladasha.'

He chuckled, and then they were beyond my hearing. I had Billy at the top of the stairs now. He was still shaking and his gaze still seemed frozen, so I moved him forward and down as carefully as I could. A couple of cops who edged past us on their way up the stairs gave us funny looks. But then, in minutes, we were back outside on the street. I walked Billy toward Fifth Avenue, away from the activity, and by the time we reached the corner he started to come back from the land of the lost.

'It happened again,' he muttered.

'You remember?'

He shook his head. 'It leaves me with a sickish feeling. That's how I know.'

'You don't remember what you said?'

'What did I say?'

He had been talking to Chali's body: 'I didn't want to do it. You didn't give me any choice.' But how could I repeat that to him? It was bewildering, disturbing. I didn't know what it meant. On

Sunday night when I'd found him in a kind of fugue state in which he'd been tossed right back into the past, he had repeated verbatim the words he had spoken to Jasmine right before she'd shot his eye out. But what he'd said tonight was new to me, as if conjured from a different reality; I couldn't recall him saying anything of the sort to her that night on the roof. It was as if he had killed her in retribution and was apologizing. A sickening feeling rippled through my stomach.

'I don't remember what happens,' he said. 'It's like I disappear.'

'As soon as you walked into the room. It seems to be triggered by . . .' I couldn't say it: dead women.

'I can't even remember what I saw. How bad was it?'

'Bad.'

'Chali, of all people.' He shook his head. 'She's not exactly his type.'

'Up until the other day, all his victims were sex workers.'

'Could be a copycat, some other nut out there who got hold of the same kind of knife.'

'Didn't you tell me those knives haven't been made in decades?'

'eBay, maybe.' He rubbed his eye. 'Who knows?'

'I wonder what Abby would tell us if she could talk.'

He looked at me; thin red veins had laced the white of his left eye.

'Monday night, after I got home, Chali wanted to tell me something. It sounded important, but I was too wiped out to talk. I asked her to wait until Tuesday.'

'Any idea what it was about?'

'None at all.'

We walked back down the block and stood close together in the cold as Chali was carried out. Detective George Vargas joined us, puffing steamy breath onto his bare hands. We watched as her body, now zipped into a black bag and strapped to the gurney, was quickly shoved into the back of the ambulance and the doors were slammed shut. It was freezing out and they wanted to get on their way.

'She have any family you know of?' Vargas asked me.

'A mother, a daughter and a brother, back in India.'

His eyebrows slid upward. 'That'll be a fun conversation. They speak English?'

'I think the daughter does; don't know about the rest of the family.'

I knew little about them other than details of Dathi's upcoming visit. When I thought of that, my heart sank deeper. Chali had been anticipating their reunion for months and my guess was that Dathi had also looked forward to it with special enthusiasm. They hadn't seen each other for a long time. I wished there was some way to keep the news from Dathi and Granny, but that, of course, was impossible. The idea of an unexpected call from a New York City detective seemed equally impossible.

'I'll make the call,' I offered. 'I'll just need the phone number for her mother's house. There was an address book on Chali's desk upstairs. Her last name is Das, and her daughter's name is Dathi – Arundathi is the full name. Arundathi Das. Chali's full name was Panchali Das. And her mother's name was Edha . . . but I don't know her last name. It must be different.'

The warmth of Billy's hand on my shoulder reminded me to slow down; I was talking fast, the little I knew spilling out, as if fast-pedaling backward could somehow change things. Bring Chali back to life. Tears trickled down my cheeks and I wiped them off with the cold back of a leather glove.

Vargas nodded. 'Okay. Thanks. I'll see if I can find you the number.'

Later, when I got home with Ben, Mac was half sitting on the couch in the dark, fast asleep, with his face tilted toward the ceiling. His breathing sounded like sawing wood. He was fully dressed, his winter boots tied in double knots.

My mother sat on the armchair near the couch, an open book in her lap, the upturned beam of her book light accentuating her puffy face and the purplish saggy skin beneath her eyes. She had been crying. So she knew.

'He couldn't make it out the door,' she whispered.

Clearly, though, he'd tried.

As I leaned over to touch my frozen lips to Mac's burning forehead, I felt the firm touch of my mother's hand on my back. Tears rushed to my eyes, and I heard her gasp for breath in the way she always did when she was determined not to break down.

CHAPTER 8

At quarter to six the next morning I slid out of bed as quietly as I could, hoping not to disturb Mac, only to learn that he was already awake. When he moaned, I also learned that he still wasn't feeling any better. I reached out to touch his forehead: still feverish.

'This is lasting a long time,' I whispered so my voice wouldn't wake Ben down the hall.

'Day five.'

'At least you can still think.'

'I'm not thinking. I'm just lying here.'

'Well, you counted to five.'

He managed a small laugh that digressed into a coughing spree.

'I think you should see Dr Velasquez, let her listen to your chest.'

'Karin – it's the flu. It'll pass.' Another series of wet, raspy coughs barreled through him.

I wasn't going to argue; I would just go ahead and make the appointment. Convince him later.

'Do you want some tea and toast, or do you want to keep sleeping?'

'Tea and toast would be nice.'

'Be right back.'

The house was freezing at this early hour; the thermostats weren't set to raise the temperature for another fifteen minutes. I put on my robe and slippers and went quietly upstairs to the kitchen. It was dark outside and the overhead light, when I turned it on, felt overly bright. I put on a kettle of water, started a pot of coffee, and sat at the table to wait.

The pad of paper where I had written Edha Sengupta's full name and phone number in India was sitting where I'd left it last night after George Vargas had called with the information. Edha and Dathi lived in the small house in the village of Sahalwada, where Chali had been raised along with her brother, Ishat. India was ten and a half hours ahead of New York, making it four-thirty in the morning their time when George had called me last night. I'd decided to wait to make the call, to allow them one last night of good sleep.

I had been awake half the night thinking about how I would break the news. It would devastate them, I knew that. But it had to be done, and it had to be done by me. At this point not a single close friend had materialized to mourn Chali in this country. I was beginning to understand just how quietly she had lived her life here: Outside of working for us a steady twenty-five hours a week, and freelancing around babysitting for others to fill in her off hours, she had kept to herself. Her recent life had been an exercise in preparing for her daughter to join her. I'd begun to suspect that Chali's plans for Dathi might have been more urgent than I'd realized; she herself had been married off at the age of thirteen, and Dathi was now twelve. Perhaps she was hurrying to save Dathi from what seemed like an inevitable trajectory toward a dreaded fate.

It would be almost four-thirty in the afternoon there now. I wondered if Dathi would be home from school, or if I might catch Edha alone, which would be better. That way, she could react, gather herself, and decide how best to tell Dathi, the depth of whose disappointment was now growing to uncomfortable proportions in my imagination.

I dialed in the international codes and then the number. There were a couple of halting, faraway sounding rings, and then the line went dead. I tried three more times, always with the same result. Finally I called an international operator, who told me that the phone number had been disconnected.

The kettle whistled and I jumped to turn it off before it woke Ben too early. I needed a few minutes to think. Then I opened my laptop on the kitchen table and searched old e-mails for Dathi's name. She had contacted me once, about two months ago, just after my miscarriage, to send a poem she'd written for my lost daughter. I'd been touched by the sweetness of her gesture and the eloquence of the poem, written in English, which she studied in school:

123

She rides a tiger
Away from the fire
Into the sky
A lotus flower in her hand.

On the petals
Are her name
And your name
Written in water.

I reread the poem before hitting reply to open a blank e-mail. My first reply, two months ago, had been a simple thank-you. This time my note was equally simple, and bore a request.

Hi Dathi,

I need to speak with your grandmother. I called the house but the phone number no longer works. Would you please ask her to call me?

Warmly,
Karin

I hoped that the directness of my note, and the total omission of any mention of Chali, didn't alarm her; but it seemed that less information was best until I had a chance to speak with Edha. I hit send, then made Mac his tea and toast.

★　　★　　★

The next morning, I sat in Dr Velasquez's waiting room with Mac, who shivered and coughed at times uncontrollably. It had taken me a full day to argue him into this visit, but finally he'd stopped objecting. He couldn't deny he was getting sicker.

When his name was called, he insisted on going alone – giving me *that look* to remind me I wasn't his mother. I waited for what felt like a long time, constantly checking my BlackBerry in case Dathi finally responded – but so far no luck. It had now been four full days since Chali's death, two days since I'd found her, and over twenty-four hours since I'd first tried to reach the family. I decided to give it until the end of the day before trying to track down Chali's brother.

When Mac finally reemerged, he was holding a prescription. 'Bronchial pneumonia,' he croaked, 'on top of flu.'

'What did I tell you?'

He wouldn't admit how right I'd been, but he handed me the prescription slip in a gesture of acquiescence. I just managed to get him home, give him the first double whammy of his Z-Pak, and tuck him back into bed before it was time to pick up Ben.

I hurried along Smith Street toward the nursery school with a sinking feeling edging on panic. Too much was happening all at once. Flu was one thing, but pneumonia? Then I thought of Chali and braced against another plunge of anxiety. It stunned me every time I recalled the sight of her corpse in that tub of bloodied water. Mac would recover. But we would never see Chali again.

Once, a few years ago, I'd overheard someone at a party refer to me as a 'murder magnet.' I'd almost spun around to protest before realizing that it was true. Up until then, my life had indeed attracted mayhem, and I had jumped right into it when it arrived. But in each case there had been special circumstances: first, to protect my remaining family; and second, to find my missing husband. I wasn't a passive person and I'd had no real choice but to pursue evil when it had touched my life.

But why now? When things had finally calmed down and life had found a normalcy, why had murder found me again?

Because of Mac's and my now indirect connection to law enforcement and thus to crime – our work, my studies, our friendship with Billy – the dark side was always near. But these days we were only observers, watching it overshadow other people's lives, not our own. Even Sunday night's murder on Nevins Street and the Dekker tragedy, while eerily close to home, were not exactly personal. I'd thought we'd found solid footing on safer ground. But Chali's murder *was* personal. Her brutal loss was an undertow pulling us back into a darkness I'd thought we'd banished. Apparently, for unfathomable reasons, I *was* a murder magnet.

Why?

Chali, though a practicing Christian, had told

me once that she believed in karma, that your actions in a previous life determined your destiny in your next incarnation. I'd almost laughed when she'd talked about karma while wearing a crucifix around her neck. She'd grown up in a Hindu world and was the sum of different belief systems, even if they were at times contradictory. In fact, not being religious myself, her philosophical contra-dictions made her all the more likable to me. She was as complicated, ridiculous, and sincere as the rest of humankind. It was what made the world work and not-work. Who was I to argue?

The thing was – and it struck me now as I opened the front door of the nursery school, where the noon crowd was starting to filter out into the winter afternoon with their mothers or fathers or babysitters – if Chali had really believed in karma, why had she continued to work for me once she'd learned my history? *I was a murder magnet.* Hadn't that worried her? Maybe it was the Christian in her that had inspired her to stay.

As soon as I walked into the classroom, which was festooned with colorful holiday decorations, Ben flew into my arms. I hugged him and kissed him and for a moment the sweet warmth of his cheek against my lips melted away all my uncertain-ties. He still hadn't challenged my claim that Chali, who was usually the one to pick him up from school, and whom he adored, was home sick with the flu 'like Daddy.' Sooner or later, I would have to tell him the truth, or at least some version of it. Death, in its permanence, was not in the conceptual scope of such a young child. I would tell him she was gone or away, and hope he didn't ask me why or for how long. Later, when the moment was right, I would tell him the precise truth.

We headed outside where the noontime life of the neighborhood was in full swing: freelancers populating cafés; a Fresh Direct truck blocking an intersection and stirring a chorus of frustrated honking; the Three Musketeers making their way along Smith Street, chattering like a clique of preteen girls.

I ran a few holiday errands on our way home, trying to support our local stores and also find a few unique gifts to supplement all the stuff I was ordering online: books, a sweater and a hat/scarf set for Mac; books and chocolate for my mother; vintage LPs for my brother, Jon, who had redis-covered the joys of vinyl; jewelry for his wife, Andrea; and toys galore for all the kids. I'd shipped some directly to L.A. but some we'd have to carry. We were leaving in a week, by which time, according to Dr Velasquez, Mac should be well enough to travel.

After lunch, while Ben napped in bed with Mac, I ordered the last of the gifts. Went through a few dozen more résumés before deciding not to bother; I'd interviewed two people I liked well enough and it would be easiest just to choose between them. As I was almost finished sorting through the day's pileup of e-mails, a new one came in.

My heart jumped when I saw Dathi's name appear on the screen.

Dear Karin,

I am so glad you wrote to me. I did not think of it but I should have written to you, because Mommy still hasn't called anyone back. I'm living with Uncle Ishat now. There is some quite bad news. My dear Granny has passed away. It was on Tuesday, from a heart attack, the doctor said. We had her funeral today without Mommy knowing. I'm not sure if you should tell her. But I don't want Uncle Ishat to tell her, either, because he is not nice about anything. Let me talk to her please. Or do you think I should wait until I get there? That way we can comfort each other. I have not been allowed to cry in my uncle's house. I am not happy here, but it doesn't matter, because soon I will be there with Mommy.

Please tell her to call us here at Ishat's house. Here is his phone number.
Dathi

But she forgot to include the number. I immediately began to respond, and then in moments another e-mail from her appeared with her Uncle Ishat's contact information. I transferred it into my cell phone and immediately dialed. I wanted to speak with Dathi. Not to tell her about her mother's murder, but to reassure her by the sound of my voice that someone was out there thinking of her, just as her sweet poem had once reassured me that I was far from alone. Now that she'd lost both her mother and grandmother, and hearing that she didn't feel welcome in her uncle's home, I also hoped at least to learn that there was someone in her life she'd be able to count on now.

As the phone rang I realized that it was nearly midnight in India, and I almost hung up, but then Ishat answered. I introduced myself.

'Ah, yes,' he said. 'My sister has spoken of you.'

I couldn't claim that Chali had spoken to me much of him, because she hadn't, except dismissively. Apparently, growing up an Indian boy turned you almost automatically into a misogynistic man, according to Chali, who had learned to express herself openly since landing here. I'd sensed she didn't think much of him, but lied anyway.

'Yes, she's also spoken highly of you.'

'I never mentioned that she spoke *highly* of you, madame.' And then a tepid laugh. 'In any case, I'm glad you called because we have had no luck reaching my sister. She has simply not returned any of my messages.'

I wasn't sure whether or not to mention that Dathi had just contacted me; it seemed late for her to be up, at the age of twelve, and true to her assessment he didn't sound like a very nice man.

I didn't want to cause any trouble for her, so I decided to avoid telling him that I'd already heard about Granny's heart attack.

'That's why I called you, I—'

He cut me off before I could deliver my own wretched news.

'Our mother has passed away,' he said, 'and I wanted Chali to be informed. Since she can't find a moment to return my calls, I would ask you to inform her of the development. Our mother has been buried. There is no inheritance. The child is here with me until she travels to the U.S.'

'Does Dathi have any aunts? Any other relatives?'

'Why would you ask me that?'

'I also have some bad news.'

I steadied myself, and told him. I could hear him breathing heavily as I spoke but he said nothing and I couldn't discern his reaction. There were no tears, no questions. All he said was, 'I told Panchali not to go to New York City.'

'I was hoping to speak to Dathi. I know it's late, but I'd very much like to say hello to her.'

'The girl has been asleep for hours.'

His outright lie, the cumulative effect of his arrogance, incensed me. Against my better judgment, I blurted out, 'She just e-mailed me. It's how I got your number.'

'I see. Well then. That computer her school gave her has been a nuisance from the start.' His icy tone alarmed me.

'She was answering my e-mail. I'm sure she's gone to bed by now. She's just a—'

Child, I was going to say. *She's just a child*. But before I could get the word out, he hung up.

Ben walked into the kitchen holding Mac's empty glass. 'Daddy's thirsty.'

'Why are you awake so soon, sweetie?'

'I didn't sleep.' He handed me the glass and darted away. Putting him in for naps these days was wishful thinking; at almost four, he wanted me to understand that a 'big boy' like him could make it through the day without extra sleep. I was almost ready to buy into the fact that he was growing up. But not quite. *He was just a child*. At his age, there was no disputing that; but how could you tell when it was time to step back? At what point was a mother supposed to loosen the reins of nurturing?

And when you didn't have a mother anymore, at what point did the rest of the world start tugging the reins in the opposite direction? Who would be there to offer protection when the only people who loved you were gone?

As I filled Mac's glass with ice and water, I couldn't help thinking about Dathi, wondering about her. How had Ishat reacted to my (poorly timed) newsflash that she had been up past her bedtime using the computer? I hoped he wasn't punishing her too harshly. And then I thought about the kids in the Lemony Snicket books I'd read aloud to my niece Susanna last time we'd visited – three orphans who endure a domino effect of loss and danger.

What was Dathi up against now?

How could I get ahold of her without inflaming Uncle Ishat?

I was a little afraid to send her another e-mail, in case he intercepted it, but decided to risk it.

Hi Dathi,

I hope you're okay. I care about you. I know that sounds strange since we don't really know each other. But I do care about you – a lot. I hope you'll call me as soon as you can, or at least write back to me. Here is my address and both my phone numbers so you can reach me in any way, at any time.

Love,
Karin

I typed in my home number, my cell number, and my mailing address. Now she could reach me any which way, and I sincerely – desperately – hoped she would try.

CHAPTER 9

By Sunday morning the wheel had turned, and turned, and turned.

Mac's fever had broken, his coughing had eased, and he was up and around.

I had hired an assistant, to start the next day: a thirtyish woman named Star who had three years of administrative experience at an investment bank and had lost her job in a flurry of corporate layoffs.

The first blizzard of the winter had hit the East Coast.

And the investigation into the Working Girl Murders had moved forward a couple of notches. Billy came over to fill us in . . . and to help me shovel.

I tackled the front stoop and the ground-floor entrance while Billy did the sidewalk in front of our house, as the people upstairs had already left for the holidays. Ben helped, using his little shovel to push remnants of snow into the street. Mac stood at the window watching us, feeling guilty, I supposed, that he wasn't doing it himself or at least helping; not wanting to risk a relapse, Billy and I had insisted he stay inside and keep warm. Finally, we convened at the kitchen table for a brunch of scrambled eggs, croissants, and hot chocolate.

'We should start eating better.' Mac scooped some eggs onto a torn-off piece of croissant and popped it into his mouth. 'Mmm, that is really good.'

'You look like you lost about ten pounds this week. Eat better later.' Billy's smile was a flash of white; I realized I hadn't seen him smile for weeks.

'So, how are *you* feeling?' I asked him.

'Well, I'm not at a crime scene right now – so fine.' He exhaled a thin laugh. 'I've been thinking it might be time for a new line of work.'

'Like what?' Mac leaned forward, interested; after all, it was the course he himself had taken out of the job when it had grown too intense.

'No idea.' The smile was fully gone now, the gloom returned.

Mac sat back in his chair and glanced at me.

'You still haven't called that number,' I said, 'have you?'

'Actually, I did call. Left a message. Happy?'

'I know it's irritating that I keep reminding you, but you have got to deal with this.'

'She's right,' Mac said.

Billy dropped his face into his hands, swallowing up his eye patch, and for a moment I saw him as he was when I'd first met him almost four years ago. At forty, he'd looked a decade younger than his age, and he'd had such an ease and confidence. He'd been arrestingly handsome, the way he looked at you with those deep brown eyes. Lately, all that implicit vigor suddenly seemed missing. The skin on the backs of his hands now was lined and powdery dry. When he lifted his face, his one functional eye looked bleary and sad. It took a moment for the creases on his cheeks, left by the pressure of his hands, to dissolve away.

'I know,' he said. 'That's why I finally called. I know I need to get to this somehow – but it's so damned powerful when it hits me. I mean, I come to, and I don't even know where I went or what happened. I don't see how some stranger can reach inside my head and flip a switch and turn it off. If it were that easy, I'd do it myself. I don't see what the point of putting this on the record is, except maybe to bomb my career.'

'Maybe that's the reason to do it,' Mac offered with a wry smile that elicited zero response from Billy.

'I don't know what I want.'

'There won't be a switch,' I said. 'Sometimes talking just helps – a lot.' I knew, having talk-therapied my way through several crises. 'Anyway, it's not like you can hide this forever from the people you work with. Sooner or later they'll figure it out.' What I didn't say was that Ladasha probably already had.

'Well, I made the call and no one's returned it yet.' Billy sipped his hot chocolate. Took a deep, exasperated breath. And shifted the conversation in another direction. 'So, about the case.'

Mac swiveled to Ben, who was coloring in his drawing book at the table. 'Hey, Benster, want to go hang some of your drawings in the gallery?' The gallery being our downstairs hallway, where one wall was filling with Ben's artwork.

'Good idea.' I crossed the kitchen to get a roll of masking tape from an under-counter drawer, and handed it to Ben. 'Remember: two-inch pieces, the size of Maretti.'

Ben 'vroomed' his way out of the kitchen, thinking now about his favorite yellow race car Maretti, and we listened as he thumped his way downstairs. Then Mac and I both pulled up close to Billy to hear the latest developments. I had barely slept the past two nights, thinking about it all. The woman on Nevins Street, and Chali, with those knives buried in their chests. The bloody scene at the Dekker house. Abby, with her blue fingernails and rainbow toenails, unconscious in her hospital bed. Dathi, alone in the world, and so far away. I drained my hot chocolate and filled my mug with coffee, leaning in to let a puff of steam warm my face.

'The lab came through with something on Abby.' He reached into his jeans pocket, pulled out a flash drive, and put it on the table.

I opened my laptop. While it booted up, Billy explained.

'There were traces of black paint and sawdust residue on her pajamas. Turns out there was a security camera inside that bodega on Nevins;

guess they're tired of getting broken into in the middle of the night. It pivots back-to-front and caught some of what passed by on the street. Got a good shot of the license plate of a black car, and the paint matches. So does the sawdust – owner of the car parks it in his garage in Queens, where he also has a woodshop.'

An image of tools and knives cluttered my mind; the idea that a man good at carving up wood might also like to carve up women sickened me. 'He's a carpenter?'

'Woodworks as a hobby,' Billy said. 'Guy's a mortgage broker. Married. Three kids.'

Mac grimaced. 'Here we go.'

'What was he doing in Brooklyn that late on a Sunday night?'

Billy handed me the flash drive. 'He can tell you himself.'

I plugged the drive into a port on the side of my laptop and we waited while the media player loaded. Billy reached over to guide the mouse and click on the video he wanted to show us. A rectangle appeared, and he clicked play. On the screen, a pudgy, middle-aged man wearing a crumpled business suit was raking fingers through a mousy comb-over. You could see that his scalp was freckled. He wore a thick gold wedding ring.

Billy and Ladasha sat across from him in the Eight-four's small interrogation room. The lighting and relatively poor quality of the tape made it feel even grimmer than it probably had been in reality.

Ladasha opened the interview with the standard recitation of date and time, for the record. Then she spoke directly to the man.

'Please state your full name.'

'P-P-Patrick John R-R-Ryan Sc-Sc-Scott.'

His hands, now resting on the table, visibly trembled. I felt a little sorry for him.

'That's a lotta names.'

'We're I-r-rish-Am-merican.'

'They call you Patrick or Pat?' she asked.

'P-P-Pat.'

'So Pat, you wanna tell us what you were doing in Brooklyn on Sunday night?'

'Dr-dr-driving home.'

'From?'

'D-d-dinner with friends.'

'Just you alone?'

'M-my wife, she wasn't f-f-feeling well, she st-stayed home.' Pat glanced at Billy, who was taking notes.

'Where did you eat?'

Pat hesitated. 'S-someplace nearb-b-by, can't r-remember the name. It was It-t-alian.'

Billy's eye stayed on the paper, jotting notes, but I knew him well and could see his reaction of disbelief. Anyone would have looked harder at the man claiming, to the cops, not to remember where he ate the night of a murder when he was caught on tape driving through the scene of the crime. But Billy held on to his restraint and didn't flinch.

Ladasha tapped the table with a short pencil she

139

held more as a prop than a writing implement, since Billy was taking all the notes. 'Well, how about when you do remember, you let us know. We'll give the restaurant a call. And maybe you mentioned it to your wife when you got home that night, maybe she'll remember. We'll give her a call. What's her name?'

'Andie.' Pat's eyes skipped from Ladasha to Billy and back to Ladasha, and then he blurted out, 'But d-d-d-don't call her. She w-w-w-won't remember. Sh-she was as-sl-sleep when I g-g-got home.'

Ladasha stared at him as his stutter rapidly worsened when he spoke about his wife.

'Whenever you're ready,' she said.

'R-ready?'

'To tell us the truth.'

She leaned back in her chair, her lips pursed. I could picture her talking to her kids this way, as in, *Cut the crap, this is me talking to you, and I don't have time for your bullshit.*

'Well, when you're ready, you let me know.' She stood up and left the room in a classic interrogation move to see if the interviewee would open up better one-on-one.

Billy put down his pen and looked at Pat. 'She means well.'

Pat nodded, and even smiled a little. 'She m-makes me n-nervous.'

'Join the club. You want a soda or a coffee or something?'

'Just some w-water. Th-thank you.'

Billy left the room, and returned with a plastic cup of water, which he handed to Pat. Another classic technique: Disarm your suspect, make him feel he can trust you even if he can't trust the other cop. You are different, kinder, more understanding, safe to talk to.

'So,' Billy said.

Pat stared at him a moment, and then spoke in a nearly stutterless rush: 'I didn't eat out that night. I didn't meet anyone. I went out alone. I drive over to Nevins Street sometimes looking for hookers, okay? Don't tell my wife. Pl-please, pl-pl-please don't t-t-tell her.'

'Hey, man, you're only human. I get it.'

'I s-s-saw the g-g-girl and I w-w-wanted to try s-s-someth-thing dif-different. So I f-f-fol-lowed her in my-c-car.'

'Pause it a minute, Billy,' I said.

He stopped the video so Mac and I could take that in: *Something different.*

'Is he saying what I think he's saying?'

'You bet. He saw Abby and figured she was working the street.'

'She's *eleven.*'

'Welcome to reality, Karin.' For a split second Billy's expression hardened, as if a mask had suddenly appeared over my friend's face: his skin, an impenetrable plastic coating; eye, burnished, unreal. Then the Billy I knew returned: all too human, flesh and blood.

141

I caught my breath. 'All right. Show us the rest of the interview.'

Billy hit play.

'Th-then she d-d-d-arted in fr-front of my c-car s-s-sud-denly. I sh-should have st-stopped when I h-h-hit her b-b-but I was sc-scared and I k-kept g-g-going. I d-d-didn't even s-see th-that wom-m-man. I d-d-didn't even kn-now about her until the n-next d-day, in the n-n-newsp-paper. It was d-d-ark out. I j-j-just dr-dr-drove.'

'It *was* dark out,' Billy echoed.

'R-r-right before she r-ran in fr-front of my c-c-car, I saw a sh-shadow. A man, I think. A d-d-dark man. R-r-running up to th-those pr-projects on Third Avenue. He c-came out of n-nowhere. I w-w-was s-s-surprised. Then the g-girl shot out and she sc-sc-scared me and I t-t-took off.' Pat let his eyes drop off Billy's face and shook his head slowly, regretfully. Then he looked up and his tone toughened. 'I shouldn't have d-d-done it!'

Done what? Considered sexually victimizing a young girl? Or hitting her with your car and taking off? Or murdering several women? My guess was what he regretted most was *getting caught*.

I didn't feel sorry for him anymore.

Across from Pat, Billy held his cool and shook his head. 'Sounds freaky. I would have been spooked, too.'

'I kn-know wh-wh-what she thinks. She th-th-thinks I have s-s-something to do with those m-m-m-murders. B-b-but I d-d-*don't*.'

'You were just driving by.'

Pat nodded, closed his eyes, and began to weep.

Billy stopped the video as Pat's hands rose to cradle his balding head.

'There were traces of Abby's blood on his car, which you would've expected, given how badly banged up she was. But no one else's blood. So he could be telling the truth.'

'What about the dark man running up toward the projects?' Mac asked.

Billy shrugged. 'It's not exactly a new story for white folks caught in a bad situation to say some black guy came out of nowhere and made their world spin out of control, now is it?'

He had a point. Two famous cases from the past leaped to mind:

In 1989, Chuck Stuart reported that an armed black man appeared at the car window, robbed his seven months' pregnant wife of her jewelry before shooting her dead (and ultimately their unborn son, too), and then ran off into the night. A ferocious manhunt in Boston's black communities ensued for weeks. Stuart's brother later admitted to throwing the jewelry into the Charles River at Chuck's request. Chuck then killed himself, having conjured up a black man everyone now realized didn't exist; he had shot his wife and unborn son himself, to avoid the responsibilities of parenthood, and hopefully date a coworker.

Then, in 1994, Susan Smith, a young Southern mother, begged the country to help find the black man who had carjacked her SUV with her two young sons strapped into their car seats in the back. The manhunt continued until the car was found submerged in a lake. Both little boys had drowned. Smith finally confessed that she had invented a fictional black man to distract from the truth: She had forfeited her children's lives in the hope of pleasing her boyfriend, who didn't want kids.

'You're right about that.' Mac threw up his hands.

I sat back in my chair, embarrassed.

And then I thought twice. 'Wait a minute. He said he saw a dark shadow, not a black man. He mentioned the projects. A dark shadow running toward the projects. He didn't say "black man running into the ghetto." Let's just be clear. If we're going to try to avoid stereotypes, we have to really avoid them.'

Billy grimaced and reluctantly nodded.

'Pat thought Abby Dekker was a prostitute just because she was walking on Nevins Street. I mean, *really*.'

'It was nearly midnight.'

'So anyone walking on a seedy street late at night is selling sex?'

'Karin,' Mac interrupted, but gently, 'I see his point.'

'She was wearing pajamas with *sheep* on them.' I stared, hard, at Mac and Billy, my two favorite men in the universe – did I have to steer even them away from some base male instinct?

144

Billy pitched forward in his chair now. 'And you're shocked because it was a *white* girl in pajamas with sheep on them, and he thought he could buy her.'

'*No.*'

'Because little black girls, let me tell you, they're used to it. You wouldn't believe the things I've seen in this city. Black guys pimping little black girls to your white neighbors.'

'*Whoa.*' Mac now rested a hand on both our arms, as if his touch could regulate down to harmless the high voltage of this forbidden conversation. 'Both of you, get off the race and gender shit. Patrick Whatshisname is a pig. But he's a pig because he's a pig, not because he's white or builds bookcases for fun or lives in Queens. They come in every size, shape, color, and gender. You both know that. So get off your high horses.'

Billy and I both sat there, grudgingly corrected.

I felt an amorphous rage deflate as shame settled in. Billy was upsetting me, but was this really why? So much had happened this past week to test my idea about who he was; I had always regarded him as reliable, unshakable, and here he was turning out to be fragile as thin glass. I didn't know if I was disappointed by his troubles, or bewildered by his needs, or afraid of the new reality that his challenges were slippery and frightening. Why *was* I upset with him? Obviously, he wasn't personally responsible for the narrow-mindedness that gripped our society; we were all in it together.

145

'I'm sorry, Billy. I didn't mean to lash out at you. It's just – men who use prostitutes, even if they're kids . . . Who are they? How can someone use another human being like that, and not understand that there's a real person at the other end of the transaction? It just makes me sick.'

'I'm also sorry, Karin,' Billy muttered. 'And for whatever it's worth, I don't get it, either. I've had to think about it so much in the last year, it makes me sick, too. Those kids going missing, then turning up as dead hookers. *Sick*. Abby Dekker lying there on the sidewalk so close to another one – how close did she come to being one of them? And Pat, from Queens, with blood on his car. It just doesn't make a lot of sense to me that this wormy guy could be responsible for so much damage, going back years. I mean, *human trafficking? P-P-Pat?* The guy's scared of his own wife. He's scared of himself. Something doesn't factor, I don't know what, but it doesn't feel right.'

'Let's look at the facts,' Mac said.

Billy nodded. 'Okay, here are the facts on Patrick John Ryan Scott, as it stands right now. He was arraigned and held on a class E felony for hit and run. Since it's tied into a serial murder case *and* the Dekkers' murders, the judge denied bail – flight risk. If Abby dies, the charge escalates to a class D felony and he goes to jail, and that's just for the hit and run.'

'Pat's wife hire him a lawyer?' Mac asked.

'Nope. Looks like she's cutting him loose, which tells us something right there.'

'How old are his kids?' I asked, thinking of *all* my kids – Ben, and Cece, and Madeleine or Elizabeth or Catharine – and wondering what kind of burden a parent placed on their children when they worse than misbehaved.

'Two are teenagers, the other one's younger, around eight I think,' Billy said. 'Two boys and a girl.'

We took that in with a moment of silence. Boys who would become men, hopefully not like their father. What were the chances of that, once the seeds of his arrest were planted in their imaginations? I shivered at the thought. On the other hand, maybe they'd look at their father and run in the opposite direction. You just never knew.

'What I keep wondering,' I said, 'is whether Abby ran before or after her parents were killed, what exactly went on in that house that night.'

'Exactly. We've been over the Dekkers' e-mails and phone records, talked to neighbors, talked to colleagues, trying to put together what was going on in their lives lately. The last call from Reed Dekker's cell phone was to . . .' Billy pulled out his iPhone, tapped it a couple of times, and read from the screen. 'Father Ximens Dandolos.'

'And I thought Seamus was a tongue twister,' Mac said of his own given name.

'I looked it up – Ximens is Spanish for Simon; means the listener. But everyone calls him Father

X,' Billy said. 'They were good friends. The Dekkers were active in Father X's church, St Paul's up on Court Street. Did a lot of fund-raising – helped finance the methadone clinic at Mary Immaculate, the teen outreach program at the local Y, things like that.'

'What time did they talk Sunday night?' Mac asked.

'Eight fifty-three. So whatever happened went down after.'

'What did they talk about?' I asked.

'The Dekkers needed someone to paint a radiator in their house. Father X likes to throw odd jobs to some of the guys in the rehab program, and the Dekkers liked to support that.'

Mac and I looked at each other and cringed. Billy shook his head. We had all heard about too many inside jobs by cons on do-gooders like the Dekkers to feel comfortable granting access to our homes by this particular class of strangers.

'Who'd he recommend for the job?' Mac asked.

'Said he'd call them back in the morning with a name.'

'Did he make that call?'

Mac and Billy looked at me when I asked that.

'Maybe he left a message before he found out they were dead.'

'He left them a lot of messages that day,' Billy said, 'but not to recommend a handyman. He was trying to reach them because of Abby. The whole family was close. Father X has been spending a lot of time with her at the hospital, sitting by her side.'

'Our family priest would have done the same thing. He and my mom were like this.' Mac twined his fingers. 'My dad used to joke that she was going to leave him for "the Father, the Son, and the Holy Ghost, but mostly the father."' Mac chuckled at the memory of his late parents.

'Kind of creepy,' I commented.

'Not really.' Mac's tone stiffened. 'What's going on with the church these days is only part of the story.'

'It's been going on a long time, from what they tell us,' I said.

'Karin the social evangelist.' Billy glanced at Mac, who quickly suppressed a little smile. 'Really, it's the same shit as we were talking about before.'

'It's true, Karin,' Mac said. 'You shouldn't cast aspersions on all because of the bad deeds of some.'

'Are you quoting your family's priest now?'

He shot me a look. But he was right: Righteousness in any form was out of line.

'All right.' I straightened in my chair. 'The facts. We clear our heads of all the noxious fumes. How is Abby doing?' Thinking of Abby made me remember Dathi, and anxiety tightened in my chest. My BlackBerry lay on the table and I glanced at it for the umpteenth time to see if she'd e-mailed back. But still nothing. It had been two days now since I'd spoken with Uncle Ishat and I was starting to really worry.

'I'm heading up there after this to see for myself.'

My pulse spiked. I looked at Billy suddenly, and he sighed.

'Yeah, sure, why not. You can come,' he said, before I even asked.

I turned to Mac. 'Do you mind hanging out with Ben on your own this afternoon? He could always stay with Mom, but you shouldn't go to the hospital yet until you're twenty-four hours past your fever.'

'Wouldn't want to spread the joy,' Mac said. 'You go. Fill me in when you get home.'

The priest was standing outside Abby's hospital door when we got there. Before we were close enough to really see his face, I noticed that everyone who passed in the hall smiled at him. He acknowledged every greeting with a small nod, but kept his attention focused on the middle-aged couple with whom he was speaking: a trim man with blond-gray hair, wearing pressed chinos and a plaid flannel shirt; and a woman who was slightly taller than him, in jeans and a fluffy white sweater. A pale blue headband pushed her shoulder-length (obviously dyed) blond hair off her face. Billy caught the priest's eye just before we reached Abby's door.

'You must be Father Dandolos.' Billy extended his hand with a smile. 'I'm Detective Billy Staples, Eighty-fourth Precinct.'

150

'Yes, of course. Good to meet you in person; I always like to match a face with a voice. And please, call me Father X; everyone else does.' Father X took Billy's hand but instead of shaking it, clasped it between his own smooth, liver-spotted hands. He had a thick head of white hair and small eyes that appeared to sink into a doughy face. When he smiled, his cheeks tightened and flushed pink; otherwise his skin was slack, hanging in jowls off his jaw.

'This is Karin Schaeffer,' Billy introduced me, 'a private investigator consulting on the case.'

Father X clasped my hand; his skin was cool and damp.

'Let me introduce Steve and Linda Campbell,' he said. 'They were close friends of Reed and Marta.'

Steve's lips pressed together, igniting deep lines astride a mouth that was unusually wide; I recognized him from somewhere, but couldn't place him. 'We still can't quite get over the shock of what happened to them.'

'I don't think we ever will. They were our very best friends.' Linda smiled sadly and nodded for what seemed a long time. Her skin made her appear older than she had from a distance: nearly sixty, I guessed. Steve looked younger, but appearances could deceive. 'And all the good works they did, well, it's going to be hard to step into their shoes.'

'Did you know them from the church?' Billy asked.

'Just about all our friends are from the church.'

'That's right,' Steve agreed.

'And to think,' Linda said, 'if Marta and Reed had gone to the party with us Sunday night, they might still be alive. Marta said she wasn't feeling well. If anyone had imagined this could have happened, we would have *insisted* they join us.' She shook her head and dissolved in tears.

'It's past, Lindy,' Steve told her, patting her shoulder; the back of his hand was blanketed with pale hair. Her tears escalated, and he wrapped his arm around her. 'It's been a tough day. We were at Reed's lawyer's this morning to hear the will. They named us as Abby's guardians.' There was no word for the emotion that consumed his face when he said that: sadness, joy, regret, gratitude, panic. I couldn't read him. All I knew was that I felt sorry for the Campbells, who struck me as ill equipped to take on any of this: first their best friends' murders, and now their child.

A nurse rattled a cart along the hall and then veered into Abby's room. With her was the small red-haired woman, the care coordinator Sasha Mendelssohn, whom we'd met on my other visit.

'Bath time for Abby,' Sasha cheerfully announced. Though obviously it wouldn't be too cheerful a bath, given that the nurse would be sponge-bathing a battered, comatose child. 'Good to see you again, Detective. And hello to you, too . . .'

'Karin.'

'Right.'

152

'Any improvement?' Billy asked.

'Still waiting for the brain swelling to go down more than it has. I can tell you it isn't worse, if that's any consolation.'

'Last time you mentioned the possibility of taking her out of the coma temporarily so we could—'

'I realize how eager you are to talk to Abby about what happened. Believe me, the hospital's been fending off pressure from every direction all week. Reporters hound us every time we step out the front door. But the message doesn't change: We won't consider bringing her out at least until the swelling's gone down, and it hasn't gone down enough yet. I'm sorry.'

It was true: You couldn't walk down the street or turn on the television without an update on Abby Dekker's status. Everyone in the city wanted to know what she knew, if anything, about the Working Girl Killer. Was the media frenzy right: was Patrick Scott guilty of all the murders, or was someone else lurking? Everyone was afraid she or a loved one would be next. And everyone wanted it to stop. Something about it being so close to Christmas seemed to accentuate the communal anguish and hope for a miracle in the form of a resurrected child.

'I understand.' But Billy's tone betrayed impatience.

'If you want to see her before her bath, now's your chance,' Sasha said.

'It's been a long day,' Steve said, 'and tomorrow's a school day for me – I'm a middle school teacher, we start bright and early. Think we'll be heading home now.'

'Mind if I take your phone number?' Billy asked. 'Love to talk to you tomorrow.'

Steve dug his free hand into his pocket for his wallet and managed to slip out a business card with one shaking hand, while Linda continued to sob at his side. 'Call anytime.'

Father X patted Linda on the back as Steve led her away. 'It has been a very long day.'

'I think I saw *you* here pretty early this morning,' Sasha said to Father X as we all headed into Abby's room. A big, cheerful hand-drawn collage crowded with goofy class photos and kids' signatures now hung on the wall facing her bed. Half a dozen Mylar balloons were clustered in a far corner of the ceiling. She lay there silently, oblivious to it all.

'Oh yes. I was here before nine. I've been reading aloud to her.'

Sasha glanced at a book spread open, facedown, on the guest chair. *A Wrinkle in Time*. That was one of my favorites when I was a kid.'

'It's as good today as it ever was,' Father X agreed. 'They say people in comas can hear. I thought reading to her might help, somehow.'

'Well, it can't hurt.' Sasha smiled.

Billy and I stood a few feet from Abby's bed, looking at her. Her wounds had healed somewhat, and the bright violet of her bruises had faded to a greenish yellow. She was thinner now, and paler, with her hands lax at her sides and her blue nail polish as fresh as a week ago from disuse. I wondered how she would feel when she learned that the Campbells were going to be her new parents. And I wondered how long it would take for her to stop thinking of herself as an orphan, if she ever would.

Abby and Dathi both – two girls orphaned in twenty-four hours. I didn't know them, really, but a word from either one of them, or both of them, was suddenly high on my wish list. As a mother who had lost two daughters, I felt I stood with them at the lip of their echoing void; ours was the kind of loss that couldn't be filled by anyone but the people who were gone. No one else would do. And you never stopped yearning.

Billy, meanwhile, was lost in his own set of pre-occupations as we watched Abby, so still and quiet in her deep, deep sleep.

CHAPTER 10

Early Tuesday morning, Billy stood in the foyer, breathing puffs of cold steam into the air even with the front door shut. He had on the same gray sweatpants and battered sneakers he'd been wearing to his and Mac's biweekly basketball games for the past two years. He marched in place to warm himself up as he waited for Mac, who was downstairs with the new assistant, Star, who had arrived late.

'Hopefully it won't be long. She started yesterday so she's got the basic idea . . . I think.' I leaned close to whisper: 'Just between us, she seems kind of flaky.'

'Weren't you the one who interviewed her?'

'Oops.' I shrugged. 'Come in for some coffee while you wait?'

He looked at his watch. 'No thanks.'

'At least come sit in the living room with me.'

He followed me into the next room, but didn't sit. I curled up on the couch where I'd left my laptop, mid-search for a new babysitter. I still hadn't figured out how to explain any of this to Ben without breaking his heart. I had tried telling him that Chali might not be able to come back, only to field a demand to call her up. I'd changed the subject. We would have to tell him, really tell him, soon.

'Any news from Dathi?' Billy asked me.

'Nothing.' I didn't elaborate; he knew how worried I was.

'We've got a new development in the case.'

I shot to the edge of the couch. 'Why didn't you tell me?'

'Relax – I'm telling you now. Women.'

'There you go again.'

'Just kidding.' He held up a flattened palm, and flashed me a smile.

I almost laughed, and fell back into the couch. 'Start talking, Billy.'

'New guy hit the radar last night: Antonio Neng. Upper East Side, personal investor. Correction: *disgruntled* personal investor. Neng's been harassing four different bankers, including Reed Dekker. Ranting and raving in e-mails, calling Dekker a "fat cat banker" who "ruined his life," yada yada yada. He was in Brooklyn that Sunday night.'

'Witnesses?'

'*Thirty* witnesses saw him. He was freezing his ass off at a Bargemusic concert on the East River, down by Brooklyn Bridge Park. We checked it out: He was alone. People who know him say he isn't into classical music. Likes hip-hop, rap, punk.'

'You said he was a personal investor—'

'Yeah, well, that's what he calls himself on his

Facebook page. A dozen years ago he sold a dry cleaning business he built up, and spent his time since then investing the profits into a small fortune. Lost a lot of it in 2008 and had to go back to work, but this time not as an owner. Now he's behind the counter taking in people's dirty clothes. Guess he doesn't like it.'

'Harassment? Or stalking, too?'

'We're finding out. The visit to Brooklyn makes us think he was getting into stalking, early stages though, because he was still building in excuses for being somewhere off his beaten path. Still not sure. Dash is working it this morning; I'll get back on it after the game. Where's Mac?' He took another look at his watch.

I went to the top of the stairs and called down: 'Billy's waiting!'

'Just another minute!' Mac called back up.

'So what are you thinking?' I returned to the couch. Billy had given up on Mac, and now sat in the chair across from me. He'd even halfway unzipped his jacket. 'Are you looking at this guy for Nevins Street, too? Or just the Dekkers?'

'I don't know – seems like a stretch. Dash and I, and just about everyone else on the task force, in our guts we think it's two cases that intersected because Abby was hit by a car in the wrong place.'

I looked at him, processing that.

'Not that anywhere is the right place. But you know what I mean.' A slash of sunlight moved along the carpet; the room suddenly brightened and Billy squinted his eye. 'Man, this room lights up. You look like you just dissolved into that couch.'

'I'm still here.'

'Karin, if you weren't, I wouldn't know what to do with myself. And I mean that.'

I smiled. 'Well, thanks. But what was that for?'

'Met with someone yesterday – a peer counselor. He got me to promise to sign up for Tai Chi, for starters; I'm supposed to do it today when I'm over at the Y.'

'It'll be good for you.'

'Maybe, but it'll suck more time out of my day, when already there aren't enough hours.'

'Everyone's busy, but you still have to give yourself time to—'

'How many people do you know who've got a serial killer on their to-do list?' He leaned back abruptly and slid his hands into his pockets. You could see his knuckles moving on tight fists under the thin fabric of the sweatpants.

'What I'm trying to say,' I tried, 'is that time is relative. 'When you have one of your attacks, and you break with what's happening and go to wherever it is that you go . . . what happens to time then?'

'Poof.'

'In the overall equation, that's time lost, right? So think of it as substituting planned Tai Chi sessions for unscheduled hallucinations.'

A genuine smile blossomed on his face, and you could see his hands relax in his pockets. 'He also set me up with a psychiatrist who specializes in what ails me.'

'What ails you, Billy?'

'As if you don't know.'

'I haven't actually heard you say it yet. Maybe it would be good to practice, so you can be honest when you start therapy. Otherwise it doesn't work.'

'You know what, Karin? You should be a therapist yourself.'

'I don't want to be a therapist.' I sank into the couch cushions. Stared at him. Waited. 'Go ahead: Say it.'

He enunciated each word awkwardly, like moving a stone around his mouth: 'Post traumatic stress disorder. Satisfied?'

'Do you really think I'll ever be satisfied?'

We burst into laughter, and just at that moment Mac walked into the living room wearing his basketball shorts and a T-shirt. His winter jacket hung open. 'Ready?'

Billy stood up.

'Mac.' I followed them. 'Are you seriously going outside in just your shorts?'

'No time to change, Karin.'

'You have pneumonia!'

'*Had* pneumonia.' He grabbed his keys out of the bowl by the front door.

He was much better, it was true; but still, I didn't like it. 'It's just common sense to take it easy for a while. At least to keep warm.'

Billy laughed. Mac kissed my cheek, and they were gone.

I lowered the shades halfway to block out some of the blinding light, and settled back into the couch with my laptop. The e-mailed résumés, this time for babysitters, just kept flooding in. It was astounding. It would have been easier to have just a few replies and carefully pick among them; this deluge was overwhelming, and I feared I'd make a mistake. How could anyone replace Chali? It didn't seem possible.

There was a crash downstairs and the sound of glass breaking.

'Oh shit!' Star shouted.

I found her standing in the downstairs hall, slumped against the gallery of Ben's drawings. On the opposite wall, where we'd hung framed family photos, were two empty spaces. The glass in one of the frames had shattered into a spiderweb of cracks over a shot of me and Mac on our honeymoon in Greece, wearing our bathing suits; Mac in the ubiquitous T-shirt that covered his array of scars left from his near miss with a very bad criminal; I, round with pregnancy. Luckily the second frame's glass was intact though one corner of the frame itself had broken.

'Are you all right?' I asked Star.

'I did a pirouette and I lost my balance.' Her lipstick was smudged.

'A pirouette?'

'I'm a dancer. I mean, I want to be.'

'I thought you worked at an investment bank.'

For three years, as I recalled from her impressive résumé.

'Day job.' She smiled sheepishly, her short haircut curved like parentheses around her narrow face. 'I'm also compulsively honest. I might as well tell you that, too.'

'Good to know.' I forced a smile. 'Why don't we clean this up?'

'I'll do it! Just point me to the broom.'

I took her to the kitchen and, just as I was showing her where to find what she needed in the pantry closet, the house phone rang.

'I'll answer it!'

'No! No need. Here.'

She grabbed the broom and dustpan and rushed back downstairs.

I took a calming breath, and answered on the fourth ring.

'Mrs Schaeffer?'

'Speaking.'

'I'm calling about your reference,' a man said.

'If it's about the job, it's been filled.' Though I almost regretted saying that, sensing it might not stay filled for long.

'Job?'

'Are you calling about one of the ads we ran?'

'Chali Das, my tenant, she listed you as her reference when she applied for the apartment.'

I felt suddenly cold as my mind shifted gears back to last week. I could still see her body lying on the gurney. That horrifying wound.

162

'Yes, Chali.' I didn't know what else to say.

'Someone's got to come and clean out the apartment. The cops are finished here, they told me. I have to rent it out or I can't pay the mortgage.'

The thought of going through her things made me uneasy. I pulled the phone away from my ear, pulled myself together. 'How is tomorrow morning?'

'Tomorrow's fine. Friday by the latest. I've got people coming to see it over the weekend.'

I hung up the phone and stood there. After taking a few deep breaths, I went to my purse, found Detective Vargas's phone number, and called him to confirm that they were really finished with the crime scene.

'Yup,' Vargas confirmed. 'We're all done there.'

'How is the investigation going?'

'Aren't you getting regular updates from your colleagues at the Eight-four?'

'I don't work with them.'

'Could have fooled me.'

'So?'

'Whatever Billy and Lalala told you, that's the way it is. We're working together, so what they know is what I know.'

'Thank you.' I didn't mean it, though; I thought he was presumptuous, and rude, and he made me feel useless.

'My pleasure.' He didn't mean it, either.

We hung up at the same time.

★ ★ ★

A toothless beggar in a Santa hat stood in front of me on the moving subway, his hand held out: a craggy map of a life of failures, pallid from addiction, brown tendrils of skin like parched rivers fading to extinction on a bloated pink palm.

'For the children,' he murmured, trying to catch my eye; but I wouldn't look at his face. I hoped this man was lying, that he didn't have any children. I dug into my coat pocket, found a crumpled dollar bill, and gave it to him, just so he would go away. He lurched along the train to the next cluster of riders, leaving behind a fetid smell.

Across the aisle, a young woman in a purple jacket, purple scarf, and purple hat smiled her sparkling blue eyes at me. I smiled back. At her feet were four overflowing shopping bags with two rolls of colorful wrapping paper sticking out of one. The smell and the man and the sad, sad moment evaporated.

Chali's stop was next, and I got off.

The afternoon was sunnier and warmer than it had been in a week; the graying snowbanks left over from Sunday's blizzard were starting to melt along Fourth Avenue. Steady dripping from awnings and scaffolding made it sound like rain, though the sky was perfectly clear. I stopped in a deli to buy a box of large, heavy-duty garbage bags. The sun, as I turned up Chali's block, blinded me for a moment. I lifted my hand to shadow my eyes just before I would have run into a pair of young boys wearing backpacks, chattering as they showed each other illustrated cards, if they hadn't nimbly darted out of the way just in time.

I stood a moment in the long shadow cast by Chali's building, awed by the quiet. A woman came out from next door with a frill of layered satin hanging below the hem of her coat. She wore red patent-leather high heels, and as she passed me I saw that her lipstick and fingernails matched her shoes.

It was as if nothing had happened.

As if a murder hadn't changed the world, right here, just a week ago.

As if Chali had never existed.

Well, it was true: She didn't exist anymore.

I found her keys in my purse and let myself into the ammonia-clean front hall. All the way up to her apartment, I thought about how Chali had made this climb daily, and how Dathi would never see this place. That it would be up to me to describe it to her hit me suddenly – how her mother's final home looked, how it smelled, how it sounded when she walked up the stairs and down the hall to her apartment. How many rooms she lived in. The colors of her walls. I felt a wave of desperate emotion; I *had* to talk with Dathi, to tell her all this. Hearing back from her felt as imperative as it was beginning to seem unlikely.

Chali's door had, ironically, been left locked, as if it still mattered to try and protect what was inside. I turned the key and let myself in.

The first thing I noticed was the metallic smell of dried blood that filled the space like an olfactory fog. A glimpse into the bedroom, and through the partially open bathroom door, confirmed my guess that no one had bothered to clean up.

Shafts of sunlight from the living room windows illuminated a riot of dust kicked up by my sudden presence in the otherwise abandoned space. The cops had left the apartment a mess. But it didn't matter. I wasn't here to clean; I was here to excavate. I sloughed off my coat, opened the box of garbage bags, and got to work separating out the stuff that seemed worth saving. I lit a half-burned cone of incense I found in a little dish on the windowsill, and played the CD that was already in the stereo: the Beatles' *Abbey Road*. That surprised me, I'll admit, but the more I learned about Chali's life and her tastes, as I dug through what was left of her world, the more I realized how little I had actually known her.

She was a fledgling poet, and had been working on a manuscript, which I'd noticed when I was here last week. I read a few sheets and learned that she was as secretly heretical as she was openly religious. Her dissent appeared practical, not theoretical, and as she had written lately in English my guess was that her social views had evolved significantly since landing in America. I stopped to read 'Arundathi,' because it was named for her daughter, and I was curious.

As for her, I say
Do not ask her to open her eyes
Before
She is ready to look.

As for her, I say
Do not try to reach her
Before
She comes to you.

As for her, I say
Overlook her, if you please
And
Resurrect us both.

I wasn't a poet, or a reader of poetry, so I couldn't judge its merits as art; it was short, and it was simple, and I had no idea if it was any good. But as expression it reached me: It was about the life Chali had left behind in India; it was her hope that Dathi's childhood would not have to end as quickly, and harshly, as had her own. Every mother wanted the best for her children and Chali was no exception.

I gathered her neat, handwritten pages into a large envelope I found in a desk drawer. Dathi would probably like to have them, as she dabbled in poetry, as well.

To the tune of 'Something' and then 'Maxwell's Silver Hammer' I got to work.

First, I bagged a pile of things to keep: the

envelope of poetry; three ornately hemmed silk saris in jewel colors of emerald, ruby, and gold; a beautiful barrette with an ornate design in turquoise and orange enamel; the prettiest of the throw pillows from the bed; a pair of traditional-looking leather sandals I suspected Chali had carried with her from home; and a small, worn Bible in which she had written her name in tiny script. These were all things I could pack up and send to Dathi as keepsakes. In addition, I put two wrapped Christmas presents, both marked for Dathi, into the bag.

I changed the CD to *Benny Goodman's Greatest Hits*. As I sorted through the mismatched plates, glasses, pots and pans in Chali's cramped kitchen, to the swing of Goodman's clarinet, my mind wandered and I forced myself back to the moment, refusing all distractions from the task at hand, disallowing thoughts that wandered too far, and there were many.

The still unidentified dead woman on Nevins Street.

Abby Dekker, half alive in her hospital bed, under vigil of her parents' priest.

Chali, soaking in a bath of her own blood.

Dathi, orphaned from afar, adrift in India.

Antonio Neng, the banker-hating stalker.

P-Patrick Sc-Scott. *Especially him.* I could not think about that man, and the sordid breadth of his comfort zone as he sought to *try something different*, without my pulse surging.

That was when it hit me: What Chali had

endured as a child bride, what she had feared her daughter would also have to endure if she stayed in India too long, Patrick Scott's taste for *something different* at the sight of eleven-year-old Abby alone on Nevins Street, stolen girls, the serial murder of prostitutes – they were all threads of the same pitiless knot.

I put my money on *him*: the double life, the guilty rage; johns' infamous taste for violence toward the women (and girls) they both desire and detest. It was self-loathing misogyny in its purest form.

He was the Working Girl Killer; I felt sure of it.

But if I was right . . . he was only one man. It wouldn't solve the larger problem. It didn't reveal how or where the missing girls had been trafficked, or why they had later been killed with such ostentatious violence. It didn't solve the Dekker murders. And it couldn't bring Chali back.

The thing was, even if Antonio Neng *had* murdered the Dekkers, and even if Patrick Scott *was* the Working Girl Killer – Chali wasn't a prostitute. Yet she had been killed in the same manner as all the others. Where did *she* fit in to all this? It didn't make sense.

Confused, heartbroken, overwhelmed, I leaned against the kitchen wall and slid down to the floor until my face was buried in my knees. I wrapped my arms around my buckled legs, and wept.

After a while, exhausted, I maneuvered to stand, and a glint of something caught my eye nestled in

169

the corner of the floor where two baseboards met. It was a ring: Detective George Vargas's silver bar ring. I picked it up and put it in my jeans pocket for safekeeping.

I changed the CD and continued working. Hours slid past. Mac was supposed to send Star to Open House to pick up Ben, which made me nervous, but I pushed it away. Changed the CD: Vivaldi's *Four Seasons*. Continued sorting and bagging the rest of Chali's stuff, either for Goodwill or trash, until the place was mostly empty except for the poignant scent of sandalwood over blood.

On impulse, at the last minute, I also threw into the bag I was bringing home the *Abbey Road* CD and the half-full box of incense, since I now associated both with Chali's home, and once her front door closed and locked for the last time, home for her would exist only in other people's memory. We'd have to carry it with us in small, intangible ways.

Since the Seventy-second Precinct was just four blocks away, I decided while I was in the neighborhood to pay Detective George Vargas a visit and return his ring. It was easier than packing it up and mailing it back to him, or playing phone tag until we could arrange a time for him to come get it. If he wasn't in, I'd leave it with someone else in his unit.

The precinct was a squat two-story building at the corner of Fourth Avenue and Twenty-ninth

Street, fringed with blue-and-white squad cars parked vertically so they could nose quickly into traffic. Inside it was like a lot of other once-modern, now-forlorn precincts, dusty and airless, milling with workaday cops and buzzing with that sickening combination of stultifying boredom interrupted by bursts of sudden activity. When I walked in, a pair of uniformed officers were leading in a new arrest, a shackled Latino kid, barely old enough to shave. I stood at the front desk beside them, waiting my turn to be noticed.

The boy eyed me. 'You a law-yer?' The way he said it: splitting the word into two overly defined halves: *Law. Ya.*

'No.'

'Cop, then.' He scowled.

'Visitor.'

The desk sergeant finally noticed me. 'Can I help you?'

After a phone call and a couple of questions, I was directed up the stairs at the side of the lobby and told to go to the second door on the left down the hall.

It was a kind of a conference room: long and low-ceilinged, with a table in the center and the cluttered look of long hours and possibly days of an unresolved investigation. The photos taped to the wall showed grim images from Chali's apartment, intermingled with graphic pictures of her decimated body, sodden and gouged down the middle. I turned away; it was not how I wanted to remember her; yet, even without the visual aid, I couldn't stop seeing her that way. My eyes landed on an easel in the corner of the room on which sat a dry-erase board charting elements of the case.

This was before I noticed George Vargas standing at the far end of the table, in the act of standing up, surprised to see me. Then my eyes adjusted and I realized that the woman seated beside him was none other than Ladasha.

'What are *you* doing here?' I blurted.

'You askin' *me* that.' Then she softened her tone as she, too, stood up. 'I didn't know you were coming.'

George came around the table, smiling, but it was forced. 'Karin—'

'Schaeffer,' I reminded him.

'What brings you to our neck of the woods, so to speak?'

I dug into my pocket and brought out the ring. 'Found this at Chali's. Her landlord called me. I told you: He needs to rent it out. I just finished cleaning up.'

'Oh, right.' He took the ring and slipped it onto his pinky. 'My girlfriend wasn't too happy when she heard I lost it. Thanks.'

'No problem.' I looked at Ladasha, who stood with us now. The shadow of faded lipstick told me she'd probably been here awhile today, working without a break. At the other side of the room, three people pored over a computer screen, studying something, one of them taking notes. 'So it's official – Chali's case and yours. I didn't realize the teams were working together now.'

'We are and we aren't.' She held my elbow and tried to steer me toward the door, but I resisted.

'Does that mean Chali's knife matched the others?' I hated hearing myself say it that way: as if that gaudy, brutal weapon that finished off her death was *hers*.

'Thanks for coming by, Karin.'

'Where's Billy?'

I twisted back to take another look across the room, but I would have noticed him if he'd been there; he was pretty distinctive-looking. What I did see now that I hadn't caught on first glance was Billy's name on the dry-erase board on a list with Patrick Scott's and Antonio Neng's, under the heading *POI* – persons of interest.

Suspects.

'*Whoa*.' It came out higher than my natural voice. 'What's going on?'

'Nothing, Karin.' Ladasha's grip on my arm tightened. I shook her loose.

'Why is Billy's name there?'

We faced each other, her large, dark pupils drinking me in, tiny red veins sprouting through the bright whites of her eyes like minuscule unreadable maps.

George leaned closer. 'All you need to know right now is it's a complicated case.'

'You can't possibly think Billy had anything to

do with this. Dash – he's suffering from PTSD. You know that, right?'

George glanced sharply at Ladasha. 'He is?'

'Seems like it sometimes,' she mumbled. 'But on the other hand, the way he tunes out, gets all spooky and weird . . .' She stopped talking when George turned sharply and went over to the board. Using the tips of his fingers, he rubbed out Billy's name.

'PTSD, man. That's tough. A guy here killed himself over it last year.' George shook his head, as if disappointed, and looked at Ladasha. 'I told you it was an out-there idea. I won't be responsible for pushing another cop over the edge.'

'Sorry, I just thought . . .' Again, her sentence faded, which was unlike her. 'All right, fine, we nix that direction.'

'Yeah, well, I don't want to waste any more time.' George wiped his inky fingers down the front of his jeans.

It felt like a show improvised to appease me with the ending I wanted. But at the same time, I needed to believe they were willing to abandon their insane suspicions of my friend. I had known Billy a long time, and I knew him pretty well; he was not a killer. I was sure of it.

'You and Billy are partners,' I reminded Ladasha. 'It's insane dragging his name into this.'

'Yeah? Well, why didn't he talk to me about supposedly having PTSD? I'm sitting there thinking the man's going psycho on me every time we hit a crime scene. What's with that? Why didn't he just *say so?*'

'The stigma – you know it as well as he does.'

'Right. Uh-huh. So he keeps it to himself and goes postal every time he sees a body? Doesn't even tell *me?*'

'He didn't tell me, either. He only told Mac. I figured it out. You could have figured it out, too; actually I thought you had.'

'Huh.' She shook her head. Rolled her eyes.

'He's getting help now, Dash. I put him in touch with someone. It'll get better.'

'All I know is maybe you better not mention any of this to him. Not a good idea 'cause me and him, we still have to work together.'

It felt dishonest, but I knew she was right: Billy wouldn't be able to handle the betrayal by his partner when he had already lost so much trust in himself. He would have to know eventually, but not now.

I left the precinct and walked quickly along bitterly cold Fourth Avenue toward the nearest R train. My mind reeling.

Billy, a suspect?

They may have erased his name, but I wouldn't forget. In fact, they probably restored him to the POI list the minute I was gone. This was exactly the kind of thing he was afraid of: You show weakness, you crack even a little, and the vultures circle.

CHAPTER 11

I got Ben dressed for school while Mac stirred oatmeal at the stove. We were back to our usual morning routine, which would have been a relief except that I hadn't slept at all. The revelation that the *other* task force, the secretive *ghost* unit (as I had taken to thinking of it) at the Seven-two had its eye on Billy really threw me. I hadn't even told Mac, knowing that it would upset him twice as much as it had upset me. I didn't want him to experience any hint of the betrayal I'd felt a year and a half ago upon learning that my good friend Jasmine wasn't who she'd seemed to be. I didn't want Mac to suffer that same treachery because in his case, when it came to *his* friend, it wasn't true. Billy was not only Mac's best friend, he was a bona fide good guy. Nothing could convince me otherwise.

We ate, and I hustled Ben out the door to school.

The dissonance between the pre-holiday excitement crackling in the frigid winter air and the sight of Abby Dekker's photo on every newsstand along Smith Street was jarring. 'Will the Angel Wake in Time for Christmas?' one headline asked above a photo of a smiling Abby wearing a fairy costume and waving a toy wand at the photographer. Where had they gotten that picture of her? I stopped to look at it: She appeared about six or seven; that it was an old picture seemed just as off-key as using it to tweak people's heartstrings.

Ben waited for me at the corner and I jogged to catch up to him.

A neighbor from my block passed us and smiled.

The Three Musketeers came around the corner and turned right onto Smith.

Somehow, life went on.

I gripped Ben's shoulder to hold him back from crossing the street so I could turn and watch the three derelicts go along their merry way. Wondering why I thought of them as derelict when they always wore clean, new-looking clothing. Wondering why they bothered me as much as they did. Wondering if there was even a chance of seeing anyone, or anything, clearly when we were all lost in the subterfuge of our own misperceptions. I thought, again, about George and Ladasha and Billy. Pushed it out of my mind.

After dropping Ben at school, I abandoned plans to start packing for our trip to California, and instead headed to the Y for a yoga class. I had to clear my mind – or at least try.

I unrolled a mat and set up the usual props – block, strap, and folded blanket – in the far corner of the room. As I was about to sit down and wait for class to begin, I glanced through the half-open slats of the blinds on the glass wall separating the yoga studio from a cavernous basketball court one flight below – and thought I saw Billy. Prying apart two slats improved the view, and there he was, standing in front of a young woman with long russet hair pulled back into a ponytail. He had on the same sweatpants and T-shirt I'd last seen him in yesterday on his way to play basketball with Mac. The woman wore black leggings and a loose cotton shirt; she wore no makeup or jewelry of any kind, which gave her a compelling plainness. No nonsense: That was exactly what Billy needed right now. Their feet were bare and they faced each other, holding each other's eyes as he mirrored her every careful movement. So it was true, he *was* trying to cope with his PTSD. To me, it was just one more confirmation of what I'd told Ladasha and George in the Seven-two conference room: Billy was dealing with it; case closed.

I sat down on the mat, on the soft folded edge of the blanket, closed my eyes, and felt a warm flush of release, like a thawed river, pass through my brain.

A little more than an hour later, as I walked through the sun-flooded lobby, feeling limber and relaxed and glad I'd dragged myself over here, I heard my name and turned back to the stairs.

'Karin!'

It was Billy. He was with the woman who had been teaching him in the gym. Both were bundled into their jackets and hats. 'I saw you from the yoga room,' I told them.

'This is Mary Salter, my Tai Chi teacher.'

'I'm Karin.' We shook hands. Hers was soft and dry and I immediately liked her. Face-to-face she appeared taller than she'd seemed when I'd spotted them earlier, though she was medium height at best. She had a big smile, and oozed security and confidence. The warmth of her brown eyes was deepened by the dark shadows under them, and made her look older than I had guessed from afar. She wasn't young, or particularly beautiful, but she exuded an undeniable prettiness.

'First lesson?' I asked.

'Yup.'

'How'd it go?'

'He did great.' Mary smiled at Billy.

'Don't know about that,' Billy said, 'but I tried.'

'Getting started is half the battle,' I said.

Billy rolled his eyes. 'You want to embroider that on a pillow, or should I?'

'I'll do it!' Mary laughed, and gathered her green knit scarf high up to her chin, as we rotated one by one through the revolving door into the cold. 'Well, nice meeting you. Off to my next gig – I juggle three different jobs, with never enough time in between.' She waved good-bye as she turned toward Court Street. Billy and I walked together in the opposite direction, toward the Atlantic Avenue and Boerum Place intersection where a steady flow of traffic siphoned off the Brooklyn Bridge.

'You two make a nice match.' A little voice whispering in the back of my mind told me things would look better for him if he wasn't perennially single; people tended to be suspicious of someone who couldn't seem to couple-up. Mary was great. It was perfect.

'Karin!' But he was grinning and shaking his head.

'She's awesome. Are you blind?'

'Actually, I *am*.'

'I didn't mean that, and you're only half blind, anyway.'

'Karin – she's a single mother and—'

'So?'

'She's gay.'

'How would you know that? You just met her.'

'She told me.'

'Oh.'

'*Oh*,' he mimicked, still chuckling. 'See you guys after you get back from California.'

He kissed my cheek at the corner, and jogged off while I waited at the light to cross the street toward home. I deliberately didn't turn to look at him, partly because I felt like an ass, and partly because I realized now why I'd made such an awkward stab at playing matchmaker: I was desperate to see Billy as normal and untroubled and unburdened. I didn't watch him leave because I didn't want to look at him any other way. He was Billy. Just Billy. Nothing had changed.

★   ★   ★

It was barely sweater weather on Christmas after-noon on Venice Beach. Jon and Andrea had bought a three-bedroom house on Appleby Street, a long walk or short bike ride to the beach where the cousins spent hours running around the play-ground or swimming or both. Susanna was eight now, David five, and with Ben about to turn four they were a high-octane trio. I lounged on a faded striped towel on the sand beside Mom, who sat upright on a beach chair – the long plane ride had done a number on her back – in a wide-brimmed straw hat. Andrea was splayed out on a low-slung chair at the edge of our umbrella's shadow, the lower half of her tan legs shot out into the sun. Pregnant for the third time, her round middle glistened with oily sunblock between the scant parts of her bikini. She was more relaxed than I'd ever seen her. The beach was crowded today. I leaned forward and squinted at Mac and Jon jogging down the undulating dry/wet seam where sand met ocean, growing smaller the farther they got. It all seemed to blend together in the wavering heat: ocean, sand, sunbathers, boardwalk, palm trees, the graphic edge of a bustling town.

Susanna was showing the boys how to dribble wet sand into turrets on the sandcastle they'd been building for the past hour. She wore glasses now, which kept fogging up in the heat, and strands of her long blond hair blew across her face, but she ignored the obstacles and stayed focused on super-vising her crew. She had evolved into the kind of smart, bossy girl any mother would be proud of. At one point, while Mom and Andrea discussed the prospect of shoehorning a soon-to-be family of five into a three-bedroom house (the third bedroom being more a glorified walk-in closet occupied by David), my mind drifted from Susanna to Cece.

She would have been nine years old now, had she lived.

I scanned the beach for a girl who looked the way I imagined my daughter would have, until I spotted a stalky brown-haired girl in the shallow water, mercilessly splashing a younger boy and laughing hysterically. There she was, and I was so proud of her for the split second before she was gone and I was staring at a stranger. Glancing again at Andrea's swollen belly, I refused to think about my *other* daughter.

Shadows, everywhere, even in this blinding sunlight.

'I'll put Susie and Davie together in the bigger room at first,' I heard Andrea saying when I tuned back in, 'and set up the crib in the little room. And then, depending on whether the baby's a boy or a girl, we'll figure out who to double up for good later on.'

Her confidence that her new baby would arrive in due course and join their family thrilled me. Now that I'd experienced a late-term miscarriage, I would never be secure about a pregnancy again.

I refused that thought, too.

It was a beautiful day.

Ben ran up and threw himself into my lap. 'We're hungry!' Sand and salt water mixed with sunscreen had turned his skin to glop, but I hugged him anyway.

'Is it lunchtime already?' Mom asked.

Andrea flipped her wrist to see her watch. 'It's after one.'

'Time to head back to the house, then,' Mom said.

'No!' Susanna now stood before us, hazy in the brilliant sun, hands planted on her hips. 'We're not finished with the castle yet. We have *a lot* more to do.'

I liked her royal *we*, since she had mostly been supervising. She was a relentless crew boss without a drop of mercy for her workers.

'I'm hungry, too.' David stood beside her.

'I'll tell you what.' I got up, bending to knock sand off my legs. 'I'll go back to the house and pack some sandwiches. You kids feel like a picnic?'

After a chorus of yeses, they raced back to their sandcastle.

Where the beach ended and the boardwalk began, I slipped on my flip-flops and started up Rose Avenue. A skinny man in a Santa hat, wearing shorts and a T-shirt, stood on the curb ringing a bell. He swung a collection can with a Salvation Army sticker at everyone who passed. I dropped in a dollar and kept going.

I couldn't resist stopping at the edge of a crowd

that had gathered around a band of drummers, five teenage boys creating an edgy, cacophonous rhythm so infectious it made you need to dance. Before long I was bouncing along with everyone else, dipping right, swaying left, nodding my head to the rhythm. And then I noticed one little girl, holding her mother's hand and moving her whole body side to side, and couldn't take my eyes off her though at first I wasn't sure why.

She was around six or seven years old, I guessed. Her hair had been dyed blond, the recognition of which was the first thing that registered as off kilter; I had never understood why anyone would dye a child's hair. She was dressed in white short-shorts and a snug pink halter top. On her feet were pink flip-flops, but instead of the usual flat kind they were wedges, elevating her height. She had a bright red pedicure, and her long hair was swept off her face in a too-perfect coif, as if it had been blow-dried. Large hoop earrings dangled from her pierced ears. Then I noticed that she was wearing a touch of mascara and a thin layer of pink lipstick, and my stomach turned. I thought of JonBenét Ramsey, the miniature beauty queen who was found in her parents' basement in Boulder, Colorado, in 1996, on Christmas Day. She was six years old, and had been murdered in a brutal crime that was still unsolved.

I stopped dancing, stopped hearing the music, and moved away from the crowd. Continued up Rose Avenue. Along the way, I saw no fewer than three other girls who had been similarly dolled up to resemble little women – unsuspecting seductresses, attached to their mothers' hands.

Why? Because this was Los Angeles? Where people famously came to get discovered for stardom? Or were all the precocious little girls noticeable here simply because so many people were out at once – a statistical certainty? If so, then why hadn't I observed the same phenomenon in New York? I reminded myself that *of course* this place was a legendary magnet for stage mothers – it was, essentially, Hollywood – and reassured myself that there was no reason to feel so surprised.

I opened the front door to my brother's house and stepped into the cool interior of the front hall. It felt good to be out of the sun. I always liked California the first week I was here before I started yearning for the East Coast again, with its moody weather and where unbridled cheerfulness is the exception and not the rule; but this time the longing seized me not two days into our visit. If it wasn't lunchtime I would have made myself a drink, and for a moment I considered it before deciding it really *was* too early in the day. If I felt so vulnerable to every dark, passing thought, what I ought to do was give my old therapist Joyce a call. I had spoken to her once right after my miscarriage, and the conversation ended with a promise that I'd call again if I felt the need. So much had happened lately, it was hard to process it all, and the truth was that sometimes now I did feel that old sinking feeling coming on, pulling me into a dangerous, familiar quicksand. Maybe now was the time to make that call.

I reached into my shorts pocket for my BlackBerry, and was about to look for Joyce's number when my phone shivered with an incoming e-mail.

I saw Dathi's name. Everything else flew out of my mind.

CHAPTER 12

Dathi's e-mail lacked the careful politeness of the last one; she had clearly dashed it off in a hurry:

uncle sold me for R10,000 to an agent for hotel work in Mumbai but granny warned me about such agents and so I left uncle's home

I answered her immediately in the hope that she was still at a computer:

Dathi, what do you mean? Are you safe?

I waited, staring at the screen. But she didn't answer.

I read and reread her message, trying to elicit more information than was actually there. Having spoken with stone-cold Uncle Ishat, I wasn't surprised he didn't want her. But *sell* her? For ten thousand rupees – how much was that, anyway?

I went to the den, where Mac and I were staying on a sofa bed (Ben was happily camping in a

187

sleeping bag on David's floor), and pulled the laptop out of my backpack. Cross-legged on the floor, I booted up and started Googling.

I began with a literal search, based on what Dathi had told me, and typed *girl sold to agent in India* in the search box. At the top of the list was a link to the *Times of India*: 'Young girls sold for Rs 2 lakh.' A lump formed in my throat at the mere suggestion of girls being actually *sold*, though I had no idea what a lakh was.

I clicked through to the article, which described an active marriage market for young girls and women. Price depended on things like age, virginity, looks, prior marriages, etc. A quick search told me that Rs 2 lakh equaled about five thousand dollars.

The lump cascaded into my stomach, igniting a sensation like seasickness when you realize your balance is suddenly off: dizzy, queasy, light-headed. I closed my eyes. Breathed. Opened my eyes. Continued searching.

One lakh equaled one hundred thousand rupees. But Uncle Ishat had supposedly sold Dathi for ten thousand rupees. I looked at her e-mail again to see if I'd gotten that right. I had.

Ten thousand rupees, it turned out, were worth about two hundred dollars. Was that the going rate for a girl these days in India? You couldn't even buy a television in America for that little money.

My head began to pound but I didn't stop. I had to know more, to convince myself that I wasn't exciting my imagination with the typical Internet poison that so easily passed as brutal honesty and truth. I quickly discovered that blogs, chats, and testimonials about human trafficking were legion; exploring them felt like an endless fall down a bottomless well. Finally I decided that it was only worth reading well-researched articles that had been written by reputable journalists and published in respected journals; it was the only way to glean any reality unvarnished by paranoia.

The more solid the information, the more I trusted it, and the worse the story got.

Because it was, apparently, *true*.

It wasn't news that young girls in India and Africa were sold into marriage, often to much older men, as Chali had been. But it *was* news to me that they were also regularly sold for 'hotel work' or 'housecleaning,' which were euphemisms for the pipeline into prostitution. I was aware of human trafficking but what I hadn't understood was how huge the problem was, how many girls and boys, but mostly girls, were sold into commercial sexual slavery by their very own families.

The magnitude of one number, in particular, shocked me: *1.3 million*. That was how many children were sexually enslaved in India alone. About half came from India; the rest were imported from other countries.

Some were as young as my Ben. Many were girls Susanna's age. Girls on the cusp of puberty – like Dathi, who was twelve – fetched the highest price.

When they tried to run away, they were beaten into submission, forcibly drugged, and turned into addicts as a form of chemical restraint.

'First time rights' for a child's virginity went for around R25,000, or about five hundred dollars.

After that, they were tortured. Held in cages. Raped.

In India, a typical child prostitute 'serviced' about ten 'customers' a day, seven days a week. It was the most horrifying math problem I'd ever faced: seventy men, every week, who bought sex from a child for the price of a cup of coffee. Scratch that: It was the brothel that sold the sex and kept the money; the child got nothing.

I sat back, away from the laptop, my mind reeling, my body shaking like a leaf in a storm.

What would Uncle Ishat buy with the two hundred dollars he got for Dathi?

A sudden wooziness overcame me; I had barely eaten any breakfast and it was already late for lunch. I closed my eyes, leaned against the end of the sofa bed, and waited for the sensation to pass.

I didn't know Dathi – but now I knew something about her. She had run away, understanding essentially what was in store for her. Unlike so many children in her position, she had been educated and forewarned. A path out had been painstakingly carved by her mother and grandmother – until it all fell apart. I pictured her now, a spirited child in an unforgiving circumstance, running in place as in a nightmare, when the harder you try, the farther you fall behind. And then, in my agitated imagination, I saw the other girls – the missing girls; the dead prostitutes – running beside Dathi. Abby, too. All those girls joined by ghostly throngs whose lives had collided with avarice or violence or both. Trying so hard to run away, getting nowhere. Vanishing and forgotten as if their existence barely mattered.

Everything had been arranged for Dathi's departure: the visa secured; the airfare paid; a one-way ticket scheduled for New Year's Day; the airline already informed that a child would be traveling alone out of Nagpur and met in New York by an adult. I had watched from a distance while Chali made the arrangements, never imagining how important it would be that I knew what she had done.

The only thing left to do now was get Dathi on that plane, and pick her up at the airport. The rest could be figured out later.

But it was ridiculous. Wasn't it? Impossible. Insane.

And yet it was such a small thing to do for another human being.

I got up and in the bathroom splashed cold water on my face a few times, dried my skin, then went to the kitchen for a glass of water. After a few sips and a few deep breaths, I was calm enough to dial Uncle Ishat's number. I leaned against the sink, listening to the ghostly ringing of his phone nearly nine thousand miles away.

Finally, he answered.

'You again.'

'Please, don't hang up.' I forced calm into my tone, when what I really wanted to do was scream obscenities at the man.

There was a pause. He was still there. I didn't know how to begin a conversation like this, but sensed that if I didn't talk fast I'd lose him.

'Let me have Dathi.'

His laugh bubbled, acrid and murky as burning rubber. 'Good-bye.'

'Wait! I'll give you twenty thousand rupees for her. Just put her on the plane to New York, that's all you'll have to do.'

His silence now thickened with interest. '*Twenty* thousand, you say?'

I hadn't thought it through, I'd simply doubled what I knew he'd gotten for her, but immediately realized that it was only four hundred dollars or so, not an impressive sum, possibly not worth the trouble to Uncle Ishat to track her down and buy her back.

'Thirty,' I said. 'Forty.' Bargaining now with myself. 'Fifty.'

'Done.'

Just like that: I had bought a child.

'Tell me where to wire the money and I'll do it right now.'

He gave me the particulars for his bank, which I jotted on the bottom of a shopping list magnetized to the fridge. I knew I had to send the money immediately. I also knew he might not comply with his end of the deal, or even try to find her.

'The flight leaves on Saturday,' I reminded him. Just six days from now. 'Do you know where her visa and ticket are? Do you have any idea where she is? Will you be able to find her?'

The more questions I shot at him, the denser his silence became on the other end of the distant line. Finally he said, 'Which question do you want me to answer first?'

'The ticket, do you know—'

'Yes, yes, I know what to do. I will wait for the money.' And he hung up.

I listened to a few moments of crackling silence before ending the call on my phone.

It took ten minutes on the Western Union Web site to transfer fifty thousand rupees from my credit card into Uncle Ishat's bank account. My price tag was $1,140.31, which included a twenty-dollar fee to Western Union. It was about a third of our monthly mortgage payment. Less than the cost of our four round-trip tickets to L.A. A relatively insignificant amount of money to people like us: average middle-class Americans. It was like letting the water run when you answered the phone, not realizing that to a big part of the world you were allowing the equivalent of pure gold to swirl down the drain. The comparisons were absurd, unthinkable, and painful to take in. I closed the Web site, letting my finger rest a moment on the smooth surface of the touchpad while the cursor shivered helplessly on the screen, before realizing that someone was in the room with me.

Startled, I turned around.

'What did you just do?'

Mac was standing there in the den, sweating profusely, looking down at where I sat on the floor with the laptop. The screen was faced in his direction; he must have seen the Western Union logo blink off. I heard the plumbing activate upstairs, which told me that Jon was in the shower.

'How long have you been standing there?'

'Did you just make a money transfer for something like a thousand bucks?'

'I did.'

'Why?'

There was no easy way to say it, and I wasn't going to lie.

'I bought a kid.'

'What do you mean *bought a kid*?'

'Chali's daughter, Dathi.' I launched into the whole story, giving him the blow-by-blow of my conversation with Uncle Ishat, leading him through article after article about the commercial sexual exploitation of children in India, illuminating Dathi's fate if we ignored the golden opportunity of flight Chali had so painstakingly arranged for her beloved daughter.

'We have no choice,' I told him.

'We?' He ground his jaw in the way I hated; it meant he was angry, felt cornered, and I'd hear more about it later. 'I'm not part of this.'

'Mac—'

'It's kidnapping.'

'You're wrong. Chali arranged everything. It's perfectly legal.'

'Until Dathi steps off that plane in New York. Does she even know her mother's dead? Did anyone tell her?'

I didn't know.

'What happens after she gets here? We take her home and keep her – like a pet?'

I couldn't answer.

'They're all waiting for you down at the beach,' he said. 'Everyone's hungry. They seem to think you came back to the house to pack a picnic lunch.'

'I did.'

He stared at me a moment. 'She won't be ours, Karin. She won't be yours. You can't replace . . .' But he trailed off before he said it: Cece. Audra or Tara or Lily.

I stood up and reached for him but he turned abruptly and left the den. Moments later, I heard the clank of plumbing again, this time from the first-floor bathroom down the hall.

'Well, screw that,' I said aloud to no one. To myself. Because I was on a quest now, this was something I had to do because it had to be done. I would have saved all the children in the entire world if I'd had the money.

But I didn't. I only had the power to save one: Arundathi Das.

Chali's only child, her one hope for a redeemable future.

Dathi: a girl I didn't know, but had to help.

In my mind, at that point, it was simple.

And I would not turn away.

I replied a second time to her last e-mail:

Dathi, I just spoke with your uncle. Everything's been arranged. He's going to look for you and put you on the plane to New York, as planned. Let him find you, or just return to his house. Trust us, please. Trust me.

But was it true? Would Uncle Ishat follow through with his end of our agreement? Or would he keep my money and still sell her to the agent? Increase his profits? Never answer another call from me? Write off his young niece as a spoiled asset and move on with his life?

A wave of cold passed through me.

I pressed send.

During the next four days, until we flew home on Thursday, every time my phone vibrated with a new e-mail I rushed to check it but it was never from her. I didn't know if she ever read my last e-mail. All I knew for sure, via a confirmation from Western Union, was that Uncle Ishat got his money.

We arrived back in Brooklyn late Sunday afternoon, into a twilit world that felt vastly different than the warm, sunny coast we'd left behind. I helped my mother into her apartment, then returned to the taxi and headed home. Another snow had frosted the brownstones and our block looked like a row of gingerbread houses festooned with colorful lights. The deep post-holiday quiet betrayed that strange, sad pause between Christmas and New Year's. Tired from all the fuss, you rested; but there was still more to come.

Released from the taxi, Ben raced up the nearest snowbank and slid down to the sidewalk, where fresh snow had accumulated sometime that day. He was about to mount the icy stoop when Mac dropped his suitcase, grabbed Ben's hood, and steered him toward the ground-floor entrance. I followed with my backpack and the other suitcase, hoisting it above the snow to the door. Over the past few days Mac's and my disagreement over Dathi had calcified into the worst kind of polite silence. He picked up his suitcase, deposited it inside the front hall, fetched a shovel from the vestibule, and started clearing a path along the sidewalk. I closed the door but didn't lock it, and followed Ben inside.

The thing about East Coast winters is that it turns the inside of a house into a warm paradise. All the sunshine California has to offer will never compare to that blast of gratitude you feel when you come inside from the cold. I was glad to be back.

Liberated from his slushy sneakers and jacket, Ben ran to his room to greet his toys. I went upstairs to sort through mail that had accumulated below the slot in the front door. Outside, I could hear the scrape of Mac's shovel, steadily clearing snow from the cement sidewalk. How could I convince him that rescuing Dathi was an imperative, not a whim? I wanted him on my side. Even though I figured that the chances she'd actually turn up at the airport on New Year's Day were slim, if she *did* arrive I wanted her to feel welcomed by the entire family, not just Ben and me. I had decided not to worry in advance about the legal implications of bringing her over using the pre-arranged paperwork of a mother who no longer existed. I was focused on getting her out of India. Nothing else. I hoped that Mac would come around to seeing the simplicity, the urgency – the *humanity* of my quest.

I phoned in a dinner order to the Middle Eastern place down Smith Street, and while we waited, I called Billy to check in with him. I couldn't help wondering if Ladasha and George had really dropped his name from the POI list; if not, by now Billy would probably have figured something out.

'You home?' He sounded groggy, or maybe a little drunk.

'Where are you?'

'Brooklyn Inn, bellied up to the bar.'

'How was your Christmas?'

'Spent the day at my sister's. It was nice. Yours?'

'Really good. I love spending time with all of them. We hung out a lot at the beach.'

'Hope you brought me back a box of sunshine.' There was a silence, a click of ice on his end, a swallow.

'So, you catch your killer yet?' I'd meant it as a joke, because we would have heard, and was surprised when he answered:

'Maybe.'

'What?'

'We're taking a real hard look at Pat Scott.'

'Did the lab connect him to Chali?'

'Still waiting on that.'

'It's been almost three weeks!'

'Yeah, well, the holidays . . .'

It was true: This time of year, everything took twice as long to get done.

'Here's one you'll like: We put Antonio Neng the stalker in lockup yesterday. Found a judge who doesn't celebrate Christmas, got ourselves a warrant on the first try. Turns out he's got weapons in his apartment, guns, and a journal he keeps that reads like a hit list.'

'Bankers?'

'Each and every one.'

'Any forensics putting him in the Dekker house?'

'I'm telling you, nothing's coming out of the lab right now. Still recovering from their Hanukkah party, and their Kwanzaa party, and their Christmas party. Probably planning for New Year's just about now.'

'How's Abby Dekker doing?'

'Still in her coma.'

'I'm sorry.'

'Yeah, well.'

'That priest still there, reading her books?'

'Every day.'

'Maybe she'll come around.' I paused, then said, 'Well *I* have some news,' and told him about Dathi.

'Wow, Karin. You know what? *Way to go.*' Another clink of ice, another swallow.

'Thanks. I could use a little support, to tell you the truth.'

'Mac's not on board, huh?'

'He calls it kidnapping.'

A bark of laughter from Billy made me laugh, too.

'Well, you do what you do, Karin. You wouldn't be *you* if you sat back and waited.'

He might have been plastered, but I liked the sound of his encouragement.

'Stop by tomorrow and visit,' I told him.

'Working all day.'

'Then stop by after work, have dinner with us.'

'Can't. Got a *psychiatrist* appointment at eight.' The way he said the word: as if it tasted bad. But I was very glad to hear it.

'Well, then how about Saturday? We don't have any plans.'

'I'll give you a call.'

I hung up and went to the window. Mac had finished paths along the sidewalk and to our ground-floor entrance, and was working on the stoop now. On impulse, I opened the front door and told him, 'I just talked to Billy. He's having a drink at the Inn and said maybe you'd like to join him.' A white lie in the white snow. But so what? It would do them both some good, and maybe Billy would rally for my cause.

Mac leaned the shovel against the railing and clapped his gloves together to shake off some ice. 'Thanks. I just might do that as soon as I'm done here.'

I didn't see Mac after that until almost eleven. Meanwhile the food arrived and Ben and I ate dinner together at the kitchen table. Then I gave him a bath and read him a book and put him to bed. I was lying on my own bed, reading, when the downstairs door finally creaked open.

'Karin!' Mac sounded more awake than when he'd left. I heard him stomp his feet energetically by the front door before his footsteps thumped down the hall toward our room. I had the feeling that something was wrong, and sat up to face the door.

'What is it?'

His face was flushed from the cold, and his eyes

looked shiny; he'd had a couple of drinks, but he wasn't drunk.

'They're waking her up tomorrow morning. Billy just got the call.'

'Who?' But I knew who, because there was only one person whose awakening could possibly merit that much excitement right now: Abby Dekker.

CHAPTER 13

We arrived moments after Abby opened her eyes – her pale eyes, flickering around the room with a vague, uncomprehending expression, suggested she didn't know where she was or what had happened. The bandages had been removed from her head, and her hair was growing back prickly and blond.

Sasha Mendelssohn, the care coordinator, stood back against the wall, hugging her clipboard to her chest, smiling tentatively as she watched a doctor who leaned over Abby's bedside. He was tall, with a fringe of longish gray hair, and his name was embroidered on his white coat: *Daniel Alter-Jones, MD, Pediatric Neurology.* Hovering just behind her were two young residents wearing pinned-on name tags. Opposite them, across the bed, stood another white-coated doctor, short and portly with a halo of grizzly orange hair: *Mark J. Miller, MD, Pediatrics.*

Billy walked into the room and greeted the others with a nod; apparently they had all met before. Mac and I hovered in the doorway. We weren't officially part of this, though a glance from Sasha

Mendelssohn acknowledged me with a note of reluctant acceptance. Mac, however, was another matter; Sasha's gaze stayed with him a moment before crossing to the doorway.

'You are?'

We shifted into the hall, and spoke in whispers.

'This is my husband, Mac MacLeary.' I watched her eyes as I introduced him: moving from my face to his and back to mine, her wariness softening. 'He's also a private investigator; we work together. And just by chance, Mac knew Reed Dekker – Abby's father.'

Sasha looked at him now with interest. 'Does Abby know you?'

'No,' Mac said. 'I was acquainted with her dad from the gym. He was a good man.'

'She doesn't know anyone in that room.' Sasha hesitated, glancing at the doorway as if it could offer guidance. 'We're hoping the Campbells will get here soon. We'd like to get some sense of how she's really doing, but it's hard when she's nervous.'

'Where's Father X?' I couldn't remember his last name – something complicated, possibly Greek – but X was easy.

'He's in the cardiac unit. He had chest pains last night when he heard Abby was being brought out this morning. This has been very stressful for him, and he isn't exactly young.'

'Heart attack?'

She shook her head. 'Chest pains, dizziness,

blood pressure shot up. Admitting him was precautionary. He's being monitored.'

'Well,' Mac said quietly, 'they say stress is contagious.'

Sasha's eyebrows shot up. 'Welcome to my world.'

'Has she said anything yet?' I asked.

'Nothing. She's disoriented, but that's pretty normal. It can take a while.'

An orderly wheeled up a tiered cart stacked with foil-covered breakfast trays. 'Heard she was awake. Taking solids yet?'

'Probably not, we still have to monitor her swallowing; but hold on, let me check on something.' Sasha scooted back into Abby's room.

Mac and I followed.

Sasha was speaking with Drs. Alter-Jones and Miller, who then looked at Abby, smiled, and spoke to her directly. 'Hungry?'

It seemed like a strange question, if swallowing might be an issue, but then it occurred to me that maybe they were just trying to get a reaction from her – any reaction. So far, it appeared she hadn't said a word, and if she had made eye contact with anyone, I hadn't seen it.

Abby's eyes clouded. It was unclear if she'd understood. The IV drip that had nourished her the past three weeks draped from the crook of her elbow to a half-empty bag of clear liquid suspended at the side of her bed. It was hard to imagine a growing child not craving real food. But nothing in her demeanor suggested a claim on any desire or intention at the moment. She seemed deeply perplexed. Lost. And something else about her reaction, or lack of it, compelled me . . . I couldn't put my finger on it. The more I wanted to cross the room and hug her, the harder I pressed myself into the wall in an effort to make myself invisible. The last thing this kid needed was more strangers insinuating themselves into her space.

'Let's bring in some breakfast,' Dr Alter-Jones said to Sasha. Then, turning to smile at Abby: 'If you feel hungry, it'll be right here.'

Sasha disappeared in the hall and returned with a tray. She put it on a small table in a corner of the room, next to the guest chair.

Abby's gaze followed the tray, then returned to Dr Alter-Jones.

'You can try eating something, if you feel like it.' The doctor smiled.

Again, no response.

'That's okay.' Dr Alter-Jones touched Abby's forehead lightly with his fingertips: pinkish clean and neatly trimmed. I noticed now that in his other hand he held a penlight; one of the first things he would have done was to check her pupils for indications of brain activity. The way he was trying to reach her suggested that he believed she was reachable.

'I'd be quiet, too,' Dr Miller said with a chuckle, 'waking up in a hospital to a bunch of people I didn't know.'

Everyone laughed, but it was forced, and kids were famous for their bullshit meters. I watched Abby's face as the strangers surrounding her tried to humor her into speaking. *Could* she speak? Seeing her so adrift and listless made me uneasy. Brain injury had been the big worry and now its specter seemed to fill the room.

I recalled seeing her for the first time: lying on a stretcher in the dark, being attended to by EMS techs; her wheat-blond hair spilling off the side of the stretcher in a waterfall. Now, the swelling that had distorted her face and parts of her body had subsided and you could see the willowy shape of an eleven-year-old who hadn't yet tripped up the steps of puberty. She was also paler, with the color wheel of her injuries mostly faded.

'Can you tell me how many fingers I'm holding up?' Dr Alter-Jones held up two fingers directly in Abby's line of vision.

She glanced at his fingers, and looked away.

'How about now?' Just one finger this time.

Lines formed across her forehead and she seemed to shrink, as if she wanted to scrunch deeper under her covers. Mac reached over and squeezed my hand. I looked at him: He seemed shaken.

Was he thinking it, too? How sad it was watching this injured, orphaned girl alone among strangers. Was he also connecting her to Dathi, another helpless girl, orphaned through violence? Was he thinking that you didn't turn away if you had a chance to help? I squeezed back and we stood there, our hands clutched. The truth was, I had no idea what he was thinking, and I doubted that he shared my preoccupation with Dathi. Mac was a tough cookie, even-keeled in the best and worst of times. I was tough in a different way: I had been called reckless, even ruthless, and my stubbornness was a matter of record. I knew that I followed my gut instinct in a way most people wouldn't dare, and that Mac both admired and distrusted me for it. I didn't *know* what he was thinking; but something shifted in that moment, and I felt (hoped) I might have finally won his heart on the matter of lost little girls.

Billy stood in the far corner of the room, his one-eyed gaze fixed on Abby. His pupil was pinprick small; though it was bright in the room, it wasn't *that* bright. A thin layer of perspiration shone on his face. He had that masklike look again, and a now familiar apprehension swept over me. I tugged Mac's hand and directed his attention to Billy. I felt his alarm as his fingers abruptly released mine.

'Can I talk to you a minute?' Mac whispered to Billy, who looked at him with a kind of surprise that registered interruption. He'd either been deep in thought or I'd been right: He was about to go off.

Reluctantly, Billy allowed Mac to lead him out of Abby's room. I was about to follow, but changed my mind when the Campbells appeared. I didn't want to miss it, if this was the moment Abby would finally speak.

The Campbells looked haggard, having now two bedsides to attend to, and I wondered if they had slept at all last night. Linda's bubble of dyed blond hair was deflated. Steve's pale yellow dress shirt was tucked in but badly wrinkled, with a lopsided brown stain soiling the pocket from which protruded the top of a cigarette pack, which surprised me.

'Sweetheart!' Linda hovered over Abby's bed as if unsure how close she could come to the fragile girl. Abby barely glanced at the woman who was to be her guardian, her new mother.

Didn't Abby want to know why her parents weren't there?

Did she expect them to sweep into the room? Was that what she was waiting for?

Or did she know they were dead?

What did she know about what happened that night?

Steve stood back with his hands in his pockets, watching his wife try to connect with Abby. Finally Linda lowered her hands, gently cradling Abby's face.

'We're so happy to see you,' Linda said. 'Don't be scared. Did they explain you're in the hospital but you're okay?'

Both doctors and both residents nodded. 'We did,' Dr Miller said. 'But it can be pretty confusing coming out of a coma. It might take Abby a little time to get her bearings.'

'That's right,' Dr Alter-Jones agreed. 'Abby, would you like to spend a few minutes alone with Linda and Steve?'

Abby didn't answer. Didn't even look at the doctor when he spoke directly to her.

'Okay,' Dr Alter-Jones said. 'We'll be back in a little while.'

As the doctors filed out, it was impossible not to overhear their conversation:

'Can't know yet if we're dealing with neuro-logical damage.' Dr Alter-Jones. 'But her vitals are good. She's basically alert. I'm hopeful.'

'Watch and wait.' Dr Miller. 'Buzz me if . . .'

And then they were out of earshot.

I joined Mac and Billy where they huddled by a vending machine across from the nurses' station. Billy was twisting the cap off a bottled water. He looked fine now. I wanted to ask him what had happened in there, though I was pretty sure I knew: He had ricocheted back to that frozen moment on Nevins Street when he first saw her, and from there back into the episode that had seized him that night, in a cruel double whammy. And I wanted to ask him, *Why now*, when he'd visited Abby before without incident. But my intention to reach out to Billy was cut short. Linda could be heard sobbing in Abby's room; Steve was loudly shushing her.

The wall clock ticked forward to exactly ten-thirty and I was starting to wonder about the wisdom of having Star fetch Ben from nursery school and drop him at my mother's apartment. She was often clumsy and usually late. It didn't feel right entrusting her with our child, which reminded me how badly we needed to correct our slipshod child-care situation. The thing was, I didn't *want* to hire someone new; I, *we*, wanted Chali.

'Let's go,' I said to Mac. 'We shouldn't be here.'

'You're right.' He turned to Billy. 'Come with us?'

'Think I'll stay,' Billy said.

I looked at him, and it felt just as wrong leaving him here alone as relying on Star to get Ben.

'Mac, why don't I hang out here with Billy? You can go home and get some work done.'

'You sure? Because I can stay.' But I knew he felt pressured, having fallen behind on his cases when he was sick.

'Absolutely. But will you check on Mom before leaving Ben with her? Her back was bothering her last night.'

'Will do.' Mac kissed my cheek. 'I'll catch up with you later, Billy.'

'I don't need you to babysit me, Karin.' Billy tightened the cap on the water bottle so hard I thought the plastic would break.

'Seriously? Because you nearly zapped off into la-la land before.'

He uncapped the bottle and drank some water. Capped it again, but not as tightly. 'Do what you want; it's a free country.'

After a minute, Steve and Linda Campbell emerged from the room. He had his arm around her shoulders and led her down the hall – just like last time. It was strange. I wondered why Reed and Marta Dekker had assigned guardianship to a woman who couldn't seem to hold herself together.

'What's with her?' I asked Billy.

'Don't know.' His voice sounded almost back to normal, but not quite, as if the shadow of whatever had overtaken him before had not fully passed.

And then something hit me: Abby's disconnected behavior had reminded me of Billy when he was falling down the rabbit hole of one of his PTSD episodes. You were not present; you were someplace else entirely, in the grip of something invisible to others, completely unreachable.

We stood in the door, watching Sasha watch Abby, who seemed to stare at the window – a view of the cityscape, covered in ice crystals – but who knew if she was really seeing anything? It was no surprise she'd be traumatized after what she'd experienced that awful night: hit by a car alone on a derelict street; and for all we knew, she had witnessed her parents' murders. Maybe she wanted to go back to sleep. Maybe she didn't want to be awake in a world without her mother and father. Maybe. If only she would open her mouth and tell us.

'Well, sorry to drag you all the way up here for nothing.' Sasha noted something on her clipboard. 'We'll call you if things change.'

'Can I hang out a bit?' Billy asked. 'Read to her, maybe? Since Father X is—'

Sasha lifted a finger to her lips in a silent *shh*. She shook her head.

Right: Just because Abby wasn't speaking didn't mean she couldn't hear, and it might upset her to learn that the priest was also hospitalized.

'I'm supposed to exercise my good eye,' Billy said.

At that, Abby's attention brushed across the room and she looked at him quickly. The worry lines deepened across her forehead; she didn't seem too pleased by the sight of the tall black guy with an eye patch slung across his face like an urban pirate. And then she looked at me and I could have sworn I saw the flicker of a smile at one corner of her mouth before she looked away again.

'Or *I* could read to her,' I impulsively offered. 'I read to my son all the time. I love reading to kids. Are they still working on *A Wrinkle in Time*?'

The book was on the table beside the breakfast tray. Sasha picked it up.

'Looks like it. But we'll get a volunteer in to read to Abby, I think.'

Abby looked at me again and as her gaze lingered, I had the strangest feeling she was reaching out.

'What if I read to her a little bit until the volunteer gets here?'

Sasha sighed; she must not have been used to visitors being quite this pushy, or maybe she just didn't see a problem with the idea, but she didn't push back.

'I'll be on the floor for the next hour or so, and you're with him, so I guess it's okay.' *Him* being Billy who, despite Abby's seeming discomfort, was an NYPD detective and as such qualified as official protection. It would also, obviously, offer Billy a chance to observe Abby a little longer – and whether the hospital liked it or not, she was potentially a key witness in a serious investigation.

Sasha handed me the book on her way out, and I pulled the guest chair close to Abby's bedside. Billy tucked himself into a corner, out of her vision, turning himself into a nearly invisible observer. I opened to the bookmarked place where Father X had stopped – Chapter Seven: 'The Man with Red Eyes.'

Abby's blank gaze stayed glued to the textured grayish squares of the dropped ceiling as I read aloud to her. I'd forgotten how much I loved this novel about Meg's stubborn journey into the fifth dimension in search of her missing father. In fact, I now recalled that when I'd read the book in middle school, I had been so enchanted that for a day or two I actually imagined myself to *be* Meg. Her intelligence and courage inspired me: She was a girl hemmed in by the misogyny of midcentury America, but she was uniquely stubborn, intelligent, and courageous; she didn't skew to the obvious if she thought her own ideas were better, and she didn't take no for an answer. Reading the novel in the 1980s, I didn't see what the big deal was until my mother explained how unusual it was when *she* was a girl, back in the fifties, to be taken seriously in any way. Visiting Meg's world again made me tingle with an old, familiar excitement of discovery. And a vivid memory I'd forgotten until now: I had decided, back then, that if I ever had a daughter I would name her Margaret and call her Meg. How had I forgotten that when I did have a daughter and named her Cece, short for Cecilia, in memory of my first husband Jackson's late mother? We'd had other things on our minds then; his mother had just passed away, and we missed her.

Tomorrow was New Year's Day, the due date of my lost pregnancy. Would I have remembered to name my new baby girl Meg?

I read for almost an hour before Abby drifted off to sleep. Then I looked over at Billy, leaning into his quiet corner of the room, arms folded across his chest. Calm now. Thinking. When I couldn't find the bookmark, I dog-eared the page and set the book down on the chair. I didn't want to make any noise so left the chair where it was. Billy followed me out of the room.

'It's New Year's Eve,' I said as we walked down the hall. 'What are you doing tonight?'

'Throwing a big party at my place. Sorry, you're not invited.'

In all the years I'd known him, he'd never once thrown a party of any kind.

'You're not spending the night alone at the Brooklyn Inn. You're coming over to our house for some champagne. When the clock strikes midnight, we'll let you leave.'

'Taking me hostage?'

'If necessary.'

We reached the elevator. Suddenly he looked at me.

'Isn't tomorrow the day Chali's kid's supposed to fly in?'

'Yup.'

'Are you going through with it?'

'Are you kidding me?'

'Think the uncle will put her on that plane?'

The elevator door dinged open. Billy stepped in first.

'We'll see.' I joined him and pushed the button. On the ground floor, the doors yawned open onto the cavernous, bustling lobby. We walked into the crowd, toward the main entrance. Through a wall of shining glass you could just see the murky image of a shoveled path bordered by mounds of slushy gray snow.

'Karin, you can't get your daughter back this way. You know that, right?'

There was no relevant answer to that question, as far as I was concerned.

'I said I'd be waiting, and I will.'

We passed through the revolving door into a gust of cold air, but I didn't zip my jacket; I walked right into it.

CHAPTER 14

I paced the area just beyond the bay of luggage carousels, the closest they allowed you to get to arriving passengers. My head pounded from drinking too much champagne last night; Billy and my mother had hung out with us in our living room until one A.M., playing game after game of cards. After that, Billy walked home and Mom went to sleep on the sofa bed in our living room. No one had bothered trying to talk me out of my mission today; they all knew me, and understood that I planned to go to the airport, regardless of any commonsense arguments that it would be a fool's errand. But still, I knew what they were thinking. Mac's parting words when I left the house at just past noon rang in my ears:

'If you can, swing by the car wash after the airport. The car's crusty after all that snow.'

He assumed I wouldn't have anything better to do after leaving the airport, because Dathi (obviously) wouldn't be getting off that plane.

Her Air India flight was due in at two thirty-five in the afternoon. After customs and luggage, I figured the soonest she'd appear would be about three-thirty. I decided to wait until six o'clock, at least, in case she was held up for any reason inside the airport. She was only twelve. I was sure she had never traveled this far alone before, if she had traveled at all. Did she expect Chali to meet her at the gate? What would she do when no one was there? I had no idea what to expect of this child; I knew so little about her. I didn't even know if she understood that her mother was dead. It wouldn't have surprised me at all if Uncle Ishat had taken the money and left the bearing of bad news to me.

But I knew what I wanted to believe; what I needed to believe: that she was on that plane, approaching New York right about now; that she was following instructions, buckling her seat belt and preparing to land; that she was waiting in a line of passengers in the aisle to start moving toward the hatch; that she was in the detachable tunnel making her way into the belly of the airport; that she was somehow finding the right lines and the right counters and presenting the right paperwork, getting all the right stamps of approval; that she was standing at the correct luggage carousel waiting for her suitcase to wend its way to her; that she had the physical wherewithal to hoist it off the moving conveyor belt, or the gumption to ask someone for help.

I had worked up a sweat pacing for so long, and held my coat draped over an arm. When I dropped it and a man accidentally stepped on it, I tugged so hard it surprised him. The sharp look he gave me could have cut glass. My eyes rimmed with tears – I was so nervous and felt like such an idiot, waiting around an airport for a girl I didn't know, who would never appear – that instead of saying something, the man closed his mouth and walked away. I was sure he thought I was crazy.

Was I?

Finally I found an empty seat on an otherwise crowded bench, folded my coat on my lap, rested my head against the wall, and closed my eyes. Over and over, I reviewed the litany of documents Chali had arranged to smooth Dathi through this trip: passport, visa, plane ticket, a letter stating that she had permission to travel alone, complete with a notary's stamp obtained from an official at the Indian Consulate. Grandma Edha had even gotten a local doctor to write a letter stating that Dathi was in perfect health. My mind searched for potential holes in the paperwork, something that might snag her on her long journey and prevent her from arriving – if she had ever left. I don't know how much time had passed in these obsessive thoughts, when I heard it:

'Karin Schaeffer? Karin Schaeffer?'

I leaned forward. Down at the far end of the row of benches was a girl, calling my name.

'I'm Karin Schaeffer!' I stood up and started walking.

She smiled tentatively before turning around to drag her suitcase forward on a strap. It didn't appear to have wheels, but it wasn't very big and she seemed to manage fine.

'Dathi?' I asked, almost close enough to touch her now.

'You were expecting another girl?' Her round face erupted into a smile. She had big, crooked teeth and black eyes that shone like wet coal. Her skin was smooth and lighter than her mother's, but her hair was as thick and black and she wore it just as Chali had: swept off her face in a pony-tail. She was dressed in a full yellow skirt and a gauzy black shirt embroidered with white thread in a complicated symmetrical design that looked like a flower but wasn't. She wore dangling silver earrings with white beads at the ends, and on her feet, newish black sneakers. She wasn't pretty, exactly, but she was beautiful. She seemed to glow.

'I'm so happy to see you! You have no idea.' I couldn't help myself: I wrapped her in a big hug, which she instantly returned . . . another relief, because among my pile-up of worries had been that even if she did arrive she wouldn't want anything to do with me; I would be a disappointment in the way of seeing her mother. And then I would have to break the news. Her hair was so soft, and she smelled like the same sandalwood incense I'd burned at Chali's, cleaning out her apartment.

'Oh, I *do* have an idea,' she said, squeezing me. 'I am quite happy to see *you*.'

And then I realized that she knew. But still, I had to ask.

'Your uncle, did he explain—?'

'No, but I saw online after Granny had her heart

attack. She wanted to tell me something before she passed on. I think her heart exploded trying to tell me such a terrible thing. I have had a *very* bad few weeks. But my mother trusted you, so I trust you. And here I am.'

I wondered how Granny had learned about Chali's death. But the stillness of Dathi's face, the depth of her eyes, told me not to pursue it. She had made it here. I could hardly imagine what she had endured these past weeks. Losing her grandmother. Dumped on an uncaring uncle. Learning that her beloved mother had been murdered. Sold to a trafficker. On the run, alone, in a country merciless to girls like her. In time we would talk about it; but not right now.

She reached for the suitcase's looped handle and tugged it forward along the polished floor.

'How was your trip?' I tried to take the suitcase from her, but she resisted.

'No, I can do it. Please.'

I let go and backed off, though it made me uncomfortable that this slender child was hauling a suitcase while I was empty-handed. When we got outside, I realized she had no coat. I tried to give her mine, but she refused.

She stopped automatically at the first line of people we came to for a bus, and looked at me hesitatingly.

'I have a car, it's parked over there.' I pointed to a metered lot in the near distance.

'Luxury!' She started pulling her suitcase in that

direction. 'At home I walked everywhere. I had hopes for a bike but Granny told me not to spend our money that way; she told me when I got to America to live with my mother things would be different. Everyone in America has a bike. No problem. In India things are not so easy for most people. But look: Today is my lucky day! Driving home in your car, and driven by Uncle to the airport in his Nano. Red, still shiny new. You should see him: he's like a king in his little car.' Her laugh was filled both with humor and disdain. She got her uncle's picture. And now I knew what he'd done with the money he'd gotten for her.

She helped me load her suitcase into the back of our MINI Cooper. Then she stood by the driver's side and waited for me to unlock the door. For a moment I was startled, before understanding.

'Dathi, here the driver sits on the left and we drive on the right side of the road.'

She grinned and her eyes rolled up in her head. 'Of course you do. How stupid of me! Granny had a video of *The French Connection* and how many times have I imagined myself sitting beside Popeye Doyle racing under the canopy road in his old car.'

I was momentarily startled that she knew the movie so well. 'You mean the chase scene under the elevated highway?'

'Yes! In Brooklyn. I am really quite excited to be going to Brooklyn.' She beamed at me as I unlocked the passenger door, slipped right in, buckled up, and waited for me to start driving.

'You know,' I said, navigating out of the parking lot, 'Popeye Doyle's car wasn't old when the movie was made. Things have changed a lot since then.'

'Of course.' Gazing through the car window, she seemed to study everything she saw: the multitude of cars driven by people of every nationality; the roads looping toward and away from the gigantic airport; the constant roar of airplanes overhead. 'Forty years have elapsed since Mr Doyle's escapades in that funny rust-colored car.'

'Was it rust?' I asked. 'I remember it more as red.'

'Shall we say rusty red?'

We laughed and I felt something wonderful happen between us, as if we had clasped hands and jumped through a looking glass together.

'Agreed,' I said.

'I have the video with me, in my suitcase,' she announced. 'We will watch it and we will see whose memory is sharper, though I venture to say it will be mine.' She winked at me so fast I wasn't sure if I'd imagined it.

'We don't have a VCR. We have a DVD player. We can rent it on Netflix, how's that?'

'Netflix?'

I explained, realizing that it was just the beginning of a long, steep learning curve.

'So you're a fan of police movies?' I exited the lot onto the Van Wyck Expressway.

'Just *good* ones,' she said with a note of seriousness that was charming coming from a girl her age. 'Film noir of that era interests me, in particular *Klute* and *Chinatown*, but I have yet to see everything.'

'No one has,' I said, 'or hardly anyone, but we'll work on it.'

'So, I'll live with you, then?'

I glanced at her long enough not to crash the car.

'Yes.' I felt a little dizzy promising that, as if I had jumped off the edge of a very high cliff. I had no idea what the laws were for international adoptions, or if Mac would even agree to it. For all I knew, he was right and this *was* kidnapping. The only thing that was really clear was that a journey had begun, and it could take us anywhere. I would start making calls tomorrow. Hire a lawyer, if I had to. Whatever it took.

'Where is my new school? Can I walk there? Or shall I take the bus? Or will I ride a bike to school?'

Did I imagine it, or had her eyes really twinkled when she said *bike*? She was asking questions faster than I could think of answers. By now, before we were even home, I knew I had a remarkable child on my hands. The thought of Dathi being trafficked into prostitution seemed ridiculous and unbelievable. My imagination was already spinning future professions for her: She could be a researcher; a diplomat; an executive. But I told myself to calm down and slow down; first things first: She needed a winter coat.

*   *   *

When I came in the ground-floor entrance with Dathi and her suitcase, Mac's first words, called from upstairs, were 'Did you remember to get the car washed?'

Dathi looked at me. 'Shall we go back out?'

'That's just my husband,' I told her.

I heard Mac's footsteps cross to the top of the stairs, and the pitter-patter of Ben's steps following. They stood together and peered down at us.

'Mac, Ben?' I steered her to the foot of the stairs, and we looked up together at my startled family. 'This is Arundathi Das. Dathi, meet Mac MacLeary, my husband, and our son, Ben.'

Her smile radiated up the stairs at Mac, who stood there looking stunned, with Ben clinging to his legs. Dathi resembled her mother; I could only imagine what my little boy made of this.

'Is that Ben, short for Benjamin?' Dathi asked, with a note of humor in her voice. 'Or just *short*.'

Ben's giggles escaped at first like a hiss of steam, then erupted into full out laughter.

'In my village there is a boy who is a dwarf, just your size, but he is fourteen years old!'

She followed me upstairs, keeping a polite distance; but when she passed Ben, who had held his ground at Mac's legs, her hand darted out and she rifled her fingers through his hair. He giggled again. Her hand shot to his underarm for a quick tickle – and just like that, he belonged to her.

Mom was sitting on a chair by the windows with the newspaper on her lap, catching the last of the daylight. She peered over her reading glasses and her mouth dropped open, just for a moment, when she saw us. But she quickly gathered herself, pushed herself to standing, and came over to meet our visitor.

'Chali's daughter.' Mom's eyes teared as she took Dathi's slender hand and clasped it between her own. 'Welcome.'

Dathi bowed her head, just slightly. 'Mrs . . . I don't understand the names here.'

'I'm Pam,' Mom said. 'Technically Mrs Castle, but Pam to you, dear.'

Dathi nodded. 'Pam.'

'I was Karin Castle, growing up,' I explained. 'And then I was Karin Schaeffer, when I got married the first time. My husband is Mac MacLeary, I didn't take his name, but Ben did. I know that's all pretty confusing.'

Dathi smiled, shrugged; she had heard every word, got it, and was ready to move on. 'My mother told me that things were different here, but that I would like it once I adapted.'

'Bright girl,' Mom commented, and gave me a thorny look: *Trafficked into child prostitution, this kid? No way.*

'You must be tired.' She took Dathi's hand and led her to the couch. 'How long was your flight?'

'Fourteen hours and a little more. I slept a bit on the plane.'

Ben jumped up next to Dathi to occupy the opposite side of the couch, getting closer, but not too close. Mac was a harder sell. It didn't take him long to get me alone in the kitchen.

'I admit, she's a charmer,' he began, 'but she's a human being; you can't just take her in like a lost pet. Maybe it's fine that you got her this far, she'll be safe now. But don't mislead her into thinking she's now part of this family.'

'Then whose family will she be part of?'

'I don't know. We'll have to call the Indian Consulate on Monday and find out what to do.'

'No, we won't! They'll send her right back, and you know what will happen to her then. I'm hiring a lawyer – whatever it takes to keep her here.'

'Karin, honestly, this is insane.'

'The alternative was insane. This is sane. Chali worked years to set this in motion.'

'But Chali's gone.'

'Right. And we're here. That's how it worked out. Life sucks. Next?'

'You want her to join the sea of illegals living underground in this city? You know what happens to those kids when they grow up without papers: They're paralyzed. Sometimes they're deported. They live in fear.'

'We'll find a way to work that out. Meanwhile, we'll protect her.'

'I know you're hurting, Karin. I realize today was your due date. But it's just a coincidence that her plane ticket was for today.'

'Our due date. Meg was your baby, too.'

'Meg?'

I froze. He stared at me. It wasn't often I couldn't figure out what to say. And then I burst into tears, and he had to stop arguing with me. He pulled us together and we held each other for long minutes, until the kitchen door opened just a little and two faces peered in through a narrow crack: Ben's below, Dathi's above.

'May we help?' she started to say; but when she saw that she had interrupted something, she pulled Ben out and quickly shut the door.

'See?' I said. 'She's special. She'll bring a whole new point of view into this family. She'll help Ben learn not to be as self-absorbed as *all* our nieces and nephews.'

'Maybe.'

'Definitely. You *know* I'm right.'

'Until she loses her original culture and becomes just as narcissistic as every other American kid we know.'

'Which won't happen.'

'Which will happen. It's inevitable.'

'Well,' I looked at him, lifting a hand to gently touch his face. 'We can at least give it a chance, can't we?'

He thought a moment, and when he said, 'Where will she sleep?' I knew I had him.

'I was thinking: Now that you've got an assistant, and your business seems to be growing, don't you want an office out of the house?'

His laugh was fast, like a shout. 'Oh, *I get it*, I see *exactly* where you're going with this.'

'Well, it doesn't take a detective . . .' Our private joke: *to figure out the obvious*.

'For now, she can bunk in Ben's room,' I said. 'As soon as we find you an office, she can move into the spare room.'

That night, while Mac was putting Ben to bed, I sat with Dathi in the quiet living room. Her eyes looked droopy; she had to be exhausted after such a long trip. And not just the flight itself, or the distance, but the breadth and depth and challenge of the many transformations she was being called upon to navigate all at once. I wasn't sure if now was the time to give her the Christmas gifts Chali had readied for her; but if I waited, she would wonder why.

'Be right back,' I told her. Moments later, I returned with two brightly wrapped presents: a medium box, and a smaller lumpy package that was fairly heavy. I had no idea what was inside either one.

'Oh!' Dathi jumped back a few inches when I placed the gifts beside her on the couch.

'They're for you. From your mother.'

She stared at them. I waited for some expression of surprise – joy or grief – but nothing came. Her face held still, so smooth and quiet I wanted to throw my arms around her, but held back.

'Open them,' I prodded her.

She carefully picked off the tape sealing the smaller box, peeling back the green and silver foil paper to reveal something metallic wrapped in heavy clear plastic. It looked like some kind of chain. She turned it over and her eyes lit up.

'A bicycle lock!' Her eyes flashed at me. Then she ripped the wrapping off the box. 'And a helmet!' Her fingers shook as she pried open the stiff cardboard to get to the orange and blue striped helmet. Snapping open the clasp, she thrust it onto her head. 'I am ready.'

'Dathi – are you sure you're okay with being here? It's not what you expected.'

'I will not be a burden to you,' she said quietly. 'I promise.'

'You're not a burden. Your mother mattered a lot to me. *You* matter a lot to me.'

'I will work and help you as much as I can.'

'Honestly, you don't have to. Just be a kid for now.'

Her hands flew up to hide her eyes.

'I'm sorry.'

'For what?'

'I think perhaps I have jet lag.'

'Sure you do. You're only human.'

She gathered herself, that helmet perched on her head, and suddenly she was no longer a little girl.

'Granny is gone. Mommy is gone. My uncle never liked me. I knew I would have to look out for myself the moment I saw the man from Mumbai put money next to Uncle's teacup on the table. I knew what it meant; Granny had warned me. My karma changed that day. This was meant to be.'

But was it really possible to so blithely accept such shattering change? Maybe it was, for Dathi; I didn't know her well enough yet to judge. She struck you as the kind of kid who could grow up to be a world leader, she was just so together. I cringed each time I thought of the fate that had awaited her on the other side of that plane ticket. And I was starting to understand what Chali had meant by karma: it was a force that arrived on its own, like a hurricane, and your job was to bend to its winds because there was no stopping it. Your grace, your survival, was in your flexibility.

By Monday morning, we had found a spare room in an apartment on our block that Mac rented as a workspace on a month-to-month basis starting immediately, so his home office could be turned into a bedroom for Dathi. Billy came over to help Mac move into his new office while Dathi and I set up her new room.

I had left a message with the Indian Consulate first thing that morning, and jumped when the phone rang, leaving Dathi alone to arrange her clothes in the dresser we had salvaged from the basement.

As carefully as I could, I explained the situation to the consulate representative who had returned my call. I was passed on to someone else, who passed me along again, but finally a friendly woman told me that if I filed the right paperwork in just the right way, we would be eligible to open adoption proceedings. It would require an immigration lawyer here, a custody lawyer in India, a death certificate for Chali, a notarized letter from Uncle Ishat, and a six-month waiting period for other 'interested parties' – long-lost relatives – to file a counterclaim. Dathi would have to go before an immigration judge. It would be a lengthy, expensive, complicated process.

'Are you sure you're prepared for this?' the woman asked me.

'Yes.' I didn't hesitate.

Later, over lunch at the kitchen table, I recounted the conversation to Mac and Billy.

'Go, Karin.' Billy chuckled. 'You're actually doing this. I admit it: I admire your courage.'

Mac glanced at him when he said that, but he didn't argue, which told me his own attitude was continuing to shift on the matter of Dathi. I felt like a runner who had passed the halfway mark, though in reality it was just the beginning.

As we ate our sandwiches, Dathi told us about her best friend from school, Oja, whom she had left behind. Oja also came from a poor family, Dathi explained, but her father was still alive and so they were able to live together – both parents and Oja, who was also an only child – and managed to scrape together her tuition. Dathi's gaze rested a moment in her hands, folded in her lap, when she told us about her friend. 'Oja will miss me,' she said quietly. 'I was unable to say good-bye to her, but I know she will understand.'

'She *will* understand,' I reassured her.

She smiled, trying to reassure herself that it was true.

After a while, Ben lured Dathi away to play with him in the living room.

Billy glanced at the doorway, to make sure the kids weren't listening, and then looked at us. 'Seems Abby did *not* know her parents were killed. Someone told her up at the hospital. They said she cried.'

'When?' I asked.

'Just this morning, right before I came over here.'

'I can't believe you didn't tell us.'

'In front of the kids?'

I glanced through the open door at Dathi and Ben. He was sitting on her lap on the couch and she was reading a picture book to him. 'So Abby doesn't know what happened that night.'

'Not necessarily. We don't know what she knows, but she's not a happy camper.'

'Definitely not,' I agreed.

'We had to let Tony Neng go,' Billy said, looking defeated. 'Don't have enough to hold him. He hired himself a pricey lawyer. They've got a court date pending while they do discovery. Man, this case is going nowhere fast. *Both* cases – stuck. Patrick Scott swears he was an innocent bystander to the murder on Nevins . . . speaking of which, we still haven't ID'd that last dead hooker.' He glanced at his watch, stood up, and cleared his dishes to the sink. 'Didn't realize it was this late. Told Dash I'd be back by two.'

'Innocent bystander. *Right*.' Mac pushed back his chair and followed Billy out. 'Anything I can do to help?'

'Take over the case, how about that?'

'I wish.' Mac snorted cynical laughter. 'It'd be a lot more interesting than the crap I'm always scraping up for people's divorces.'

'I'll trade you any day.'

We followed Billy to the front door. 'I mean it,' Mac said. 'If I can help you out somehow, let me know.' Implicit in the offer, of course, was that he was still there if Billy was hit by another PTSD episode. We both were.

After Billy was gone, and Mac had also left to join Star, I went to the kitchen to clean up.

'Karin?' Dathi came up behind me so quietly my heart jumped. I turned off the faucet and faced her, expecting her to insist on finishing the dishes, as she had before. But this time, that was not what she wanted.

'Yes?'

'Who is Abby?'

My pulse galloped; so she *had* overheard.

'A girl from the neighborhood.'

'And her parents were also killed? That man, Mr—'

'Billy?'

'Yes. Billy. I heard him say Abby didn't know her parents were killed. Is it usual for parents to be killed here in America? No one told me about *my* mother, either, until I found out for myself.'

I dried my hands on a dish towel and reached out to push away a frazzle of hair that had strayed over one of her eyes. 'No, it isn't usual for parents to get killed here. It's very *un*usual. It's relatively safe here.'

'Then why?'

'Abby's parents, you mean?'

'Yes, and Mommy. How can that be?'

'That's what Billy's trying to figure out.'

'Were they killed together?'

'No. Separately, on different days, in different places, and in different ways.'

Dathi nodded slowly, thinking that over. 'But it's very strange, even so.'

'I agree about that.'

'How old is Abby?'

'Eleven.'

'Then I must meet her.'

I hesitated a moment before answering. 'Sure, but she's in the hospital right now.'

'Was she injured when her parents were killed?'

'Not exactly, but sort of.'

Dathi didn't challenge the ambiguity of my answer, and she didn't ask me anything else. She sat alone at the kitchen table, thinking, while I finished the dishes.

Later that night, long after I'd thought Dathi had fallen asleep, I heard sobs coming from her new room. I stood quietly outside the door, listening.

It was another reminder that I really had no idea what I had gotten us both into. But still, hadn't I done the right thing for her, considering the alternative? I stayed focused on that: I had saved Dathi from a human trafficker who was probably going to sell her into a network of child prostitution so vast it was unlikely she would ever have been heard from again. I had to believe I was doing the right thing by her; the alternative was too treacherous a prospect.

Dathi lucked into an available sixth-grade spot at what was supposed to be a good public middle school in Park Slope, a short bus ride away. On her first day, I dropped her in the office, where the principal met her and promised to send her home with a supply list at the end of the day. I left the building feeling hopeful. But as young students flooded into the main entrance, sophisticated beyond their years in skinny jeans, short metallic jackets, Day-Glo sneakers, nostril rings, eyeliner, and bright green hair, my optimism began to dissolve. Dathi would not fit easily into this trendy crowd.

When I returned with Ben at three o'clock, she came out the side entrance in a river of other sixth graders, her jacket unzipped in the cold, clutching an old backpack of Mac's to her front. She looked mildly traumatized. I was about to reach out to give her a hug when she glanced at me sharply before her eyes flitted away. I held still. A girl ran up behind her and tugged her ponytail.

'Bye Dathi, see you tomorrow! *Remember*.'

'Remember what?' I asked her as she jostled through the crowd to the corner. Our bus stop was directly across the street.

'*Shh*.' She wouldn't look at me. Then I noticed that almost none of the other kids had been met by adults: she was embarrassed. I held my silence to spare her further shame until we were nearly at the bus stop.

'Is everything okay?' I whispered when no other kids were around.

She nodded, and whispered back: 'May we shop for a few new clothes, please?'

'Is that what that girl was telling you to do?'

'No. I promised to meet her on Facebook later.'

'Oh. I guess that would be okay. We can shop first, then make you a page.' The idea made me queasy, though. Twelve-year-olds on Facebook? Was that normal?

'Karin' – she kept her voice a low whisper – 'I am already on Facebook. Everyone is.'

I didn't know what to think, so kept my mouth shut for now.

We got off the bus at the Atlantic Center and shopped our way through Old Navy and Target for a few new outfits that would help her blend in better at school, and also picked up some supplies. At home, she packed her new purple tie-dye backpack with everything she needed. Meanwhile, she logged onto her Facebook page and merged it with a new one on the U.S. domain.

Dathi, just like that, was off and running. I let her use my laptop again after dinner; two hours sped by before I suggested that it was time for bed.

I went into her room to say good night to her at nine-thirty. She was lying on her mattress in the dark, and when I opened the door, a shaft of light from the hall fell on her yawning face.

'Okay if I come in?' I asked.

She nodded.

I knelt on the floor beside her, and tentatively stroked her forehead, as a mother might. She let me, silently at first, and then she said:

'I friended her and she accepted.'

'That girl from school?'

'Yes, her too. But I meant Abby.'

That took me by surprise. I was sure I'd never mentioned Abby's last name to Dathi. Anyway, she was in the hospital; it wasn't possible.

'Maybe it was a different Abby. That's a common name.'

'Abby Dekker. I read about *her* family's tragedy online. And then I found her on Facebook.'

It didn't surprise me that Abby had a Facebook page, now that I knew that 'everyone' that age had one, but it was unlikely she'd gotten her hands on a computer at the hospital. Still, you never knew. I would ask.

'Well, I guess anything's possible. What did Abby say to you?'

'Nothing. We didn't message or chat. She just accepted my friend invitation. She has five hundred and seventeen friends of all kinds. I noticed she hasn't updated her status recently. When was she hurt?'

'More than three weeks ago.'

'Yes, that's about right. I only have twenty-six friends, all girls I knew back home, but I am sure I'll catch up fast. My whole class was on Facebook tonight, I think. Oja was there, too. I introduced her to my new friends.'

'Were Abby's friends girls and boys?'

'Girls, boys, women, men. Everyone is Abby's friend. I already like her very much.'

I felt a little dizzy by the time I left her alone to go to sleep. It was all moving so fast. Before going to bed, I went online and created a Facebook account for myself; I hadn't been tempted by it, or felt any need for it, until now. I found Abby easily and sent her a friend request; but unlike Dathi, I didn't hear back, and so couldn't see past her photo and her name into the world she had created before the accident.

The next morning, Dathi appeared ready for school in skinny jeans and a T-shirt featuring a drawing of a bicycle and the legend *Cool Rider*. She had also chosen a pair of feathered earrings in sherbet colors and a cupcake charm necklace, both of which she wore now. She almost looked like all the other tweens at her new school except for one thing: She didn't have the attitude yet; she was still the eager, friendly girl who had greeted me at the airport. But she was working on it. When I tried to get onto the bus with her, she stopped me.

'Karin, please, I can do this myself.'

My mind reeling, I stepped back onto the curb and watched the bus pull away. Mothering a twelve-year-old girl, mothering *this* girl, was like nothing I had ever experienced. Her fierce independence frightened me, even if I recognized myself in her. She was a child, but she seemed right on the cusp of that moment in childhood when you left it behind. Still, I had brought her here; I needed to keep her safe. The challenge was going to be figuring out how.

Back at home, I checked my Facebook page to find out if Abby had accepted my friend request. She hadn't. I called Billy and told him about it.

'Abby's still staring at the ceiling,' he said. 'She can't even talk.'

'Can't or won't?'

'You think I know?'

'Just ask Sasha Mendelssohn if there's any way she might have been online. I'm trying to figure out if Dathi made this up.'

'She seems like a sweet kid; I don't take her for a liar.'

'Neither do I – but we really don't know her very well.' I didn't like saying that about Dathi, mixing doubt into the irrational affection I already felt for her. But it was true. 'Find out and let me know, okay? I'm really curious.'

Twenty minutes later, just when I'd stepped out

of the shower, my cell phone rang. I picked up my jeans, where I'd dropped them on the bathroom floor, and fished in a front pocket for the phone: Billy calling me back.

'Mendelssohn says no way. Abby doesn't leave her bed unless someone's with her, and then she pretty much just goes to the bathroom or hobbles down the hall on crutches. And all the computers in the hospital are password protected.'

'So either Dathi made it up, or someone else is controlling her Facebook page.'

'Ask her to show you when she gets home from school.'

'I will.'

'If it's true, Karin, call me. Sometimes stuff slips past the CCU.'

These days, a detective could hardly get through a case without calling the Computer Crimes Unit for help. It was a no-brainer that the CCU would have been monitoring the Dekker family's online profile, but Billy was right: They might have missed something.

'I'll call you either way.'

CHAPTER 15

We crossed Bergen Street with the *Don't Walk* sign flashing. Ben reached the corner first and scootered ahead, nearly colliding with the Three Musketeers.

'Whoa!' The short guy with dagger sideburns and yellow and red sneakers threw up his hands. Jutting his jaw forward, he attempted a semitoothless smile. 'Fast little bugger.'

His friends gurgled laughter, and together, in their usual chattering clump, they turned up Bergen in the direction of Court Street. I paused to watch them. Where did they go every day, back and forth along the same path, at the same time, like clockwork?

Looming at the far intersection of Bergen and Court was St Paul's, the big Roman Catholic church I'd passed dozens of times. Father X's church. The church where the Dekkers had been members. I wanted to follow the Musketeers all the way, to see if that was where they were going, but Ben was already at the next corner and I had to hurry to catch up with him.

As I rushed forward it struck me that these three

242

men, these derelicts in their clean little-boy clothes, could be the very men (or kind of men) Father X recommended out for odd jobs. Reed Dekker's last call before he was killed had been for just such a reference. The idea of one of these men entering the Dekker home to repair a broken radiator made my skin crawl. I imagined him spotting Abby – and then what? That was exactly how Elizabeth Smart's abductor had found her, focusing on her as his target before abducting her for nine months as his 'wife': Elizabeth's parents had given the down-and-out man, a homeless Bible-toting pedophile, work fixing their roof.

Maybe I'd come too close to some seriously bad guys in my years in law enforcement, but the rehabilitation of broken people struck me as a deluded pursuit. Protect your family first and keep troubled strangers at a safe distance, that was my philosophy, having learned the hard way that surface assumptions about people were often wrong. Kindness and forgiveness were *not* always what it took to restore a person's dignity, because some people just didn't have any.

'Ben!' I called. He turned around, far at the opposite corner, and saw me waving him back in my direction. 'Come here!'

He zoomed to catch up with me as I turned in the opposite direction, quickly shortening the distance between us. When he got close, I broke into a jog. He easily kept up.

We crossed Court Street at the light. I managed

to catch a glimpse of the last Musketeer going through a gate on Congress Street before vanishing from view. Ben and I followed until we were at an iron gate leading into a small yard with a concrete statue of a girl at prayer: the entrance to a chapel. A plaque outside the gate read *Burial Site of Cornelius Heeney, Founder of Brooklyn Benevolent Society and Benefactor of St Paul's Parish 1836.* We went around to the main entrance, on Court Street, where a sign announced the *Roman Catholic Church of St Paul and St Agnes.*

So the Three Musketeers *were* projects of Father X's. *Had* they known the Dekkers?

'Let's go home, Ben.' As I started walking, I pulled out my cell phone.

'Can we get ice cream?' He stood on his scooter and pointed now in the direction of Blue Marble.

'Later. First we have to eat lunch.'

Reluctantly he turned around and zipped past me. Billy answered his phone as I was picking up speed in an effort to catch up with my very fast son.

'Just what I like,' Billy answered, 'a call from a heavy breather.'

'Listen, Billy, there are these three creepy guys I see all the time, and they just went into Father X's church.'

'So?'

'Didn't you tell me the Dekkers supported the church's work with the needy?'

'Yeah, so?'

'You told me that Reed Dekker's last call was to the father about getting someone over to fix a radiator.'

'Paint a radiator.'

'Whatever.'

'Details matter, Karin.'

'If any one of those men was inside my house, I'd worry. I'm just saying that if I were you, I'd check it out.'

There was a pause. A sigh. 'Sure. Why not? I'll just put it on my list, right under Dathi's phantom Facebook activity.'

That floored me. 'Phantom?'

'You caught me at a bad time. I'm busy. We'll talk later.'

That was three lame zingers in a row, and each one stung.

We'd reached our block. I slowed down, watching Ben glide toward our house. I didn't like Billy's dismissive attitude, but I understood it: when you were working an impossible case, or in his situation three impossible cases that had rubbed up against each other, everyone was an armchair detective; everyone had the next great lead for you to follow so you could catch your guy. I knew all about how hard it was to politely listen before getting back to the leads you were working on before the interruption. But it was *me*, not some random busybody. Billy knew I was a good investigator even if I wasn't official anymore. So why had he blown me off like that? I wondered if he was too distracted by his PTSD and the looming shadow of its discovery by his colleagues to focus fully on work. Maybe, I thought, unlocking the downstairs door and pushing it open so Ben could get inside, just maybe next time I had a good idea I would call Ladasha, instead. She would love that; it would feed her distrust of him. But I couldn't do that to Billy. And I wasn't going to let go because at this point I *wouldn't*.

More and more, I believed that Chali's murder was part of a larger picture that had burst into view on Nevins Street that December night. More and more, the shadows overlapped, implicating each other: dead prostitutes who had vanished as girls; Abby, just eleven, found half dead so close to a crime scene, on the night her parents were killed; Chali, once a child bride in a country infamous for human trafficking, murdered; and now Dathi, the imperative of whose rescue burst into my consciousness as all these pieces clicked together in a new, brutal logic. Girls were vanishing and then, somehow, returning, transformed by whatever had happened to them. It was something you expected in the third world. But here? On the sophisticated East Coast of America? In one of the wealthiest pockets of New York City? It was a ridiculous thought bordering on paranoia.

And yet . . . the shadows thrown by the neighbors, friends, creeps, priests – all the people whose lives swirled around the dead – shifted restlessly. There was something to see hiding in the shadows.

Someday Dathi would crave answers, and I wanted to know what to tell her. Especially now that she was a very real part of my family and my life, I felt a powerful urgency to find out who had killed her mother. To give her answers. And to stop whoever was destroying all those innocent girls.

Dathi barely got her jacket hung up in the hall and her sneakers off before I asked her if she could log into her Facebook account.

'Of course!' she said, a little too perkily, I thought. Something told me she was more depleted than she was letting on. Another trying day at her new school? My heart sank for her; I wanted this to be easier than it was or probably could be.

She sat at the kitchen table with my laptop. After a moment, she called me over.

Abby's profile photo showed her face in close-up, with her blue fingernails pulling her cheeks like lumps of clay. Her eyes were bright and her hair looked blonder than in real life.

'That's a funny picture,' I commented.

'She probably took it herself with her webcam.'

I looked at the array of thumbnail photos showing her various friends who were currently online. Most of the kids' pictures were goofy, improvised, like Abby's, whereas the adults tended to be more studied even if they were relaxed.

'You're right: She *does* know a lot of different kinds of people.' I was especially surprised to see how many of them were adults, and wondered if that was normal for a kid in the world of online networking. My gut told me it wasn't. Some may have been teachers at her school and parents of friends. But then it struck me: Too many were men.

'You see, her last status was on the day of the accident.' When Dathi's slender fingertip touched the screen, I saw a drop of purple fingernail polish that hadn't been there in the morning, dead center in the middle of her nail. She must have noticed my attention because suddenly she held up all her fingers for me to see: Each nail had been targeted with a purple dot. She smiled tentatively. 'Tiffany did it at lunch.'

'It's nice,' I lied. It wasn't either nice or not-nice. It was silly. I could only imagine the kind of social pressure she was under and how bewildered she must have felt.

She clicked to her own page; her profile photo showed her as a little girl, back in India, wearing matching orange saris with a young and smiling Chali. My stomach tumbled at the sight of them together. Then she clicked on a little earth symbol in the toolbar and a list of notifications popped up.

'See here? She accepted my friend request last night.'

I nodded. 'Okay.' But it was another disingenuous response: It *wasn't* okay. I didn't believe that it was Abby who confirmed the friend request. It couldn't have been, unless she had a laptop hidden somewhere in her room, or someone visiting her had brought in a computer or allowed her to use their smartphone. But all those possibilities seemed doubtful to me. Abby did not seem tuned-in enough to social network at the moment, even if given an opportunity.

'I would very much like to meet her,' Dathi said, again.

I looked at her: loneliness came off her like a vapor. I wanted her to have a friend, a real friend, so badly. But why Abby? And *how* Abby?

'We'll see. Do you have homework?'

She pulled a stack of heavy textbooks out of her backpack, and set to work.

A few minutes later, when I followed Ben downstairs to make sure he wasn't getting into anything, I ducked into my bedroom and called Billy.

'The Facebook page is there,' I told him. 'I saw it. Someone definitely confirmed Dathi's friend request last night.'

'Karin, about before. I'm sorry. I was just, you know—'

'It's okay.' Though it wasn't, really. 'Listen: Do you think maybe whoever broke into the Dekker house the night of the murders somehow got Abby's login and password?'

'I'll get the CCU on it. This is enough of a red flag to subpoena the account. Shit – they should have seen this themselves.'

'They weren't looking.'

'I'll say.'

'Listen, Billy, before you go – I also want to say that I'm sorry, too.'

'What for?'

'Pushing you so hard, in different directions.'

'I don't really know what you mean.'

But I knew that he did: pushing him to feel better, pushing him to do better; pushing him to delve into the murky waters of his deepest self and catch a serial killer at the same time.

'Go back to work, Billy.'

'Stop telling me what to do.'

We laughed. And hung up.

The next day, Dathi took herself off to school in a morning routine that had already fallen into place. We all ate breakfast together; at eight-ten Dathi left for the bus; at eight-fifty I left with Ben to drop him off at school; sometime while I was gone, Mac took himself to his new office. By the time I got home at a quarter past nine, I would be alone in the house.

Only today I didn't get there. On my way back home, my attention or obsession or paranoia or whatever you wanted to call it was snagged, once again, by the Three Musketeers making their way along Smith Street. For some reason, their regularity infuriated me this morning. They clearly had sucked from the bottom of life's shoes, so how was it that their days cycled forward so reliably? There appeared to be a peacefulness to their routine that I felt, intuitively, they didn't deserve.

Every day at around nine A.M. they walked up Smith Street in one direction. Every day at around noon they walked down Smith Street in the opposite direction and went to St Paul's.

Where did they go in between?

What exactly was their involvement with Father X, his church, the Dekkers?

Today, as I was about to turn onto my block and they passed me in their prattling nicotine cloud, I hesitated. Watched them move down the block toward the next corner. And without exactly deciding to – followed them.

I just had a feeling about this. A strong feeling that it was crucial to peel back every shadow. Not just to solve the murder cases, but for Billy's sake: It wasn't enough for the POI list to shrink with the omission of his name: it also had to grow and grow until his name's place on it was all but forgotten.

They crossed Pacific Street and kept walking, all three nodding to the orange-vested crossing guard as they passed her.

'Yo, boys,' I heard her say.

At the corner of Atlantic Avenue, they turned east. I held my pace and continued to follow. As I turned the corner onto Atlantic, I realized that this was the same path Dathi followed every morning to her bus, the B63. The Musketeers gathered around the bus stop, waiting. Did these men ride the B63 every morning? What if one day, for some reason, Dathi was late for school – and rode with them? A chill zippered through me: I didn't like this; I had to know.

I casually stopped near the bus stop and pretended to wait as if that had always been my intention. Their juvenile chattering never ceased. When I managed to overhear them, their conversation was remarkably insipid: at one point, they fervidly discussed shoelaces and double knots; next, the topic was ketchup and how many times you should knock the bottle to get it moving. I started to find them almost charming, an impulse that dissolved when the tallest Musketeer stepped out of the group and moseyed to the recessed doorway of a copy shop that had not yet opened for the day. He wore pressed blue jeans, bright white sneakers, and a black jacket with a white sweatshirt hood dangling down his back. His back to sidewalk traffic, he unzipped his fly and that was when I turned away. After he returned to the bus stop, I glanced over to where he had stood and saw a stream of urine meandering along the ice-mottled sidewalk. Any possibility of charm vanished.

The B63 came and went. The Musketeers continued to wait. Another bus also used this stop, the B65. I had never taken it and I didn't know its route. But when it arrived a few minutes later and the men lined up, I got on behind them, swiping my MetroCard as if I had always planned to make this journey today. I sat near enough to keep my eyes and ears open, but not so close that I would catch their attention.

They sat together at the back of the bus and never stopped talking. They reminded me of middle school girls. It wasn't the first time I'd had that thought, but now it really struck me what that meant because of Dathi. I hadn't known any preteenagers since having been one myself, and that was a long time ago. Now, suddenly, with Dathi in my home and life and family, I was being plunged back into that world; it was like getting tossed into the deep end when your swimming skills had been untested for too long. I vaguely remembered what it was like: any blood, any sharks, and you were a goner. Cruelty was the name of the game. Social pressures were like tides that pulled you and pushed you according to their own internal rhythms. Survival meant navigating the forces until graduation – and then you were free (until high school). That the Musketeers reminded me of a claque of tweens interested me now more than ever. *What was the bond between these three men?*

At Third Avenue, the bus turned and continued up Dean Street. Just before the stop at Classon Avenue, the men stood up and gathered at the side door. I waited until the last minute before following them out onto a derelict street of abandoned-looking warehouses, an auto body shop with its gate pulled down, and a few low brick buildings where you'd only live if you had to. I didn't know whether to feel nervous or comforted that I wasn't exactly alone here: Across

253

the street, a larger group of men and some women, much like the Musketeers in their cheerful decrepitude, stood gathered in front of a nondescript door of an unmarked brick building. I walked slowly up the opposite sidewalk, focused forward, deciding what to do when suddenly the door opened and the people waiting formed what could pass for a line.

I watched as the line snaked through the door until they were all gone. When no one was left, I crossed the street and read a small sign on the front of the door: *St Vincent de Paul Treatment Center, Mary Immaculate Hospital, Hours: M–F, 9:30–4:00.*

If I remembered correctly, this was the methadone clinic the Dekkers had been involved in funding. Apparently no one had considered it important to spend much on signage – but when you thought about it, it really didn't matter. All those people had found their way here. My guess was that they'd had little choice in the matter; at least some of them had most likely been sent here by a judge.

I opened the door and walked in.

A big room with scuffed beige walls and a low dropped ceiling was filling with people waiting, some of whom had seated themselves in rows of bolted-down plastic chairs. The rest had formed into an unruly line in front of a little window that opened onto an office. Not knowing what else to do, and hoping not to bring attention to myself,

I got in line. People were signing in on a clipboard at the window, then taking a seat. As we moved steadily forward, I formulated a plan: Since I was here, I would find out who the Three Musketeers were exactly. Take it from there.

There were five people between me and the last Musketeer; luckily the trio had stayed together in line. When I got to the window, a man in a green medical smock, with dark shadows drooping down his long face, looked at me with interest. I didn't smile, just looked away, hoping he wouldn't question me. At some point, I assumed, they would need identification; no one handed out methadone without it. Right now the addicts were just queuing up for their fixes, and my guess was that they were ID'd when the drug was dispensed. I wouldn't be here that long.

I took the pen and started to sign my name. Well, not my name: *Janice Doen*. It was the first thing that sprang to mind; a variation of Jane Doe, it was one of the aliases I used sometimes working undercover back when I was a cop. I signed slowly enough to count up five spaces.

Marty Brilliant

Iggy Black

Jose R. Seraglio

I silently repeated the three names – Marty Iggy Jose, Brilliant Black Seraglio – on my way out the door. Alone on the sidewalk, I pulled out my BlackBerry and typed the names into an e-mail which I sent to myself. Then I slipped my phone back into my purse and headed back along Classon. I found the bus stop just a block away and stood under the Plexiglas shelter. The barrenness of this place unnerved me; there was no one else around. And then, suddenly, I heard my name.

'Karin! What are you doing in my neck of the woods?'

I looked up, for a moment recognizing her before realizing who she was.

'Mary. Tai Chi. Right?'

'At least I've still got *that* job.'

We smiled at each other. With her was a tall black teenager with a barely visible mustache and a floppy knit hat that swayed to the right. He stood close by her side. A sharp gust of wind sent them closer to me under the bus stop shelter. We barely knew each other, but we instinctively huddled for warmth.

'You lost your other jobs?' I recalled now that she'd mentioned she had three.

'Yup. Two in one week. Fremont's looking for a part-time job now, but there isn't much out there for teenagers.' I looked at the boy, and she remembered to introduce him: 'My son, Fremont.'

'Karin.'

We nodded at each other, refreshing our smiles.

'Fremont's got the day off from school,' Mary said. 'Teacher prep or something.'

The bus came and we all piled on.

By the time we reached my stop, just outside the YMCA where they also got off, I'd been reminded that Mary was a single mother and learned that Fremont was her only child. I didn't know it as a fact, but I had a feeling she'd never been married, particularly since Billy had told me she was a lesbian. Still, you never knew. They had lived in Prospect Heights since 'before it started getting gentrified,' which told me it had been *really* desolate before, as not a single sign of gentrification had leaped out at me during my brief visit.

'So what were you doing all the way out there?' Mary asked. We stood together on the sidewalk as the bus pulled back into traffic.

'Kind of an informal investigation.' I explained briefly, but enough to capture her attention.

'I've been following those stories in the news. I'm a true-crime *nut*. I read all those articles and sometimes I even read the books.'

'She hides them when people come over,' Fremont said.

'A lot of people think it's twisted to be interested in stuff like that. And I don't know why I am – but I am.'

'Then you know my story.' Before I could stop myself, because I rarely talked about it anymore, I told her about my first family and how it ended. Mary linked arms with Fremont, listening intently, pulling him closer as I got to the end. Her eyes teared and now, forty-five minutes into our fast friendship, she used her free arm to offer me a hug.

'Listen' – I pulled away – 'maybe this is crazy,

but if you need work, and you aren't proud, I have a job. It could even be two jobs: babysitting in the afternoons for my son – he's almost four – and office work in the mornings for my husband, Mac. He's a private investigator.'

Mary's face glowed so brightly she could have lit up Atlantic Avenue all on her own. She looked up at Fremont. 'Pinch me!'

He had a musical laugh.

'I mean it, Karin,' Mary said. 'I was just telling Fremont how much I miss playing with him when he was a sweet little guy. And you *know* I'd like nothing better than to work for a private eye. I mean, *really*.'

'So you will?'

'I was starting to wonder how I was going to pay the rent.'

Fremont looked at her, alarmed. 'I didn't know that, Mom.'

'It's okay: I just got two new jobs! What did I tell you – a window closes so a door can open.'

'Can you come by tomorrow afternoon? It's Saturday so everyone should be home. You can meet Mac, and we can go over the details.'

'Okay. I'm giving a Tai Chi lesson right here at three o'clock. How's four?'

'Perfect.'

We parted ways, glancing back at each other to smile and wave. I knew it was risky to offer so much at once to someone I hardly knew, but I had a strong gut feeling that this was an excellent idea. Anyway, how could Mary not be a better assistant than Star? Even if it didn't work out, it was worth a try. In fact, maybe this was the real reason I had followed those men all the way to Classon Avenue this morning; maybe it had nothing to do with Father X or the Dekkers or any of that. Maybe my karma had meant for Mary and me to run into each other at just the right moment, when we needed each other. Or maybe both impulses had led me in a meaningful direction: finding Mary *and* following the Musketeers.

As I crossed Atlantic onto Boerum Place, I speed-dialed Mac with the news. His reaction was immediate and strong.

'You what?'

I told him again: I'd been to a methadone clinic in Prospect Heights; and I'd hired Mary Salter to work for us.

'We'll talk later,' he said, hanging up abruptly at the sound of something crashing in the background. Star must have been there. I reminded myself: He would thank me.

Next I called Billy and told him about my surprise encounter with Mary, but left out the part about following the Three Musketeers to rehab. I was worried he'd distrust my impulse to connect those far-flung dots on the Dekker map, and I would need his help finding out who they were. I'd have to play that one right.

'Oh Jesus, Karin. You hired my Tai Chi teacher to work for you?'

'She needs the work, and she's great.'

'That she is.' A phone rang in the background and a voice called out to someone; he was in the detectives unit. Good.

'Did you know she has a black son?' I asked Billy.

'Half-black. She told me about him. Had herself inseminated back when she was living with her ex-girlfriend. It was a long-term thing but it didn't survive parenthood.'

'Well, he seems like a nice boy. They seem really close.'

'She's crazy about him, that's for sure.'

'So Billy – I need a favor. Can I stop by the precinct?'

'When?'

'How about right now?'

'What if I told you I wasn't at the precinct right now?'

'I'd tell you you're a really bad liar.'

After that call I texted Mac, asking him if he could pick Ben up from school at noon, as I had an errand to run. He answered immediately that he could. Then I slipped my phone back into my purse and turned around in the direction of the Eighty-fourth Precinct.

CHAPTER 16

It was the first time I'd been inside the Eight-four conference room that had been given over to the search for the Working Girl Killer. The task force had been at it for a solid year here in Brooklyn, after a year based in Manhattan, and it showed in the comfortable familiarity of the dozen or so people working the case. Informal personal areas had been carved out along the big table that dominated the room and on the two credenzas against a far wall. Laptops, printers, coffee mugs, even a few photos of the cops' smiling families – a shocking (to me) leap of faith given the array of grisly crime scene photos taped to the walls in the work-in-progress that was an endless investigation like this one. I still shuddered to think how many cops felt immune to the violence they encountered on a daily basis; but I also understood that, to do the job, it helped to convince yourself it would never touch you. You had to believe you were safe in a sea of brutality, and your family was your island hideaway. Look at their smiling faces, and for a split second you felt liberated from the realer-than-real world that was your daily job. How badly

I wanted to tell them that they were deluded to feel safe. No one was safe; I had learned that the hardest way possible. But I would not be the one to break their bubble. Billy knew, though; his delusions of invincibility had exploded with his eye when the woman he'd loved had tried to kill him.

Ladasha was seated at the far end of the long table, working at the room's big desktop computer; this would be the one 'secure' connection where sensitive permission-only searches were preferably done, though it was doubtful that protocol was strictly followed anymore. Popping up from behind the monitor I could see the wide spray of Ladasha's latest hair extension; it was Friday, her long-standing 'date night,' which I knew she nearly always spent with girlfriends or family, going out for early dinners or maybe a movie; knowing her, she'd probably had a manicure, too.

She glanced up from the monitor and saw me walking in behind Billy, who had met me in the lobby.

'Hi Karin!' There was no sarcasm in her tone, for a change, which told me she either felt guilty for cheating on Billy with George over at the Seven-two, or she just didn't want to tick me off.

I followed Billy to her end of the table, where I could see that her manicure was a hellacious red, and she was in the ViCAP database – the FBI's Violent Criminal Apprehension Program that collected, collated, and analyzed information on violent crimes throughout the country so investigators could track patterns quickly. I recalled the hours I'd spent with my head buried in ViCAP back when I was searching for the Domino Killer, not once thinking I'd ever find the handiwork of that psycho in my own house. As if she could read my thoughts, Ladasha clicked on another tab to bring up a Zappos page where apparently she'd been browsing high-heeled boots.

'If it's lunchtime, I'm in,' she said.

'Not quite yet.' Billy navigated a chair to get in front of the computer. 'Borrow this a minute?'

'Go ahead.' Ladasha yawned, exposing her gold tooth. 'I'm not getting much of anywhere.'

Coming around to see the monitor, I was distracted by a section of wall covered in photographs of footprints in mud, dirt, snow, gravel.

Billy noticed me looking. 'P-Pat's footprints at nearly every crime scene.'

'You linked him?'

'I shouldn't have said that.' As we talked, Billy got out of ViCAP and logged into the CRS database – the Criminal Records Section documented every single police encounter from a stop-and-frisk to an arrest to a point on your driver's license. You could plug in a name and see if anything popped up. 'He's got a size ten shoe, like our guy. That's all we know.'

'MR1123.' Ladasha rolled her eyes. A couple of the other investigators chuckled.

'Unfortunately P-Pat wears a popular model of a popular brand of sneakers,' Billy explained. 'New

Balance MR1123, same as our guy at five out of the eleven crime scenes. But our guy wore Clark's desert boots, too, sometimes.'

'And Patty Scott doesn't own any of those,' Ladasha said with a note of frustration. I watched her a moment to see if she'd glance at Billy's feet, but she didn't. She wouldn't, in front of me. But you didn't have to look to know that his shoe size was much bigger than Patrick Scott's.

'Which means squat,' I said. 'He could have them stashed in a locker at Port Authority, for all we know. He could—'

'Slow down.' Billy glared at me.

'Sorry.'

'Never apologize,' Ladasha forced a laugh, 'and never explain. Who said that, anyway?'

'The Duke.' We all looked at the guy with a jet-black comb-over, sitting across the room nursing a Styrofoam cup of something.

'The who?' Ladasha asked.

'John Wayne,' a young woman answered, swinging a flowered Doc Marten boot onto the corner of the table and tugging a quick retie.

'Yo, peeps,' Ladasha barked, 'shut down the movie streaming and get your faces back to work.'

'Right, Dash,' the young woman snapped back, but with humor. 'As if we do anything else.'

I pulled up a chair beside Billy, aching to take over the mouse but forbidding the impulse. This was a favor and I needed his cooperation; push too hard and he'd shut me down.

'Whaddya got.' Billy's hands poised to type.

'Marty Brilliant, Iggy Black, Jose R. Seraglio.'

'Who's that?' Ladasha stepped close enough to peer over Billy's shoulder.

'Neighborhood drug addicts,' I said. 'Friends of Father X.'

'Where are you going with this?' she asked.

'Have you thought maybe you're focusing too much on the wrong people, Dash?'

She stared at me.

'You know, Patrick Scott and the other guy.'

'Antonio Neng,' she said. 'So far they're the best we got, like it or not.' She was a good actress in front of Billy; she knew her lines.

'They're both placed at or near the scenes on the same night,' Billy said. 'Why wouldn't we work them?'

'I know,' I said. 'I'm with you on that. But I was just thinking . . .'

'Uh oh.'

'Billy, don't you see? I'm thinking whoever got into Abby's Facebook knows something and is sitting back, watching. I'm thinking it all somehow filters through the Dekkers.'

'Fucking CCU; they still haven't called me.' You could see Billy's jaw muscles ripple as he ground his teeth.

I touched his hand. 'I'm thinking it connects to their church, through their ties to Father X. And maybe to some of his, you know, human projects.'

'Oo-wee.' Ladasha shook her head. 'The priests,

265

they ain't just child rapists, now they're killers, too! *Here we go.* Maybe you've been taking in too much news.'

'I didn't say anything about the priest killing anyone, did I?'

'No, but—'

'All I want to do is check out these three guys, see what they do for Father X, and find out if they ever did odd jobs for the Dekkers. See who's who in the bigger picture. I leaned closer to Billy. 'Think about it: *Human trafficking, right here in Brownstone Brooklyn.*'

'*Billy,*' Ladasha's tone shifted from mocking to serious. 'I thought we agreed you weren't gonna talk out of school.'

'I didn't.'

'Then how—'

'So you're already thinking along the same lines.' A spark caught inside me: Something was happening here.

'We're thinking what we're thinking, Karin,' Ladasha said. 'But you are not a part of this. You only think you are.'

'Chali,' I reminded her, 'made me a part of this. She recognized Reed Dekker, remember? She wanted to tell me something the night she was murdered by the Working Girl Killer.'

'We don't *know* the same person killed Chali,' Billy said.

'Yeah, Karin,' Ladasha said, 'and bottom line: You're a bystander to all this. You're not technically family of a victim, and you're not on the case, either.'

'Chali's daughter lives with me now. I need to be able to tell her why her mother died.'

Billy and Ladasha glanced at each other. She reluctantly nodded.

'All right.' Billy's hands returned to the keyboard. 'What were those names again?'

'Marty Brilliant, Iggy Black, Jose R. Seraglio. The Three Musketeers – that's how I thought of them until today. They get their rehab at Mary Immaculate, one of the Dekkers' pet projects, run by Father X out of St Paul's Church on Court Street. Every day of the week, these guys go from St Paul's to Mary Immaculate in Prospect Heights, and back again, like clockwork. What was Reed's last call to Father X about?'

'Needed an odd job done.'

'Right. And who do you think he sent out on odd jobs?'

Billy glanced sharply at Ladasha. 'Got that list?'

She turned to a stack of files and pulled one. Opened it and read aloud: 'Yup, all there: Brilliant, Seraglio, and Black. Among others.'

'Okay, Billy,' I said. 'Go ahead: Look them up.'

He did. And they were all there in the CRS, with enough of the blanks filled in to sketch out their histories.

Martin Brilliant hailed from Mill Basin, Brooklyn. His record showed fourteen arrests for petty crimes like pickpocketing, jumping the subway turnstiles, and possession of illicit drugs. He had done a year in prison for the drugs, but had pled out on all the other charges. He'd been ordered into rehab by the last judge he'd faced on a charge of disorderly conduct. About a year ago, he transitioned from a halfway house in Brownsville, Brooklyn to a building in Red Hook, called Sons of St Paul's, used to house recovering drug addicts who had found the Lord.

Ignatius Black, Jr., grew up on the Upper West Side of Manhattan, in the Amsterdam Houses, one of the city's sprawling low-income housing projects. He was the son of a taxi driver and a garment worker who divorced when he was two. He'd dropped out of high school, found work on the streets selling heroin, and ended up in prison for six years. He came out faithful, but gravitated back to drugs; he had lived at Sons of St Paul's for the last year and a half.

Last but not least, Jose R. Seraglio was a native of Boerum Hill, part of a big Dominican family of blue-collar workers that had mostly stayed in the neighborhood until rampant gentrification had put the store leasers out of business and made the homeowners rich enough to get out of the city, which had treated them shabbily. Jose had sat out the big migration of his family to New Jersey, stayed in the neighborhood, and been in and out of jail on a series of minor arrests. Like the others, he ended up a junkie of one kind or another, and ultimately found his way to Father X's Red Hook parish-within-a-parish for semirehabilitated misfits. He had lived at Sons of St Paul's with his BFFs Marty and Iggy for coming on a year now.

'So it is what it is.' Billy leaned back in his chair. 'They are who they are. Doesn't mean squat.'

'What about this guy?' My fingertip touched another name on the list of Sons of St Paul's residents who shared quite a few arrest dates with Jose Seraglio, and had left the Red Hook residence a few months ago. 'Edward Walczak – he was on the same rehab schedule as the Three Musketeers. Why did he leave?'

'Maybe he *graduated*.' Ladasha's sarcasm was back in town.

Billy checked out recent arrests and current arraignments. 'No sign of him anywhere in the system since then. But I wouldn't worry about that; maybe he straightened out. Sometimes they do.'

'Look at that.' I picked up the mouse and clicked on a link: *Witness*. 'The file is sealed because it involved a minor.'

Ladasha and I leaned in close enough to read the sparse information available about Edward Walczak's brief run as a witness in a sex crimes case, five years ago, leveled against none other than Ximens Dandolos – Father X. Walczak had been subpoenaed but ultimately dismissed as unreliable based on his history with drugs and petty crime.

'There you go,' I said. 'There it is.'

Ladasha folded her arms over her chest and stood there, silent. She didn't so much as glance at Billy, who was staring hard at the screen. I couldn't tell if this was new information to them, or if it bothered them that I had figured something out that they didn't want anyone to know.

'I wonder where he lives.' I started to maneuver the cursor across the screen.

Billy reached over and took the mouse out of my hand. 'Karin, listen: time for you to go.'

'It said Walczak grew up in the neighborhood. Is he still here?'

'You see' – Billy stood up now – 'this could get real messy.'

'I know how to handle an investigation,' I argued, 'and you know I would never invalidate evidence.'

'Evidence of what?' Ladasha challenged me. 'You don't seem to know better than to make up your mind in advance.'

'Why did Father X nearly have a heart attack the minute Abby woke up?' I looked from Billy's face to Ladasha's. Neither flinched. 'What is he afraid she knows? What is she afraid to tell?'

They glared at each other but didn't answer – either because they didn't know, or there was something they couldn't, or wouldn't, tell me. I knew that my unofficial visit was a distraction. I knew that Ladasha was right to be irritated with me. I knew that Billy was under enough stress and I shouldn't be adding to it. If I couldn't help, I shouldn't be here. I knew all that. But still – there was something no one was seeing. Did it matter who saw it first?

I stood up and scanned the gruesome photo-montage depicting repetitions of the same horrifying crime: young women, all prostitutes except Chali, strangled and then bludgeoned with a replica of a 1963 Bowie knife made by a long-defunct Mississippi company called Stark. Chali, though, had been stabbed with a different make knife. Photos of both knives were taped side by side on the wall. Someone had arranged them carefully, straight and level, so your eye focused on the subtle differences: the newer knife's elongated blade curving at the tip, the shiny new wood grain handle, was exactly like the one I'd seen protruding from Chali's chest. My own chest clamped at the sight of it. The Stark Bowie that was almost exactly the same, but not as shiny or sleek. It wasn't a fancy knife or particularly popular, which was why it had been discontinued, and it was impossible to find them now even on eBay. Anyone's best guess was that the killer had a stash of them. Maybe his stash finally ran out and he'd needed a close replacement. That, or there were two killers now.

To the right of the twin photos of the almost-matching knives were photos of Reed and Marta Dekker shot point blank in their home. Which begged another question: Was it one crime, or two, or – when you factored in the vanished girls from long ago – *three*?

'I'm going to the ladies',' Ladasha announced. On her way, she steered me out of the conference

271

room, into the hall, and toward the nearest exit. At the top of the staircase she leaned to my ear and whispered, '*Careful.*' She stood there, watching, as I made my way out.

Mac and Ben were just finishing lunch when I came in. I joined them, and after Ben left the table to play in the living room, I filled Mac in on my morning. He listened, half smiling, shaking his head from time to time; but not once did he challenge any of the instincts that had tossed me around the morning like a Ping-Pong ball.

'I think you can probably leave it with Billy and Dash now,' he said, after I was through telling him about my visit to the precinct. 'Let them take the lead. It's their case, and you have other things to do.'

'I know. I should.'

'You did good; now move on.'

I nodded.

'I mean it, Karin. I know Chali meant a lot to you, I cared about her, too, but we have to let the cops handle this.'

There was a strain of annoyance beneath his reasonable tone; and then something occurred to me. 'Are you angry that I hired Mary without asking you?'

'Are you kidding me? I already fired Star.'

'That was fast.'

'I couldn't take it anymore. She wasn't competent, bottom line. I hope this Mary person is better.'

'Well, she won't be worse.'

We left it at that. Mac was on board with giving Mary a try for both jobs, so long as he liked her when they met tomorrow. And I had done what I could, identifying my Three Musketeers and launching, or at least reinforcing, a new line of thinking for the task force – preferably steering it as far from Billy as possible. Now I would (try to) back off.

Except . . . I couldn't stop wondering about that fourth Musketeer. Seeing him in my mind, picturing him with the others, the clump of men bigger and noisier as it moved along Smith Street to turn on Atlantic toward the bus stop.

And I couldn't stop thinking about the impression Abby had made on me last time I'd seen her: how she had reminded me of Billy's PTSD when it flared up. The silence. The shining cloaks of eyes that look inward but not out. That backward traveling to a scary place you wished you could forget, but it kept rearing up and dragging you back to the time you least wanted to revisit. The suspicion people felt in the face of that eerie silence, as if it was an omission of something hidden – a secret or a lie – instead of an indication of blankness because you weren't really there anymore. You had been swept away.

Mac went back to work and I hung out with Ben. I couldn't resist a quick Google of Edward Walczak.

There was only one listing for that name in the

online white pages for Brooklyn. If it was accurate, then he still lived right here in Boerum Hill. I noted his address in my BlackBerry. Just in case.

At about three-thirty I heard a key rattle in the front door and knew that Dathi was home. Ben and I went to greet her in the front hall. She toed off her shoes and set down her backpack by the wall.

'How was school today?' I asked.

'Good.' But she didn't seem good; she seemed exhausted. The sparkle she had carried off the plane with her was dimming. As the days passed I became more aware of how much effort every small and large adjustment took for her, from unlocking a new door to wearing different clothes to acquiring a taste for different food to adjusting to the relative flamboyance of her new school-mates. She kept a brave front, but I knew she was struggling. Still, whenever I wondered if I had done the right thing by luring her out of her own country, I rephrased the worry and reminded myself that I had intercepted her from a terrible fate in what was essentially a rescue.

She followed us to the kitchen, where we sat around the table and the kids had a snack together. Then Dathi cleared her dishes and Ben followed suit, standing on a stool watching her hands care-fully wash each item and set it in the dish drainer to dry.

'Let's play Maretti,' he said, when she was finished.

The longing glance she cast the laptop, where it

sat open on the table, told me she wanted to get online. I was learning to read her, and it felt important to respond positively, to build as many lines of communication and trust between us as we possibly could.

'Want to check your Facebook before you do homework?'

She smiled, and I saw it: a flicker of the spiritedness with which she had first greeted me.

'I want to play Maretti!' Ben said.

'I'll play with you.' I got up and pushed the laptop to Dathi.

She started typing before she had sat all the way down. The whole time we zoomed our little cars around the living room, I could hear the keyboard clacking in the kitchen. Dathi was a focused typist. Finally she appeared in the doorway.

'I now have eighty-three friends.'

I looked up, my little race car frozen mid-race along the edge of the coffee table.

'You mean Facebook friends?' I still couldn't quite convince myself these were actual *friends*.

She nodded.

'That sounds good.'

'Beyond my friends from home, I only know seven of my new friends. The rest are friends of friends who friended me. It's very exciting how quickly it grows here. There are so many more people my age online than at home. The thing is . . .'

'What?' I sat back; parked the car on my bent knee.

'The one person I'm still hoping to hear from is the one person who is the most silent.'

For a moment I thought she meant Chali: that she was waiting, hoping, yearning to find her dead mother on Facebook of all places. Then I corrected that thought.

'Abby?'

'Yes. She is my best friend here. *Don't* tell Oja I said that.'

I suppressed a smile. 'I won't.'

She crossed the living room to the front hall, where she got her backpack. On her return to the kitchen, where she had taken to doing her home-work in the afternoons, she paused and dug into her bag. She pulled out a paper on which she had drawn something, and handed it to me. Standing very still, she watched me look it over.

It was a charcoal sketch, black on heavy white paper: a knot of elegant lines that revealed two women . . . or, the longer you looked at it, a woman and a girl. When I realized that it was a mother and daughter, embracing, emotion welled up suddenly. Dathi missed Chali more than I could imagine, and in a way I could hardly grasp. I knew the desolate hopelessness of a mother yearning for an absent child. But the inchoate misery of a child yearning for a mother? It was a sister universe, but a different one.

Sensing something, Ben came up behind me and looked over my shoulder at the drawing. The visceral closeness I felt as he pressed up against my back, the warmth of his breath on my neck, filled me with such powerful affection it almost hurt.

'It's beautiful,' I said softly.

'It's for her.'

For Chali, she meant. But again my assumption was corrected.

'For Abby.' Dathi took back the drawing. 'I sent her a message about it a few minutes ago. I think she'll like it, don't you? Shall I mail it to her?'

'We can do better than that.' I stood up and hoisted Ben onto my hip in one arduous movement. 'Come on. Get on your jacket and shoes.'

'I have homework!' But the way she said it, with such buoyant abandonment, told me that she understood what I was thinking and she knew as well as I did that her homework could wait until later.

We dropped Ben off to wreak havoc on the quiet of Mac's new office, then headed back into the darkening afternoon, through the cold, to the subway. If there were no delays, we'd make the last half hour of afternoon visiting hours at the hospital.

CHAPTER 17

Abby was alone when we got there. It was the first time I hadn't walked in on other visitors or at least Sasha Mendelssohn. The desk nurse had recognized me and waved me on before reaching to answer her phone.

We walked through the open door and there she was: propped on a pile of pillows, reading *The Giver*. Not only was she reading on her own, but she was holding the book herself, which had to mean her broken collarbone was almost healed though you could still see a rainbow of discoloration through the open neck of her hospital gown. The cast on her leg had collected a few signatures and doodles, but not many.

Her eyes shifted to peer over the top of the book when she heard us enter.

'Hi Abby. I'm Karin, remember me? I was here a couple times before. I live down the street from you. This is Dathi; she's twelve. She wanted to meet you.'

Her eyes flicked from me to Dathi, who smiled.

'I brought it.' She held out the rolled-up drawing.

'Did you get my message on Facebook? I tried to chat you but you're never on. Here.'

Abby let the book fall out of her hands and Dathi jumped to catch it, dropping the rolled drawing onto the bed. She laughed, and Abby's face lit with the slightest hint of humor.

'Where is your bookmark?' Dathi looked around for it: rifling the pages, checking the bed, the floor, peeking under Abby's covers. Finally she found it halfway across the room. 'Here we go! But how will we find your page?'

Abby reached out for the book and Dathi gave it to her. Flipping through, she found her spot and Dathi stuck in the bookmark. Then Abby wiggled back on her pillows, trying to sit up straighter.

'Here.' Dathi rearranged the pillows to make it easier. 'Better?'

Abby moved faster and sat straighter than I'd seen her these past weeks. But she still didn't speak. I had warned Dathi about this and was impressed by how maturely she was handling it.

The single visitor's chair had been pushed into the corner, and when I repositioned it beside the bed, Dathi stood back as if I was going to sit down.

'You sit,' I told her.

'No, I will stand.'

'Go ahead. I feel like stretching my legs.'

Dathi acquiesced and pulled the chair even closer. She had decided even before meeting Abby that they would be friends, and so they were, simple as that. But it wasn't just Dathi who had evidently made a quick decision: Abby also leaned closer.

'Karin told me about you,' Dathi said. 'I found you on Facebook, and now we're friends. After school today I wrote you about this. I go to Middle School 51. Where do you go?' She unfurled the drawing and held it as flat as possible in front of Abby, whose eyes quickly took in every inch of it.

'Can you tell what it is?' Dathi watched Abby's face. 'You see? It is a girl with her mother. That's the thing about our mothers: When you get close to them they are soft like no one else. Mine smelled like cloves. A girl at school told me her mother smells like cookies. I like cookies very much. Back home in my village in India a cookie was a rare special treat.'

Abby's gaze now moved from the drawing to Dathi, and appeared to study her. Dathi's hair was swept off her round, earnest face with an elastic band. Her feather earrings dangled. Despite her new American clothes, she still looked a little backward and forward at once: unable yet to wear that second skin of tween style (or what passed for it), and unwilling to belittle her intelligence by turning speech into a version of text message slang. At Dathi's middle school, I had overheard one girl say to another: 'BTW she used to be my BFF but she's so *random* I can't stand her LOL!' I did a double take and then decoded the sentence enough to figure out that another kid had been harshly condemned. Probably a 'friend,' since now it seemed *friends* were virtual while real-life social pressures at school turned many into *frenemies* faster than they could befriend or defriend each other. I had learned a lot in a single week of hovering around Dathi, who, despite being an outsider in her new world, was a different kind of outsider than I was. That was evident here, right now, in the way the two girls clicked.

I hovered near the door, watching, trying not to intrude on the bubble they were forming around themselves and each other; that special world young girls create when they become instant citizens of the same secret planet.

'Do you want me to hang it on your wall, right there, so you can see it?' Dathi pointed to a spot across from Abby's bed, a few feet beneath the suspended television.

Abby hesitated, then nodded.

'I will need some tape.' Dathi glanced around the room as if she might spot some.

'I'll ask at the desk,' I offered.

On my way, I ran into the Campbells. Linda looked less stressed than last time I'd seen her, when she'd broken down and was led away in tears. Father X was with them, looking paler and thinner than before his own recent hospital stay.

We greeted each other and I asked after his health. He told me he had spent only two nights in the hospital before being released with a 'prescription to reduce the stress in my life,' which made all of us laugh.

'How do you do that?' Linda said. 'Do doctors think you can just pick up and move to a desert island on permanent vacation?'

'It's called blood pressure medication.' Father X's smile lifted his face, transforming his cheeks into red apples.

I hated him.

I didn't know him, and maybe the onslaught of news about pedophile priests had poisoned my thinking, and obviously I shouldn't have judged *this* priest based on the crimes of others – but I couldn't help myself. What was he doing hanging around this orphaned child's hospital bedside? Didn't he have a whole congregation to think about?

'I take it Detective Staples is trying to talk to Abby again,' Father X said to me, with a tinge of mourning in his tone; and I wondered who the mourning was for: the Reeds, Abby, or himself.

'No, I came up here on my own. My daughter is in there, visiting with her.' I surprised myself, coming right out and calling Dathi my daughter.

'I didn't realize you had a daughter,' Father X said.

'Yes, she's about Abby's age. I also have a three-year-old son; well, he's practically four.'

'Do your daughter and Abby know each other from school?' Linda asked. 'I have to try to gather up as much information as I can about her life and friends if I'm going to be her mother now. Not *if*. I meant *because*.' Linda's skin blushed a vivid pink.

'You'll get the hang of it over time,' Steve reassured her. I was impressed with what a doting husband he was, and imagined he'd make an equally doting father to Abby. The Dekkers had evidently believed he could, though their faith in Linda baffled me.

'Marta and I were good friends but I've realized how little I really knew about their day-to-day lives.'

'We abide in shadow,' Father X remarked in a tone meant to be soothing, but wasn't. But then nothing he said or did could pass by me now without skepticism or even outright distrust. A line from my brief foray into Sunday school sprang from memory, when the teacher read aloud in a ridiculously ominous tone from the King James Bible: *He who dwells in the secret place of the Most High shall abide under the shadow of the Almighty*.

But as soon as I thought that, I recoiled at my own arrogance. Maybe Ladasha had a point; maybe I had already decided before the evidence was in. Maybe the ideas I considered instinctive were really knee-jerk judgments that would prove detrimental to the case the more I hung around. Maybe she and Billy were right: Maybe I shouldn't.

'That we do.' Steve patted Father X's back. 'I suppose we'll ferret out what we can about Abby's life, and make up the rest as we go along, right? You're going to be an awesome mother to her, Lindy.'

'We'll certainly have to make plenty of adjustments' – Linda gathered herself – 'but I'm eager to do it. I don't want anyone to think I'm not. Darling, since I'm thinking of it, what about Brazil?'

'That's been booked since last year.'

'Well, I'll stay home while you're gone.' To me, she added: 'Every spring for years now, the boys head out on their annual fishing expedition off the coast of Brazil, and we girls jet to *Paris* for a week – boo hoo.' She grinned.

'Great fishing off Brazil.' Steve smiled at the thought of it. I recalled that he'd mentioned he was a teacher. The trip sounded like a well-earned vacation, possibly the highlight of his year.

'Of course' – Linda's cheerful tone crumbled – 'it wouldn't be the same without Marta. I don't mind staying home this year, not at all. In fact, I'd rather.'

'We'll tag team our trips next year,' Steve thought aloud, 'or alternate years. We'll work it out.'

Now I realized why I'd recognized Steve the first time we'd met: He was the other man in the photograph with Reed in the Dekkers' living room. The photo had been taken on what had appeared to be a boat; I recalled their relaxed, tanned faces.

'What about you, Father?' I asked. 'You must need vacations, too.'

'I rarely take time off, and when I do, I like to stay within driving distance.' He pressed out a smile and looked at the Campbells. 'Shall we?'

I followed them into Abby's room.

Dathi was partially leaning on the mattress now, talking to Abby in the dramatic whisper of a story-teller just getting to the good part, and Abby was pitched even closer than before, intently listening. When they heard our footsteps, they pulled away from each other.

'Oh, honey, you're looking so much better!' Linda hurried to Abby's bedside and leaned in close.

Abby kept still, a blank expression frozen on her face. Any animation she had shown with Dathi had vanished.

'How are you feeling? Almost ready to come home?' Just like last time, Linda hesitated before touching Abby's forehead lightly with her finger-tips; but this time, she didn't burst into tears. She pulled away and continued to smile at Abby while Dathi stiffened in her seat, trying not to get in the way of the adults who had swept so force-fully into the room.

I could see the bafflement in the expressions of Father X and the Campbells as they took in Dathi, who looked nothing like me. It was none of their business, but I had called her my daughter just now, so I stepped forward.

'Dathi lives with me now. Her mother used to work for us, before—'

Father X's effortful smile softened his surprise. 'Yes, of course. Let me welcome you.' He held out his hand to her until she acknowledged it with a quick shake.

'I called her my daughter before,' I said, 'because I'm hoping she will be.'

Dathi's expression cracked with emotion a moment. Then she looked at Abby, whose light eyes seemed to darken.

'Well,' Linda said softly, to me, 'then we have something in common, don't we?'

'I guess so.'

Suddenly we were all talking but not-talking about the murder of two mothers in the presence of their orphaned daughters. A chill crept through the room, as if someone had opened a window, though no one had. I became aware of the institutional airlessness of the hospital, where temperatures were regulated in a constant transfer of air that never left the building. It was the same dusty sourness that made me dislike staying in big hotels: it suffused your lungs and before long seemed to be in your blood, replacing oxygen with a sensation of gradual suffocation. In fact, standing there in that fragile moment, I realized how much I had grown to despise institutions in general, having spent years sworn to the army and then the police force. I hadn't recognized my disdain for other-enforced boundaries until I had been so free of them I had no choice but to rely on myself almost completely. Maybe that was partly why I was having so much trouble finishing school. Why all I really wanted these days was to bury myself in family, more and more of it, all the time. Why I found Father X, an authority figure from one of the world's most entrenched institutions, so creepy.

'Dathi, I think it's time for us to go home.'

She stood up, leaned down to whisper something into Abby's ear, crossed the room, and took my hand.

Dathi and I traveled home packed into a rush-hour subway, standing inches apart, grasping the same pole.

'*The French Connection* came in the mail today,' I told her.

'Oh?'

'If you can get your homework done by the time Ben's in bed, we can watch some of it tonight.'

'I will try my best.'

After that, we didn't talk. She seemed absorbed in thought, but so was I: My desire to speak with Edward Walczak, the fourth Musketeer, and find out what he knew about Father X was gathering an obsessive momentum in my mind. What would be the harm? Maybe there was something to learn from him. Something important that I could pass on to Billy and Ladasha, in case they hadn't already ferreted it out on their own. And then I would do what everyone seemed to want and mind my own business, leave it to the professionals, and get back to my own life.

That night, sharing a blanket with Dathi on the couch in our dark living room, munching from a bowl of popcorn between us, I tried to understand her attraction to a story so far flung from her own world – a 1970s New York narcotics detective on the trail of what turns out to be an international drug ring – but instead understood something else: her fascination with Popeye Doyle. It was his irreverent persistence, and the innate imperfection of his quest. He shouldn't have dug his nose in so deeply to a dangerous underworld, but he did anyway, and the end result was nothing like what anyone might have predicted. It was, essentially, the same thing that drew me to Meg in *A Wrinkle in Time*: She's driven by her anger and stubbornness and that is how, ultimately, she arrives at an unexpected truth.

At four o'clock on Saturday afternoon, Mary and Fremont Salter arrived on our front stoop. Fremont had a guitar strapped across his back, and he carried an amplifier that looked heavy. His band had a gig later that night; Mary was driving the equipment, which he hadn't felt safe leaving in the car.

The kids gathered around the guitar while the adults moved to the kitchen to talk in relative silence. It was a short interview, if you could call it that. Mac evidently felt as intuitively comfortable with Mary as I did and asked her only the most perfunctory questions about her professional background. She was one of those people who had followed many paths before having a child and never really settled into any particular career: a jack of all trades, master of none, but competent at many. Along with having learned Tai Chi, karate, and aikido with enough proficiency to teach beginners, she had also studied social work (before dropping out), been a waitress, and done administrative work in all kinds of offices, including a six-month stint as a secretary at the downtown Manhattan bureau of the FBI.

'So you went through the security check,' Mac asked her.

'Oh yeah, the whole rigmarole. It was actually kind of fun – I'd never been fingerprinted before. I don't know if Karin mentioned it' – she looked at Mac – 'but I'm kind of a junkie for that kind of stuff.'

'You have a reference over there at the bureau?'

'Sure.' She pulled out an old-version iPhone. A moment later, she had sent him the contact information. She then tapped in a text message to her reference. Half a minute later, her phone buzzed with a response.

'Gary says go ahead and call him anytime you want,' Mary said. 'You can even call right now if you want to.'

Mac's eyebrows shot up. I knew that one of his frustrations (among many) with Star had been her lack of efficiency. 'Why not?'

While he called, Mary joined the kids in the

living room. I shut the door for privacy and stayed in the kitchen with Mac, listening to his end of the conversation. He asked the usual questions and each time nodded at the answer. By his positive tone, I already knew the outcome before he signed off with 'Thanks for doing this at such short notice. She sounds pretty amazing.' After hanging up, he told me: 'He said he wanted to hire her, but her son was young and she didn't want to work full-time.'

I smiled at him. 'So let's do it?'

'Let's do it.'

We went to the living room, where Mac gave Mary a thumbs-up. 'According to Gary, you're the one who got away.'

'Aw, shucks.' But there was nothing shy about her; she seemed to know she'd been a good worker. 'I can give you another reference or two if you want.'

'Not necessary,' he said. 'If you want the jobs, both of them, you're hired.'

Mary beamed at us. 'I think this was meant to be; I really feel great about this. So, when do you want me to start?'

'How about right this minute?' I blurted out, seeing how comfortable the kids were with her and Fremont.

'I *could*, actually. We have a few hours before Free's gig. You guys can grab a quick date and it'll give me and the kids a trial run together before you have to commit to anything.'

Without wasting a minute, we put on our jackets and boots and headed out into the purple twilight.

'It's early for dinner.' Mac pulled on his leather gloves after locking the front door behind him. He jogged down the steps to join me on the sidewalk.

'Are you hungry?'

'Not really. You?'

'Not at all.'

'Do we have time for a movie?' he asked, walking beside me toward Smith Street.

'I don't know. But here's what I'm thinking: Let's see if Edward Walczak's home. Maybe he'll want to come out and play.'

Mac laughed, filling the space between us with a cold fog. 'You really don't give up, do you?'

'Why should I?' There was an edge to my tone, which he met with a snap of aggravation.

'Karin – if you want to be a cop again that badly, then get back on the force. If not, then back off. Really.'

I stopped walking and waited for him to turn and face me. I wasn't hurt by his tone, just resolved. I had held it back too long. The way he looked at me, I could tell he understood that something was about to shift.

'I know why you think I've been overdoing it, but there's a reason I've been poking around on my own.' And then it just spilled out: My visit to the Seven-two that day to return George Vargas's ring. Finding Ladasha there. Seeing Billy's name on their POI list. Arguing them out of it but not knowing if I really had. My urge to protect Billy.

'Un-*fucking*-believable.'

'So now you get it.'

We started walking again, our pace picking up.

'Yeah, I get it. You know where that Walczak guy lives?'

CHAPTER 18

*E*ddie *Walczak, Jr.* read a crooked, hand-scrawled label beside the buzzer on a plain door that shared an address with a local hardware store. The door led to the apartments upstairs. I pushed the button. After a wait, I rang again.

'He ain't there.' A young man with short, grizzled hair stood just outside the store, beside shovels and stacked bags of calcium chloride, watching us. His eyes were older than his face, which gave him a spooky look I didn't like. Mac answered him first.

'Do you know when he'll be home?'

'After work, probably.' He plucked a piece of something off his tongue and flicked it onto the sidewalk.

'What time is that, usually?' I asked.

'Seven.'

'Like clockwork?' Mac smiled.

'He works real close by.'

'Where's that?'

'Hardware store.' The man now grinned. And I knew.

'Are you Eddie?' I asked.

He nodded, holding the weird smile. 'Who wants to know?'

'Mac MacLeary' – he offered a gloved hand – 'and this is my wife, Karin Schaeffer. We're private investigators, working on a case.' You could have said that was a lie, but to me it signaled something else: Mac was angry; he believed in Billy as much as I did and was unwilling to sit back while he was demonized for his suffering. You could almost feel the heat of his outrage. The detail that we weren't officially working the case was unimportant.

'I don't know nothin'.'

Mac stepped closer. 'Listen, it's about Father X. You know, the thing from five years ago.'

'Yeah?' Defensively. But he didn't leave.

'Can we talk somewhere, do you think?' Mac asked.

Eddie glanced behind him into the shop. Then he called: 'Yo, Tony, back in a few minutes. I'm taking my break.'

Without his jacket he led us across the street and over a couple blocks to the Dunkin' Donuts on the corner of Smith and Bergen. We passed from the cold gray outside into the bright warmth of the orange and pink plastic interior, and parked ourselves at a table for four.

'Coffee?' Mac peeled off his jacket and draped it over mine on the spare seat.

'Milk, no sugar.'

I sat down beside him.

'How long you been a cop?'

'We're not cops. We used to be, but no more. Now we're in business for ourselves.'

'Who you working for?'

'We're helping the detective working a murder case,' I told him, and watched for his reaction. He held his poker face.

Mac returned with a tray and distributed paper cups of coffee and sugar crullers. Eddie picked one up and used it to stir milk into his coffee. When he lifted it out, the end had disintegrated.

'Which one?'

'Both. Nevins, and also the couple.'

'Yeah, I've been following it all in the papers. When I was a kid this wasn't such a safe neighborhood. Then it was. Now, I don't know.'

'Did anything strike you about the couple, the Dekkers, who lived on Bergen Street?'

Eddie hesitated, then shrugged his shoulders. 'Like what?'

'Well, like they were active members at St Paul's. Their pastor was Father Dandolos.'

Eddie smirked and dunked the rest of his cruller so fast the entire thing immersed in coffee. His short-bitten fingertips emerged dripping wet.

'You know him,' I said.

'Father X, you mean?'

'That's right.'

'Sure. So what?' But there was little conviction in his defensive response. We had found him, of all people. He had to know essentially why we were there. After a quiet moment, he asked us: 'Father X have something to do with that?'

'We don't know,' I answered.

'You were a witness,' Mac tried, 'in a sealed case.'

Eddie looked at us with a new, somber expression; the sheen of defiance had drained off. 'It was about a kid, so they sealed it. But they wouldn't listen to me, so he's still out there, doing his thing.'

'What happened?' I asked.

'I've been clean and sober a year now. It took a while, but I cleaned up for good.'

I nodded. Mac bit his cruller, not taking his eyes off Eddie as he spoke.

'I was an altar boy for six years, since I was ten. My mother was really into it, and yeah, I liked it at first. I felt proud, you know? After a while, I dunno, it got boring, but I was sticking with it 'cause of my mom. A lot of us kids over at the church were doing shit, you know what I mean – drugs and shit. And holdups – nothing serious, just local shit. No one ever got hurt; that wasn't the point.'

'What *was* the point?' Mac asked, before a shiver of what looked like regret passed over his eyes.

Eddie's expression stiffened. 'There was no point. Okay?'

'You were a kid then,' Mac backpedaled. 'Now you're an adult. Working. A law-abiding citizen.'

'In *every* way,' Eddie said.

'It must have really irked you reading about what

happened to the Dekkers,' I said. 'In your own neighborhood. Active members of Father X's church. It must have brought back some bad memories.'

Eddie nodded. 'Maybe if it happened now, they'd listen to me.'

'Maybe they would,' I said.

'If *what* happened, Eddie?' Mac leaned forward slightly.

'Here's the thing,' he began, 'and maybe they were right: I was basically a smartass thieving junkie and it wasn't like I actually saw his face. I was what you'd call a crap witness. Well, that wasn't how they put it.'

'Unreliable witness,' Mac said. 'But now things are different; you *are* reliable. What did you see?'

'Well . . .' He picked up a white sugar packet and carefully folded over one edge, creasing it again and again. 'Okay, it was like this: I'm in high school, right? And half the time we got football practice in the afternoon. So it's already dark out when I come out of the subway, and I remember *shit* I was supposed to drop off some flyers my mom made right after school so the church lady could make copies. So I remember this, and I head straight over to the church office to drop it off. And I do it: I drop it off in this box on the desk. But I hear a noise in the storage closet and I'm wondering about it, and also, you know, that's where they keep stuff and sometimes I'd like take a look just to see if there was anything worth – Well, anyway, so I open the door. It's dark, and I never turned on a light when I walked in so all youse got is moonlight coming in the windows, and in the dark closet I see a couple people. A man and a kid: this girlie-looking boy, Joanne. Real name's Joey but Joanne's what we called him because of his looks. Skinny. These baby-blue eyes. Pretty blond hair. I swear, he looked like a girl.'

'Who was with him?' I tried to get him back to the main point.

'The father.' He stared at us.

'What was happening in the closet?' Mac asked.

'What do you mean, what was happening? What do you think happens in a closet with a priest and a half-naked girlie boy?'

'What did you do?' I asked.

'Shut the door. Went home. Told my mother I dropped off the papers. Ate dinner.'

The air in the donut shop got heavy. Eddie turned the sugar packet over and creased a short end in the opposite direction.

'What happened to Joey?' I asked quietly.

Eddie shrugged, his eyes fixed on his busy fingers, the now-mangled packet beginning to leak sugar onto the orange Formica tabletop. 'Nothing. Saw him the next day on Court Street with his mother, holding her hand. Kid was such a wimp.'

'How old was he, do you remember?' I asked.

'I dunno. Ten, maybe eleven. Something like that.'

298

'Did the same thing happen to you,' Mac asked, 'as happened to Joey?'

Eddie's gaze snapped up. His eyes were clear, angry. 'No way. I never woulda let him do that to me.'

'Do you know if he ever did that again to Joey? Or to any other kids?'

'I only know what I saw that one time.'

'And you're sure it was Father X?' Mac sipped his coffee without taking his eyes off Eddie's face.

'Who else would it be? He was the only priest in the church, and he was wearing his robes, the creep.'

'But you didn't see his face?'

'No.' Eddie's eyes watered and I thought he was going to cry, but instead he sneezed. 'Someone got a dog in here?' He turned around to see if someone had snuck one into the shop, but no one had. 'You got dog hair on your clothes or something? I'm real allergic.'

'No dogs in our house,' I said.

'Must be someone else. Anyway, I know what I saw, and it was him.'

'Listen, Eddie, can I ask you something?' Mac said.

'What?'

'Were you high that afternoon?'

'I told you, I just came from football practice. You showed up stoned for football practice and you were off the team – *gone*. Trust me: Much as my mom loves the church, my dad loves football. No way was I gonna risk that kind of beating.'

'But even though you were straight that day, no one believed you.'

'Some people believed me, some people didn't.'

'When did you tell what you saw?'

'The next night. It was eating at me, you know? I told my mom, and she screamed at me, told me to shut the fuck up basically, Father X wouldn't do something like that. But when my dad got wind of it, he listened. He's the one called the cops. And then it went from there.'

'So what happened to Joey?'

'I dunno. I stopped going to church; I was sixteen, my mother couldn't make me anymore, and my dad, what did he care? Me and Joey, we didn't travel in the same circles. I saw him around now and then, but that's about it.'

'Did he ever say anything to you about it?' I asked.

'Just once. He was coming outta the park with some of his friends – he was always hanging out with girls, jumping rope, shit like that. He saw me and ran up to me and kind of whispered, "Thanks anyway, Eddie."'

'Nothing else?'

Eddie shook his head.

'You didn't say anything back?'

'What was there to say? But it was nice he said something to me, you know? I mean, when he said my name it was kind of sweet, like he meant it. I think I was the only one who really knew.'

'So, later,' I pressed for the rest of the story, 'you ended up living at Sons of St Paul's? That must have been awkward for you.'

'Shit. Awkward ain't the word for it. But when I got out of prison – ten months, petty larceny – that was part of the deal. I had to live there for a whole fucking year before I could "enter society," total bullshit, but that was the deal.'

'We understand you made some friends there,' I said.

'Shit, you *did* do some digging on me, didn't you?' It seemed to make him feel important. We didn't deny it. 'If you mean the guys – you know, Jose, Marty, and Iggy – I didn't meet them at Sons. We knew each other since we were kids. They were friends with my older brother and we kind of hooked up. They're not bad guys, but I don't really see them anymore.'

I didn't ask why; obviously they were still using, even if they were using legally through the clinic, and it seemed as if Eddie was trying to distance himself from that crowd and those times. There was no need to shine too bright a spotlight on his association with those losers. Eddie, at least, had a job and an apartment; it was probably a minimum-wage job, and it was probably a lousy apartment, but it was a start.

'They were friends with one of Joey's older brothers, too, now that I think of it,' he added. 'Joey had like four older brothers, no sisters, lucky shit.'

'Any chance,' I asked, 'you could tell us where he lives?'

'The Espositos? Over on President Street, between Hoyt and Bond, right across the street from the school. They got the most lights on their house. Put 'em up right after Thanksgiving and leave 'em until Easter. You can't miss it.' Eddie flipped his wrist to check his watch. 'I gotta go.'

We stood to shake Eddie's hand. Mac opened his wallet and took out a business card. 'Call me if you think of anything else. Any chance I can get your number?'

Eddie recited his phone number, which Mac keyed straight into his BlackBerry. 'If it's him, if he did it, I'll testify on the stand. For whatever it's worth.'

Mac stood and I sat, both of us watching Eddie Walczak brace his shoulders against the cold as he hurried coatless across the street and out of view.

It was deep twilight when we walked up to the Esposito home on President Street. Eddie had been right: You couldn't miss it. The small brick house blinked like a sales pitch for Times Square in the middle of the quiet block, rhythmically flashing streaks of color into the drab winter evening.

'Here goes nothing.' I headed up the stoop, with Mac right behind me.

The doorbell rang with a recorded choir singing 'We wish you a Merry Christmas!' over and over.

'It's past *New Year's*,' I mumbled.

'Guess someone here didn't want to see Christmas end.' Mac glanced at me with a wry smile just as a burly man with a graying comb-over opened the door.

'Are you Mr Esposito?' I pulled off my glove and thrust out a hand.

'Yeah.' He shoved both his hands into his pants pockets. 'How can I help youse?'

We introduced ourselves first as neighbors, then as investigators, watching his expression roller-coaster from almost friendly to borderline hostile.

'Whaddya want wit' me?'

'We were hoping to speak with your son Joey.' I smiled. 'Is he home?'

'Joey didn't do nuttin'.'

We explained some more, nipping at the edge of the five-year-old scab of Father X and the case that went nowhere, because like hungry scavengers we wanted to see what was underneath.

'We ain't openin' that can a worms again.' The door started to close when someone appeared on the stairs behind him.

'Pop?'

'Get upstairs, Joey.'

In the diminishing sliver of open door I saw Joey Esposito. Eddie had been right: He looked like a girl, a very pretty girl, slender with shoulder-length blond hair. It was almost impossible to believe that he and his father were related. Joey was also considerably taller than his father, whose height was average at most.

'These cops wanna talk about You Know What,' Mr Esposito grumbled. 'That crap again. Listen, youse: none a that happened. The Walczak boys were a bunch a troublemakers. You wanna know what really happened? Willy Walczak's girlfriend Kim went with my son Johnny, and the Walczaks rigged a story to break our hearts.' He pounded his chest once with his fist. 'It wasn't bad enough Joey here's a little different? They had to rub it in our faces even worse?'

I tried to catch Joey's bright blue eyes as his father slammed the door, but he drew them away. A loud click told us they had turned the lock on the inside.

'This whole Father X thing' – Mac turned quickly to avoid a blast of colored lights, but I'd seen the frustration in his glance – 'it isn't going to lead anywhere, Karin. The Walczak-Esposito thing sounds like a personal vendetta.'

'I know, but—'

'This isn't a pedophile case, Karin. Whatever went on with that – whether it's true or not – all that's irrelevant.'

'But all those missing kids ending up in the sex trade, ending up dead. And the way the Dekkers died – they knew something. I'm convinced of it. And Abby getting hit by a car like that, on Nevins Street, so close . . . Father X hardly leaves her side. Why won't she talk?'

'Maybe she can't.'

'They don't think there's anything wrong with

her vocal cords, and neurologically she's been checking out okay.'

'Except for not being able to speak?'

'*Come on*. You know there's something to it: She saw something; she's scared.'

'Sure she saw something. Maybe she saw her parents get killed. Maybe she saw Patrick Scott eyeing her from his car. Maybe she saw Billy when he was freaking out. Anything could have scared her that night.'

'How would she have seen Billy? He didn't get there until after Abby was hit by the car.' I glanced at him, the side of his face flashing red, red, red.

'I was just making a point.'

Down on the sidewalk, Times Square at our back and the dark Brooklyn evening in front of us, we left the block and kept moving. Back up on Smith Street, cafés and restaurants beckoned; the early shift was starting to come out for Saturday night.

We arrived home to the chaos of a happy home. Dathi and Fremont were huddled over the laptop at the kitchen table, sharing a bowl of tortilla chips. Mary and Ben were sprawled out on their stomachs on the living room floor, placing stones we'd collected last summer at the beach inside a dollhouse Mary must have carried up from downstairs.

'I hope you don't mind.' Mary scooped up a handful of stones from the floor: faces had been drawn on each one with marker.

'Why would we mind?' I kissed the top of Ben's

head, but he didn't turn around. He was happy, so I was happy.

'I'm having a party,' he said after a moment, still not looking at me, 'and all these people are invited.'

'A stone party. Good idea.'

'I think he means a birthday party,' Mary said. 'He told us his birthday was coming soon.'

'It's true, his birthday's in a couple of weeks. A party – okay.' It *was* okay; in fact, I'd been feeling guilty that I hadn't done anything about it yet. 'Okay, Ben, we'll have a party on your birthday.'

Soon, we all stood in the front hall, cheerfully bidding each other good night. Wishing Fremont luck at his gig later. Making plans for Mary to return on Monday.

Just as they were about to leave, Dathi turned to me. 'Perhaps we could watch Fremont play?' Her eyes were so bright.

'Tonight?'

'Perhaps.'

If she had demanded it, I probably would have said no. But the way she asked, with such careful diplomacy, made me want to please her. 'I guess we could eat a quick dinner and get over there in time.'

'It starts at eight,' Mary said.

'Go for it,' Mac called from the living room. 'I'll put Ben to bed.'

'See you guys later, then,' I told Mary and Fremont as they carried their equipment out the door and down the front stoop.

By seven-thirty, Dathi and I were in the car on our way to Park Slope.

Perch Café on Seventh Avenue was packed with teenagers. The narrow storefront opened onto a spacious rear area, where the first band was getting ready to play. It was too crowded with teenagers to see Fremont, but Dathi plunged right into the crowd in search of a spot with a view. For all her politeness, she wasn't shy.

I found Mary sitting at the bar, drinking a yogurt smoothie, waiting. All the parents, and there weren't many, were clustered by the front. There were half a dozen small tables where some people sat eating dinner; a couple of waitresses zipped around serving and clearing. I ordered a cup of coffee and joined Mary, pulling up a stool.

The sound of an electric piano pealed through the space.

I leaned back and tried to see above the packed bodies, which were jostling and hopping to the music, but couldn't see the band. I couldn't see Dathi, either.

'She'll be fine.' Mary had read my mind.

'I'm actually not worried about her. She's got so much common sense and resilience.'

'I noticed that. It's unusual.'

'I hear her crying at night, but she hardly ever talks to me about it. She doesn't know me that well, I guess, but still. You'd think she'd need someone to talk to.'

Mary swallowed a long sip of her smoothie and put down her glass. 'People in that part of the world think differently. I've been in India; before having Fremont I used to travel a lot. In the East, death is part of life.'

'I've heard that.'

'It's hard to get it until you see it. Their whole belief system is different than ours.'

'Dathi's mother, Chali, used to talk about karma. I mean, she was a practicing Catholic and she still believed in karma – I couldn't get over that.'

'Yup. It seems strange to us. But all those things can be true at once. Just like life and death can coexist at the same time – it's a concept that's just alien to us. In the East, people mourn as deeply as we do, but it's different. It's hard to explain. It's like, for them, when someone dies they don't really lose them. The life force doesn't end, it transfers, kind of.'

I thought about that for a minute; it was such an appealing concept. The deaths of loved ones I'd endured had been horrible blows, permanent losses. Even my miscarriage – the loss of someone not yet fully formed, more the prospect of someone I would have come to cherish – had been devastating. Each loss was a brutal injustice. It had never occurred to me to think of it in any other way.

'Does Dathi know how her mother died?' Mary asked softly.

'She does. But you're right: She seems to accept it in a certain way I don't quite understand.'

Mary smiled elusively. 'Karma means intentional action, good or bad. It's all-important. It all adds up. Dathi probably assumes she'll see her mother again, in one form or another. Or maybe not *see* so much as *experience*. She probably also assumes that whoever murdered her mother will be avenged in kind, one way or another, sooner or later.'

'Karma.' I nodded. 'Right.'

Bands changed and there was some movement in the crowd. I couldn't help looking for Dathi again; and again I didn't see her. But I did see someone else I recognized: Joey Esposito. His head flashed blond and blue above the crowd. And then he turned and saw me, too. He started to turn away, until I smiled. He hesitated, waved, and pushed his way out of the pulsating bodies to come over and speak with me.

'Sorry about that before. My dad doesn't like cops.' His eyes rolled up. Without the damper of his father's presence, he was funny, even flirtatious. He was also flaming. If I wasn't mistaken, he was wearing sparkling green eye shadow and a touch of mascara.

'I understand,' I told him. 'But we're not cops; we're private investigators. And we're not digging into the old case against Father X. This is new, about the recent murders.'

Mary leaned forward, listening intently.

Joey stepped in closer, his eyes twinkling under the bar lights. 'I don't mind talking about it. No one raped me, okay? Maybe I exaggerated that part a little bit because I hated going to church. But it was true about the priest. And Eddie wasn't the only one who didn't see his face; I didn't see it, either. The man was wearing a mask, one of those plain white face masks you pick up cheap for Halloween. He only got me into that closet one time. Lucky for me, Eddie opened the door – that's when I ran out.' He sounded sincere, until he added with a whimsical flourish: 'That's my story and I'm sticking with it!'

I didn't know what to think; Joey seemed like a fabulist. It was easy to see why people weren't confident in his side of the story. But did that mean it never happened at all?

'Do you have any reason to think it *wasn't* Father X?'

'Now? Who knows. Then? I was a little kid. It was the priest, at the church, I'd seen him around that afternoon. Why wouldn't it be him?'

'Any other kids ever come forward, telling the same story?'

When Joey shrugged his shoulders, a slender silver chain glistened on his neck. I thought I saw a crucifix dangling off it before realizing that it was a little silver penis. He seemed to notice, and enjoy, the way my attention froze on it a moment.

'What about your brothers?' I asked.

'According to them, *nada*,' Joey said. 'It was just *moi*. And *of course* some people thought I deserved it.' He batted his eyelids.

I tried not to laugh. If he had been anywhere

310

near as hard to read as a young child as he was now, it would be a blatant lie to claim that no one could possibly doubt him.

'Thanks for talking, Joey.'

'What's your phone number?' He pulled his cell phone out of his jeans pocket. He dialed in my number as I recited it, then called me. I answered and hung right up. Now we had each other's numbers, though I wasn't sure if that was a good thing or not. I hoped he wouldn't consider me a confidante for his storytelling, but then I corrected myself: What if he was telling the truth?

He leaned forward to air-kiss my cheek, like we were girlfriends, and went to find his coat. I turned to Mary, who was smiling, watching Joey dance his way toward the door.

'His father is the polar opposite of him,' I said. 'It's like he landed in that family by accident.'

'That kid needs to grow up and start his own life as soon as possible. It's the only way.'

The next song ended. Dathi pressed herself out of the crowd and stood at its edge, looking around. Her eyes smiled when she saw me. I waved, and she disappeared back into the undulating throng.

That night I lay in bed a long time, thinking about Joey Esposito. Was there any chance it was true? Had a masked priest tried to assault him when he was a young boy? Or was he still processing the Walczak family's grudge against his family? As for the legal case, it was easy to see why it had been dismissed: Despite the onslaught of sex abuse cases being brought against the Catholic Church, even five years ago, this one obviously had dubious merit. Eddie Walczak's father had leveled an accusation, not the Espositos; and the rivalry between the Walczak and Esposito sons complicated the whole thing. Even Joey, who claimed it was true, couldn't say who had been behind that mask.

Over the next few days Mac and I tried to find out what we could about the Dekkers' connections with the church, but nothing appeared unusual. Billy and Ladasha, for all their hard work and all her bravado in her secret shadow investigation with George Vargas, also appeared to have nothing to show for it. At least, nothing anyone was sharing with us.

The dead were receding farther into the past, as they tended to do. And our lives notched forward day to day to day.

Then, on Tuesday, Abby grabbed for a lifeline.

CHAPTER 19

Sasha Mendelssohn called to say that Abby had drawn a picture of herself and Dathi.

'I think it's a good sign,' Sasha said. 'She's doing so much better now – physically, at least. Her cast is coming off her leg, and there's been some discussion about discharging her to the Campbells, possibly as soon as next week . . . but we're still hoping for a better assessment of her true neurological function. The problem is, she doesn't relate well to any of the adult staff here, and she hasn't bonded as well with any of our other young patients as she did with your daughter.'

'You want me to bring Dathi by for another visit after school today?'

'If you don't mind.'

'I'll ask her. But I guarantee you, the answer will be yes.'

We were back up at the hospital that very afternoon.

Abby wiggled up in her bed the moment we walked in. Dathi hurried to pull up a chair and soon the two girls were huddled together. Abby moved better; her body was healing if her mind hadn't yet. Knowing that the cast would be removed soon, the girls set about decorating every blank inch with pens borrowed from the front desk. Dathi then used my phone to take pictures, which she e-mailed to herself. They were uploaded to her Facebook page within hours.

We visited again on Friday after school and then again on Sunday afternoon. Each time, it was the same: They enclosed themselves in a private bubble of drawing, lanyard weaving, Dathi reading aloud or talking and Abby listening. I took to wandering the halls, visiting the cafeteria and gift shop, even sitting in the waiting area sometimes to give the girls privacy.

After what felt like a particularly long visit, I waited while Dathi zipped herself into her jacket and rattled off another round of good-byes to her new 'BFF but don't tell Oja' – when Father X and Steve Campbell arrived and the atmosphere radically shifted. Abby's discomfort was swift and obvious: Her gaze swiveled to the ceiling, her body stiffened.

'Hello!' Steve reached out to shake my hand; his leather glove felt saturated with cold from outside. 'I heard you've been here a lot lately; guess we keep missing you.'

'The girls have really hit it off,' I said. 'We've been to see Abby three times this week, but we don't stay late.'

'We'll have to make a point of getting them together when we get Abby home, on Tuesday,'

Steve said. 'Just got the good news on my way in. Isn't that great, Abby? Linda's home right now, getting your new room ready.'

Abby held her muteness like a life raft.

'Well, they've got a stack of papers for me to sign. Back in a minute.' Steve turned to me with a smile. 'See you soon, I hope.'

The thought of leaving Father X alone with Abby made me deeply uncomfortable. But before I could think of an excuse to stay, Dathi did it for me by sitting back down in the chair.

'We weren't leaving,' she said, zipping her jacket all the way up. 'I'm just cold.'

'It seems warm in here to me,' Father X said. 'But you're used to a hot climate, aren't you?'

Neither Abby nor Dathi responded or even looked at him, but I couldn't take my eyes off his face: hating him: the high pink draining from his cheeks as his temperature adjusted, his eyes shining wet, the wrinkled grid of his forehead.

Leaning against a wall, I crossed my arms over my chest and got as comfortable as I could in an uncomfortable position. Dathi stayed planted in the chair, uncharacteristically refusing to offer it to an elder, and read aloud from the end of *The Giver*. Father X hovered quietly, occasionally yawning. As soon as Steve returned, holding a large envelope, Father X went for his coat. Steve seemed surprised that the visit was already over.

'So soon?' Steve asked.

'She seems tired.' Father X glanced at Abby with

a gentle smile that gave me the creeps. 'We'll be back tomorrow, dear.'

'Linda will come with us, okay?' Steve promised. 'She said to give you a kiss.' He did not, however, try to deliver it.

As soon as they were gone, Dathi whipped off her jacket. She had sweated so much her shirt was wet.

'Abby, honey.' I stepped away from the wall and moved closer to her bed. 'Does Father X scare you? Don't you like Steve and Linda?'

She looked at me quickly, and for a moment I was convinced she was going to say something. But instead her gaze moved away, returning to the wall opposite her bed, where the first drawing Dathi had made for her was now surrounded by four others.

'That's okay.' It wasn't, but what could I do? I turned back to Dathi. 'Come on, now we really do have to leave.'

Dathi whispered yet another good-bye in Abby's ear; but when Abby nodded in response I got the feeling it had been more a question and answer than a relay of good-byes. Dathi carried her jacket to the elevator, while I slipped mine on. Riding down alone to the lobby, she blurted out:

'Abby isn't scared of Father X. She likes him. It's the other priest she's scared of.'

That stunned me. 'What other priest?'

'She just wanted you to know that.'

'Okay – but how do *you* know?'

'She told me.' Dathi's smile was bright and proud. A chill flashed through me.

'Has she spoken to you?'

'Yes. Of course. She is my best friend.'

'You mean she actually *talked* to you? Not wrote, or drew a picture, but *spoke*?'

'Yes.'

'When?'

'Every time I visit. She has a lot to tell me. For instance, Abby doesn't want to go live with those people.'

I couldn't be sure if it was true – it seemed to me that Dathi had a vivid imagination – but I was willing to suspend my disbelief for now. It was also a matter of stubborn hope: *Of course* Abby would talk eventually; why wouldn't she? She was terrified of something she felt she couldn't say, but she wouldn't be able to hold it in forever.

'Why not?'

'Her mother's coming back for her. How will she know where to find her if she's been moved?'

'Dathi – her mother isn't coming back for her.'

'Oh, but she is.'

'How can she?'

The elevator doors dinged open and people started pressing in. The lobby was busy with visitors and hospital personnel coming and going. It seemed that just beyond the rotating doors of the main entrance, there was some kind of confusion outside.

'Dathi, what did she mean by "the other priest"? What other priest?'

We pushed together through the revolving door and walked into a scene of chaos: reporters and rubberneckers jostling for the best view.

Father X was surrounded by uniformed police, trying to tell them something, but they didn't appear to be paying much attention. One of the cops pushed the father's left shoulder to turn him toward the open door of a waiting squad car: his hands were shackled behind his back. The undersides of his palms were lined and swollen. I looked around for Steve Campbell, but he was nowhere in sight.

'You're making a mistake,' Father X pleaded. 'Please, hear me out.'

The cop pushed him all the way into the car. Another one kicked it closed.

They weren't listening to him: an arrest had already been made; their job was to get him to their precinct where he could talk all he wanted – or not.

I stepped forward and asked the nearest uniform, 'What's going on?'

His expression hardened. I knew the look: He had no intention of answering some nosy lady from the crowd. He shut himself into the front passenger seat and the squad car drove away.

'Son-of-a-bitch!' I shouted after him, regretting it as soon as it slipped out. I glanced at Dathi, ashamed of myself; but her quick, delighted smile made me laugh. We stood there, staring at the pair of taillights blazing red into the gathering darkness before vanishing around a corner.

'I'm getting to know you better, Karin.' Dathi took my hand. 'I like you best when you're at your worst. Does that make any sense?'

'Do you think you've seen me at my worst?'

'Perhaps I didn't mean *worst*. Perhaps I meant *unguarded*.'

I gave her hand a squeeze. As we walked toward the subway, I called Mac and told him what had happened.

'I know,' he said. 'It's all over the news.'

'What are they saying?'

'Karin, you're right there! Don't you know?'

'No one would tell me anything.'

'The cops are saying he's a "person of interest" in the Working Girl Murders.'

'Since when do they arrest a person of interest?' But it was a rhetorical point; we both knew they only arrested you if there was serious reason to believe you were directly involved in a crime. I felt vindicated: So I had been right. But I wanted to hear it from the source.

I called Billy's cell phone and left him a message: 'Why did you guys arrest Father X, exactly?' But he didn't call back before we descended into the dead zone of the underground tunnels.

CHAPTER 20

It was fully night when we came up out of the F train station at Bergen Street. I waited for my BlackBerry to chime the news that I had a voice mail waiting, but there was nothing: Billy still hadn't returned my call. I tried him on his landline at the precinct but whoever answered said he hadn't been seen all day.

When we walked into the house, the first thing I heard was the television news being delivered in an urgent tone.

Mac appeared, looking worn out. 'Dathi, you must be hungry. There's some takeout in the kitchen. Ben's in there—'

'He's eating all alone?' I interrupted.

But before he could answer, and as Dathi went to join Ben, Mac steered me into the living room. I sat on the couch without taking off my coat.

'Watch this. They're about to loop it again. Maybe they'll add something new.'

I sat beside him on the couch, my attention fixed on the clean-cut anchor who filled the screen.

'We're still waiting for the chief of police to come out and make a statement,' he announced. His white hair blended with the snowbanks behind him, turning him ghostly pale. The whole city was so snowbound now, I couldn't tell where he was.

'To recap: Breaking news in the hunt for the Working Girl Killer that's kept the city wondering, and looking over its shoulder, for two years now. Father Ximens Dandolos of Cobble Hill, Brooklyn, was arrested tonight in connection with the case. This after the source of the murder weapon used in the latest murder, of a nanny in Brooklyn two weeks before Christmas – the first nonprostitute killed in this case – was traced to a hardware store in Brooklyn where illegal knife sales have been under scrutiny by the district attorney's office. That's all the information we have now; no word yet on whether that knife is considered an exact match for the ones used in what is thought to be the work of a single serial killer, or how Father Dandolos might fit in. Stay tuned.'

I soughed off my coat and left it puddled behind me where I sat. 'Wow.'

'Walczak.' Mac grimaced. 'Selling knives under the counter. Looking us right in the eye and giving us a load of –' He glanced back at the kitchen, where the children were eating, and stopped himself from fully indicting Eddie Walczak without any evidence. And then that weak thread of suspicion snapped when the anchor reappeared on screen with an update:

'This just in! We're told that the knife used in the latest murder by the Working Girl Killer was

321

purchased just three weeks ago at a Lowe's hardware store on Second Avenue in Brooklyn. A credit card used to make a purchase of other supplies at the same time confirms a witness's allegation that the supplies and the knife were bought by the same person – the superintendent of St Paul's Roman Catholic Church in Cobble Hill. The super, Rustilav Chuikov, often shops at Lowe's on errands for the church. He was questioned earlier today by the police – they specified that he is *not* a suspect, but a person of interest.'

'How can he even say that with a straight face?' I shook my head. 'Person of interest, *right*.'

They segued into a report on the New York State law making the possession of a knife that 'looks like a weapon' illegal without a hunting or fishing license, and the outright ban on the sale of switchblades and gravity knives. Bowie knives fell under the first category: legal to purchase, but not to carry without the proper license. Because an employee at Lowe's had been running a black market on the illegal knives, any knife he sold, over or under the table, had been tracked in a special investigation. Before long, there was more about the case:

'The man you see here—' A square-jawed Russian, with a gold front tooth that flashed in the spotlight when he spoke, filled the screen in a close-up I guessed he could have lived without. 'Rustilav Chuikov, who's called Rusty, says he knows nothing about the purchase of any knives at Lowe's or anyplace else. Listen.'

Rusty spoke into a microphone so close to his mouth that it was enclosed in bursts of vapor each time his breath hit the cold air. 'I have not bought any knife, in December, today, or any other day. What would I want with a knife like that? Nothing! That is all I can say right now.'

As soon as he was done, the anchorman's voice returned, discussing the knife. As he spoke, a photograph showed an exact replica of the Bowie knife purchased from the now-arrested employee at Lowe's – the knife that killed Chali. The knife, with its elongated blade curving at the tip and shiny new wood-grain handle, was just like the one I'd seen protruding from her chest.

'For more on the phenomenon of serial killers, here is CNN criminologist . . .'

The camera switched from the knife to the face of a spiffily dressed man with short salt-and-pepper hair, sitting at a desk in a newsroom, smiling at the camera. Mac muted the volume.

'Well, either the press hasn't caught on to the possibility of a copycat, or they were asked not to talk about it,' I said. 'I kept expecting them to show a picture of the Stark Bowie, too.'

'They also didn't mention the souvenirs.' That an item of clothing was missing from each victim was valuable information only if no one else knew about it; it was the trump card for separating copycats and wannabes from the real McCoy.

'Billy still hasn't called me back.' I checked my phone again. 'Did you talk to him at all today?'

'Not since yesterday.' Mac dialed Billy on his own phone, but there was still no answer.

'I wonder if he's still mad at me,' I said.

'He's just stressed. He'll get over it.'

By the time Ben was asleep and Dathi was tucked into her bed, the recycled story had picked up a few more details. The news crew was now stationed on Court Street, just a few blocks from our house, in front of the Congress Street entrance to the church. I recognized the plaque behind the journalist who now addressed the city:

'In a shocking twist to a notorious case, the priest who presides over this storied Roman Catholic church in upscale Cobble Hill, Brooklyn, has been arrested in connection with the serial killings, known as the Working Girl Murders, which have terrorized New York City for nearly two years now. Father Ximens Dandolos, who has been the pastor of St Paul's and St Agnes for twenty-five years, is now said to be the very person who signed a credit card receipt at Lowe's hardware store when the knife that was used to brutally murder this woman was purchased.'

Chali's smiling face appeared on the screen. I froze, seeing her alive and happy – I hadn't thought of her that way in so long. Mac's hand landed gently on my back.

The sound of footsteps alerted us that Dathi was on her way upstairs.

'Turn it off!' I fumbled for the remote, and found

it wedged between the couch cushions; but it was too late.

She stood at the top of the stairs in her new flannel nightgown, staring at her mother's face.

'What are they saying?' she asked in a hoarse, sleepy voice. 'Have they found my mother's killer?'

'Maybe,' I said. 'But they're not sure.'

I went back downstairs with her and sat beside her bed in the dark until she was almost asleep, holding her hand. There was a charged quality to the silence; I felt there was something she wanted to tell me, but wasn't ready to speak.

Finally I leaned over to kiss her forehead. 'Good night, sweetie.'

'She knew my mother,' Dathi whispered.

'Who?'

'Abby. She knew my mother.'

I assumed Dathi was embellishing, weaving her old world with her new one, adding invented details to create a better picture. I knew how hard it was to think, starkly, in one *before* and another *after*, to accept that you had to let go of what was gone.

I didn't argue with her. I kissed her forehead. Shut her door and went back upstairs. The anchorman was back with the latest.

'In a new development on a roller-coaster night as police scramble to finally identify the serial murderer known to all of New York City as the Working Girl Killer, a close friend of the priest who was just arrested as a person of interest in the case has reportedly committed suicide. Public middle school teacher Steve Campbell was found by his wife just hours ago, hanging from a pipe outside the service entrance of his apartment in Carroll Gardens.'

A headshot of Steve Campbell popped onscreen, the kind taken by school photographers in front of a wavy blue background. It was presumably an old yearbook photo from an earlier era in his teaching career, because he looked a good decade younger than he had this afternoon. *Dead?* It was hard to process, having just seen him. He had seemed so happy and hopeful about the plans for Abby to move in.

The news anchor went on to report the little he could about Steve Campbell, which wasn't much. He had been found by Linda two hours ago. When the image of an unattended podium appeared on screen, and a voiceover said they were still waiting for the police chief to appear for a news conference, I turned off the TV. If the press had found out that the Campbells were Abby's guardians, and made any connection between her parents' deaths and the Working Girl Murders, they weren't saying.

Steve Campbell – was *he* the 'other priest'? I recalled my surprise at not seeing him anywhere near Father X during the arrest this afternoon. Had he sprinted off at the first sign of trouble? I could see it: something hidden suddenly revealed as a curtain is pulled back; the naked horror of being caught on a stage where you never wanted to be seen.

What was going on at that church?

Mac and I were both working our phones now, trying every number we could think of to find Billy. Mac was so frustrated to reach Billy's voice mail again that he threw his BlackBerry on the floor; the back popped off and flew across the living room. I held mine in my hand, squeezing it, as if I could force it to ring with the call I wanted.

Silent seconds blurred into silent minutes. Mac turned the TV back on and rewatched the relooped replay of the same story.

I badly wanted to talk to Dathi, to press her harder about whether Abby had told her anything else. But when I returned to her room and cracked open her door, I could hear by the slow rhythm of her breathing that she had finally fallen asleep. For a moment I thought about waking her up, but didn't have the heart.

CHAPTER 21

Not untypically, the morning clock ran ahead of us and there was no time to talk before Dathi had eaten, and was dressed and ready to run out the door to catch her bus. Our conversation would have to wait until after school. I wasn't sure what could be gained from it now, anyway; the investigations were heating up fast and whatever there was to find, they would find it – that was what I told myself. *Back off.*

After dropping Ben at nursery school, and like clockwork passing the Three Musketeers on their way along Smith Street to their morning bus, I watched them recede in the direction of Atlantic Avenue. Now that I knew who they were – now that they had names and backgrounds and challenges – they didn't repulse me anymore. They saddened me. Like a mother, I hoped for the best for them while bracing for the worst.

A siren caught my attention: A cop car driving along Smith turned sharply onto Bergen in the direction of Court Street – and St Paul's Church. Standing at the intersection, I looked up that way to try and see what was happening, but it was too far. All I could make out were parked cars and revolving police lights. It was no surprise that the investigation would have wrapped its arms around the church buildings by now, and dug a few tentacles behind the altar and every pew. I knew I should have minded my own business, but I couldn't resist walking up to Court Street, just to see.

Both the main entrance of the church and the rectory had been cordoned off with yellow crime scene tape, and pairs of uniforms stood guard.

'What's happening in there?' I asked the first cop I saw, as if I didn't know.

'Move along, please, ma'am.'

I walked around the corner to the Congress Street entrance, and asked again.

'Move along, lady.'

Across the snowy courtyard, through the leaded glass windows, I could see people moving around inside with a workaday efficiency: methodically searching, discussing last night's movie, imagining today's lunch. I recognized the young woman with the flowered boots from the task force. At this point, I pretty much knew that they'd be in there for hours, if not days, combing for anything that might be evidence in any of the three intertwined murder investigations. I wished I could go inside and be that proverbial fly on the wall. But even I knew there was just no way.

I decided to head over to Billy's. We still couldn't reach him, and I was worried. On my way there I texted Mac to let him know where I was going.

I walked along Bergen Street, crossing Third Avenue into a strip of newly constructed high-rise 'luxury' apartment buildings that were in the early stages of uniting two gentrified brownstone neighborhoods previously separated by industrial blight. Billy lived just on the other side, where Park Slope began.

'Karin!'

I turned around and there was Mac, breathless from jogging.

'I thought you were working that new case?' Another wayward husband, another angry wife, another bitter divorce in the making.

'Can't concentrate; I'm worried about Billy, too. Anyway, Mary's there and she's amazing. I've already got her skip tracing. She's a natural.'

We crossed Fourth Avenue onto Billy's block. He lived in a ground-floor studio apartment of a brownstone on St Mark's Place, just shy of Fifth Avenue. The building had a blue double door leading to the foyer and upper floors. Billy's entrance was below, separate from the other apartments. We opened the gate, passed through the small front area where the building's garbage cans were kept, and went down a few steps to ring his bell.

After a couple of tries, I put my hand through the bars on his front window and rapped on the glass with my knuckles. 'Billy? Are you there? Billy!'

'Looks like there's a light on.' Mac shaded his eyes to peer inside. Squinting, I saw the glow from a lamp in the living room, but it was hard to focus past your own reflection in the glare of sunlight. 'I think he's in there.'

The lock on Billy's outside door gate had been broken since we'd known him. Mac pushed it open, dug into his pocket, and took out the jackknife pick set he'd started carrying when he went into business for himself. I stood just outside while he got to work in the small, enclosed area between the inner and outer doors, deftly fiddling in the keyhole of the front doorknob until he found the right pick. The door popped open. I walked in behind Mac, closing the door behind us.

It was a large, open space: living room area on the street side, bedroom area on the garden side, galley kitchen in the middle. Two half-wall partitions split the spaces into almost-rooms; but it didn't matter where you stood in the apartment: You could see everything.

Scanning the living room, the kitchen, and then the bedroom, the realization of what I really feared crystallized: that I would find Billy hanging or slumped or splayed. We hadn't said it but it was why we were here: the possibility that his volatile misery may have lured him to the easy solution of ending his life. In the shadow of Steve Campbell's suicide, the prospect felt even more urgent: There was the catalyst of PTSD, and then there were the lurking, looming suspicions that Ladasha and George Vargas had planted in my mind that Billy could be working both sides of the murders. I did

331

not believe it. I knew that Mac didn't believe it, either. And yet it simmered inside me as an impossible possibility.

We opened closets. Pushed back the shower curtain. Got down on our knees and looked under Billy's double bed.

'He isn't here,' Mac said.

'What's that?' Over in the corner of his bedroom area there was a big shopping bag filled with a jumble of clothes. I pulled out the topmost piece: a low-cut purple shirt with an eye patterned out of rhinestones. The fabric felt cheap, and there was a noticeable rip along one seam and a smudge of lipstick along the neckline. 'Why does he have all this?'

I leaned closer to make sure I was right: the bag was filled with women's clothes: slinky gold leggings, black fishnets, skimpy halter tops, skirts so short they looked like strips of cloth. Old perfume wafted up out of the bag. I felt like vomiting.

'What's going on with him?' I dropped the purple top back into the bag.

'Strange.' But that was all Mac said, unwilling to put into words what we couldn't help thinking.

'Let's go talk to Dash,' I said.

'We should call her first.'

'I don't think so. If they turn this place into a circus and it comes to nothing, that's it for Billy.' His career would be over: unemployment by innuendo. 'Let's go over there and talk to her in person. Make sure.' I was tempted to bring the bag of clothes with us but knew better than to touch anything else. That was the moment I realized that I was still a cop (even if I wasn't one) before I was a friend. If those clothes had belonged to the victims, Billy was on his own.

My heart nearly stopped when we walked into the task force conference room at the Eight-four and there was Billy, leaning back in a swivel chair at the far end of the table, his muddy cowboy boots crossed at the ankle and propped on the table. George Vargas was sitting with him, studying something on the desktop computer. Ladasha was standing at the wall, looking at some photos I hadn't seen before, talking to a man who was taking notes.

'Jesus,' Mac muttered, when we walked in and saw him.

'Hey! Compadres!' Billy swung down his feet and leaned forward, smiling. 'What brings you to Dodge City?'

'We've been trying to reach you.' My tone was stern, almost accusatory, but I didn't regret it.

'Yeah, sorry. My battery ran out and my sister's basement flooded – a pipe burst in one of their bathrooms. I've been there helping them bail out. What a mess.' He stared at us, his smile fading. 'What's going on?'

I didn't know whether to be angry or relieved, but there wasn't time to decide, and it didn't matter now. 'Why do you have a bag of sleazy women's clothes in your bedroom?'

'Whoa!' Anger flashed across his face. 'You were in my apartment?'

Mac stepped forward to get between Billy and me. 'We were worried about you so we went over.'

I thought Billy was going to try to push past, but he didn't. Instead, he deflated. 'Those clothes were my niece's; they were hand-me-downs for Dathi – but forget it.'

'Janine lets her daughter dress like a streetwalker?'

Billy shot me a hard look. Someone across the room stifled laughter.

'You actually thought Dathi would wear that stuff?'

'I didn't even look in the bag, Karin. I just grabbed it and brought it home, dumped it off, and came to work.'

Ladasha spun to face him. 'Yo, Billy, we're *busy* here.'

'What the fuck, Dash? You just spent twenty minutes on the phone with one of your kids!'

'You disappear when all this is going on and you walk back in all *yo baby* and you think the rest of us who been here *all night long* shouldn't talk to their kids?'

'Gimme a break – I had the day off.'

'Well, it's not your day off now! Maybe you ought to tell your friends to visit some other time.'

George Vargas looked up from the computer; the stubble peppered across his shaved head glistened greenish under the fluorescent lighting.

Billy's pupil, sharp as a grain of sand, fixed on Ladasha. 'You know what, Dash? I am not your husband, in case you haven't noticed.'

Her eyes narrowed. 'I wouldn't marry you if you were the last man on earth.'

'Good. Then we agree on something.'

'Let's get out of here,' Mac whispered to me. 'We found him, and it looks like those clothes are—'

But just at that moment the young detective I'd spotted through the church windows came in carrying a cardboard box. 'Hey Karin, glad you're here; something I want to show you.' I didn't recall having actually met her, but Mac and I had taken on a kind of urban legend status around here, after the catastrophe with Jasmine a year and a half ago. She dropped the box on the table with a thud. 'I'm Sam, by the way. Detective Sam Wright.'

'*You're* Sam. Billy's mentioned you, but I thought—'

'Yeah' – she grinned – 'it's kinda cool having a guy's name. Well, it's really Samantha.'

'Mac,' he introduced himself. 'Karin's husband.'

'Great to meet you.' Sam shook his hand vigorously.

'What do you have there?' Vargas came around to peek into the box.

'Goodies,' Sam said.

Item by item, the box was unloaded: a laptop; three CDs in unmarked paper sleeves; a guest book; a stack of loose photographs; a locked metal box; a paper bag containing a comb trailing gray hairs; another paper bag with a used toothbrush inside; some crumpled-up tissues.

'Gotta get that laptop right over to CCU,' Vargas said.

Billy looked at Mac and me: 'Guess what? CCU traced a hacked user for Abby's Facebook account – it wasn't her operating it. The e-mail address routes through an overseas server with an IP in the Midwest. We haven't matched it to a hard disk but maybe . . .' He glanced at the scuffed black laptop that had been pulled from the box.

But that would take time; the computer would have to be logged and then sent over to the CCU. Meanwhile, other items in the box might yield instant gratification.

Mac used his lock-pick set to open the metal box.

When I saw what was inside, it was hard to believe what I was looking at. But pictures don't lie.

CHAPTER 22

Photographs: lots of them. Men, including Steve Campbell and Reed Dekker, aboard some kind of yacht, looking groggy and contented in their baggy short-sleeved Hawaiian shirts. Fishing poles. Beer bottles. Mixed drinks. And lots of children, some very young, some barely pubescent, scantily clad in bathing suits you wouldn't feel comfortable passing in a Victoria's Secret storefront. Wearing things that were supposed to be shirts but were more like scraps of cloth dripping off their mostly exposed bodies. Toothless smiles trying to look happy for the camera; dull eyes that revealed the disorientation of a situation that is innately surreal; children who were not children because their eyes said otherwise. Sitting on the men's laps, legs loose, hints of wandering hands, giddy drunken smiles, little shoulders tensed below stunned-smiling little faces. Children on beds. Naked.

I couldn't look at any more.

'Oh my God,' Sam mumbled.

Ladasha turned away, hiding a face distorted by

anguish, muttering, 'What is wrong with this crazy fucking world?'

'Steve Campbell mentioned something about annual boat trips off the coast of Brazil,' I remembered. 'His wife called them fishing trips – *the guys' time off* kind of thing.'

'Gross.' Sam grimaced.

'This is un-fucking-real,' Vargas muttered. 'You think you've seen it all – think again.'

Even Mac looked stunned, and he had seen a lot. Maybe these past few years, working mostly cases of errant spouses, he had forgotten how sordid it could get. I know I had. But the contents of the locked box reminded me how deep some people's undersides went, how malevolence could become a way of life.

Billy was last to move away from the box, shaking his head. 'Man, that is some crazy shit.' His tone was so soft, so low, you could hardly hear him.

Mac stepped closer to the group at the table now. 'Where were those fishing trips again?'

'Isn't Brazil a hub for the commercial sex trade?' A shadow seemed to fall across Vargas's face as it dawned on all of us. Suddenly I recalled some of the sordid facts I'd picked up researching trafficking, when I was deciding what to do about Dathi.

'It is,' I said, 'along with India, Africa, and Thailand. Those are the biggest markets. Victims are trafficked through from just about everywhere.'

'When I used to work domestic violence,' Sam

said, 'there were pimped girls who told us some of their friends got trafficked out, never seen again – poof. If the girls surfaced back in New York, we'd just arrest them. No one bothered the pimps or the johns. Nothing changed.'

'Load of *crap*.' Ladasha reset her tone to surly, but she wasn't fooling anyone.

'What about the hooker on Nevins?' Mac asked. 'Did her DNA ever match up with any missing kids?'

'I wish everyone would stop calling them *hookers*,' I blurted. Hookers. Whores. Sluts. The words were so ugly; but how did those women, sometimes just *girls*, earn those judgmental labels? There was a societal transaction, a collusion, that started as early as middle school if not sooner: Girls tarted themselves up for approval, and it went from there. But everyone was born innocent. It wasn't right.

'Yeah,' Ladasha backed me up. 'They're sex *workers*.'

'Technically speaking,' I said, 'they're commercial sex trade *victims*. Not workers; that isn't *work*.'

'People *pay* them,' Billy said.

'People pay *pimps*,' Ladasha argued. 'And people who do that ain't *people*. They're pigs.'

Billy raised a hand to rub his eyes. 'I'm just saying that's the perception, okay? I know you're right, but we're not here to change the world.'

'Why not?' But I was roundly ignored.

Billy finally answered a rephrased version of Mac's question: 'No, the *commercial sex trade victim* on Nevins didn't hit as a missing kid. She doesn't show up in our system at all.'

'Buddy of mine is a cop in Brazil – Rio,' Vargas said. 'I'm giving him a call, get him to look for her over there. And I'll check Interpol, too.' The International Criminal Police Organization. Suddenly there was an elephant in the room: Why hadn't anyone thought of running the Working Girl Victims through Interpol before?

'Tell him to check the system for the other ones, too,' Ladasha said.

Vargas flipped open his cell phone, shaking his head. 'All those missing kids who found their way home just to get themselves killed by some psycho with a hunting knife.'

'You still think it was *some psycho*, George?' Ladasha's voice bubbled with frustration as she seemed to realize, along with everyone else on the task force, what I had suspected for a while now: that it wasn't your garden-variety serial killer they were hunting. The person who had killed those women, and possibly the Dekkers, too, wasn't the likes of Patrick Scott, trolling for sexual thrills, or Antonio Neng, stalking a banker in vengeance. It was someone with a secret he was desperate to hide.

Someone like Father X. Reed Dekker. Steve Campbell. The other men in the creepy photos.

And the secret had just peeked out at us from inside a little metal box.

Vargas reached his friend on the phone and

launched into a conversation in Portuguese that eluded me, but the urgency in his tone was unmistakable.

'What I don't understand,' I thought aloud, 'is what Chali had to do with any of this. I'm sure she was never trafficked – not like that, anyway. She was sold into marriage when she was thirteen, but by the time her husband died, she was a mother, and she came here to work as a babysitter not long after. How does she fit in?'

Sam went over to the box and pulled out the church's guest book. 'I was looking at this before' – she flipped through pages as she walked over to me – 'and there's something I wanted to show you.'

She edged the tip of her short-bitten fingernail beneath a name in the guest book: *Chali Das*. I recognized the painstaking handwriting. It was dated the last day I saw her. Under 'Reason for Visit,' she had written: *Confession*.

'I didn't think Chali ever went to church near our house,' I said. 'She used to mention a church in her neighborhood. She loved talking about it; she was pretty religious. I'm sure she would have mentioned it if she went to St Paul's or knew Father X.'

Billy stood behind Sam and together they fanned through the rest of the book. 'Nothing,' he said. 'It looks like that was the only time she went there, or at least the only time she signed in.'

'Chali was a stickler for rules,' I said. 'If she

signed the guest book once, she would have signed it every time.'

That was the day Billy and I discovered the Dekkers' bodies. The night Billy received his award. Chali had been with Ben all afternoon and evening . . . had she taken him with her to visit the church? I felt a shiver of cold, imagining that.

'Maybe she didn't go for confession,' Vargas said. 'Maybe she went to talk to Father X. He'd be the one sitting in the confession booth, right?'

'That's what they told us over at St Paul's.' Sam closed the book.

'She told me she needed to talk to me.' I walked around the table to stand in front of the gory montage, scanning it for new clues, fresh under-standings. My gaze landed on the photo of Chali, dead in her apartment, and I remembered Dathi, just last night, telling me that Abby had known Chali – insisting on it: 'She knew my mother.'

I turned to look at Mac and Billy. 'I need to check something at home. And then we need to talk to Dathi – I think Abby might have told her other important things we should know.' I looked at my watch: It was almost noon; Dathi would be home in a few hours.

No one was home when we got there but you could see that Mary and Ben had stopped in for lunch: a frying pan that hadn't been there earlier was drying in the dish drainer; evidently she had cooked him something before heading out to his music class.

'Chali kept a calendar here.' I pulled open the crowded kitchen drawer.

'Why?'

'She'd forget hers at home sometimes.' I found the pocket-sized calendar and started leafing through the pages. 'She did odd jobs for people around the neighborhood occasionally, babysitting, cleaning . . . I'm wondering if . . . *Here.*' I showed him the page for July 24. '"Marta Dekker, six P.M., 234 Bergen, Abby." She *did* know Chali!' I flipped through the rest of the calendar, but there were no other entries for the Dekkers. 'It looks like it was just that one time.'

'What did Chali want to tell Father X?' Mac wondered aloud.

'Dathi also said Abby told her that "her mother" was coming back for her. It sounded like a fantasy to me – Abby never spoke. But what if Abby really *was* talking to Dathi? What if she *did* tell her things that were true? What if she told her all about . . .'

It was hard to voice what we'd seen in those photographs of Reed Dekker and Steve Campbell. But having seen them, beginning to realize now the stark probability that Abby's father was not an innocent victim in his own murder, it was impossible not to wonder if, and how, she might have been victimized. It made me sick to think it. But the way she reacted around adults, the recognizable signs and symptoms of having been traumatized . . . it was all right there on her face, and in her silence. Had Chali stumbled onto something the night she babysat, something that clicked for her later, after the Dekkers were killed? She had been agitated the last time I saw her; she had needed to tell me something. Had she tried to talk to Father X about it? A priest – she would have trusted him without question. Had that turned out to be a fatal mistake?

'And to think that Abby was supposed to go live with the Campbells tomorrow.' A shudder ran through me. 'Steve Campbell – Mr Nice, a *teacher*. I'm glad he's dead.'

Mac went to the cupboard to get a clean glass and filled it with water at the sink. 'I can't get over it – I *knew* Reed Dekker. Well, I sort of knew him. But one thing he did not strike you as was a pervert. He was a stand-up guy. Remember I came home from the gym that time, saying we should invite them over for dinner?'

'I remember. What else did everyone who knew those people not see?'

'What time does Dathi get home from school?' Mac asked me.

'Three-thirty, three thirty-five, depending on the bus. Maybe we should pull her out early.'

'What for? We're solving a crime, not stopping one.'

'How do we know that?'

'The damage is done, Karin. Dathi's boat's been

rocked enough. This can wait a couple more hours.'

I hoped he was right.

Mary came home with Ben just after two-thirty. We filled her in, and we all waited together. And waited.

Three-thirty came and went. Four o'clock. Four-thirty. At four thirty-two, I called the school, only to be told without a moment's hesitation, by whoever answered the office phone, that all the kids had left the building together at three o'clock today just as always.

I hung up the phone and looked at Mary and Mac, whose expectant faces watched me, waiting to hear that all was well.

'Something's wrong,' I said. 'I feel it. Mac, why haven't we gotten her a cell phone yet?'

'It doesn't help to think that now.' But I could tell by the tension rippling across his forehead that he wasn't as calm as he sounded.

'We could have called her, at least. We could have tracked her via satellite—'

'I think we should go together to see Abby,' Mary said suddenly. 'No police. Just you and me, Karin. No men.'

Mac nodded soberly; Mary had a point: Abby switched to mute every time a man came near her. It was worth a try, especially if her silence had anything to do with a fear of Steve Campbell or Father X, who were no longer a threat. I wondered if she knew that.

'Leave a note for Dathi here,' I told Mac. 'Give Ben his scooter and go out on foot, retrace her bus route, see if you find her anywhere along the way. Maybe the bus broke down. Maybe she got off. Maybe she's lost.'

Ten minutes later, Mary and I were in a taxi racing up the FDR, paying the driver extra to go as fast as he could.

CHAPTER 23

We pushed through the revolving doors at the hospital's main entrance so fast it kept turning after we'd rushed into the lobby. Waiting for the elevator to arrive felt like a small eternity. But finally . . . finally . . . we were at Abby's bedside.

She cracked a tiny smile when she saw me. At the sight of Mary, a stranger, she stiffened.

Mary moved back until she was standing almost against the wall.

'Abby, honey,' I said. 'Did anyone tell you yet that you won't be going to the Campbells?'

Abby shook her head. I could have sworn she brightened at the news, just a bit, but enough to embolden me to continue – gently.

'Steve died.'

She didn't appear upset; on the contrary. I plunged forward.

'And Father X was arrested.'

A simple nod.

'We're starting to figure it out.'

She closed her eyes.

'Are you ready to talk, sweetheart?'

I couldn't tell if she was retreating into her hard, lonely silence, if she really *couldn't* talk, or if she was thinking it over. I turned to look at Mary, deciding on a different tack, and beckoned her forward.

'Abby.' I spoke softly, carefully. 'This is my friend Mary. She's a mom, too.'

Abby opened her eyes. Mary smiled warmly, making sure not to come too close. Her hands floated open in a gesture of friendship, and I was taken off guard by the dime-sized tattoos in both her palms: a flower in her right palm, a smiley face in her left. I hadn't noticed them before. It occurred to me that she was offering them to Abby, showing them, so she would have to ask.

Abby's gaze fixed on the tattoos, shifting between them like a metronome.

'This one,' Mary said, 'the lotus, symbolizes detachment from your surroundings. Plus I think it's really pretty.' Her whole face smiled, melting a layer of Abby's wariness; Abby leaned closer to see the other hand. 'The smiley is a reminder not to worry too much.'

Suddenly Abby laughed: a chain of tinkling bells that skipped out of her with surprising ease. One hand, the blue polish now chipped mostly off, flew up to cover her mouth.

But we'd heard it – the beautiful, miraculous sound of her voice.

'Abby,' I said, 'Dathi told me yesterday that you've been talking to her. We can't find her anywhere. Can you help?'

Abby's gaze flickered across my face.

'*Please* talk to me. Tell me anything you told her that might help us know where to look.'

She took a deep breath, and locked her eyes to my face with resolve. You could feel the tendrils of a conversation about to start. I came in closer.

'My mother has a nose ring.' Her voice was small at first, tender, hesitant. 'An itty bitty diamond or something.' She reached up to touch the outside of her right nostril.

But I'd seen pictures of Marta and didn't remember a nose ring; it would have stood out on a banker's wife.

'She came that night. She wanted to know where Daddy kept his things, so she could get the ones that were hers. She wanted them back. And she wanted *me*.'

'But you lived with your mother,' I said. 'What do you mean?'

Abby stared at me, appearing to realize the breadth of what we didn't know, what she'd have to explain. 'Marta wasn't my real mom. They said she was, but she wasn't.'

'I'm confused, Abby.'

'Marta was Daddy's wife.'

'Your mother – who is she?'

'Daddy had lots of kids, but we didn't always know each other. But my mom remembered me, and she came back to get me, and also to get her stuff, 'cause she wanted it back. I knew where it was. I found it a long time ago, but no one knew I knew. I pretended I didn't know. I was scared.'

I felt as if we were going in circles; but Abby was trying, finally, to tell us something. And I had to listen patiently and carefully until I understood.

'Who's your mom?'

'Tina.' She said it carefully, like turning a candy in her mouth. 'I never met her before that. She's so pretty.'

'Do you know where she is now?' But suddenly I knew the answer, even if Abby didn't: the dead woman on Nevins Street; I could still see the tiny sparkle of her nose ring in the dark. If I were Abby, if I had had a long-lost mother who came back for me out of the blue, I would run barefoot at midnight on a winter night to follow her, too. But if I was right, if the murdered woman I'd seen that night was Tina, why did Abby think there was a chance she'd come back? The car must have hit her before Tina was attacked, in which case she wouldn't know that *both* her mothers were dead.

'What happened that night when Tina came to get you?'

Abby's voice started small and thin, gaining confidence the more she spoke, as if issuing the memories robbed them of their power to terrify her. 'They had an argument. Tina accused Daddy of tricking her. She said he stole me from her. She said Mommy, Marta, needed to know where I really came from. Mommy got *so mad* when she heard what Tina told her.' Abby's eyes slammed shut, but she kept talking. 'She called him lots of names. I hated him, too, so I didn't care.' Her chest began to quiver and then shake, and then sobs rose up in waves. I leaned over to hold her, and she let me. 'Tina got scared and left. I ran after to tell her I knew where her things were. I could show them to her. She could have them back. But it was dark and I got lost and I had to find her.'

After a few minutes, when Abby had calmed down, she said, 'I asked Dathi to get Tina's things for me, from the place where Daddy kept them under the stairs. So when she comes back for me, I'll have them for her. Dathi told me she'd do it; she'd go at lunchtime, it would just be a quick errand, and then she'd go right back to school.'

'Honey.' I spoke softly, knowing that sometimes the most obvious questions were the hardest to answer. 'Why didn't you tell us all that?'

'I was afraid if I told' – her voice was so small – 'I'd be like the girls in the pictures, when Uncle Steve got me home. Daddy never hurt me because I kept quiet. At least I think that's why. I never really knew.'

CHAPTER 24

The first call I made, as soon as Mary and I were in a taxi speeding back to Brooklyn, was to Dathi's school to find out if she had ever come back after lunch. The school had an open lunch policy, during which kids were let out for an hour. Attendance was taken twice a day, in the morning and after lunch. I waited a few minutes while a school secretary put me on hold, then heard exactly what I expected:

'She was here on time for A.M. attendance, but she wasn't marked in for P.M. attendance.'

'Why didn't anyone call to tell me she never got back to school after lunch?'

There was a pause. A sigh. 'We don't always call. But we keep a record.'

Which apparently the person who answered the phone when I'd called earlier hadn't bothered to check. What was the point of all that record keeping if you weren't going to use it?

Next I tried to call Mac, to tell him to look for Dathi at the Dekker house. But he didn't answer his cell phone and he didn't answer at home, either.

I thought of calling Billy, but decided against it. But I did call his sister; something had been bothering me and I wanted to find out. I tapped my phone's Web browser and in moments located her number through the online white pages.

'Hi Janine, I'm Karin,' I introduced myself, 'a friend of Billy's?'

'Oh, sure. He's told us all about you. Your little boy sounds like a hoot.'

'He is.'

'Little boys that age – yummy.'

'Janine, thanks so much for the hand-me-downs for Dathi. She needs clothes. We really appreciate it.'

'Don't mention it; sorry it isn't more. I hope she doesn't mind Catholic school chic.' She laughed. But I thought it was a strange thing to say.

'Dathi's trying to be more American,' I said, 'though maybe not *that* American.'

'You telling me she's too uptight for a navy blue skirt with pleats and a matching sweater?'

'Oh – I didn't see those.'

'The good thing about school uniforms is you don't have to fuss about shopping, except for a few weekend clothes. The bad thing is, no one wants most of it afterward, except other Catholic schoolgirls. But I figured the skirt and sweater were versatile and Dathi could probably use them.'

'Thank you. By the way, I'm wondering if Billy's there; I've been trying to find him.'

'Billy? No.'

'He'd mentioned helping you bail out from a broken pipe – what a nightmare.'

There was a pause. And then: 'We just got back from Jamaica this morning. All our pipes seem fine.'

I fudged my way out of the rest of the conversation. cutting it short. I had what I needed to know: Billy had lied about where he'd been yesterday and last night, why he'd been incommunicado. And that bag of trashy clothes – they hadn't belonged to his niece, from the sound of it.

I called the Eight-four conference room and asked for Ladasha.

'Oh Jesus, Karin. What do you want now?'

'Dathi might be in trouble.'

'Honey, I got five kids, and I can tell you I never knew a teenager who *wasn't* in trouble.'

'She's only twelve.'

'Same difference.'

'Listen to me, Dash. Dathi didn't go back to school after lunch today. I just talked to Abby and—'

'You *talked* to Abby?'

'Yes. I'll tell you everything later. But right now, we need to find Dathi.'

I rattled off everything Abby had told us. What worried me now was that other men were involved, besides Reed Dekker and Steve Campbell, who were dead and harmless, or Father X, who was in jail. The question was: Who were the other men in the photos?

354

'Dash, maybe you already know this – but don't tell Billy for now, okay?'

She sighed, or snorted, or a combination of both. 'Yeah. I got that one figured out.'

'Can you get over to the Dekker house to check?'

'I'm on it.'

'See you in a few minutes – on my way.'

The cab pulled up in front of the quiet brownstone that exuded a forlorn abandonment. The windows were dark. Recent snowfalls had buried the house in untouched swaths of white, thick bands of it edging the roof and the lintels above each window and the front door. A narrow path of packed snow had been trampled by the inevitable stream of passersby. I was surprised that none of the neighbors had shoveled the sidewalk, knowing that the Dekkers were gone and the house was unoccupied now. They must have thought it was still a crime scene, and therefore shouldn't be touched, though that in fact was not true.

Mary and I got out, and the cab drove away. A few people walked by on either side of the street, but mostly it was quiet and peaceful. Evening was quickly descending, sucking away all the light.

'Where are they?' I snapped. Ladasha had told me she was 'on it.' By the look of it, no one was on it. And I wouldn't fool myself by thinking anyone had come and gone – the pristine blanket of snow up the front stoop said otherwise.

'Look at that.' Mary pointed at the snow-covered front yard leading to the ground-floor entrance.

You could just make out, in the thickening twilight, a steady trail of smallish footprints.

We opened the half gate and entered the yard, where a large flowerpot was mostly buried in snow.

'It looks like someone was digging behind the pot,' Mary said.

When we came closer, you could see that a hand had burrowed all the way to the bottom by the back. On one side, settled lightly across the top of the snow, there were bits of snapped-off twigs from the dead plant in the pot.

'The pot was tilted over,' I said. 'Abby must have told her where to find a key.'

The outside lower gate was unlocked; it opened to an easy push. The inner door, however, was locked, but with the kind of flimsy doorknob locks you tended to find inside on hollow doors. A lot of the brownstones still had those, relying for safety on the heavy iron exterior gate. I wished I had Mac's lock-pick set, but I didn't.

I fisted my hand in my leather glove and punched through the pane of glass closest to the knob. The glass shattered. After knocking out the jagged teeth of broken glass, I reached in and turned the pinch lock.

'When are people going to learn not to use these cheap doorknobs?' I said to Mary.

'Well, *I* won't, that's for sure.'

It was still and quiet inside the house. The low-ceilinged ground floor, with its carpeted hall and three doors off a narrow hallway, looked as if it had served as the Dekkers' utilitarian space: work-rooms, guest room, storage.

Dathi's black sneakers, wet from tracking through the unshoveled snow to the door, sat side by side, neatly, by the wall. It was too quiet. Was someone with her? Had he heard us come in?

'Shh,' I cautioned Mary, whispering: 'Check the rooms down here. Abby said "under the stairs," so keep that in mind. I'll go up.'

I went upstairs to the parlor floor. Light from a passing car outside shimmered on the high, ornate ceiling. The round glass coffee table had gathered a thick coat of dust as undisturbed as the snowy front stoop. Something I hadn't noticed last time I was here popped out at me: a cookbook had been left open on the couch, a pair of reading glasses hooked over the topmost page. I wondered what the Dekkers had been doing that Sunday night when Tina appeared at their front door. It struck me how shocked Marta must have been – a doorbell setting in motion the abrupt destruction of her world. But had she really been an innocent bystander? It was hard to understand how, living with such a man, you would fail to notice or even suspect that something was seriously amiss. It seemed beyond reason. But in these cases there were really only two choices: She was either deluded beyond the pale, or his accomplice.

There was no sign of anyone else here. I started to relax; then warned myself not to.

Hidden under the stairs, Abby had said.

I looked around.

As in all brownstones, a staircase zigzagged up the flights, this one rising in elegant bends of polished banister. I walked to the bottom of the stairs and looked up, thinking it was possible that one of the steps opened; but for the kinds of things these men had been up to, such a small hiding place seemed unlikely. Careful to avoid the orange-and-red vase on the pedestal near the foot of the stairs, I slowly walked the length of the wall that sided the staircase on the parlor floor, where old-fashioned carved wood paneling had been restored to a dull luster, a decorative checkerboard landscape of circles within squares within larger squares. It was the kind of pattern you'd imagine a young child taking the time to count the parts of, but you'd have to really concentrate or you'd lose track; there was no way to ascertain the number of circles at a glance. I stood there, staring at the hypnotic repetition. Each circle was ringed by two other circles, and had a convex center.

Stepping closer, I moved my fingertips along the surface of the nearest circle, dipping toward the center. They were like inverted buttons. How many hands, over how many decades, had explored the crevices of the pattern? The longer I looked at it, the more I saw: a dozen circles graced each panel, and each panel was the size of approximately half a door. Between each panel was a hairline separation so thin it was barely visible.

When I was a child, Jon and I would spend hours

exploring our grandparents' big old Victorian house in Montclair. When we eventually moved in, we discovered on our own that there were secret compartments built into the house in seemingly random places; Grandma and Grandpa always denied it, but with a sly wink. By the time we outgrew our curiosity about secret places, we had mapped every one of those compartments in our minds. Some had slender handles that would lift up leverlike out of the edge of a panel, while others popped open on tension springs if you pushed them just right.

I pressed all along the edges of the closest panel. Nothing moved. Stepping right, I kept trying until one sprang open to my touch.

CHAPTER 25

Inside was a musty compartment piled with bike helmets, tennis rackets, a bucket, a coil of hose still in its packaging – the kind of random stuff a family accumulated over time. The stink of decay was terrible; it was the same smell I recalled from my first apartment in Brooklyn where mice had died in the walls. It was too dark to see across the entire space, but I thought it was worth a look, so I went to the kitchen and rooted around until I found a flashlight in a drawer along with other household tools: a ball of twine, packing tape, a stapler.

Illuminated, I now saw everything, and realized that this was where the family stored a lot of its shoes: white sneakers in various sizes; high-heeled black leather boots; Crocs in different sizes and colors; purple rain boots; large brown suede Desert boots, edged with mud. I couldn't resist knocking one over with the flashlight to see inside: My heart jittered when I saw a whitish *10* imprinted on the leather interior. I swung the flashlight to the pile of sneakers and was sure I spotted at least one pair of men's New Balance. I didn't remember the exact model of sneaker Ladasha had mentioned matched the footprint at many of the crime scenes, but I remembered they were a size 10 and sometimes, instead of sneakers, the killer had worn Desert boots.

I was about to back out of the space and call Ladasha when I thought I heard something knocking around inside. I swept the flashlight back and forth, but saw nothing new. A live mouse must have been trapped behind a wall. With no one living here anymore, the place must have become infested.

But then I heard something that with certainty was *not* a mouse.

'Hello? Is someone there?' The voice was small and muted; but I recognized it.

'Dathi?'

'Karin – in here!'

'Where?'

'Push the inside wall, the one with the sticker.'

Three quarters of the way up the back wall of the crawl space, along the far left edge, was a decal from a bank. It looked innocuous enough, as if stuck there accidentally by a mischievous child; but when I pressed it, I could feel that it was in fact covering some kind of hardware.

The inner wall sprang open in my direction, just an inch, but enough for me to get my fingers through. I pulled it open and shone the flashlight into the darkness: and there was Dathi, cross-legged, the top of her head touching the low slanted ceiling. You could see from her puffy face that she had been crying.

'I shut the door behind me so no one would see me, and I couldn't open it again. Abby didn't warn me.'

'Who was going to see you in here?'

'I don't know. She told me to be careful. Look.'

I swept the light across the space beyond her and saw how far back it went, diminishing to a sharp angle at its deepest point. Shoeboxes were stacked against the wall, along with some larger boxes that looked worn with age. Nothing was labeled, and Dathi had opened a few of them, assumedly to find what she had been sent for.

Her hands shook as she held up a flimsy book of photographs, the kind drugstores used to give you for free when you had your prints developed there. 'These are Abby's baby pictures with her mother – her real mother. They are so much like my own baby pictures: our mothers were both girls.'

Then, from the floor beside her, Dathi picked up a cloth doll, the color so faded it looked almost white, the fabric of its face so thin there were no features, just a blank webbing through which you could see clumps of stuffing. 'I think this is the doll Abby meant. She said it was her mother's, and then hers. I had to find it in the pictures first. The *other* pictures, Karin . . . in the other boxes.' Her expression froze in a denial of whatever it was she had seen in the photographs.

Behind her, photos lay scattered across the floor where she had emptied shoeboxes, searching. It looked like more of the same kind of filth that was in the metal lockbox from the church. But this time I caught a glimpse of two things that made my insides quiver: In at least two photos, there were black-robed men, like priests, wearing the kind of white Halloween mask Joey Esposito had described; in another photo, you could see the arched back of a young girl with long brown fingers curved around her middle like a cage.

She whispered, 'Thank you so very much for saving me, for bringing me from India, so I wouldn't have to . . . Well, I am worried about Oja.'

'Oja's family will protect her.'

'Why didn't my family protect me?'

'We'll discuss that later.' Instead of launching into vitriol about Uncle Ishat, I reached in to pull her out. Her hand was tacky-wet, as if it had touched something syrupy.

Before she had moved more than a few inches, we were startled by the clacking of footsteps.

'That's just Mary,' I whispered.

But something felt wrong. Mary was wearing crepe-soled boots; her steps would be spongy, not the hard clomps of what resonated across the wood floor of the foyer, coming closer.

'Karin?' Mary's voice sounded distant – she was calling up from the bottom of the ground-floor staircase. She must have heard the footsteps, too.

The walking stopped.

'I'm scared,' Dathi began to say.

I pressed my hand over her mouth. Shut off the flashlight. Pulled the inner door closed; it locked with a click, trapping us both inside. We listened as someone rooted around the exterior crawl space.

'Oh shit.'

It was Billy.

I pressed harder against Dathi's mouth: *Not a sound.*

'*Motherfucker.*' He sounded bitterly angry.

'Billy?' You could hear Mary's voice in the near distance, beyond the wall.

There was some jostling in the crawl space as Billy backed away. You could hear him exit the space, his unbalanced footing as he came to standing.

'Mary! What're you doing here?'

'I came with—' She stopped talking so abruptly I thought my heart would explode.

There were a few loud clomps of Billy's hard footsteps. The sound of something heavy falling.

'Oh man, what were you thinking?' you could just hear Billy mumble. 'That is definitely not good.'

If he had hurt Mary . . . *if he had hurt her . . .* Furious, I looked at Dathi and mimed a fast zipping across my lips: *Keep quiet.* Then I released her, grabbed the flashlight, leaned as far back as I could – and kicked open the inner door. The wood shattered. I kicked twice more to push away the shards and create a big enough opening to crawl through. Then I hunched forward and sprang out of the crawl space.

Billy and Mary both stood there gaping at me. On the floor between them lay jagged pieces of orange and red glass, remnants of what had been, until moments ago, a slender vase.

'Karin!' Billy said. 'What the hell?'

'Ditto.'

'I came to look for Dathi – and for you.'

'Why?'

'Because I was *worried*. What, do you think you have a monopoly on caring about your friends?'

'How did you know to come here?'

'Did you think . . . oh, fucking Dash. What a piece of work. What did she say to you?'

'How did you know to come here?' I asked again.

'Sasha Mendelssohn up at the hospital's been talking to Abby. She called me.'

'Billy,' I spit it out, 'I called your sister and—'

'Yeah, she told me.' He sighed. 'Okay, I lied to you about her pipes breaking. I had something to think about and I needed to get away, all on my own; I didn't want to talk about it with anyone. I went out to Greenport on the North Fork. Got drunk. Took some long walks. Shook some cobwebs out of my head.'

'You're sure that one's true?'

'Why wouldn't it be?'

'Those sleazy women's clothes in your apartment.'

Disbelief crossed his face like a shadow. 'Oh *no*. Is that what you were thinking? Karin, seriously, you thought *that*? About *me*?'

'Dash and George Vargas, they've been investigating you. The way you've been falling apart at crime scenes, well, they thought maybe it was more than PTSD.'

'Yeah, I know. I found out about it this morning after you left. I had it out with her. It was bullshit, what they were doing. I could probably sue them for harassment, you know? But I won't. I just want out.'

If he was saying he'd had enough of police work, good for him; but this wasn't the time to have that conversation.

'Billy, what are those clothes?'

'I am not the killer, Karin.'

The look on his face: I wanted to believe him. And yet I knew that if he were a true sociopath, proficient with the kind of manipulation and deception he'd have to be capable of to pull that off, then he'd still be doing now what he'd mostly always done in the past: convincing me he was a good person, my true friend.

'What about those clothes, Billy?' Gently, this time.

'I'm telling you: Janine gave me a bag of stuff for Dathi. It was last week, before they went on vacation. I brought it home. Put it in my place. Went to work.' His eyes rolled up, as if remembering something, and he dug his cell phone out

366

of his jeans pocket. He pressed a speed dial and waited for an answer. 'Eartha? It's Uncle Billy. That bag of hand-me-downs sitting in the hall by the front door, last time I was visiting – did you put some other stuff in there before I took off?' He listened, his face lighting with humor. 'Uh-huh, yeah, thanks honey.'

Mary and I glanced at each other: truth or dare? How could we be sure he was really talking to his niece? It would be easy enough to find out later, if necessary . . . and he knew it. Which pretty much convinced me. Billy was complicated these days, but he wasn't stupid.

'Costumes from her school play. She thought the bag was going to Goodwill; she didn't know her mom was passing the stuff on to anyone to actually wear.'

'What was the play?'

His smile broadened. '*Rent.* Satisfied?'

'You really didn't notice what was in the bag, Billy?' It was hard to believe, given how flashy the clothes were. 'It didn't strike you as the kind of stuff Eartha doesn't usually wear?'

He shrugged his shoulders. 'Honestly, Karin, I didn't notice. I didn't even look; I just grabbed the bag and left. I haven't been in the greatest state of mind lately. I've been missing a lot of details.'

I knew it was true; and just like that, whatever doubts I may have grudgingly nursed about him evaporated.

'I'm sorry, Billy, I—'

'Karin, forget it. Let's just get past this, please. Let's find Dathi.'

'I am here!' She must have been hovering in the crawl space, waiting for the right moment to come out. She emerged, crawling, with a shaky smile on her round face. I wished she didn't think she had to be so brave all the time. She had just spent hours locked in a putrid space filled with child pornography. She had every right to protest in any way she felt like; but Dathi, being Dathi, wouldn't.

She came to my side. I put my arm around her shoulders and kissed the top of her head.

'How did you find me?' she asked.

'Abby.'

'She told me not to tell anyone; she was very afraid of Mr Campbell.'

'He can't hurt her anymore.' I noticed Dathi's hands, which had been sticky when they touched me before in the dark: Some of her fingers and part of her right hand looked blackish red. 'Dathi, are you bleeding?'

She shook her head. 'There's a box, inside is a plastic bag, but it wasn't tied very well. There are some items of clothing inside the bag, some a little bit damp. I smelled mildew.'

I stared at her a moment, horrified – what had she stuck her hand into? My mind flew to the photographs on the task force wall: all those young women, brutally murdered, partially dressed, each missing an item of clothing. I pulled Dathi close.

'Karin,' Billy said, 'let me have that flashlight.'

Mary stayed in the hall with Dathi while I followed him to the crawl space. I could hear them chatting, Mary trying to distract her from the bitter truth she would eventually know by heart: that it wasn't just her, but girls everywhere who were in danger. She and Abby had more in common than she had imagined. I only hoped this wouldn't sour Dathi on her hopes for her new life in America; things *would* be better for her here, despite all this. She would learn to absorb and navigate the complications, some of them paradoxical, over time.

Billy got to his knees and crawled in. I crawled in behind him.

There was barely enough room for both of us to squeeze together through the second, smaller door. He jostled the flashlight in and forward, switched it on, and swung it back and forth in the small space.

And then we saw the box.

The partially faded stamp on the side of the old cardboard read *Stark Bowie #23 (MS-63)*.

He held the light on those words: There it was.

He had finally found his killer – a man who had been dead for three weeks.

Which meant that someone else had killed Chali, thus the copycat knife. Trying to make it look as if the Working Girl killer had finally run out of his signature weapon? Someone who had been determined to carry on the legacy? What had Chali seen or heard or thought or discovered that night she'd spent with Abby in this house? Why hadn't she mentioned something sooner?

'I wonder if there are any knives left in there,' I said.

Billy scooted forward on his knees, his head hunched to accommodate the sloping ceiling. Fingers shaking, he pried apart the four folded flaps.

'Billy, you're getting your prints over everything.'

'Fuck it,' he said. That was when I knew for sure that he had given up on being a cop.

I pressed in beside him as he maneuvered the flashlight so we could see inside the box.

At least a dozen small, narrow boxes were nestled neatly together at the bottom, each imprinted with a Stark logo in a fattened italic that had been modern in the 1960s and was retro now. Billy reached in with his free hand.

'I don't think you should,' I warned. If he touched anything else, put his fingerprints on one of the boxes housing an individual knife, it would be even worse for him.

He pulled his hand out.

The light flashed off suddenly.

We backed out of the interior crawl space and sat back, hunched among the now disarranged pile of the Dekkers' stuff. I knelt across from him, hands on knees, about to get up. And then he looked at me. I looked at him. We stared at each other in the kind of empty silence you feel sitting on the beach when another winter is behind you and you're not sure what to make of the murky distance of an indistinguishable horizon.

CHAPTER 26

M aybe it shouldn't have, but it felt like an honor when Mac and I were invited back to the task force the next morning to witness Billy and Ladasha's interrogation of Father Ximens Dandolos; after two days of stubborn silence, he had finally agreed to talk. Though in fact it was not so much an honor as a practicality: Having unofficially met and spoken with Eddie Walczak and Joey Esposito, Mac and I were in a position to know things the task force didn't. Transcripts could not replace the nuances of a face-to-face conversation. And so, just in case something Father X said triggered a connection that might otherwise be missed, we were there to listen and observe. After that, we promised to 'keep our noses out of it,' in Ladasha's words.

We sat behind the one-way glass separating the Eight-four's dingy interrogation room from a row of chairs in what felt like a closet. In front of us – me, Mac, Sam, and George – Billy and Ladasha prepared.

It started like a show, in a way: You shuffled your chair around, sound-checked the video recorder, made sure your bra wasn't sticking out of your V-neck sweater and tossed your coiled hair extensions back off your shoulders (if you were Ladasha), straightened your belt and took a long sip of water (if you were Billy), generally and dramatically ignoring Father X on the other side of the stained, scratched table. You made the interviewee nervous by delaying the start of something dreaded, in a reverse psychology that was part torture, part payback, part groundwork. Basically, you tried to seize the power before they did. There was a lot at stake: You were fighting for the truth, but the guy on the other side of the table was fighting for his life.

Father X waited in his chair, squarely facing them, sitting straight, his hands folded together on the table. In the orange jumpsuit, stripped of the authority of his collar, he looked frailer and older than I had seen him before. His hair was greasy and thin across his freckled scalp. Dark purple bags weighed down his eyes. Even from where I sat, behind the glass, his fingernails looked long and ragged.

'Ready?' Billy asked Ladasha.

'Ready.'

He switched on the video camera and she recited aloud the details of the day and hour, and listed who was present in the room. And then they began.

'Okay,' Ladasha said to Father X, 'talk.'

He took a deep breath and sighed so deeply, it sounded like a wave crashing to shore on our side of the microphone. He closed his eyes, gathering himself one last time, and then opened them.

'Where do you want me to begin?'

'At the beginning,' Billy said calmly. 'We have as much time as we need. There's no rush.'

Father X cleared his throat. 'I met Reed and Marta Dekker about ten years ago, when they joined St Paul's. They had just moved to the neighborhood, bought a house, and were settling in. Reed was a banker; despite everything, he was a very smart man.'

Ladasha rolled her eyes, and tapped her pen hard, twice, against the side of the table. 'Skip the fan club bullshit, okay?'

'Hey, Dash.' Billy touched her arm to calm her. She shot him a look. But something told me they were working together on this. Billy was going to be the listening ear for Father X, Ladasha the provocateur teasing his anger – she was good at that. 'Sorry about that, Father. Go on.'

'Abby was about a year old, and Reed and Marta had just gotten married. Reed was a widower. That was what he told us all, even Marta: He said that his first wife had died in childbirth, and Abby was their baby. Eventually I found out the truth.' His eyes clamped shut a moment, then he continued, 'Reed and Steve had been running their trips to Brazil for years. They got girls from wherever they could, including local traffickers, it didn't matter how. Tina was one of the kids from here. He liked her in particular. When she became pregnant by him, he kept his eye on her where she was living, in a slum in Rio where they had set up an orphanage of sorts, though no effort was ever made to find families for those children; they were housed, but barely.

'When Abby was born, Reed kept her, because she was his. I honestly can't explain to you why he wanted to have her. It's not what you think – I'm fairly certain he never abused her. I think he actually loved her, in his way. I don't know. I just don't know.' His voice began to dissolve in emotion.

'Keep talking,' Ladasha said sharply.

Father X wiped his face dry with the flats of his trembling hands.

'I have a gambling problem.' He attempted a pathetic smile, which vanished into abandonment, shame. 'I got into debt, and started borrowing from the parish. I always meant to pay it back. I did, at first. But then it got to be too much and I couldn't. So I stopped trying. By the time Reed discovered the accounting discrepancies, it had gone pretty far.'

I glanced at Sam, who answered my question: 'Dekker volunteered financial services for St Paul's.'

'Why did Father X allow anyone to look at the books?'

She shrugged. 'Protocol – someone had to, so he went with it. He isn't the sharpest thief.'

'Reed needed a way to launder the money that financed the trips to Brazil,' Father X continued, 'so he made a deal with me: He could balance

St Paul's books, erase the entire debt, and fund me when I needed, in exchange for something *he* needed. I didn't ask too many questions at first. I never imagined it had anything to do with harming anyone.'

'Well what did you think it was?' Ladasha snapped, and Billy touched her arm again, this time leaving it there.

'White-collar crime, I assumed.' Father X's head sagged to his chest, then lifted it with such effort you'd think it weighed a hundred pounds. 'Some kind of investments he wasn't supposed to be making. He was a banker. He was very wealthy. I didn't know and I didn't ask. Until . . .'

Through the glass, you could see Billy's fingers tense on Ladasha's arm. She didn't flinch. I shifted forward in my seat.

'. . . the first girl found her way back, and threatened to expose him. He tried to buy her silence, but she didn't want money. She wanted, well, I suppose, revenge. He seemed to realize that this could happen again. My understanding is that he planned it meticulously: When they found him, he would kill them, and make it look like a different sort of crime. He called it "misdirection," and at the beginning it seemed to work.'

Girls, abducted as children, enslaved in prostitution, brutally murdered to keep them quiet. And Father X just went along with it? Because of a gambling addiction? This was beyond the narcissistic self-preservation of your typical addict; even he, pushed into a corner, might have found a speck of conscience still left to act upon. This was pure psychopathology. The worst kind of silence: passive malevolence: unthinkable: unforgivable. And yet I suspected, from my fledgling studies of forensic psychology, that in a court of law Father X's claim of a gambling addiction – if that, other than his silence, was his worst contribution to the horror all those children endured – could offer just the right dose of mitigating circumstance to blur the lines of absolute responsibility. It made me sick to think it.

Billy and Ladasha, somehow, managed to hold their tongues and continue listening as if Father X was telling a reasonable story.

'It started to happen more and more over the last two years. It was getting really difficult.'

'How did they find him?'

'I don't know how the first one located Reed, but the rest? Facebook.' He grinned, and chills corkscrewed up my spine. If he wanted any of us to share in the irony of that, he was barking up the wrong tree.

'It wasn't going to end on its own. I'm glad it's over.' His voice was like an exhalation, as if now he could breathe, when in fact the worst was yet to come. Life in prison was no picnic for anyone, especially pedophiles (or their close associates). Unless he succeeded in doing his priest thing and blinding his new colleagues as to his true self. Why not? It had worked for him for years.

'So you're telling us that Reed did not sexually abuse Abby,' Billy said. 'Is that correct?'

'Not to my knowledge.'

'What about other men?'

'I believe not. He loved her. He kept her protected.'

'Did he know she knew?'

Father X's expression froze a moment. 'I don't understand.'

'She found his stash,' Billy said with such calm precision it was like cutting glass. 'She saw it all. We thought maybe you were aware of that.'

There was a pause, a bubble of quiet, in which it became clear that Father X had probably not been aware of Abby's discovery of her father's hiding place.

'No. I wasn't aware of that.' His tone was such a hollow whisper, you almost felt sorry for him, but there was no way you ever really could.

'Can you tell me why you were spending so much time in Abby's room at the hospital?' Billy asked.

'Because of Steve. I was afraid to leave her alone with him. I care about her. I watched her grow up.'

'So, what, you were gonna move into the house with the Campbells?' Ladasha blurted out. 'Jesus Christ, spare me.'

'I didn't know what I was going to do yet.'

'And Marta?' Billy asked. 'How much did she know?'

'Nothing. Which is why things got so out of

hand the night Tina turned up at their front door, looking for Abby. I believe Tina's mere presence told the whole story, in so many words. Abby bears a striking resemblance to her birth mother – it would have been impossible for Marta not to see it.'

Billy and Ladasha glanced at each other.

'We didn't see that,' Ladasha said.

'If you'd seen her before . . .' *her murder*; he couldn't bring himself to say it, '. . . well, there were traces of Abby in her face.'

'And you'd seen her before that?'

'Yes.'

'So what about you?' Billy planted his elbows on the table and leaned forward. 'After a while, helping Reed and Steve keep their cover, you developed a taste yourself?'

Father X scowled instantly. 'For children? Never.'

'We have a witness who saw you in the church closet, with a boy, about five years ago.'

Now the father's cheeks reddened. He shook his head.

'That charge was dismissed. The boy was a troublemaker, notorious for lying. He had problems with his sexual identity. *No one* believed that boy saw *me*. The priest was wearing a mask, the boy said. It was not *me*.'

'Okay. Then who was it?'

'A client of Reed's and Steve's. He had a fantasy of –' Father X averted his eyes a moment, ashamed.

'*Client?*' Ladasha now flung her pen across the room. 'Why don't you just say it straight!'

'A john.'

'A what?'

'A man . . . I don't know what you want me to say.'

'A *rapist.* How 'bout that?'

Father X stared at her in dumb silence.

'How 'bout we call you what you are, Mr High and Mighty? A *pimp.*'

'I was never—'

'What do you call it, then? I am a mother! I *know* when someone goes too far with a child.'

'Dash.' Billy's tone was firm. 'Enough.'

'Motherfucker's a *pimp* just like the rest of them. Thinks he's so holy. Take off his costume and look at him – he's just a regular convict.'

Billy didn't even try to stop her now. She ranted for a while, breaking down whatever might have been left of Father X's fragile dignity. When she was worn out, she sat back and inspected her new manicure: a vivid purple.

'Okay now,' Billy said calmly, a stiff tug at the final layer, now that the surface was pummeled soft: 'Tell us about the murders that were yours.'

He didn't even try to deny it anymore. He appeared defeated, exhausted; his body now slumped in the chair. 'Reed insisted I help him or he would turn me in. He said he had to keep an eye on Marta, he couldn't leave the house to go after Tina, so I had to do it. I took the knife he left for me outside the door, hidden behind a flowerpot, and followed Tina to Nevins Street. I thought I couldn't do it, but it was remarkably easy to kill her. I just did it. I made it look like Reed's work. And then I saw headlights; a car was coming along. I darted away and noticed Abby running up the street. I wouldn't have gone back to the Dekkers if I thought she was there. But she wasn't, so I seized the opportunity. Reed had cornered me. I had killed for him. I had to end it. I went back to his house to let him know I'd taken care of Tina. He didn't seem to realize Abby was gone, and I didn't mention it. Marta was upstairs; I could hear her crying. I was shaking uncontrollably.' He held out a trembling hand to demonstrate; he faked it so well, you could see what a good bullshit artist he was, how he had managed to fool (almost) everyone. 'He went to the kitchen to get me a glass of water. I hadn't realized he kept a gun, but apparently he did: He set it down on the counter by the sink to fill the glass. I came up right behind him and picked up the gun. It was that simple. Obviously he thought he had complete control over me, that I wouldn't dare cross him. As soon as he turned around—' He stopped talking. Swallowed so hard, his Adam's apple scraped visibly up and down his throat. 'Then I went upstairs to Marta. I had to end it. I had to.'

'What did you do with the gun?' Billy's tone betrayed nothing. None of the shock or disgust he must have felt, listening to a description of multiple murders so logically enacted you couldn't *not* think that Father X was the real thing: In his desperation to stop the killing, he had become a killer. Had it never occurred to him just to turn himself in? Stop Reed? Stop Steve? Protect the children? Why did he believe that the needs of one old man trumped those of so many?

'I dropped it in the Gowanus Canal, off the Carroll Street Bridge, where I thought no one would see me.'

I leaned closer to the glass, making sure not to miss a single word. He still hadn't mentioned Chali.

'And then what?' Billy asked.

'I went home.'

'And?'

'I don't know how to do this. It's been torture every step of the way. Watching Abby lying there like that in the hospital – it was horrible.'

'Because *you* were responsible,' Ladasha spat.

'Yes, in a way I was.'

'In a way?'

'What about Chali Das?' Billy asked.

Finally.

Father X nodded somberly. 'The next day, when the police and the newspapers were trying to find out what happened to the Dekkers, the babysitter came to confession. She told me she feared Abby had been abused, that she had sensed something was off when she babysat for Abby once, that she herself had been a child bride and she felt she detected something familiar in the girl. An anxious silence. I listened quietly, but I thought I would lose my mind. I didn't know what else she was aware of but I couldn't let it go. I realized I had to kill one more time. But I couldn't get into the house for one of Reed's knives.' He shook his head. 'The whole thing was falling apart.'

I stopped listening: In my mind I was back in Chali's apartment, looking for her, finding her dead. Wondering why she had been singled out for such cruelty. At that point, I couldn't do it anymore. I got up and walked out of the room.

Mac filled me in on the rest later that night, when we were home, decompressing at our kitchen table after the kids were in bed. We had had a drink before dinner and now we had another one; but no amount of alcohol could cloud my brain enough to dull the painful truth.

According to Father X, Steve Campbell was the Facebook expert, an allegation supported by the CCU, which had finally succeeded in tracing the account controlling Abby's page to Steve. It was he who located the resurfaced girls and Reed who silenced them, together creating the scenario of a serial killer to deflect the real problem: The girls were all connected through them and their trips off the coast of Brazil. They were tour operators, basically, having developed a business catering to mostly American men seeking sex with children.

Each year, fifteen to twenty men flew to Miami, where they boarded a chartered yacht and headed south into the Atlantic Ocean. They spent a full week together, having their fun. Then they went back to their lives as husbands and fathers, bankers and doctors, lawyers and teachers, neighbors and friends.

CHAPTER 27

Ben's birthday arrived on a Sunday. When Mac and I rolled out of bed at just past nine, we could smell that Dathi was already up and cooking in the kitchen: The rich aroma of poori wafted down the stairs to our room. She had made it once before and we'd all watched as the golden circles of dough puffed up in the pan. I had been so impatient to try it that I'd burned my tongue, but wouldn't make the same mistake this time.

When we got to the kitchen in our bathrobes, Ben was at the stove with her, standing on a stool. He was wearing his plaid pajamas and looked like a little man – four years old already; I could hardly believe it.

'Happy birthday!' I kissed the tousled top of his head.

'Happy birthday, Mommy.'

'It's *your* birthday, silly.' Laughing, Dathi flipped a poori, which sizzled when it landed. 'No one else's.'

While the poori was finishing, Mac scrambled eggs and I started coffee. Then I cleaned the strawberries I'd bought the day before as a special treat; they were so dear in the winter, we rarely got them. Soon we were all sitting around the table, a family of four, which six months ago was just what I'd expected to be doing at this time of year – but with a different daughter. Dathi was on the way to becoming ours now: We'd hired lawyers in both countries, and the official adoption paperwork was being prepared. So far there had been no objections from Uncle Ishat, the Indian Consulate, or the Indian government. Apparently she didn't matter to anyone else: She was just a girl adrift in the world. But she mattered, deeply, to me, and in growing increments she had started to matter to Mac, as well.

Mom arrived in time to snag the last piece of poori. Between her new medication and a new physical therapist, she could make the walk over by herself now. She had brought a gift wrapped in colorful paper and decorated with a curly ribbon. Ben nearly assaulted her, trying to get it out of her hands.

'Not yet.' Mom laughed. 'Karin? Mac? You better get to it.'

We had been waiting for her. I went to the front hall and opened the coat closet, where last night we had managed to stash Ben's unwieldy gift: a new bicycle, shiny royal blue, with a good loud bell and training wheels. He ripped off the badly wrapped paper and jumped on, ringing the bell nonstop. Now Mom tried to give him her gift, but he had lost interest. I handed it to Dathi to open for him.

'Ah, his helmet,' she said. I wondered if it reminded her of her own helmet, the gift from Chali, which had gone unused because she didn't have a bicycle to ride. She strapped the silver helmet, dotted with green frogs, onto Ben's head.

Meanwhile, Mac ducked downstairs to the basement. I heard him struggling up the stairs but didn't go to help him because I didn't want the kids to follow and ruin the plan.

When he appeared in the living room, a little breathless and wheeling a much bigger bicycle – a girl's two-wheeler, white with maroon trim – Dathi's jaw dropped. Eyes tearing, she ran to Mac and buried him in a hug.

We had promised Ben a party, and he would have one, but it was not going to be the kind of party he expected. Instead of games and cupcakes and balloons at home, Mac, Dathi, and I got bundled up and struck out into the brilliant blue morning. Mom was going to skip this part and meet up with us later. The temperature had risen over the last few days, melting most of the snow, and now you could move along unimpeded. Ben and Dathi, strapped into helmets, rode their new bikes on the sidewalk. Mac and I rode our bikes beside them along the edge of the street. It took a while, because we had to stop frequently for Ben, but he was a trouper on his new set of wheels . . . and by the time we reached the Atlantic

Avenue entrance to Brooklyn Bridge Park, he was getting the hang of it.

The plan was to meet everyone here. We were the first, so we waited on a bench overlooking the East River and the southern tip of Manhattan, a packed checkerboard of skyscrapers.

'It's cold,' Ben said.

'We'll warm up once we're on the move.' I kissed his cheek

'Here they are!' Mac pointed at Mary and Fremont, arriving on their bikes; he zoomed ahead while she chugged behind.

Dathi circled to meet them, a little wobbly but mastering the bicycle she had waited so long for. Moments later, when Billy rode up, she repeated the circle to greet him.

'Nice bike, kid,' he greeted her.

Grinning, she followed him back to the bench, where Ben now sat on Fremont's lap.

'Ready?' Dathi pointed herself in the direction of the path that edged the river.

'Not quite yet,' I told her. 'We're waiting for a few more.'

Mac tried to suppress his smile, but it was contagious and I struggled not to smile as well. We both knew how much this would mean to Dathi, and even though it was Ben's birthday, this was going to be our last chance to see Abby for a while. The gift for Ben was more people to lead on his procession along the water to the restaurant, and when we got there, a cake was waiting with his name on it.

After a few more minutes, Abby came riding along on her own bicycle, one of the things she'd taken out of the Bergen Street house for her imminent move to Connecticut. A middle-aged couple followed on rented bikes.

Abby had a set of biological grandparents still young enough to care for her with the energy they had once put into searching for their daughter, Tina, who vanished when she was twelve years old. It turned out that her DNA had been accidentally dropped out of the database, which was why she remained unidentified as long as she did.

The Giffords lived in a nice house a few blocks from the ocean, where they had raised four children – Tina had been their second oldest. Now there were aunts and uncles and lots of cousins living mostly nearby. Of all the cousins, Abby was the oldest, as Tina had been so young – only fourteen – when she'd given birth.

Ray and Sandy Gifford pulled up behind Abby, who had tossed over her bike and jumped off to inspect Dathi's. Abby winced a little when she moved, and she still had a slight limp, but most of the healing she had to do now was emotional; her body was well on its way.

'How on earth are we going to keep up with her?' Sandy asked cheerfully; but it was a purely rhetorical question. Their gratitude for Abby was on record in all their words and actions since the day they'd learned of her existence. When Sandy smiled, watching Abby inspect Dathi's new bike and dole out enthusiastic approval, an array of deep wrinkles flowered in an expression that was both joyous and tragic. She had mentioned to me, when we'd spoken on the phone to arrange this, how much Abby resembled Tina; how wonderful that was, and how painful.

'It won't be hard,' Ray said warmly, lifting a gloved hand off his handlebar to pat his wife's shoulder. 'It'll be one of the easiest things we've ever done. She'll be our new beginning.'

Abby smiled at her grandparents as she strode past them to pick up her bike and remount.

Dathi and Abby led the way, with Ben and Fremont following. The adults trailed close behind, six sets of eyes, all watching in case anyone stumbled. On our right, in the near distance, the steep canyon of the city. On our left, the graphite surface of a winter river shining under an unseasonably bright sky. In front of us, a smooth path that curved and curved again as we made our way forward together.